Advance Praise

Many Australians still cling stubbornly in the intended invasion of Australia and the repelling of the Japanese on the Kokoda Track prevented it, but either way the campaign was a brutal affair fought in inhuman conditions, suffered by both sides…This is the setting for INTO THE WET. The characters bring a personal dimension to the story, but its strength is the way Coker captures the experience of the battlefront in miserable conditions: the heat, the mud, the sheer helplessness, and the endless rain of the Wet, the equatorial downpour that characterizes the region's summer.

Meticulously researched and described in intricate detail, Coker's story carries a gritty authenticity as a result. It could almost serve as a manual for participation in the conflict, of the day-to-day grind. In his search for authenticity, the author has tried to capture the distinctive Aussie accent and vernacular. It's a brave attempt that most wouldn't try, but doesn't quite ring true to an Australian ear. It's the only shortcoming in a book that makes you feel you are there, going through the agony of the unfolding drama of a thoroughly unpleasant military campaign.

-Craig Collie, co-author of THE PATH OF INFINITE SORROW, THE JAPANESE ON THE KOKODA TRACK. August 9, 2015, Sydney, Australia

One of the most infuriating reads I have ever undertaken. The depth of Jerry Coker's research is remarkable and illuminating. The immediacy of his portrayals of action I have never seen equaled. I often felt I was on-site and being shot at whilst being subjected to a monsoonal deluge. Been there and done those things, in a later war, and his immediacy evoked excruciating memories. This book is real. It is rooted in the reeking mud of archival reality and grows a trueness of its own.

Mr. Coker's style is a dense read, with logistics, military overview, and both martial and personal histories interspersed with that exemplary action. Because action and personal involvement with his characters' point of view are so engaging, the reader is carried through what could have been interruptions; gradually realizing that the frustration and indignation engendered by background is a primary motivator for persisting in the read. You not only want to know what happens next, you demand to know. Those characters are alive; you have their memories and the desperation of their situations to force you to feel their fears and pains.

There are both a fine historical work and an engaging novel here, so entangled that it is necessary to really immerse in their interweaving story lines. Your attention is demanded. And you are forced to yield to it.

The author allows no escape. The sensorial intensity of his writing puts you there, whether starving while in flooded foxholes during freezing nights of unending downpour, or covered with mosquitoes in the thrall of thirst, subject to blind gunfire, or aching with fear, piloting a decrepit Gooney Bird through fighter-infested skies. You feel everything the characters feel. Inescapably. Don't pick up this book unless you can tolerate hours of captivity.

I began by saying this book was infuriating. I stand by that; not only because of the way the thing refuses to let you go, but because of the hellishness of war, the entrapping inhumanity it brings upon men and women, and the fact that you will never be able to forget this lucid glimpse of it.

-David Lloyd Sutton. Author, editor and book reviewer

INTO THE WET

Jerry Coker

Pocol Press

POCOL PRESS
Published in the United States of America
by Pocol Press
6023 Pocol Drive
Clifton, VA 20124
www.pocolpress.com

Publisher's Cataloguing-in-Publication

Names: Coker, Jerry, 1950-, author.
Title: Into the wet / Jerry Coker.
Description: Clifton, VA: Pocol Press, 2017.
Identifiers: ISBN 978-1-929763-76-4 | LCCN 2017952802
Subjects: LCSH World War, 1939-1945--Australia--Fiction. | World War, 1939-1945—Japan--Fiction. |
World War, 1939-1945--Campaigns--Pacific Area--Fiction. | World War, 1939-1945--Campaigns--Papua New Guinea—Rabaul--Fiction. | Rabaul (Papua New Guinea)--History, Military--20th century--Fiction. | Australia--History--20th century--Fiction. | Historical fiction. | Military fiction. | BISAC FICTION / Historical.
Classification: LCC PS3603 .O3963 I58 2017 | DDC 813.6--dc23

Library of Congress Control Number: 2017952802

Second printing; originally published by Black Rose writing, 2015.

To the nurses whose care and kindness reside in our hearts forever. With affection and a special salute to three from my war; Mary Ann Renaldo, Sarah Jane Hodge and my dearest friend and wife, Jan.

FOREWORD by Eric Bergerud
Professor of History at Lincoln University
Author of *Touched With Fire* and *Fire in the Sky*

Jerry Coker has written a fine historical novel set in the bizarre and vicious six-month jungle campaign fought between Australian/US forces and elite Japanese infantry in Papua New Guinea during the last half of 1942. The battle was fought between the Japanese beachhead at Buna and the key allied base at Port Moresby. Connecting the two end points was the infamous Kokoda track which became the scene of a kind of epic see-saw struggle between the Japanese and Australians. Coker's finely crafted novel serves this harsh battle well as he interweaves the narrative of fighting men (and some American nurses) from each contending army allowing the creation of a kind of diorama of this desperate struggle. The narrative is very engaging and the multiple viewpoints employed by Coker helps remind the contemporary reader of the way which WWII threw millions of individuals into utterly unexpected places to do unexpected duty and changing lives forever. Coker looks back on his characters and captures something of the way people thought and lived in the early 1940s. It was very different from our world with most people close to the farm or factory and only a minority in the educated elites. Only the main Japanese character is a young career officer – the others were civilians inserted into history's greatest war by the torrent of historical circumstance. I think this ambiance is essential to understand World War II and Coker can be applauded for capturing it.

I studied this campaign for years and am very impressed with Coker's command of the historical factors that formed this battle. Above all – as indicated by the title – Coker emphasizes the impact of brutal climate and terrain on every aspect of the war in New Guinea. The beastly heat, torrential rains, created a jungle or swamp environment that was home to insects and bacteria that continually assaulted every person in the theater. Creature comforts were almost non-existent, supplies of every kind very short, and relief from the physical pounding delivered by the land itself almost impossible to find. Logistical failure added starvation into the mix for the Japanese forces. When the campaign was in action, only a handful of combatants on either side could have been considered "healthy" in a meaningful way. This was a small unit war so violence was sporadic but almost non-stop so the fear of combat was also added to the lethal brew. There were much larger and violent campaigns during the war, but, with the possible exception of battles in the extreme cold, I can think of none more miserable. Or in the words of one of Coker's American characters the theater had "the stink of rot."

Much of the novel deals with the crucial medical effort required to allow this campaign to take place at all. Casualty rates among allied combat units in Papua surpassed 80% with the vast majority lain low by malaria or the myriad other diseases confronting poorly supplied men in the jungle or the coastal swamp. Naturally the thousands of wounded often carried a disease with them. Crucial to saving lives was rapid evacuation – to the extent possible in a primitive theater – much of that task fell on the crewmen of the C-47 transports. I applaud Coker's emphasis on the "Gooney's". Although lacking in the glamour of combat craft air transport was arguably the most use of air power in New Guinea. The pilots who measured their tours in "hours" rather than "missions" were some of the best of the war. Usually flying craft that would have failed any inspection, crewmen brought in the supplies needed to allow infantry to fight and withdrew the disabled – usually fully loaded both directions. It was a dangerous job. As shown in a dramatic episode by Coker, unarmed transports could be terribly vulnerable to Japanese fighters. But the author is quite right in noting that most planes lost simply disappeared, unseen victims of enemy action or, more likely, to the terrible weather and terrain found in the Owen Stanley's. As one C-47 pilot flying the "Moresby-Dobodura Express" told me, "in the Stanley's there's a rock behind every cloud, and they were easy to find." (Lost warplanes continue to be found in Papua.)

The experience of the wounded in hospital is well and deftly covered by Coker. There were a small number of nurses in that theater but their presence was particularly valuable for the wounded for both professional and psychological reasons. A 32nd Division vet from Buna was under the care of one of them and he told me that her presence reminded him that the real world continued to exist, even if far away. And as shown by Coker medical personnel were also vulnerable to tragic mischance that always punctuates war.

Coker does a good job of covering the factors that made the Japanese and Australian forces such formidable combat soldiers. The Aussies were proud individualists but well trained volunteers bound closely by what they called "mateship." Coker's portrait of Japanese infantry is most convincing. At one level they were soldiers like others of the era – they complained a lot about almost everything if among friends. Not many wanted to be where they were. Yet morale was solid and reflected their excellent training which allowed complex small-unit maneuver and the ability to fight at night – one of the most difficult military tasks and rarely seen in WWII. But there was also a unique ethos in the Japanese fueled by deep cultural factors malignantly influenced by a kind of ersatz Bushido peddled by Japan's military regime that, among other things, made surrender unthinkable. Obviously if surrender was impossible for the brave, prisoners were cowards to be scorned and mistreated. From the allies point of view, if the enemy would not surrender they had to be killed. This tragic dynamic helped turn the Pacific War into a kind of struggle of annihilation and this horrible reality was well displayed in the Kokoda campaign. Only a handful of Japanese escaped the campaign, an ugly omen of later battles like Iwo Jima. It is no accident that the struggle ended at Hiroshima.

In summary, Coker has written a novel with a very engaging narrative supported by the use of historically accurate details and events. Highly recommended.

Those new to the South Pacific called it the rainy season.
To the locals it was known as The Wet.

Author's Note

Although carefully based on actual events and the military units involved in the New Guinea campaign, *Into the Wet* is a work of fiction. With the exception of using the real names of certain military commanders for accuracy, the characters portrayed in the story never existed and are entirely from my imagination.

Heartfelt appreciation to the curators and volunteers who patiently and enthusiastically answered my questions at the Australian War Museum, in Canberra; the Australian Army Infantry School at Singleton, in New South Wales; and at the Puckapunyal Army Base, now home of the Australian Light Horse, near Seymour in Victoria. Many thanks to fellow pilots who ensured I learned the cabin, cockpit layout and operating procedures of the Douglas (DC-3) C-47 as it was flown in the early years of the war.

Special thanks goes to Nathan and Drew Coker, whose expertise as law enforcement weapons and drug recognition instructors offered me unique, hands-on insight about the automatic weapons used in the Southwest Pacific in 1942, and an understanding of the early development of methamphetamine and the physical effects of its long-term use.

CHAPTER 1

November 30, 1942, Dobodura airfield, 15 miles South of Buna, Papua New Guinea

Don Crenshaw stepped back under the wing and leaned against the right landing gear tire, seeking a dry spot on the muddy rubber without being burned by dripping oil coming straight down from the hot engine. The wind turned south again, bending the sudden, torrential downpour horizontal, hurling water, mud, sand and chopped Kunai grass under the wing. He cursed, dodging around behind the wheel as if it would offer protection. Five minutes earlier the sun beat down like a heat lamp, but the steaming pools of water all around the incomplete runway and the sudden appearance of the black, low clouds so dense and textured they looked like tight balls of wool gave it away. The monsoon season—*the wet*—was coming, and what were already tough flying conditions would be downright nasty.

There was nowhere to go. At least over at Port Moresby on the western side of the peninsula there were flight shacks and Quonset huts near the aircraft revetments so the transient crews could get out of the weather, sit down, and sometimes get something to eat or flop out on a cot. This Dobodura auxiliary airstrip, 100 miles away, didn't exist a week before. The engineers carved the airfield from what turned out to be an outstanding surface for a runway, a plain of Kunai grass, or elephant grass, once it was shorn right down to the stubble. The remaining turf stubble drained water naturally, was several feet thick and stayed firm even under the heavy poundings of constant take off and landings of overloaded bombers and transports. The new campaign 15 miles away in Gona and Buna demanded air transport and fighter support immediately, so the engineers pulled out all the stops. 5,500 Japanese were reportedly in the area, some seen within a half of a mile of the ever-expanding runways, but the engineers never stopped working, the dozers and hundreds of indigenous laborers barely visible in the rain, shadowy movement like curling grass in a breeze.

Don noticed the new linked metal runway material was being used on the edges of the runway and most of the taxiways. Mud oozed through the grates so it appeared the plains were really patchworks of Kunai grass and swamp. At least the plains were flat, which kept the approaches reasonably safe and level and the runways were long enough for crews to abort a takeoff. It gave them a chance, considering nearly all of the aircraft operating in the Southwest Pacific were short of spare parts, engineering support and flown by exhausted crews. Maintenance

1

was not near regulation standard, and he knew many of the airplanes would have been grounded weeks ago if there wasn't such a need for them. Chronic mechanical failure was so common crews were developing ad hoc procedures and work arounds the Air Corps Groups simply integrated into the protocols, once it was determined the procedures saved time or kept airplanes in the air. There was no effort to deal with the manufacturer or Training Command, the only operational imperative was moving tonnage as close to the fighting as possible.

The weather was spotty enough the Japanese were able to send fighters and bombers from Rabaul over on New Britain to harass the Aussies and the US 32nd Infantry Division at Gona and Buna. The powers that be figured it would be just a matter of time before the Japanese discovered the new runways at Dobobura. The revetments the engineers had built were an eighth of a mile away from this runway and well camouflaged, to protect the few P-40s staged to take on the Japanese. Nothing else was visible other than perimeter anti-aircraft positions dug in above the water table, and a half dozen wrecked airplanes dragged off the side of the runway. With no revetments or cover of any kind, transient aircraft were ordered to spread out all over the field, far from anyone else and any shelter, to simply wait for their mission load to come to them. To an observer, however, the operation was well timed and organized, the most visible element the choreographed ballet of transports sliding down out of the pattern on an invisible escalator to the runway. None of the transports were coming in from Port Moresby deadheading, all were crammed full of the disposables of war: ammunition, rations, weapons, spare parts, medical supplies and men.

Other than responding to a light signal clearing him to land from a makeshift tower, Don had communicated to no one coming in to Dobodura. A jeep drove over to them about three minutes after they had landed, a ground officer directing them to an open space by the side of the runway near two other waiting C-47s. The cargo shoved through the big fuselage double door, the manifest of which Don and his co-pilot had just a few minutes to review before takeoff at Port Moresby, was being unloaded unto a US Army Dodge six by six before he had stepped out of the cockpit. Their outbound cargo, wounded troops from the fighting 15 miles away, was on its way. *Do you need fuel or oil?*

The squall came just minutes after the last transport landed. Don heard the whine of a supercharger in the pattern, peeking up over the leading edge of the wing not believing anyone, especially a fighter, was trying to land with the rain and strong gusting winds. If you just wait a few minutes conditions would change, as they say in Papau. *Dehori.*

2

Wait awhile. It was as true as rain. But Don heard the miss and sputter of the whining motor clearly now, realizing a man was being forced to do something of which he had no choice.

Don's co-pilot, Jack Cooper, dropped down from the cargo hatch and slid close to the fuselage until he dipped under the wing. Cooper realized his mistake, getting soaked with the next thudding gust of wind and rain, spraying them both with a sheet of gritty cold water. The misery on their faces said it all—fatigue, anger, disgust; but Cooper, a very experienced former airline pilot was a talker.

"What a fuckin' shithole! A couple of minutes late, we would've been trying to land in this squall, like this poor bastard in the pattern, you hear em'? It's gonna' quit for good any second!" Don nodded, his eyes on the sky.

The wind sock was darting frantically 90 degrees from the useable runway heading, with the crosswind runway nowhere near completion or long enough. The bottom of the cloud deck, black, rolling like boiling oil, was down to maybe 300 feet. That was where Don spotted the fighter, a mud-brown P-40, circling, trying to decide which direction the wind was blowing. The supercharger was surging, with staccato bursts of power amidst a choking, mechanical gargling as the pilot tried to work the throttle and keep the airplane in the air just a little bit longer. Another engine could be heard, strong, steady and powerful as a second P-40 swept past the first, circling protectively, his wingman.

Don could see both fighters were Aussies, the paint schemes virtually the same as the USAAF, since the Air Corps Fifth Air Force and the Royal Australian Air Force created a joint management and replacement pool in mid-summer. There were only a few P-40s available, so airplanes went back and forth between the air forces as operational need demanded. The Americans painted white stars on the wings and fuselages, but the Aussies had Royal Air Force roundels with the kangaroo in the middle.

The squall seemed to stall right over the airfield, twisting and snarling in darkness above with hurricane bursts of wind down closer to the ground. Any airman experienced with New Guinea weather knew these squalls were highly localized, incredibly strong and dangerous storms of short duration. You avoided them at all costs, skirting them by miles if possible. You never try to land or take off in one. Don had spent countless hours over the last six months circling at altitude or close to the surface of the water out at sea watching and waiting them out.

The engine quit with a quick series of loud snorts and coughs, turning silent as the P-40, down to about 250 feet and slow, gently carved around to line up with the main runway heading. The wind direction no longer mattered to the Aussie strapped into the tight cockpit.

Don and Jack both stepped out into the gusting rain, staring. The wind swept up from the south, but jerked easterly so abruptly Don couldn't hold onto his overseas billed cap, even when he clamped his hand firmly on it to keep it on his head. It blew away, but he didn't even glance towards it, his eyes locked on the tiny dot dropping lower and lower.

The nose of the P-40 dove to the runway as the pilot tried to keep the airspeed up. He was doing a good job of it, the airplane slipping level with the nose now pointed into the gusting easterly wind. Just before touchdown the pilot pressed the rudder to force the nose to line up with the runway, the upwind wing low, the deadstick fighter's upwind wheel touching as the gusting wind kept pushing the airplane across. Huge rooster tail geysers of water were being displaced by the bouncing single wheel. Don wanted to close his eyes but couldn't. A quarter of the way down the runway, both wheels were on the ground, the tail still up. Don could see the pilot was trying to offset the direct crosswind with his rudder as the P-40 slowed down. Without an engine to give him a burst of airflow over the surface of his rudder, the rudder ceased to be effective as the tail slowly settled and weather cocked against the gusts. The P-40 began to skid first into the wind, then abruptly in the opposite direction, leaving the runway and into the mud. The machine flipped over so fast Don would have not believed it possible.

There was a weak *crump* and *bang* followed by complete silence. There was no explosion or fire. Moving at 50 to 60 mph when it departed from the runway, the P-40 did not slide or move an inch once it flipped. The forward momentum stopped. *Like the life of the pilot,* Don thought. He was aware, slowly, of the supercharger whine of the Aussie's wingman as he continued to circle for a full minute. The wingman suddenly pulled up into the cloud deck and disappeared for what Don assumed, was a strong desire to climb away from the scene, the storm and to seek calm air and sunshine.

"Poor bastard," mumbled Cooper. They could hear a couple of jeeps heading down the taxiway towards the crash, but there didn't seem to be any ambulances or fire engines responding. The strip was not even officially operational yet, the cart not caught up with the horse.

"What do you think?"

Cooper had been a pilot of the line for eight years before being called up as a military reservist, with 1,000 hours in DC-2s, the immediate predecessor of the DC-3, and a few thousand in DC-3s, the civilian version of the very machine they were flying. Like their fighter brethren, once the Air Corps determined transport aircraft were more valuable than combat airplanes in the Southwest Pacific, they worked with the Australians to steal, confiscate or requisition every available transport airplane they could get their hands on. Since the US Army Air Corps was the only legitimate supply line available for the allied forces, the Air Corps blended this ragtag collection of aircraft, many of them DC-2s and DC-3s from Australian and Dutch airlines stranded by the war, into the first viable transport group to supplement the few machines in theatre. The confiscated airplanes were stripped of parts if non-flyable, the remaining machines refitted and repainted as USAAF transports.

Cooper, in this way of thinking, was a refit. Most US airlines and their line pilots were being drafted into a federal transport service. They would fly the same airplanes they flew for the airlines, but the missions were strategic and under the direct control of the US government. They were not real military pilots. Pilots like Cooper, who enlisted in the Air Corps during the time of peace in the reserves, were called up after Pearl Harbor and utilized like any other military pilot. Having nearly five times more hours in type than Don himself, you would think a man like Cooper would already be an aircraft commander. They were in fact the same rank, first lieutenant, but Cooper came to New Guinea as a new C-47 pilot in the squadron, and SOP dictated a pilot with Cooper's experience but new to the operations of the SWP would fly awhile as a co-pilot. That was *four months and hundreds of hours* ago, and Don, when pressed by the squadron CO or a group operations officer, could only say the same thing: *He's not ready.*

"What do you mean, *he's not ready*?" they demanded, "It's your job *to make him* ready! The man has 7,000 hours, for God's sakes!" Twice now Cooper was temporarily assigned to fly with first the squadron CO and then a group training officer on regular resupply missions. In both occasions Cooper was returned to Don without comment, no further questions or inquiries in tow. For his part, Cooper, if he knew what was going on, appeared to be perfectly content. When he was first assigned to Don, Don was gracious and a little awed by Cooper's experience. He explained, as did the squadron CO, that as soon as Cooper got the feel of the New Guinea operation and the way Group wanted things done, he would have his own airplane and crew. Don had apologized, looking forward to the opportunity to learn from Cooper. And he did, as the man was silky smooth on the controls, knowing how to finesse the engines and trim as only a man who spent the equivalent *of seven months* non-stop in a particular tiny space would know.

Despite his extensive experience, including military, Cooper was not prepared for the type of flying they did here. Many of the daily, routine operational flights they flew challenged basic flying instincts. But mostly Cooper couldn't handle *being shot at.* For Don it meant there were situations where he would be flying the airplane by himself.

Six months before Don arrived at Archerfield Airport, in Brisbane, with a small group of newly minted transport pilots. June is the middle of winter in Australia, and it was cool and raining the day they arrived. Some had arrived by ship, like Don, and a few managed to get to Brisbane by a haphazard series of connecting military flights. Getting to the war was not much of a priority ticket in getting a seat, they found. In all cases it took weeks to cross the Pacific, and the pilots felt rusty. They were assigned to a newly formed squadron, the 21st Troop Carrier Squadron, based in Brisbane on paper, but most detachments were flying out of Port Moresby, 1,500 miles to the north on New Guinea. Most of the pilots, including Don, had to find it on a map, having no idea where it was.

What about training, orientation flights, that sort of thing? they asked. The harried operations officer stared at them, not unkindly, nodding back towards the flight line where there was not a single transport in sight. *You'll get all the flying you can stomach soon enough. If it's flyable, it's in the air or in maintenance at Moresby.* They got the message, waiting for days before finding themselves on a mud spattered C-47 for the cold, seven-hour flight to Port Moresby. They surveyed the stripped cabin, which didn't even have the toilet seat paratrooper pans on each side of the fuselage, with dismay. It seemed every square inch of the cabin forward of the cargo door had boxes of spare parts. The 40 or so square feet left in the narrow tail section was the space available for the five officers and their bags. It was tight.

The loadmaster and flight engineer, a young man with a three or four day growth of beard wearing a strange mix-match of sweaters and coveralls, plugged his headset into the intercom and told the pilot they were ready. The new passenger pilots, freshly trained on the dangers of flying overloaded or unbalanced transports, stared at one another. The loadmaster checked their names off his clipboard, respectfully pointing to the floor of the airplane. As he closed and locked the door the pilot was starting the left engine. Without another word, the loadmaster pulled a sleeping bag from behind the cargo and stretched it out right beside the five officers, all still upright, crouched forward, their heads barely clear of the overhead aluminum ribs. The loadmaster crawled inside the bag, pulled up the zipper and did not move again. One by one the officers laid down their stuff, realizing the luggage constituted the seating or sleeping arrangements. If the war in the Pacific was screaming for pilots, this was not the welcome they had anticipated. They also understood within 30 minutes they were woefully underdressed for winter flying, certainly as passengers of a drafty transport with the ambient cabin temperature hovering around 50 degrees. They had their leather flying jackets, but their tropical khaki uniforms felt like tissue paper against the heat-robbing ice cold aluminum airframe. No one slept much, except the loadmaster, snoring peacefully throughout the entire flight.

The real shock came when they landed on Seven-Mile airfield north of Port Moresby, in between rain squalls, to find their way to squadron operations. There they viewed the flight line for the first time to discover what constituted "flyable" in the SWP. They heard the stories from the instructors on how squadrons made do, and they were not disappointed. *Shit,* remarked one pilot, *we are flying junk!* Wrinkled, dented aluminum sheet metal was in evidence on every visible surface, with varying paint schemes on panels clearly from different airplanes. The undersides of the engine nacelles were streaked with smeared oil, and the more sharp-eyed pilots noted the neat round holes in the aluminum roughly patched with fabric. *These are fuckin bullet holes...goddamn!*

Bullet holes, appearing suddenly on wing surfaces, or the *TINK TINK TINK* as the armor-piercing rounds punctured the fuselage, somewhere, on *your airplane*. There was nothing quite like it. Not what you expected flying unarmored, slow moving buses with wings. What stopped Cooper cold though, Don was pretty certain, were the orange-yellow golf balls. They had just transitioned to the new technique of air-dropping supplies to the troops on the Kokoda Track, all Aussies, and the procedure went from hair-raising to straight out, nerve-busting scary. They heard the Air Corps was developing a parachute system for delivering supplies, but nothing showed up. For the time being, supplies were delivered directly by either landing on tiny scraps of bare earth designated as forward airstrips, or more recently when the Japanese overwhelmed the grass Kokoda airfield in mid-winter, pushed out of the cargo door to free fall to the earth.

There were problems, of course, just getting into the rugged terrain the troops were fighting in. Frequent storms, intense, mountain-hugging fog and poor radio reception between the ridges made the 50 mile trip from Port Moresby across the Owen-Stanley mountain range risky enough, especially if the weather to the east allowed for Japanese fighters from Rabaul. The Zeros hunted transports, the loss of one machine gunned out of the sky reported as "Missing, Failed to Return", unless there was a visual confirmation, which was rare. Airplanes, lost or shot down, simply disappeared into the green jungle. They occasionally flew in pairs and sometimes had fighter escorts, but mostly the missions were singles for routine resupply. The Aussies wrapped their own supplies in wool blankets covered with rough burlap. The Diggers would stuff the cargo, mostly rations and small arms ammunition, as far forward in the cabin as possible, until there was barely room for the

7

loadmaster. The Australians called C-47s Dakotas, but when the mission was air resupply to the troops on the Track, it was a *Biscuit Bomber*. They would thank the American pilots sitting in their cockpits with a broad, cheery wave of a hand. *Thanks, mate! God-bless ya!*

The initial technique for air drops was one based more on intuition than any past experience. They certainly had no previous training for it. Being low and slow close to the ground was something pilots avoided, but getting close to the ground was the requirement. So the procedure was to deliver the materials as near the troops as possible, therefore LOW—but to maintain safety by keeping the airspeed high, therefore FAST. The C-47s, once the friendly troops had been identified by panels, markers, smoke or occasionally radio contact, swooped in low, 20 feet off the treetops between 140 to 165 mph. Pilots didn't like coming in quite so low, but the speed ensured good control and a minimum amount of time over the target. Energy and speed could then be traded for altitude.

The problem was apparent the very first time a pilot dove down, leveled off and yelled at the loadmaster to start kicking the stuff out. The burlap-wrapped cargo, ammunition or rations, would hit the ground at 150 mph and bounce in all directions, occasionally exploding like a bomb burst. The Aussies were reporting anywhere between a 15 to 25% recovery rate. Some ground officer, most likely an engineer, suggested the supplies were being delivered at too low an altitude, and with too much speed. He turned out to be right, and after some experimentation, a new air delivery technique was established resulting in a significant increase in recovery of materials. Unfortunately, the technique placed the C-47s in a much more vulnerable position to receive ground fire.

The new procedure was to approach the drop zone much slower, around 90 to 100 mph, and much higher, around 300 feet. Instead of swooping out of the sky like a dive bomber, making a fast-moving, hard-to-hit target for machine gunners, a crew approached the drop zone in slow, stabilized level flight. At 300 feet and departing the aircraft at 90 mph, the cargo had enough time to lose forward momentum, transitioning instead to a straight free fall to the ground. Gravity took its toll, but the supplies were no longer ricocheting like tennis balls.

The new stabilized, slow and higher approach technique was an immediate success and fully adopted. The second time Don and Cooper used it, delivering supplies very accurately across a small narrow meadow between two invisible, mist-wrapped peaks, the base of the ridge on one side erupted with flashing sparkles. The ground fire, all coming from Cooper's side, started to hit the airplane as Don was cleaning the airplane up and advancing the throttles. *TINK TINK TINK,* metallic raps on the fuselage, had Don turning instantly to Cooper to ask if the starboard engine had been hit, and to retract the flaps.

What he saw was shocking, as Cooper, a man in his early 30s, had turned sheet white, bloodless, strangely shrunken like a wizened old man. His head retracted into his shoulders, hands gripped to his chest. His eyes were wide open, unblinking and staring, until the first string of heavy machinegun tracers arced around the windshield like a spouting fire hose. His head turned slightly when he saw the tracers, his jaw dropping. The tracers, fiery projectiles to aid the machine gunner's aim with a glowing dart every fifth or sixth round, looked for the world like burning yellow-orange golf balls from the receiving end. They glowed, suddenly slowing down as they came closer and closer, then instantly they were past.

"AAAAHHHHHHHH....." moaned Cooper.

Don pulled up the remaining flaps, ignoring Cooper, glancing at the engine rpm and propeller speed on the right engine, hoping it wasn't hit. He pushed the nose down as the C-47 picked up speed, grateful the ailerons and rudder felt normal. They had been level to make the drop for about 15 seconds, and it took about seven seconds to push the nine pallets out the door. The ground fire came about five seconds into the air drop sequence. Then it took about 15 more seconds to clean up the airplane and fly out of the little gorge. Don pressed his intercom to check on his loadmaster, breathing a sigh of relief when the young sergeant responded, confirming neither he nor the two Aussie volunteers were hit. Don asked him to check the aircraft for visible damage, especially the right engine, and was again rewarded with an all clear: no fire or smoke.

Once clear of the peaks and back up into the clouds, Don concentrated on his instruments and flying the airplane, alone. He noticed movement on his right with his peripheral vision, but focused on flying. Cooper was touching and rubbing his chest, as if to determine he was hit. After a few moments he leaned forward, turning his head as if he were scanning the instruments, his hands moving from his chest to his knees, the natural position of a second pilot, ready to assist or take over when called upon. At about 10,000 they broke into brilliant blue open sky, Don easing the nose down, ready to drop back into the clouds. He switched his scan to the cockpit windows, looking for fighters. Cooper, he noticed, seemed to be doing the same thing, looking slowly around, up and down. Don headed towards Port Moresby, beginning a slow descent. Minute by minute, he sensed Cooper doing what he was supposed to do, scanning the engine instruments on the ride side of the panel in front of him, then transitioning his view outside, especially to the right and behind, areas Don could not see.

After a few minutes Cooper turned towards Don. Don met his

9

eyes, not believing the change. The blood was returning to his face, his head more erect, his eyes no longer wide open. The lids seemed heavy with sleep, drowsy and droopy. He seemed exhausted, resigned.

"I'm sorry, Don," he said in a calm, flat voice, "I've never—I'm sorry." Don only nodded as his attention returned to scanning for enemy fighters.

"The first time I got shot at I didn't like it much either."

Don pushed the nose down even further as they re-entered the clouds. He had seen just enough of the pass below to know their position. They were clear of most of the high terrain. He had flown this route a hundred times, but without a reliable radio range at Port Moresby to draw a bearing, they flew a dead reckoning course and descent, time and distance, hoping to break out of the bottom of the clouds just west of Uberi, then continuing due west about ten miles north of Moresby, over the flat, safe swamps. If they did it right, they would be two minutes away from Seven-Mile airfield. He didn't know what to say to Cooper, or what to think of the incident. He assumed with Cooper's experience he could count on him, but everyone responded differently to their first combat missions or being shot at. Nothing much prepares you for that, he reasoned, hoping it would be something Cooper would learn to cope with.

He never did. When it happened again a week or two later during a supply drop, the yellow and orange golf balls came from ABOVE and DOWN at them from a gray, misty outcropping, searching for their cockpit. Cooper had frozen again, but not before gripping his control yoke and banking the transport hard to the right, instinctively turning away from the ground fire. He was not flying the airplane, Don was. They were still in the drop zone in the middle of a drop, the loadmaster and volunteers kicking the materials out when Cooper's maneuver threw them backward inside the fuselage.

It was pure luck it wasn't a complete disaster. If Cooper banked to the left, there was no doubt in Don's mind he would have lost his loadmaster, at the very least, through the cargo door. None of the men were restrained by straps in the airplane. At 300 feet there was no point in having them wear a parachute. Don, a large man, easily over-powered Cooper with a straight arm, pulling him back from the controls, gripping Cooper's wrist hard until he released the yoke. Once he confirmed the loadmaster and volunteers were uninjured on the intercom, they re-flew the valley to finish the drop. Cooper had fallen back into the white corpse mask again, shrinking down into his seat, closing his eyes. Don couldn't believe it. The hillside gunner did not shoot during the second drop.

This second incident was almost too much for even a mild-tempered man like Don. He fully understood Cooper could not handle being shot at, and never would, but the man also broke a cardinal rule in a two-seat cockpit. Airplane cockpits with two required pilots distinctively divide the functions and responsibilities of the pilot, the captain, and the co-pilot. The man in the left seat is in charge, did most of the flying, and the co-pilot flew at the pleasure of the captain. He was an assistant. Don understood Cooper had been a Captain of the Line before he was called up as a reservist, but in this squadron Cooper was a co-pilot. Don's first instinct was to immediately request a replacement after reporting the two incidents. He would let the squadron decide if there would be any charges or disciplinary measures. He was so angry he did not say another word to Cooper after they landed. He stared at the man for a long moment, then simply unbuckled his seat belt and walked out of the airplane.

As in the first incident Cooper recovered quickly once they flew out of the drop zone. Everything seemed almost normal by the time they were on their approach to Moresby. In the landing pattern, without thinking, Don asked for flaps and landing gear and Cooper dutifully pulled the levers, confirmed their position, even noted *I have a wheel* on his side, *gear down and locked*, the standard call-outs. On final, Don didn't even look Cooper's way as he called for cowl flaps, *open*, and to confirm the tail wheel was locked. Cooper confirmed both, the last words they said to one another that day.

In the end Don did nothing. He steamed and fumed, but once he cooled off knew he would not report him. Transport pilots were hard to come by, any transport pilot, and once one revealed leadership potential he was promoted out of the right seat. His fellow squadron aircraft commanders averaged two or three months with their co-pilots. Someone to break in all over again *and some of 'em ain't worth shit! Might as well be flying alone!* He heard that often enough. He had a problem with Cooper, but it boiled down to what he could accept. When they weren't being shot at, or flying real low and slow where they MIGHT get shot at, Cooper was reliable and an excellent pilot. The combat exposure was just minutes of each mission—critical minutes, but a small part of the mission. Cooper revealed no fear of flying in weather, even when they were skirting around thunderstorms close to the ridges. And he saved Don's bacon in the Dutch DC-2.

One week in mid-September there was a string of mishaps and two of the most reliable C-47s were damaged in landing accidents. Not total write-offs but the squadron was down, temporarily, to six working airplanes being flown around the clock on resupply missions by the exhausted squadron crews. Two DC-2s, both Dutch airliners, were flown down from Malaysia at night by British crews with more balls then sense. The machines, abandoned by the Dutch and stolen under the noses of the Japanese, were in fair shape and immediately commandeered by the USAAF into service. Within 24 hours the passenger seats were removed and the aircraft painted in USAAF mud brown.

The DC-2, visually similar to a DC-3, was an underpowered and less capable aircraft but there was no question of getting the airplanes on the flying schedule. The Allies needed anything with wings capable of carrying cargo. Don and Cooper, currently without an assigned airplane that day, were grease-penciled for an afternoon resupply mission with a DC-2.

Don, with zero hours in DC-2s, climbed on board two hours before the flight to familiarize himself with the cockpit. He was appalled with his first discovery. The layout of the cockpit was somewhat similar to that of a DC-3 or a C-47, but all the instruments were metric, i.e., liters and kilometers per hour. Every single gauge, label, cockpit sign and manual was in Dutch. He was saved by Cooper, who slid into the right seat and explained the differences between the machines, pointing out the power settings and necessary airspeeds for varying weights. His 1,000 hours in DC-2s were evident, yet the most valuable component was his admission of his heritage, on his mother's side, of the Netherlands. He was just fluent enough in Dutch to translate the signs and gauges. They worked together to also translate the metric gauges into values they could use and understand, developing a useable checklist of flying numbers by takeoff time.

Luckily on this mission they received no ground fire, the largest threat being the anemic response of the DC-2's engines when Don firewalled the throttles trying to clear a ridge after the drop. When they landed back at Moresby, he actually got under the wings to inspect the landing gear, expecting to find evidence of the foliage he knew they flew through.

Don returned his attention to the men crawling over the overturned P-40. Things were working out between him and Cooper. He was lucky to have him, most of the time. He could not help but wonder, though, if someday, somewhere his need for another pilot would not be met. They might both die as the result. It just hung out there. He tried not to think about it.

"Mind if I run over and see if I can give them a hand?" asked Cooper, hesitating, although already starting in that direction.

"Sure, just come back when the trucks arrive with our wounded." Don watched him hunker down against the onslaught, stumbling as the gusts blew him backwards.

The pilot of the P-40 survived but Cooper didn't think he would live. It took about 30 men, most of them natives and Army engineers, to hoist the upside-down fuselage up in the gusting wind. It was the only way to get the pilot out of the cockpit. The canopy was closed and intact. Once they propped the fuselage up a few feet, the canopy was kicked open. It was not a pretty sight. The deceleration of the flip over was so abrupt the pilot's shoulder harness failed, hurling his head into the gun sight mounted on the windscreen rail. Split it wide open. The Aussie was still alive, but he never made a sound and probably never would.

Cooper said a couple of the rescuers were asking why the pilot didn't just bail out of his Kittyhawk, as the Aussies called the P-40, when he still had some altitude. All the pilots in the group knew. He tried to save the machine. The engine was running right up to when he lined up on final. It was just bad luck, that's all. Of course the transport pilots didn't have that option most of the time, as they didn't wear parachutes on normal missions because they flew too low. They hugged the ridges and dodged in and out of the clouds to avoid fighters, and if they got shot down during an aerial delivery, the ground was seconds away.

Don got tired of the wind and rain and climbed back into the fuselage. He was cold, wishing he could get into dry clothes. In 10 or 20 minutes the storm would pass, the heat lamp return and his uniform would dry in minutes. In the gloom of the cabin he found Sergeant Larson prone dead center and asleep in the cabin passageway. He was oblivious to the drama on the runway or the brief, violent storm chucking the 19,000 pound (empty) airplane around. Don decided, after a quick consideration, to move up a little farther and join him.

Sergeant Larson shook Don awake. Don stared at him, Larson's blond hair almost white in the light, with the look of a man who not only was being retrieved from a deep sleep, but awakened by a ghostly stranger. He gripped Larson's arm hard, as their eyes locked.

"Sir—it's Larson, sir! The wounded are here and we need to get em' loaded!" Don looked past Larson, focusing on the internal ribs of the fuselage curving up to the ceiling of the cabin. *A fuckin' gooney bird, what did you expect?*

As he stumbled out Don was blinded by the yellow glare of the blazing sun. *Jeez Louise*, he thought, *this place is fuckin' insane*. The wind and rain had vanished, the steaming pools of black water on the sides of the slightly high-centered runway the only evidence of the torrents from minutes before. He brushed his hand through his short, cropped black hair to recall he lost his cap earlier in the wind.

Sergeant Larson and the medics were inserting the apparatus to suspend and stack the patient litters in the cabin. They would be taken down at the other end of the short flight to Moresby, when the transport would resume its duty as a freight hauler on the return trip to Dobodura. On these short flights up over the Owen Stanleys' the patients were attended by Army medics, either US or Australian, depending on the nationality of the casualties. On the longer flights headed for Australia, and in some cases, all the way back to the United States, the Army was starting to include nurses.

These nurses were to be specially trained to deal with the issues of patients in flight, a new category of medicine altogether. The thought made Don think of Katie. She said once she liked flying and was thinking about volunteering for the flight nurse program. He didn't know if she said that because he was a pilot, but he liked the idea. Maybe he would see her more. He'd only known her a month, talked to her maybe three or four times, but there was something there, he sensed a mutual interest.

There was zero chance for a guy to meet an American woman, nurse or otherwise, on New Guinea most of the time. Don knew he was lucky. For the combat troops, the first time they would see one would be as a patient in either a station hospital or evacuation hospital at Port Moresby. For everyone else, even pilots, it was an impossible situation. For one, there were very few women, period, but the rules and regulations for fraternization under General Douglas MacArthur were also very strict. Unlike the ETO (European Theatre of Operations), there were no nurses allowed near the frontlines, the portable surgical hospitals or even the Clearing Company base hospitals. Where they were allowed, dozens of miles to the rear, they were segregated and housed behind *barbed wire and armed guards.* Any contact with a US Army or Navy nurse was for official business only, and the few off duty occasions where nurses were allowed to mix with the men, they had chaperones.

Don was always glad to fly one of these air evac missions for just the chance the 153rd Station Hospital would send their nurses out to meet the air ambulances. If the cases were critical enough, both Army docs and nurses would be waiting to perform triage among the casualties. If nothing else, he could at least ask about Katie, no harm in that, is there? Especially since she was leaving Port Moresby any day. The 153rd was rotating with the 166th and Katie was going back to Australia. He never got a mission to Australia, so it might be months before he saw her again, if ever. He sighed, forgetting about it as the first casualties, burn cases apparently, were carefully lifted into the cabin.

Even at 15 feet, Don could smell the charred flesh, mixed with some kind of fuel. The glazed eyes of the soldiers followed his as they

14

passed, passive and withdrawn. He and Cooper stepped forward to assist the medics with the loading, not something they normally did, holding IV bottles alongside the wounded until the litters were latched in place.

The next group of litters were filled with Australians, the Diggers unusually burned brown in the sun even for Aussies. Their eyes were large, the faces skull-like, a vision of lean, tapped out men. A few of their uniforms, what was left of them after the medics cut them to pieces, were the old Australian kit; khaki shorts and shirts, not the newer green jungle uniform.

"Who are these guys?" Don asked the lone Australian medic. "They look like shit, they've been through the ringer."

The Aussie medic, who didn't look much better than his patients, glanced at Don with a sharp, weary eye. He was near exhaustion himself, the dirt on his face appearing to have been there for weeks.

"Ayes' blokes are 2/14 Battalion, 21st Brigade, 'om the 7th Division, suh'." He said this with such reverence, Don could only nod grimly. The unit sounded familiar. He was pretty sure these were some of the men the squadron had been doing airdrops for. "We 'ave been through da' ringer, mate, we 'ought da' Japs oop' da' Track all winta' an' 'opped em' dead, an' got pulled off a refit ta' go with 'is show. Not many of us left ta' 'hip home!'"

Don examined the men closely, noting most of the wounded Aussies had their bush slouch hats, the large, floppy wool and felt things that made the Australian soldier so unique lying on their chests, clutched in their hands or tucked under their litters. Many of them, even those with heavily bandaged wounds, were smoking cigarettes while talking quietly among themselves. Their eyes were bright and un-blinking. *A tough looking bunch*, Don thought, *like the horse wranglers he encountered every summer on the ranch as a teenager back in Burney, in Northern California.*

These men looked like them in a way, they lived outdoors, had the physical confidence, presence and wildness of men who could take care of themselves. And stayed to themselves. That was where the comparison stopped. Unlike the American burn casualties loaded up forward, the Aussies completely ignored him as he stood next to them. He knew they lived in a world of terror, death, filth, hunger and unrelenting exposure beyond his comprehension. He sensed they were still out there in the jungle somewhere, wary and considerate only of their own kind. He had not seen what they had seen, could not even fathom living as they had under the dark green canopy he flew over so close he could see their upturned faces. Don slipped around the medics respectfully, making his way up to the cockpit to begin his preflight checks, feeling almost invisible.

15

CHAPTER 2

November 30, 1942, 153rd Station Hospital, Port Moresby, Papua New Guinea

Disappointment, true down to the dirt disappointment was not something Kathleen (Katie) McCutcheon ever really embraced, mostly because it was not allowed in her family. You called the emotion something else and you damn well better not be walking around with that sourpuss, young lady. Scots-Irish on both sides, 40 years away from the small windswept islands their grandparents called the Old Land across the Atlantic, the McCutcheons' and the McConnells' left the rock lands of Massachusetts for the promises of the American West in the 1840s. Each family chose a different path, stopping here and there for burials, work, marriages and disaster, chronicled in long diaries and letters accompanied by dusty, faded pictures. These forbears, mostly farmers and sheepherders with an occasional seaman or two, knew a world of hard weather and hard times. Or it seemed this is all that would be remembered when a lesson was taught to the children. Katie sighed, aware she was alone in the Quonset hut, sitting down on her bunk lighting a cigarette, ignoring the NO SMOKING sign. Her single duffle bag, packed and unpacked every day for a week now, was stowed under her bunk.

It had taken her six years to get away from the cattle ranch north of Lakeview, Oregon to this very spot in New Guinea. Six years from the time her high school diploma was placed in her hand and she made her secret promise to do something with her life, something worthwhile and, well—dramatic, as far from eastern Oregon and cows and steers as she could get. Nursing was the ticket for her escape as it certainly worked for her older sister. Susan went straight up to Corvallis for a couple of years of college and then made the transfer to nursing school in Portland. It was only 250 miles or so as the crow flies from Lakeview, but a long tortured train ride from Klamath Falls, the closest station. No one did it unless they had to. Far enough, her sister said, for once you pass the dairies outside of Portland there was not a cow to be seen. It sure sounded good to Katie, who true to form, learned from Susan's mistakes and bypassed the meanderings of casual campus life for a direct route to nursing school.

Katie, even in high school, was already volunteering during the summer breaks at the little hospitals and nursing homes in Klamath Falls while staying with an aunt. This was pretty disappointing for her parents, who were hoping she would help with the ranch but recognized the path already blazed by her sister. To their credit for which Katie was grateful, they didn't stand in her way knowing she preferred flushing shit out of bedpans and giving enemas to old people to riding a horse all day, looking for lost cattle.

The bed pan experience did point Katie away from routine ward work though, guiding her to psychiatry and to the large state and private hospitals in Salem, Oregon after she graduated from nursing school. Psychiatry lost its charm quickly once she realized the patients in her care were truly chronic, with most destined to never leave the hospital. She found them tragic, pathetic beings and in the end unrewarding for her as caregiver. The human mind was too vast, too much of an enigma for her direct action, results-oriented ideals of nursing. Her knowledge, youthful enthusiasm and skills weren't enough. In the end she could not fully engage or trust them with her heart. The tipping point came when a patient, an old man in his late-60s Katie considered benign and harmless, nearly ripped the front of her white, starched uniform off trying to get at her breasts.

It had happened near the end of her shift, an hour or two after dinner and medications, his sudden appearance at the nursing station surprising her. A strange, animal-like look in his eye just before he attacked was the only warning she received. He was treated almost like a trustee compared to most of the other patients, so he was familiar with the latch to the half door leading to her station, a button under the shelf out of sight. He reached around and pushed the button and was on her before she could get to her feet. His grip was incredibly strong as he tore at her uniform, reaching for her collar and yanking the heavy cotton straight down, the buttons snapping. Katie could not believe what was happening as the man groaned, his face buried in her breasts. Her scream came suddenly and loud, just as her instincts kicked in and she fought like she used to fight with her brothers, who had taught her how to use her shoulders for power to punch and jab with closed fists, knuckles forward, making them hard, making them hurt.

The old man backed away in pain and fright as she got to her feet and followed him aggressively, mad as hell now, swinging hard but expertly, using her upper body to throw strong punches to his face. Two male attendants and a couple of the patients arrived as Katie backed the old man out of her office, trying to cover his face as she pummeled him repeatedly, her uniform dress half torn off, one breast free from her broken bra, blood dripping from deep scratches on her shoulders. It was an episode Katie didn't like to think about but it did change her direction, returning her to regular ward work for a short internship in OB/GYN and pediatrics. She decided she wanted to be around normal people for a while. Women and babies seemed safe, positive and

17

rewarding, something she could wrap her passion around for the rest of her career. This seemed a reasonable plan right up until December 7, 1941.

Some of the doctors at her hospital were military reservists who were activated almost immediately. They reported to work in uniform waiting for their orders, quite unnecessarily, but it did have the desired effect on Katie and many of the other nurses. The uniforms looked great, the doctors suddenly more important, more *relevant*, in their eyes. The young nurses wanted to do something but only a few made the big step prior to December 7th, even though most folks felt a war was coming. Katie, unattached and knowing her sister was already trying to get into the Army Nurse Corps even though she was 29 and apparently past the cut-off, went straight down to the recruiting office during lunch.

Despite the fervor of patriotism, the loud noise and talk of service to country heard from classrooms, church pulpits and radios, few women heeded the call because, in all honesty, it was not something a well-brought up young woman was supposed to do. The military was very much the domain of men, of rough men with rough edges who did not rub shoulders with polite society. The US armed services of the late 1930s were small, remotely placed organizations and inconsequential to most Americans. Anyone who lived near a military base would tell you that. Katie or her sister never listened to such talk. The immediate needs for the country meant a large Army had to be stood up, one that didn't exist yet. The few who represented the old guard would be flooded with new people and blood, a new order of things. Men would have to get used to having women work with them, because as in past times of difficulty everyone was needed. The country needed women.

Having been raised on a cattle ranch Katie and her sister were certainly not in awe of men. They considered themselves the equals to most men in just about anything you cared to imagine, certainly the superiors to some. Besides, they knew all about so-called rough men, men like their father and brothers, uncles and neighbors, young cowhands and old cowhands. A breed of man you had to understand.

The two sisters chose nursing because it was a respected profession and it gave them the necessary freedom they wanted out of their lives. They wanted to serve their country now, not just their community, the military being a vehicle for them to remain in their chosen profession and do just that. Later, when Katie realized certain of her relatives across the country, in places like Iowa and Kansas, were refusing to acknowledge her as family because she voluntarily joined the Army, she became a bit sad. Many of these folks she could hardly remember, if at all, but because they carried both the McCutcheon and

18

McConnell name she was more hurt by it than she was willing to admit.

This feeling of being let down, disappointment—unexpected surprise, whatever she was raised not to demonstrate publically—was becoming a constant reality now she was a real Army nurse. Katie had tried *to toss it aside, make do, put a smile on it,* and every other folk bandaid her family had used to bury hurt and unhappiness. It just didn't work anymore. Nothing panned out as she expected.

There was virtually no training offered by the Army when they arrived at their post at Fort Sam Houston, Texas, other than a few days of classroom orientation on how to wear an Army uniform, understanding ranks and courtesies, and an hour or two on how to stand at attention and salute. The Army, rightly, the new recruits reasoned among themselves, focused mostly on patient care the Army way, which is to say treating soldiers as mass casualties. As one snarky recruit sniffed, *this is like being trained as a short order cook for 1000 people! Sanitation! Cleanliness! Sterile fields! Tents! Big Tents! Bigger Tents! Clean! Cleaner!* The sense the young nurses received from their instructors was they were being trained to treat thousands of casualties at the same time, and girl, you better keep those tents spotless in between. This was going to be a BIG war, with BIG casualties. The faster they could get those young men healthy, the faster the US would win the war.

Only one McCutcheon would make it through the pipeline. Susan finally won a waiver to become an Army nurse even though she was past the age cutoff, but there was delay after delay waiting for the waiver to turn into orders from Washington. In the interim Katie was accepted into the Army Nurse Corps almost immediately due to her past experience in psychiatry. She was on a troop ship docked at Honolulu when she got word Susan had eloped and moving to Spokane, Washington. A handsome young man, another rancher's son, had won her heart despite her desire to serve her country. Susan was impatient, always was, making her choice almost out of spite as far as Katie was concerned.

Katie, who waited an hour to get a telephone line home, smiled sadly as she digested the news. She fired off a telegram to Susan in Portland with congratulations, annoyed as usual when the two military policemen assigned as the nurse's chaperones started droning the nurses needed to get back to the ship. The two MPs, both enlisted corporals, seemed to ignore the fact their 12 charges were commissioned officers, all second lieutenants. They herded the young ladies together like a girls' softball team, calling them *ladies* or *girls*. None of them stood up to it and challenged the MPs, instead, they jumped around like sheep to finish their cables and telephone calls. It didn't help the elderly, retread first lieutenant Army nurse in charge of all 60 of them insisted they wear their white nurses' uniforms and blue, old-fashioned capes, topped off with the flying nun cap pinned to their hair. Their second lieutenant bars were hidden on their uniform collars under the cape, so some civilian folks and even military personnel mistook them for Catholic nursing nuns, even though they wore no habits, their hair quite visibly tucked under their caps. Once the rumor got around they were nuns that was it. It was *sister* this and *sister* that, with everyone so intent on getting an outside line to the States no one cared.

Katie cared. She knew many of the new nurses cared too, assuming the Army would handle this issue once they got out in the real world, this lack of respect they sensed from everyone in uniform during their initial orientation. This meant of course, men, officers and enlisted men, who not only stared at them instead of saluting when it was supposed to be appropriate, but smiled and even laughed at them. It was embarrassing and sometimes infuriating when another officer, a man, would walk right up to them and boldly reach up to their collar and finger their shiny gold bar.

"Are you really a second lieutenant—I mean, are you in the Army?" They asked, smiling. This happened so frequently, and especially to the better looking nurses, it ceased to be a playful joke. During the orientation period the only male officers who seem to pay any attention to them as officers were physicians, and even they were slow to respond to the poorly executed salutes of the nurses out on the street. The old-fashioned starched white nurses' uniform was supposed to be replaced by a more Army-like, khaki or brown uniform for off ward wear, but they weren't issued any. When they received their orders from Texas to report to a troop train for the beginning of their journey to the South Pacific, they were also expecting to be issued some form of fatigue work uniform, similar to the work uniform for male soldiers. Instead they reported in their whites and blue capes, enduring the beginning of their new roles as Catholic nurses to the thousands of troops packed with them on the trains. What was funny, Katie would reflect later, was that the troops were more respectful to them when they thought they were Catholic nuns than they ever were when they realized they were brand new second lieutenant Army nurses.

Not that there would be much chance for military interaction between the nurses and troops once they were jammed into their cars, or later on the special decks of the troopship. The nurses were segregated completely, with armed MPs on all entrances. On the troopship, stuffed to all corners with men and materials with most of the men forced to remain below decks, the nurses were treated as officers and assigned to "officers' country" at a higher deck. Male officers could be seen and conversations with them happened occasionally during messes as they passed by the nurses' tables. There was no other opportunity. No other briefings or contacts with ships' company or officers occurred, so the nurses had no real idea where they were going after they left Honolulu. They endured the ridiculous abandon ship drills where they were at once subjected to endless catcalls and hooting when the troops, at last released to the fresh air for a brief respite to stand by a lifeboat, spotted them. No one disciplined the men when they did this, so the noise level was high for the hour and a half required to start and finally secure the drill, or certainly as long as the nurses were visible during their trek to their assigned boats.

One of the nurses wondered out loud, to the giggles of the others, *if the men are already going nuts when they spot white women on their way to the war, what are they going to be like when they hadn't seen a woman in a year or two?*

That's why they got us locked up like hens in a hen house, dumb ass, answered another nurse.

The ship arrived in Brisbane, Queensland, Australia, in late July, 1942. After a great deal of confusion where the Army appeared to not know what to do with them, Katie and 20 of the new nurses were assigned to the 153rd Station Hospital, based at a former Anglican boys prep school on the coast at Southport. The other 40 nurses were assigned to hospitals farther away at Gatton, Sydney or Melbourne. At first Katie was pretty excited about the assignment because she found out almost all of the 153rd had been transferred to Port Moresby, New Guinea. She really didn't know exactly where Port Moresby was on New Guinea, but she did know the Japanese were on the island and the Australians were fighting them in the mountains somewhere, and Americans were also fighting on Guadalcanal. What she didn't know was the reality of General MacArthur's strict rules on keeping nurses out of combat zones. The Aussies were fighting a desperate battle for survival up in the Owen-Stanley's, a battle against a superior Japanese force where the outcome was not certain. The Japanese force threatened the existence of Port Moresby, so although the 153rd was there supporting the American air crews and the Aussies fighting in the mountains, there would be no nurses until the island was considered secure.

Katie and the other newly assigned nurses joined the 30 or so 153rd nurses who were left behind. The hospital had a 250 bed capacity with perhaps 100 patients, many seriously wounded Australians who had lived or had family in the region prior to the war. Americans were fighting in the South Pacific, but the casualty numbers were still low. The evacuation chain was fairly rigid, American casualties going to Australia only because their wounds were too serious to be treated in the field, but not serious enough to warrant shipping them back to the

United States. What the 153rd had a lot of were Americans ill from tropical diseases, diseases requiring distance from hot and humid conditions. Diseases like malaria, scrub typhus, dengue fever, tropical dysentery, yaws, leprosy, bubonic plague and cutaneous diphtheria. What they were also seeing were cases of FUO, "Fever of Unknown Origin", some of which were later categorized as "Battle Fatigue". The US hospitals, building up at a tremendous rate preparing for the counter-offensive back up the island chain, had so much surplus capacity where the Australians did not, the US authorities accepted Allied casualties wherever they could.

Southport was a beautiful resort right on the coast. Even in the Australian winter the weather was balmy, warm without much humidity, the beaches long and spotless. The locals were extremely friendly, welcoming the new visitors into their homes and lives. They seemed grateful for the arrival of thousands of Americans even as their own men, Australian Army veterans of the Middle East from the 6th and 7th Divisions most recently returned, started shipping out again. Katie realized with alarm many Australians believed the Japanese planned an invasion of the Australian continent, a threat never considered seriously by the American Press. *Of course not, deary,* a middle-aged Aussie hospital volunteer said with a smile and a condescending wink. *You Yanks wouldn't be much worried about us, what with the Japs almost taking Midway about 2,000 miles away from California!*

Katie got the message, recognizing the Australians already endured an attack on their soil on the north shore at Darwin. Like west coasters back in the States, there were constant rumors of infiltrators and invasion up and down the vast coasts of the continent. The Australians were less hysterical about it but to their Prime Minister, John Curtin and many Australians the threat was very real. The big difference was proximity. The Japanese lost the naval battle of the Coral Sea only 200 miles off the coast near Townsville, on the northeast shore, turning around a Japanese invasion force bound for Port Moresby. If the invasion had been successful the Japanese would have gained complete control of the northern approaches to Australia, as the closest point of New Guinea was only about 300 miles away.

Nonetheless rules were relaxed in Australia, with plenty of free time for the American nurses to enjoy the beautiful beaches. Despite the charms Katie and the others quickly became bored and unhappy, itching to get closer to the front like their sisters in the ETO. As the battle on the Kokoda Track raged and American airmen and soldiers seriously wounded in and around Guadalcanal began to show up throughout the winter with the Aussie wounded, there was more of a sense of contribution on their part, but only so. There wasn't much of a life and death struggle going on at Southport, for the patients were well stabilized for the most part by the time they arrived.

Katie envisioned tying a tourniquet on the leg of a wounded soldier, or giving a chest massage when another had stopped breathing when she thought of handling combat casualties. The Army triage training taught them to prioritize the mass casualties they would receive and it was a sobering, thoughtful consideration for these young nurses to pick out who would be most likely to survive and therefore receive priority in treatment. The work would count then. Being on the back-end, the back-water of the evacuation chain simply wasn't satisfying to her as an Army nurse.

In October the Australians had turned the tide and were beating the Japanese assault back down the Owen-Stanleys' towards Buna. At the same time the US Army 32nd Infantry Division began moving their troops, training furiously in Australia, from Adelaine on the south coast to Camp Tambourine, near Brisbane. In mid-September units of the division were being airlifted to New Guinea preparing for the new campaign. Near the end of October General MacArthur finally released Army nurses for duty at Port Moresby, citing the closest Japanese troops were 100 miles away, contained and soon to be destroyed.

Within a week Katie and 40 other excited nurses from the 153rd were on their way to Archerfield Airport at Brisbane. Newly clothed with ill-fitting men-sized aviation coveralls, combat boots, steel helmets, gas masks and mosquito nets, the nurses stood by the side of the tarmac. They were finally going to where the 153rd really was, where the war was, but not all at once. They learned like everyone else, equipment took top priority and each airplane had only so much room for passengers.

The hurry up and wait, constant anticipation was almost more than Katie could bear. The long, endless, freezing and bumpy ride on the transport plane was acceptable only because she was finally getting to the war. With her face pressed against the only window available to them because of all of the equipment on the plane, Katie jostled with the other nurses for their first glimpses of New Guinea. The transport had stayed around 5-6,000 feet, 1,000 or so above the gray cloud deck. After six hours it descended through the clouds, bumpily, lower and lower until the C-47 was clear of the clouds and a few hundred feet off the dark, choppy water.

It felt much warmer in the cabin now, the humidity creating condensation on the aluminum fuselage and a clammy dampness on their uniforms and skin. As she watched she realized she couldn't see the surface of the ocean clearly anymore because of mist and rain, a hard rain thumping against the skin of the airplane with a frightening, rhythmic rumble. She was forced aside by another nurse trying to take a look. Tired and irritated, Katie stepping back over the packed gear and sleeping bodies to find a place to sit. The enlisted loadmaster woke up with the rain, smiling and yawning at the nurses as he rolled up his sleeping bag. He stood up and hooked up his headset to the intercom and checked in with the pilot. *About 45 more minutes ladies,* he said cheerfully. *Hopefully we'll be out of this soon and in the sun.*

He was wrong by nearly an hour. The transport droned on and on, in and out of rain showers with an apparent head wind, finding every bump in the sky. One of the nurses, her face against the glass, shrieked with delight as she pointing out the window. *There's jungle down there! We're over jungle! Everything is so—green!*

It became the trademark inside joke whenever someone asked them to describe New Guinea. They would look at them strangely, and declare slowly and with the same bright-eyed enthusiastic emphasis as the nurse at the window: *Why, everything is so—GREEN!* It was a true, no-shit moment, because as they were to find out, New Guinea, especially anywhere near the jungle, was nothing but green. Green moss, green slime, green foliage, green trees, green water—a dark, yet almost luminous green. That is, unless it's raining. In that case everything turns mud brown. They stepped out of the airplane into a straight down, waterfall deluge pelting them painfully. They followed one another directly under the wing, staring out across a tarmac of what appeared to be a huge lake. The rain was so heavy they couldn't see anything beyond the shadow of what appeared to be another airplane, 100 yards away. They could see no buildings or structures of any kind beyond the mist of the rain.

The rain stopped almost instantly after five minutes, evaporating the mist to reveal the double reflections of numerous structures and aircraft. The clarity of the moment was lost as steam began to rise everywhere, creating a new murky mist clouding the view again. The sun, totally hidden seconds before bore down on the water to shimmer and bounce the glaring white light straight under the wing, blinding them.

Jesus, thought Katie, *what a place.* She wondered how the pilot landed on the lake they were on, but noticed how almost immediately the standing water, including the water that had been an inch or two deep under the C-47's wheels, was disappearing somehow. There seemed to be some kind of a corrugated metal surface coming out of the water, big mats with large holes. *Where does this drain too?* But this thought was lost as a lumbering, splashing Army deuce and a half drove up next to the cargo door of the transport. Two soldiers jumped out of the canvas-

24

topped back and two more stepped out of the cab, all of them stopping momentarily to stare at the nurses. Finally one of them, an NCO, barked an order and the others went inside the plane. *Hi there, girls!* The NCO said enthusiastically but he too turned and stepped inside the transport. It didn't take them long to figure out no one was coming out to pick them up. They watched as the men quickly loaded up the entire back of the deuce and a half with aircraft parts and lubricating oil. There didn't seem to be any room for any nurses. Katie, impatient and growing more frustrated by the minute, approached the NCO about taking at least some of the nurses.

There was room for two nurses in the cab of the truck, jammed in tight, and two more standing on boxes near the back of the truck. They tossed in their duffels for the ride to flight operations. They would see about calling the 153rd for a ride. Katie with the two remaining nurses, hoped to get a ride with the crew of the C-47 once they secured the airplane. After about 15 minutes a lone jeep whirred along the now mostly dry, puddle-strewn tarmac before turning abruptly beside the transport, stopping close to the big tail where Katie and the others stood. The tall, dark-haired officer driving had his leather-brimmed overseas hat on the back of his head, his eyes shaded by the oversized aviator sunglasses. His smile was broad and warm as he lowered the sunglasses to peer at the nurses. They stared back at first before they realized he was a first lieutenant, shooting out their right arms for stiff, exaggerated salutes. The officer adjusted his hat, slowly returning the salute.

"Nurses!" he declared. "We heard there would be nurses soon!" The officer introduced himself, informed them he was the pilot of the C-47 100 yards away preparing to deliver supplies to the Aussies up in the mountains as soon as the weather cleared. Katie and the others, charmed by this handsome pilot and possible ride, explained their predicament. Within 20 minutes the officer delivered the nurses directly to the doorstep of the 153rd Station Hospital, a few miles away from the airfield. He went out of his way to inform them he was based right there at Seven-Mile airfield and was home most evenings. It was the first time Katie met Don Crenshaw and like the others, thought he was a pretty nice guy and kind of cute.

Katie's first impression of Port Moresby on the other hand, was not so good. What she didn't know at the time was the impression would not improve. Living conditions for the nurses were primitive although most of them lived in Quonset huts instead of tents. It kept some of the little furry four legged animals at bay. Security was good for the most part, certainly in the living quarters which were surrounded by barbed wire and armed guards, per General MacArthur. The heat and humidity were oppressive, sauna-like, with insects so thick at dusk you couldn't breathe. You had to wear long sleeved protective clothing because of the threat of malaria anyway, with the only real relief found behind screened buildings spray-saturated with DDT. Air raid alerts were constantly occurring, almost to the point folks would ignore them because actual bombing raids were rare. But they did happen. If the weather over the Owen-Stanleys' broke at all, there was always a chance of Japanese medium bombers slipping through the passes from Rabaul. There were more and more Australian and American fighters coming up the pipeline from Australia, but parts were non-existent, with good maintenance hard to come by. Many of the fighters on the ground stayed on the ground for want of both.

Everything was on the bubble; the planning for the new Buna and Gona campaign, indeed the strategic plan for the entire northward offensive, was upended on its ear. Katie and the rest of the nurses, all with less than 30 days in Port Moresby were going back to Australia with the rotation of the 153rd Station Hospital with the 166th. Despite the living conditions Katie was appalled when she heard the news. *What! We just got here! Why? Aren't we more needed here?*

What had been so imperative—getting casualty treatment facilities as close to the fighting as possible so wounded could be returned to duty as quickly as possible—was being mitigated by the air transport experiment. The lowly flying buses, the C-47s, the converted DC-3 people haulers turned into troop delivery vehicles, were now flying *everywhere* and carrying *everything*. As Don Crenshaw told her only partially joking, in the last six months the generals suddenly realized the solution for much of the incredible distances of the Pacific was air transport. It eliminated the need to build dozens of treatment facilities in horrible, disease-infested places. Troops, once their wounds were stabilized in aid stations and mobile surgical hospitals, didn't have to remain in such places as Port Moresby for 90, 60 or even 30 days for treatment and recovery before they would be evaluated for potential return to duty. In seven hours casualties would be in Australia; safe, disease and insect free.

At first all casualties from the Kokoda Track were airlifted to Port Moresby for treatment. Only 50-60 miles away in the mountains, the tiny grass airstrip at Kokoda became a godsend to wounded Australians. The survival rate shot up immediately. The earlier extraction method for wounded or sick who could not be treated in the field was a carryout. 15-20 natives were required for each casualty, the slow, treacherous trip back down the narrow trail taking several days. For some the more seriously wounded or ill Aussies, the stretcher ride, high up on the shoulders of the "fuzzy wuzzy angels", merely compounded the personal sufferings of a journey to an early grave.

In the single week the Dobodura airfield had been in operation the casualty evacuation plan was already changing. The decision ensured many pre-screened casualties would soon bypass Port Moresby completely, flying direct to Australia. As the capacity in Australia continued to grow it became apparent this tremendous resource was underutilized, certainly when more transport aircraft were made available. There were issues to be worked out because air transport of casualties created its own medical hazards, most just now being understood. But the limited experience revealed troops who could not be treated in the field recovered much more quickly when they were far removed from the sweltering jungle environment.

To Katie this meant Port Moresby would soon be a medical backwater. The 153rd with five months on New Guinea, was suffering with enough tropical disease and psychological problems among the original, all-men medical staff to be almost functionally ineffective until the nurses arrived in late October. Even then the nurses, all commissioned officers, encountered problems with the enlisted medics who provided the only direct care available until the nurses arrived. The nurses took over the care of the patients, immediately relegating the medics to the more menial support roles and creating resentment and downright hostility.

Nurses were going to stay this part was clear, as long as they were needed, but not necessarily Katie and the other newly arrived nurses attached to the 153rd. They were going back to Australia because they were part of the 153rd. The replacement unit, the 166th Hospital Station, was bringing their own 53 nurses. Katie and the 40 nurses were ordered a week ago to pack their bags and prepare to depart, making room in their quarters for the incoming 166th. This was not a big deal on a personal level, as Katie and the others were only allowed to bring a single bag in. Every day for a week the nurses got up when alerted to meet incoming casualties, waiting to be relieved. What the medical command planners could not predict were the enormous casualties sustained during the initial part of the Buna campaign, a campaign started essentially the same time as the 153rd and the 166th were supposed to be changing hands.

To the nurses it was one more sign the left and right hand of the Army did not communicate. Somehow the people who were planning the fighting part of the war moved along on different schedules to the ones who picked up the pieces. What it meant to Katie was more confusion and a rising sense of frustration. She hated Port Moresby, everything about it, and a part of her was ready to leave. The personal conditions, the working environment, the horrible climate, the suffering

27

of the men who fell under her care, it all seemed to run together. She felt guilty because she had only been there a month. She resented the cold looks from the medics when she gave them orders, fully aware of their stares at her legs, breasts and butt when they thought she was not looking. Not that you could see much when a gal is wearing baggy cotton coveralls two sizes two large. *Oh hell, some of them stare whether I'm looking or not. They don't give a damn.*

After treating mostly Australians when she was in Southport, she was surprised when they started receiving American wounded from the Buna campaign. The Australians in Southport and the ones she treated at first at Port Moresby were all veterans and somewhat older. They were sun weathered, tough and mostly silent men suffering from long exposure to combat, jungle rot and malnutrition. The Americans, all from the 32nd Infantry Division, were generally younger in new uniforms, and much more talkative if their wounds were not serious. Many were obviously traumatized by what most likely was their first combat action. Katie found herself holding back tears from the suffering of many of these boys, their cheeks smooth, eyes wide and frightened.

An Australian, a twinkle in his eye, would grip her hand momentarily as she tended his wounds and smile. *Miss, you bein' ma' Sheila fur' the day? Don't min' a bit!* Her months in Southport educated her to what an Aussie meant by that, and she smiled back. *I'm here for you as long as you need me.* An American soldier, a mere boy from his demeanor and fear, would grip her hand the same way as she stopped to check his vitals but wouldn't let go. *Please don't leave me. Please don't let me die here.* She couldn't tell the boy directly if he was going to die he never would have been flown from Dobodura to Port Moresby. At the field aid station or surgical hospital, the volume of wounded forced the medical staff to triage and set aside Expectants, or those they expected to die soon. But the new fighting push at Buna seemed to have many patients being loaded on the medevac flights that would be considered critical. A small number might die on the flight for a number of reasons, but it was very rare. The survival rate if a man made it to a medevac flight was very good. At least this boy, with an amputated leg and a punctured lung, would mostly likely survive. All he knew was he was whole 24 hours ago and was now missing one leg and it was difficult and painful to breathe. *I'll be right here. You go to sleep.* Katie would stay as long as she could. Sometimes it would be enough.

She wanted to go, she wanted to stay. *I waited six years to get here, serve a month and I'm ready to leave. A month.* The over treated water, the horrible, metallic taste which could not be covered up with coffee, tea or anything was giving her the constant runs. She was tethered to the bathrooms wherever she was, losing 10 pounds in the process. The huge malaria pills they took every day were starting to make her skin turn yellow—or orange? Despite the mosquito screens and nets around their beds all of them were bitten dozens of times every day. She scratched the bites in her sleep, slowly tearing the skin off with her nails creating wound lesions impossible to heal in the humidity. She understood now the huge craters on the veteran Australians she had treated at Southport. It took weeks or months of a dry climate for the lesions to close up. Her arms and legs, rarely exposed to sunlight now they had cotton long sleeve coveralls to wear, were covered with the small unsightly red sores making her look like a leper in the shower. *Well, with all the other lepers.* At least hers were not the size of large coins, dripping pus, like those poor wore-out Aussies.

Katie lit a fresh cigarette from the butt of the first, flipping the butt neatly into the sand ashtray hidden under the foot of her lower bunk. She needed sleep but her brain was still spun up. Her shoulders slumped with fatigue as she bent down to massage her feet. They hurt so much. She had spent sixteen hours straight on them assisting in the OR last night, had something for breakfast and went back for six or seven more this morning—or was it afternoon? The wounded kept coming, it was a factory. Garda, her boss, sent her off to get some sleep when Katie leaned over a patient she was intubating and fell asleep. There was no warning at all. Luckily the insertion was done, the patient breathing normally as she laid her head on his chest. The surgeon slid the mayo tray aside with his elbows before breaking scrub to gently lift Katie off the patient. *I think McCutcheon is done.*

It would have been embarrassing if she was awake. She did awake 45 minutes later on a gurney set aside in a corridor, then ordered to her quarters by Garda when she attempted to scrub for a return to the OR. Katie slowly laid back on her bunk, closing her eyes only briefly before she heard the drubbing drone of engines overhead, several of them, C-47s in the pattern. More wounded, had to be.

She heard the quick steps crunching down the sandy walkway between the Quonset huts, the stride of a woman always in a hurry. There certainly weren't any men around, except the bored, quiet clump of the MPs as they passed one another walking the perimeter of the women's compound. Katie sat up, swinging her legs to the floor as Garda popped through the screened wooden door.

"Did you get any sleep, girl?" Garda demanded testily, noting the cigarette in Katie's hand. Katie grinned sadly while shaking her head.

"No, too wound up. I did get some rest."

Garda was already heading out the door as she pointed skyward. "It's all you're goin' to get, girl. We got inbound wounded overhead, and

29

we don't know too much about this bunch at all. All we heard was we're getting some American burn cases from an exploding vehicle, and a bunch of shot-up Diggers from their big push yesterday. We're taking as many them as we can as the Aussies have run out of beds. Their guys were on the other side of the Gona swamps without any roads, so they were hand-carried out by the fuzzies and their own medics. They're probably a mess. The Colonel wants everybody not in scrub out there to triage. He's holding surge three and four and Captain Lewis is coming along with a radio. We're getting' kinda' backed up! Come on, get your boots on!"

CHAPTER 3

November 30, 1942, Seven-Mile airfield, Port Moresby

"Best aye' kin' do, Vic. We'll get ya' 'arm as a tick. Hang fast, old cobber. Ya' need more 'ole blood, but the Yanks 'ave me their last 'ag of A Pos for ya' so it'll have ta' do. I'm also givin ya' 'ome saline oop' da' sleeve. Fresh stuff, da' blood, so they tell me, straight froom' the yoong' nurses! You're leakin' like a sieve." The words drifted away as the medic stepped back.

Vic opened his eyes only for a moment, hoping his face reflected the smile he was trying to convey to his old friend. He could feel the wool blanket being gently tucked under his body, not too tight, leaving his arms free for the IVs. The morphine did the job, he really couldn't feel much anymore, except when he tried to breathe deeply. He was so cold just a few minutes ago, and couldn't control his shivering. Potty must have heard his chattering teeth. Potty was tending all of the Digs on the airplane yet hovered close to always return to Vic's side.

"Thanks, Pot, you're a fine Sheila."

"Aye' told ya'," Potty muttered accusingly as he adjusted Vic's pillow leaning close, "da' poosition' was too bloody strong, da' Jap in Gona is not da' fella' we knew on da' Track."

Potty reminded Vic of his mum, fussing over a long-ago arm fracture from his childhood when he fell out of a tree he was forbidden to climb. Gums are sticky, covered with biting insects, with notoriously dangerous limbs that would split on a whim. Solid, sappy but hard as granite and nearly as heavy, he was lucky he landed beside the limb instead of under it. It might have bloody well killed him. Cracking his forearm in two places he screamed bloody murder until his dad heard him. His dad didn't let him have it, probably because he was hurt badly, but he was ticked off Vic could see. He quieted down as his dad lifted him carefully across the bench seat of the Model A Ford pickup. He started whining and carrying on again when his mum got to him back at the house, aware his father did not say a word to him as he drove off. *The bloody fool probably broke it, so I'll go in to Bombola and see if I can get that new doc.* His dad was already mad at him for poking about in the gum groves instead of helping out in the stock pens. His mum shook her head, carefully guiding Vic into the house.

Like Potty, his mum talked to herself under her breath as she worked, words meant for him in a strange sort of murky signaling system, with a solid inflection of *disappointment, disapproval, distaste, dismay*—and so on. Potty—and his mum, would simply mutter around

31

you with an occasional raised, irritated eyebrow nodded in your direction. The broken arm spawned all kinds of under-the-breath discussion, not a word of it decipherable. All he knew was his mum was angry with him yet babied him for nearly two weeks until his dad lost his patience. He could say now he understood his mother and men like Potty. They cared deeply about you but you bloody well should know better, and you will hear about it! It was their way, harmless but confounding to a child until the system was understood. A true source of amusement for a grown man, most of the time. Potty—Patrick Johnson, Corporal, Royal Australian Army, was a medic. The only medic of 9 Platoon, A Company, 2/14 Battalion, 21st Brigade, 7th Division from the beginning when they formed the division in Victoria. Vic—Vaughn Evan Hickey, platoon sergeant of 9 Platoon, could not imagine life without him.

The ride in the air ambulance took about 45 minutes and was bumpy as hell. Vic could smell the burn cases, the roasted flesh mixed with gasoline and his own anemia nauseating him. The C-47 was uninsulated and unheated, so as it climbed into the altitudes necessary to clear the Owen-Stanleys' the cabin became cold and noisy. Some of the men, mostly the American burn cases, were not completely sedated so the cold was hard on them. One or two started to moan until their medic sedated or comforted them enough to quiet them as they descended into the landing pattern at Moresby. Vic took a single deep breath to control his desire to vomit, forgetting his punctured lung, finding instant, blinding pain followed by unconsciousness. One moment he was staring at the fabric of the bottom of the litter suspended over his, the next he woke to a young, feminine face with light brown hair carefully lifting his blanket. Their eyes met briefly, a penlight blinding him before she turned to Potty.

"Ayes' lost a lot of blood, miss. He 'alked 'ight into a burst o' Jap seven point seven, 'amn near point blank, 'ost of it there in 'is 'ight hip. Aye, it's a mess. One 'aught em' in the loong', poonched' clean through both sides. For' he fell, some type of charge went off besides the boonker', blowin' em' oop' an' agin' the coconut sides of the boonker'. Nice coompound' fracture of the right tibia, it is."

The nurse listened to Potty's litany before turning towards Vic, looking at him more carefully. "Is there anything else?"

"Shrap poonktures', lots of em'."

"Once the burn cases are unloaded, this man comes off first, er, Sergeant."

"Corp'l, miss. Corp'l Johnson." The nurse nodded and turned around, filling out a tag of some kind. Vic watched her, realizing she was quite young and not very big. Once finished she attached the tag to Vic's blouse, looking at him for a long moment.

"Ooh' might you be, miss?" He asked slowly trying to focus on her face. Her pupils, dark against her brilliant light green eyes, enlarged almost with recognition although Vic was certain they never met.

"I'm Lieutenant McCutcheon. I'm an American Army nurse," she said unnecessarily. A veil seemed to form across her eyes before she pulled back. "You're going to be fine, we'll take good care of you." Then she was gone, moving on to other patients.

Potty was right, the coastal positions the Japanese held at Gona were bloody murder. After the Stanleys' the lowlands were like being dumped into a flooded basement sewer of an old building with the roof torn off. There was nothing above you, no triple canopy of stinking green rising two hundred feet to blank out the sky. When the sun rose to track across the horizon there was no filter or shade to deflect the blinding yellow heat, unless you were under the cover of the banyans. The water, sometimes knee deep, sometimes over your head, gave no relief or safety in its blackness. Vile, still and murky, the mangrove swamps surrounded the Japanese positions on three sides, built on the 15 kilometer stretch of semi-solid earth on the coast, all Kunai grass. The former coconut plantations owned by the Lever Brothers planted thousands of coconut trees in neat rows very close to the edges of the Kunai grass. The Kunai marked the transition from swamp to higher ground, of dry ground, the only dry ground.

The Japanese mowed down most of the coconut groves, stacking and packing the tree trunks tightly together above the high water table to create some of the finest defensive positions ever seen. Having the only high ground around the Japanese knew the Allies would have to approach them from the swamps. The positions, mostly for medium and heavy machine guns, were built by the hundreds with the endless supply of coconut trees, their very narrow firing ports designed to mutually support other guns through interlocking fields of fire. The mangroves offered little real cover and a myriad of underwater obstacles for infantry in the form of gnarled, tortured unseen root systems of the twisted banyan trees. These created excellent killing zones filled with slow moving, stumbling men.

High enough to see their fields of fire but low enough to blend into the terrain, the coconut bunkers were camouflaged by careful and daily replacement of Nipa fronds, a low scrub plant found everywhere on the higher ground. The coconut tree trunks, many a foot in diameter, were also used for the roofs of the bunkers and found to be incredibly resistant to small arms fire. Most mortars except for a direct hit from the heavies, would have little effect on the occupants, to the dismay and peril of troops who hoped the gunners would be stunned long enough for a sapper to toss in a charge. Plunging fire, true artillery fire was not available, as the Aussies only had a few of their 25 pounder antitank guns and the Americans had only a *single* 105 mm howitzer to support the entire 32nd Division assault. US made M3 Stuart tanks operated by the Australians were being used and directed by the Americans farther south.

To Vic, the entire Buna – Gona campaign should have been someone else's problem. 2/14 Battalion was one of the first 21st Brigade units sent up in to the Stanleys' to support and relieve the militia. 2/14 arrived on the Track with 546 men in August, finding their operational end on the Imita Ridge a month later. 2/14 was withdrawn on September 16, decimated, arriving down the Track at Uberi with only 88 men, three of them officers. The battalion was reformed at Koitaki near Port Moresby, fleshed out with new replacements. A few of the replacements were recovering wounded, Kokoda veterans from other battalions sent to 2/14 instead of their original units. In either case the battalion was reforming with men who needed more training or needed more rest. It was not to be. Still understrength with only 341 men and officers when they received their orders for the Buna – Gona assault, the battalion was airlifted by C-47s to Popondetta on the east coast on November 25th.

As a platoon sergeant and acting platoon commander for 9 Platoon until a new officer was assigned, Vic knew the men were not ready and resolved to not throw their lives away. When the platoon arrived at Port Moresby in September to take on the Japanese for the first time they'd been together for over two years, including some harrowing times in Lebanon and Syria fighting Vichy French. The Australian Army, always short of the type of heavy firepower found in the American Army, made up the difference in hard, dedicated individual small-unit infantry training where men learned to rely on one another, learning individual strengths and weaknesses. The troops were originally all recruited locally, with most of the men from the 7th Division coming from the southeastern territory of Victoria. They knew one other, often all of their lives, the loyalty to their mates foremost in their character.

2/14 Battalion like the rest of the 21st Brigade, adjusted to the new men but it would take time to regard them as anything more than warm bodies in a friendly uniform. The Kokoda was small unit warfare, a corporal's war. In the Stanleys' the close-in terrain dictated the need for very aggressive daylight patrolling. There was no other way to find out what the enemy was doing in front of you. Fighting pits were close together, touching close together, because jungle light--dim, dark and shadowy during the best of the day--turned carbon black at dusk. You could not see your hand in front of your face. The jungle world was a matter of feet, sometimes inches. The day patrols on both sides discovered each other in short, violent confrontations at point blank range. Survivors were the men with tactical advantage, saw the enemy first and were ready to destroy him. In such an environment the fighting was so personal your mental safety, in Vic's mind, what kept you from going bloody mad, was keeping your weapons like extensions of your arms. You kept them spotlessly clean and loaded, or in the case of his trench knife, razor sharp, with chums on each side he knew better than his own brothers. There was nothing else, the rest you trusted to the Almighty.

The new coastal campaign placed the old jungle warriors on edge immediately. The tight-knit, almost eerily silent world of the triple canopied jungle was gone. The intermittent open sky, stinking swampy terrain forced the individual Diggers apart to reduce massing targets, the unrelenting sun cooking their brains under the slouch hats during the day. These few remaining Kokoda veterans were still weak from disease and barely-healed combat wounds. The battalion, three under-strength companies, unloaded from the American C-47s to begin the 32 kilometer force march to Gona, knowing this would be yet another unknown. The few small narrow roads, the only dry approaches between the patches of Kunai grass and the swamps surrounding Gona, quickly meandered into nothingness. 9 Platoon stepped off into the dark waters with the rest of A company on the morning of November 29th, slogging cautiously through the slime, aware the creeks fed from the sea were home to crocodiles and when they reached their objective on drier ground, Japanese machineguns in fortified bunkers.

They heard the experience of the lone US Army division in the company briefs, a division now bogged down after fighting slowly north for nearly two weeks. The 32nd ID, a federalized National Guard Division out of Ohio with no prior combat engagements, was sent up the coast in a motley collection of yachts, fishing boats and small freighters to land and destroy what was according to intelligence a small detachment of Japanese troops. Lead reconnaissance forays discovered, at high cost, the 32nd ID faced at least 5,500 Japanese. It became apparent very quickly the Japanese anticipated the assault, heavily fortifying the only high ground available. The 32nd ID in Buna was stalled in the same type of swamplands the Aussies were now entering in Gona, learning terrible lessons from their outright inexperience with resulting high casualties. This in itself didn't surprise Vic at all. Most Australians, even combat veterans like the soldiers from the 6th and 7th Divisions, liked Americans in general but felt the US Army, infantry specifically, was over-equipped and under-trained.

35

The Allies needed a foothold on the high ground to the north at Gona, with a pincer movement between the Aussies and the 32nd ID to sweep the Japanese off the 15 kilometer peninsula of dry ground southward to Buna. The assignment for 2/14 Battalion was to crack the top in a small section of fortified bunkers, killing or driving the Japanese defenders from the narrow strip of dry ground. Australian tactics never embraced the frontal assault against a heavily defended enemy unless there was no other option. What was finally starting to work for the Americans in Buna, using tanks to blow apart the Japanese coconut bunkers with 37mm guns, was not available to the Aussies on the 29th of November. There were only three Aussie Stuarts on the entire peninsula, with no way to transport them north through the swamps. Having only limited mortar support and no artillery except a few 25 pounder anti-tank guns, little offshore naval gunfire or close-air support, 2/14 was forced to take the bunkers the hard way. Destroy them one by one, getting infantry close enough to blow up the bunkers with grenades and satchel charges.

There was no wind at all by mid-morning, the sun already so hot every metal surface—weapon, link attachments to the web gear, a wristwatch—burned against the skin. The heat didn't seem to bother the biting insects, clustering near salt and moisture, mostly the eyes, mouth and back of the neck. Vic had his most experienced men with him in the forward section of this advance, all Kokoda and Middle East veterans. He appreciated their discipline as they slowly, carefully picked the insects off their faces. There was no arm waving, swatting or cursing. They approached the Japanese positions silently knowing their only safety was not being seen.

9 Platoon was on a ragged line one section wide, in visual contact with another platoon from A company on their right, to the south. Vic's second section was about 35 meters behind his, with the reserve platoon 100 meters to their rear. He couldn't see them, but he knew the other two companies were similarly configured on their left and right. It made for a fairly small front, but the staggered depth allowed for the men in the second tiers to shift right or left if the forward sections encountered a strong point. If this was a reconnaissance patrol the men would have had a much narrower front, essentially one or two deep, staggered, staying only as close together as necessary to maintain visual contact. But this was no patrol, their mission was not to explore, retreat and report. Their mission was to find the bunker fortifications in the Kunai grass ahead and destroy them.

Vic, conscious of the inexperienced replacements behind him yet dearly and painfully aware of his mates on his left and right, believed he

36

was doing the right thing. He knew Potty, Link, Scabby, Biscuit, Rocko, Jock and Red would do what was asked of them in the next few minutes, there was no question. Each demonstrated many times over their loyalty to him and to one another. There was the innate sense of brotherhood and comradeship born of shared suffering and survival on days none expected to live through. *It was this very strength and utter reliability that filled the small, shallow graves lining the trails on the Kokoda,* he thought.

It came slowly, the realization the terrain and vegetation around them were changing. They were still in the water, chest deep in many places but button clumps of earth, like giant mushroom islands were ahead, Nipa fronds clustered all around. Each section on the frontline slowed, ever wary, the only sound the high pitched buzzing and clicks of insects. Men instinctively raised their heads, noting the high Kunai grass now visible as far as they could see on the high horizon like a light green and yellow prairie. It was the edge of the plateau, the transition from swamp to dry plain.

Vic signaled to both sections to halt and find concealment. In some cases men drifted quietly left or right close to vegetation, with others lowering to the stinking black water keeping only their slouch hats and weapons clear. He noted the platoon to his right was doing the same thing as he lifted his glasses to examine the vegetation ahead, especially right below the base of the Kunai grass. Suddenly far to the right the slow, thudding stutter of a single Juki 92 heavy machinegun erupted in a long burst, immediately accompanied by a multitude of other Jukis and lighter Nambus. These were answered by Aussie weapons; Lee Enfield's, Thompsons and Bren guns. The noise and racket down by the water was deafening. All they could see on the right were clouds of insects rising, disturbed by the gunfire. Twitching involuntarily the men still did not move out of position, especially after 5 or 10 seconds with no fire directed at them.

It was just a matter of time now so Vic signaled the sections to continue moving forward. He certainly wasn't going to give their positions away unnecessarily, but they needed to get to the Kunai grass and dry ground as quickly as they could. If Japanese positions were directly in front of them it was impossible some of 9 Platoon had not been seen. *Why weren't they firing?*

Vic did not have to direct his front section to drift from one large mushroom island to the next, the earthen islands offered natural cover and concealment. No one was exposing himself more than he had to. After weeks on the Kokoda where firefights occurred at 5-10 meters and the foliage was so thick you still couldn't see one another clearly at two, 9 Platoon felt immediately at home under concealment. They knew how to use it, knowing when it was better to not be seen rather than simply seeking cover from high velocity bullets. They instinctively knew the Japanese were tracking them, waiting for them to get closer. Vic was especially sensitive to this, stopping to scan the Kunai grass transition area now less than 35 meters away.

The company to their left encountered heavy machinegun fire, although sporadic. Two of the newly assigned sappers, engineers loaded down with explosive satchel charges to blow the fortifications, trailed Rocko as he slipping from one mushroom island to the next, the two obviously believing Rocko knew what he was doing. Vic smiled as he watched out of the corners of his eyes, noting the sappers, both strapping young fellows, towered over Rocko's gnome-like figure. He couldn't blame them. Despite his size, Rocko was a Bren gunner whose reputation for killing Japanese with accuracy and speed at any range went far beyond 9 Platoon or A Company. He was most likely the best Bren gunner in the battalion and possibly one of the best in the 21st Brigade. Having such a man with you was not such a bad idea. Cocking his ear, Vic listened as the gunfire to their immediate right continued at a furious rate, cycling higher as Japanese machineguns, traversing around in their narrow slits, found new targets. He focused again on the yellow – green plain now coming close, finally seeing what he knew was already there.

Directly ahead was a small, prow-shaped cove pointing up into the higher ground. You wouldn't see it until you were within 20 or 25 meters unless you knew it was there. It appeared to be a natural, gentle slope approximately 75 meters across almost at the base of the water, climbing up and disappearing into the taller Kunai grass. Black water transitioned to Nipa fronds, then sparse, dry and short Kunai grass in the middle, providing an inviting clear path to the plain on the top. *A bloody trap*, he whistled to himself. Vic tapped the open palm of his left hand with two fingers from his right, a slight clapping sound the men closest to him heard and understood immediately. Biscuit, Scabby, Rocko and Jock stopped moving, turning to watch his hand signals. He signaled for the men on his left to move left, the men on the right to move right. *Enemy straight ahead, flank approach.* Vic turned and repeated his signal to the men behind him, waiting for their acknowledgement.

The veterans in the front section signaled to the men closest to them and the section split instantly, moving away from the little cove. It didn't take long to understand they were being observed. Sparkles of muzzle flashes, half a dozen to the left from the top of the cove and another half a dozen from the right flashed a split second before the black water erupted all around them. A hundred bullets spouting three

38

meter high geysers slashed right down the middle of where the men were a moment before.

Thank god for veterans who move instantly, Vic thought, they understood their safety came from *moving right now* when they received a command. Miraculously no one in the lead section was hit in the hail of bullets. Later, Potty told Vic a single man was wounded by the deadly swath of lead in those few seconds, a replacement in the following section who froze a fraction too long. A machinegun slug ricocheted off the water, slowing its velocity enough to skip right up and smack the forehead of this poor lad dead center, hardly breaking his skin. The THWACK of the impact was loud and the boy dropped like a rock. One of his mates dragged him to cover, only to discover to their mutual astonishment he was still alive. *Hardly rates a 'ound stripe, da' bloody 'ardhead,* wryly noted Potty, *but rose a whopper of an egg on 'is noggin, da' lucky snot!*

Their luck held for a few more minutes because the platoon to their immediate left drifted too far to the right. The gun positions on either side of the cove guns; unseen, silent, their muzzles angled 30 degrees outboard from the cove to protect the higher cove guns, opened up. Vic, who had paused behind cover to decide their path around the cove guns, was appalled to see how close the hidden guns were to the water. He couldn't believe it. *Those bloody bastards must be half in the water! How could they do it?* The gun positions were virtually invisible, exactly where he was going to guide his men. The Japanese used smokeless powder so the only indicator of the gun locations were the muzzle flashes, noise and dancing, disintegrating foliage. The flashes were accompanied by lead scything inches above the water, probing the foliage and soft cover, searching for unprotected men trying to hide.

Without being told the 9 Platoon veterans in the forward section stayed close to cover, drifting outward to the flanks of the guns whenever they sensed the gunners were probing elsewhere. They knew how the Japanese built machinegun bunkers, the firing slots narrow horizontally to defeat hand grenades or satchel charges tossed from any safe distance. The tiny slots restricted vision for the gunners, especially to the sides, so the fortifications were built in a zig zag configuration, each gun position responsible for its own field of fire yet overlapping and mutually protecting the blind sides of other bunkers. The only way to get past such fortifications was to destroy one, eliminating the protective fire it provided to the surrounding bunkers before working around outwardly behind the other bunkers, eliminating them one at a time.

A very hazardous assignment. On the Kokoda the Japanese built similar machinegun bunker fortifications but with much less hardy materials to work with. In Vic's experience on the Kokoda, the jungle provided the best form of protection by virtue of the almost complete concealment of the forest around you from the ground up to about five meters. The foliage, the uneasy twilight darkness under the shadowy green canopy above and the large, impenetrable layers of fleshy, dripping green leaves ensured patrolling soldiers on either side could stay concealed to touching range. Vic knew it all to well, having killed Japanese so close he could count the individual threads on the frayed collars of their shirts. It also meant the machinegun fortifications in the Kokoda didn't expect to be attacked by airplanes, artillery or even mortar bombs because of the overhead canopy. They merely had to be invisible right up to the time the victims walked by and were shot to death at point blank range.

In the intelligence brief days before a young American Army captain outlined what they would face in the coconut fortifications. The 32nd ID, stung from the criticism from the Australian brass and General MacArthur himself, was reeling from not only the unexpected resistance of the Japanese defenders and resulting high casualties, but the sacking of their commanding general by MacArthur. Their experience with the bunker fortifications, many miles south of Gona near Buna, propped up the hairs on the back of Vic's head. *God Almighty*, he thought. *Mortar-proof, bullet-proof and the only things that seem to work—blowin' 'em apart with a tank or burnin' 'em out with flamethrowers—we don't have. Bloody awful for this lot.*

The most useful piece of information to Vic and the rest of 2/14 was what the Yanks discovered when they started knocking the fortifications out. The Yanks hadn't fought the Japs up on the Kokoda so they had no basis of comparison. So when the young Yank captain described the interlocking, mutually supporting fires structure everyone just nodded. When he described the lack of infantry support around the fortifications, and what they found to be the single entrance door at the back of the structures, everyone perked up and started to pay attention. *No supporting infantry? No snipers?* Fixed machinegun fortifications without supporting infantry was like advancing tanks without infantry. Without walking infantry scouts to be your eyes and ears to protect your sides and back, you were blind and could be ambushed and destroyed.

Vic kept thinking of this as 7.7mm bullets from the Jukis ripped the water around him. He realized he could advance no further to the right and he could not go forward, as there was no cover whatsoever right to the muzzles of the bunkers in front. He stayed behind his mushroom island, peeking when he sensed the guns probed elsewhere. When he sent his forward sections to the sides to flank the cove approach, they moved laterally further than he before the guns opened up. He was effectively trapped in range of the dozen guns up on the cove defenses, or the guns right down in front of him on the water. If there was supporting infantry up on the top of the cove, they could drop mortar bombs on A company and specifically 9 Platoon and be done with it.

Without a radio Vic could not communicate his tactical situation. It was apparent by the racket 2/14 was fully engaged along the front of the Kunai grass. The break for 9 Platoon came suddenly, the deadly accurate fire from a single Bren gun from the immediate right silencing first one, than two gunners from the bunker directly in front of Vic. The firing slots were only 15-20 centimeters high and about 80 wide, so the bursts were extremely accurate. As expected, the machinegun fire resumed as other gunners replaced the casualties but other Bren gunners began to put rounds and pressure on the same two firing ports, forcing the Japanese gunners to turn away from the Bren gun on the right. Vic knew it had to be Rocko, spotting him with his sappers in tow less than 15 meters from the bunker, camouflaged with Nipa fronds around their heads. Vic was amazed the Japanese gunners could not see them. The other Bren gunners were laying down so much lead on the firing ports the Japanese gunners were shooting sporadically, clearly harassed by the accurate fire. Vic was very proud of his men, he wanted to cheer.

Rocko lifted out of the water, firing two quick bursts and two longer ones, punching all 30 rounds out of his magazine directly into the bunker firing slot on the right. It was outstanding shooting. One of the sappers, acting as his assistant gunner, accepted the empty magazine and handed Rocko a fresh one for a quick reload. Rocko sloshed forward, never stopping or taking his eyes off the gun port until he was two meters away, continuing his quick, deadly-accurate shooting directly into the slot until he was empty. One of the sappers stepped around him and literally shoved the Japanese machine gun barrel aside and held it as the other sapper pulled the charging handle that lit the rope fuse on a satchel charge. Rocko stepped back, fully exposing himself to the other gun port as he directed his fire into their opening. The sapper pushed the smoking satchel charge in the hole, pressing his Enfield revolver forward and firing several rounds inside before backing away.

"FIRE IN THE HOLE!" he bellowed. Rocko and the other sapper were already moving to the right as fast as they could. The three men were less than 5 or 10 meters away when the charge exploded, the shock wave flattening them into the water; the flame, debris and concussion boxing everyone's ears with a muffled, very painful and sharp WHUMP. The solidly built bunker did not fly apart, but large, jagged pieces of coconut trunks were lifted and hurled in all directions. The bunker guns

41

were already silent.

What surprised Vic more than anything was Rocko and the two sappers were still alive. With the destruction of the one bunker right down on the water, the only significant fire in front of 9 Platoon came from the guns up on the cove top. Those gunners had a clear view of the water approaches, ensuring lots of lead was filling spaces between the mushroom islands. He expected another hidden gun position, especially farther to the right of the bunker on the water, to reveal itself when Rocko and his sappers approached. Vic could only shake his head in disbelief as he and everyone who was pinned down moved laterally before the smoke cleared, hop-scotching from cover to cover until they reached the first edges of the Kunai grass, the solid ground around the destroyed bunker and out of the sight of the upper cove guns.

As the midday sun broiled their backs and exposed skin while slithering through the Kunai, 2/14 would find many surprises in store for them. Up here in Gona the battalion found only about two-thirds of the machinegun bunkers occupied. Either the Japanese had moved troops down south to face the 32nd ID which was likely, or they simply didn't have enough men to man all of the bunkers. Vic was horrified to realize Rocko and the sappers could have been killed by the crossfire from a bunker built, just like the one they destroyed, right on the water 30 meters to the right. Rocko plus about six or seven other members of 9 Platoon had followed Vic's direction to move right. They would have waded directly into the muzzles of this other invisible bunker. Only it was empty, built right at the water table and half filled with vile, black slime. He could only imagine what it would be like to spend any time in such a fortification. The one that was just destroyed was slightly higher on the water table and only had a half a meter of water in it. It was small, with two ports for Jukis, but apparently the tomb for six or seven men. It was hard to tell and no one had the time or desire to crawl inside. The defenders were most likely already dead or dying when the satchel charge went off, but there was no taking chances with Japs as far as these men were concerned.

No one knew for sure which bunkers were occupied. That in itself was a remarkably effective delaying tactic, forcing men to work right up to a fortification. A silent bunker protecting an empty one would open up, slaughtering a few more Diggers. As the afternoon wore on, 2/14 was discovering strongholds where *all* the bunkers in an area were occupied with resulting high casualties. Not so for 9 Platoon, for which Vic was very grateful. With the exception of the lad with the egg knob on his forehead from the spent ricochet, the 19 men in 9 Platoon had only three minor casualties. One gunshot wound in the forearm, through and through, and two others with shrapnel embedded in their hands, faces and neck. All three were still in their sections supporting the assault, brushing Potty away when he tried to pluck out a sliver of coconut wood or steel during a lull.

2/14 also found the US Army was incorrect in their intel saying the Japanese did not use supporting infantry to protect their bunker complexes. At least not up here in the Gona area. There were no roving infantry teams but A Company discovered some of the machinegun bunkers were protected by snipers. Two or three hours after leaving the swamps, one of the sister platoons from A Company ran into a bunker complex that left the platoon pinned down and unable to move forward. 9 Platoon, working its way through an open meadow to their northern flank, discovered a series of abandoned bunkers and were taking a short breather when a runner came looking for Vic. The request came from the pinned down platoon commander: *Could 9 Platoon fade south, engage the bunkers from the flank and the rear?*

Vic took a quick assessment of 9 Platoon's ammunition supply. In anticipation of the bunker campaign every Digger had packed extra Mills bombs and all the ammunition they could carry. As expected, Vic found the rookies still carried most of their grenades and were low on rifle ammunition. The bunkers were being taken by the veterans. They knew what they were doing and in many cases directed their inexperienced charges to *lay doggo;* take cover and provide covering fire. Vic was not one to criticize another man, never had to, choosing instead to keep the effective ones busy with tasks he knew they could do. In such small, close quarters company as 9 Platoon Vic was king and no man wanted Vic looking past him when a job needed to be done. Vic had all the men dump their grenades in a pile, handing out most of the Mills Bombs to his veterans. He left the ammunition as is with each individual, knowing men were very resistant to part with their personal supply unless they absolutely had too.

The platoon was exhausted from the heat and the strain. There was no time to brew a billy of tea or even take a moment to chew on a biscuit. Most ate their last rations for breakfast, with maybe a biscuit or two for tucker. The battalion had pushed off on the 25th with five days rations, command apparently expecting the bunkers to be taken quickly. Standing on their slight rise, Vic looked to the west and saw the foreboding, sinister dark waters of the mangroves from where they came. Other than the dark line of mud and slime on their uniforms, now dry, denoting how deep the water had been, it was hard to believe they had been down there. To his north and south there was nothing but tall, uncut Kunai, four or five meters high, with narrow paths carved by the Japanese. A Company used these paths wherever they found them, some men vaguely concerned they might be mined. The paths appeared to be very well used, downright trampled, so the consensus was they were probably safe for transit but ripe for ambush whenever they led to a clearing.

9 Platoon followed one of the narrow paths, two sections in double file, each man keeping at least a 10 meter staggered interval. It was unnerving because it was like walking down a cleared double corn row where you could only see straight ahead, behind or above. Vic, with Scabby and Biscuit in the lead, was close to the front of the first section because he wanted to get eyes on the situation. Rocko and his two sappers were right behind him, followed by Link, Jock and Red. Scabby dropped to his knee, signaling *enemy in sight* with his SMLE Lee Enfield. Every man who could see him moved away from the trail and into the Kunai grass, silently dropping lower, their weapons ready. Scabby turned slowly, his eyes forward until he made eye contact with Vic, nudging him up with his finger.

Scabby, a thin, lean man whose skin turned bright red with any sun exposure before fracturing into a horrible peeling sunburn, was an excellent scout and point. He had stopped five meters from what appeared to be a large clearing. A narrow tunnel view was the only perspective they had, remained well back in the shadows and unseen. They could hear the machineguns in the bunkers firing close by. It was hard to tell exactly where it was coming from at their position on the trail, as noise funneled down to them. As Vic crept up to Scabby, he saw a shadow cross the little tunnel view before vanishing. Vic froze for a second. Scabby leaned over until his lips almost touched Vic's ear.

"Aye', did ya' see that?" he whispered. "Aye' saw noother' one just a sec' 'efore. Both of em' carryin' stuff, but I think they's goin' the wrong way, Vic!" Vic nodded, pulling the heavy lensatic compass out of his shirt pocket, pushing it away from their metal weapons on the ground before giving it a quick glance. He oriented it to North, nodding his head in agreement.

"You're right, Scabby, the boonkers' should be to the right, to the south, an' that Jap was headed north." Vic peered over his shoulder, lifting his head slightly. With his hand he signaled the platoon to stay put while directing Rocko to join them. The three of them slipped out of their packs and slouch hats, crawling forward on their stomachs as far as their dared. Vic silently lifted his binoculars, drifting a large square of gauze like-linen over his head and glasses to ensure there would be no reflection. A meter back in the shadows, he could see most of a fairly sizeable clearing, perhaps 30 meters across directly to the other side, with what appeared to be a wider portion to the right side, to the southwest. There was another trail like the one they were on, leading off somewhere almost directly across. It was obvious the clearing was well used. There were stacks of boxes, wooden and flat he assumed were ammunition. As he watched, two more Japanese soldiers in clean uniforms and in seemingly good health hustled across the clearing carrying radio or electronic equipment on a casualty litter. They were fresh troops, no doubt about it. They didn't seem overly cautious, moving quickly without looking around.

Vic pressed his luck, creeping forward until he could see better to his right, to the southwest. There he spotted a trail opening before being forced flat when another Japanese soldier appeared, heavily burdened with a section of the gun carriage for a Juki heavy machinegun. A minute later other soldiers joined him, each carrying different parts of the gun carriage. These were followed by two men struggling with the heft of the receiver and barrel housing. When the soldiers passed Vic waited a moment before leaning forward, cocking his ears to confirm the machinegun bunkers were firing from the direction the soldiers were coming from. They were. *Are they pulling out?*

It did create a bit of a dilemma for 9 Platoon, since the path they were following would apparently lead them to the machinegun bunkers yet might be full of retreating Japanese soldiers. Vic slipped back into the shadows, conferring with Scabby and Rocko. They agreed it appeared the Japs were pulling back, but based on experience leave enough firepower to hold up their sister platoon. They still needed to get down there and put pressure on the guns. There didn't seem to be any other options but pressing on, so he placed Jock and Red, both Bren gunners, in a hidden blocking position to cover the two trail openings. Vic waited a couple of minutes before sending Scabby, Rocko and his two sappers, and then Biscuit and Link out into the edges of the clearing, creeping around the perimeter until they could get some eyes down the trail to where they believed would be the machinegun bunkers.

Slim, the second section leader and the only Kokoda veteran of 9 Platoon with the section other than Potty, slid up to Vic to get his instructions. With only a couple of veterans and the rest replacements, he knew his job was to provide covering fire and back up the lead section. His section would hold back here with Jock and Red. The first section would put enough pressure on the machine- gun bunkers to let the sister platoon move up, then the section would retreat back up to the clearing. If the Japs overwhelm the first section or pull off a full blown withdrawal, the second section and Bren guns would make quick work of them. Anyway, that was the plan.

Scabby crept into position to take a peek down the trail, suddenly raising and shouldering his Lee Enfield in one motion, firing three shots as quickly as he could operate the bolt. He turned and grinned at Rocko, right behind him, signaling three enemy down with his fingers a moment before he was shot through the forehead. Before his body hit the ground Jock's Bren gun barked with a short burst, right into a dark shadow on the opposite side of the clearing. As Jock told Vic later, he had noticed something dark moving in the grass, and had just turned his Bren in that direction when he saw the muzzle flash.

Rocko pulled his old friend to the side of the clearing, gently covering his face with his slouch hat. He looked over at Vic with a sad smile before turning away, letting Biscuit and Link take the lead, motioning the two sappers to stay close. They slipped down into the trail and out of sight. Within a minute they could hear the Bren gun stutter, so Vic, signaling the others to stay put, picking up his Thompson before carefully crossed the clearing.

The shooting up the trail created panic among the Japanese soldiers who were withdrawing. Most had their hands full of equipment with their weapons slung over their shoulders, hesitating before dropping their loads even when the Aussies were in sight. Rocko took full advantage of their hesitation and shot many of them. He took a firing range assault stance, bracing his body and shooting with the stock of the Bren under his arm. He was almost as accurate firing point of aim as he was shouldering the gun, killing a half a dozen men in seconds with only two or three round bursts. Biscuit and Link, both sharpshooters deadly with their SMLE Lee Enfields at all ranges, stood and shot Japanese coming out of bunkers as quickly as they appeared. As Vic arrived from the trail seeing the reverse slope created by the backs of the bunkers, there were eight bunkers in view, most with the escape hatches open. As Rocko stopped to change his magazine a Japanese soldier dropped his load to run right past him at full speed, his face filled with fear. Vic raised his Thompson to shoot as the man's head exploded from a .303 bullet from Link's Lee Enfield, fired off hand. The body ran forward with a leg out before crumpling in a heap. Link, his bolt flying as he ejected the empty and reloaded, pivoted to shoot another Japanese soldier turning to run away.

With the sudden appearance of over a dozen Japanese bodies in a matter of seconds, Vic felt like he was observing a casual hunting party or a shooting gallery, it was so surreal. The noise from the bunker guns was deafening and continued, drowning out the rapid small arms fire from his men who hardly moved from their positions other than reloading and firing. His brain finally processed the meaning of the open doors and pointed them out to the two sappers who stood a few feet behind Rocko with their mouths open, revolvers in their hands but not moving. He understood they hesitated because they didn't want to be shot by his men. At the moment not a single Japanese soldier was coming out of the bunkers.

"Blow these bastards! Whatcha' waitin for!" He screamed, then turning to Rocko and Link, "cover em!" Vic caught Biscuit's eye and waved him forward as he ran to the nearest bunker with an open hatch. "Cover me, Biscuit!" The rear of the bunker revealed a small depression in the earth to protect and hide the tiny door, which Vic could see was being pulled closed from the inside. With a Mills Bomb from his pocket at the ready, Vic handed his Thompson to Biscuit as he dropped into the depression. He grabbed the hatch handle with all the strength he had in one hand, wrestling with the occupant on the other side trying to close it. Off balance, Vic fell backwards, the handle still in one hand and a grenade in the other as the hatch swung open freely. He released the hatch handle to pull the pin from the grenade as the muzzle of a rifle appeared, the door opening disappearing in a blinding flash.

There was a sharp pain in his chest with a heavy numbness as he fell back again. Vic tried to get to his feet as someone yanked him back around the shoulders, twisting him around. A deafening blast came a second later from behind, slamming him against the bunker. Stunned, his ears ringing, he tried to stand up again, his lower leg in excruciating pain. He stumbled in shock to see Biscuit lying there at his feet. Biscuit's legs and buttocks were shredded red and grey like raw hamburger, blood pulsing from his muscles, his blue eyes open and blinking. He took the brunt of the blast, and Vic, reacting slowly, realized he had dropped his grenade. Biscuit had tried to pull him away.

"Biscuit," he moaned, "Ah, moother' of God, Biscuit..." A flash to the right was instantly accompanied by a jerking sensation at his hip. He glanced down at his thigh, staring blankly out of curiosity at a bit of bone and pink and purple flesh from a big hole. It took him a moment to realize it was his thigh. His legs folded, toppling him onto Biscuit's chest. Vic tried to move off of Biscuit's body but his own muscles were not responding as he mumbled and slobbered, apologizing to his chum whose eyes were dimming to glaze as his own view narrowed like a tunnel, fading gray to black to nothingness.

CHAPTER 4

November 30, 1942, Seven-Mile airfield

Port Moresby was clear as the first of the three C-47s passed Uberi to begin their letdown toward the swamps. To the east behind them the sky was full of clouds, some dark and threatening, yet the air merciful to the crews and their loads of wounded men. The bumps were passable. Don Crenshaw, leaving the cockpit door open, glanced over his shoulder into the cabin during the worst of it, noting the two medics bracing and holding on. They never left their patients.

As they passed over the swamps to begin their turn, Don picked up the microphone and called the tower requesting the altimeter, wind direction and speed on the ground. Cooper was flying this approach so Don handled the radio and did the pre-landing checklist and callouts. They were cleared for a long straight-in to the main runway which was more comfortable for the patients. Don leaned forward to peer out his side window as Cooper gently rolled out on the runway heading. Don could see one transport a mile behind them in trail getting ready to turn, with the second a tiny dot against the clouds. Since the last incident weeks ago Don and Cooper came to an unspoken peace. Cooper appreciated Don's acceptance of his failures when the shooting started, rewarding Don from then on with a quiet loyalty at all other times. For Don's part he simply let Cooper do more of the flying, except when they might expect any ground fire.

As usual, his skill and professionalism as a pilot were a pleasure to witness as Cooper flew the six mile descent to the end of the runway with practically no adjustment to the throttles. They smoothly flew to the runway as if they were on rails. The C-47 leveled across the numbers, sinking gently to the runway to touch on the mains. Cooper pushed the control yoke forward so smoothly to keep the wheels on the runway Don was not certain they were down. It was a perfect wheel landing, throttles eased back to idle as the tail softly lowered to the runway. Don turned his head towards Cooper giving him a respectful nod.

"I bet you didn't get too many complaints from passengers about your landings. That was damned nice, Jack." Cooper glanced over at Don, the broad smile genuine.

A "Follow Me" jeep was waiting for them once they were on the ground. There were a number of transports parked in the usual transient areas all loading with cargo going back to Dobodura, so to relieve the temporary congestion the jeep led the transports to the opposite side of the runway. Here there were revetments normally used by medium bombers, temporarily vacant. Cooper stood on his left brake and spun the C-47 around in the revetment they were pointed to, cutting the mixture and shutting down the engines. Don's heart skipped a beat when he saw the ambulances and jeeps heading towards them down the taxiway, the long flowing golden hair of a nurse without the benefit of a cap catching his eye instantly. That first one was a blond but there were two brunettes in a second jeep right behind it. Don slid his side window open, watching the jeeps separate as the triage team leader pointed nurses towards different airplanes. The two brunettes looked too much alike, damn. He got distracted as Cooper started working down the after landing and shutdown checklists. It didn't stop Don from looking over his shoulder periodically into the cabin.

Don unbuckled the safety belt, painfully working his way out of his seat. Considering the size of the aircraft the C-47 cockpit was surprisingly small and compact, with all of the controls within easy reach of both pilots. It meant however, a man of Don's height and dimensions needed a shoehorn to get in and out of his seat. Luckily Cooper was a slight fellow and didn't hog the space, so he leaned away as Don turned out of his seat patting Cooper on the shoulder as he passed. He brushed his hands through his hair as he glanced down the passageway, spotting Katie immediately as she stepped into the doorway. He grinned and waved but it was lost on Katie who didn't look up towards the cockpit at all, staying all business talking to the attending medics.

The passenger cabin aisle was filled with voices as nurses and medics hustled around discussing the patients before lifting them out. It was a slow process because once they started to move the litters down the aisle everyone had to get out of the way. The litters were stacked two deep, the burn cases closest to the door and going out first. Don leaned against the frame of the cockpit door hoping to catch Katie's eye as she asked rapid fire questions to the American and Australian medics. As she worked up the cabin now assessing the Aussie casualties, Don noticed her coveralls seemed to drape more loosely on her frame as if she had lost weight. She was a petite, slim person anyway, the affect being of more frailty, of vulnerability. Up in the forward cabin there was less light so she used her flashlight, her questions answered almost comically polite by the gaunt, scarecrow Aussie medic hovering right next to her. She looked up to examine and adjust a IV drip with her light, the beam flashing up into Don's face, 10 feet up the aisle. The light hesitated for a second before moving away.

"Well, hello, Lieutenant Crenshaw," she said, somewhat formally Don thought. He couldn't see her eyes as her face turned back to the patient. "Didn't know this was your plane."

"Good seeing you again, Lieutenant McCutcheon," Don said, louder than he meant to. He wanted to say more but the Aussie medic was talking to her.

"Aye' miss," the scarecrow was saying, "da' fightin' was 'oop in Gona yesterday af'noon, the pl'toon took some boonkers' froom' the rear an' got shot 'oop by snipers. We kilt most of em' tryin' ta' escape, boot' dey' had a Nambu we didn't see. Dey' shoot' up da' hole' section in a minute, dey' did!" Don recognized the medic was the same one he had talked to before they loaded the airplane at Dobodura, realizing with a start the man not only served with these Aussies during their battle, he helped carry them out.

"The pl'toon's 'n bad shape, miss, da' wounds' gone septic for some of em', and all aye' had for em' was sulfa until last night," the medic continued. "Da' fuzzies came in an' 'elped us carry da' boys back, but dey' had ta' carry em' back thru d'a swamps until we hooked up with you Yanks at your aid station. We got some plasma, an' dey' took some slugs and shrap out. It saved Vic and Rocko and Link. We lost Scabby and Biscuit." Don watched, almost enviously, as Katie gently held the medic's arm. She examined the man's face carefully, touching his neck and jaw.

"Sergeant—I mean Corporal—Johnson, right? How are you feeling? You seem to have some shrapnel wounds on your neck and throat that need attention."

The medic pulled away immediately without rudeness, gripping his neck while shaking his head. He seemed embarrassed by Katie's attention. "Tank' you, miss, but no, Potty's okay, all'be fine. All' see ta' dem' soon. These blokes we need ta' get ta' hospital!" He turned to pat the wounded Aussie's arm, "these blokes are all aye' got left, we be all that's left from the Kokoda!"

When the last litter was carried out Don started to follow it when Cooper called to him from the cockpit.

"Tower just called, Don. Fuel truck's on its way and so is our next load for Dobodura. I guess we're going back." Don grimaced with the news, shaking his head.

"Even with that weather over there? The afternoon scud is full on, they'll be squalls all along the coast!" Don complained peering out the window, looking for Katie.

"More wounded, I guess. Heck the tower said we may have to figure on TWO more trips. We'll be coming back to Seven-Mile in the dark, looks like."

Don didn't answer, hopping out of the airplane to jog over to an ambulance where Katie was talking to a captain, an army doctor. Don

50

approached, saluting the doc before nodding to Katie. The doctor waved a casual salute as he glanced at Don, then at Katie. He turned and walked around the ambulance. Katie, oddly formal, insisted on saluting and holding it for Don. Annoyed, he saluted her back. There were two or three more litters to load into the ambulance so Katie stepped away from the vehicle, walking slowly towards the runway. Don got the hint, quickly catching up.

"Well I see the 153rd is still here, I thought I was going to miss you." Katie glanced up, her face tired and a little sad, Don thought.

"No," she sighed, "we're still here. I think the big push over there in Buna and Gona kinda' messed up the move, at least temporarily."

"You look like you've lost some weight—and not getting enough sleep," he said lamely, hoping she would take it the right way. She turned her head towards him again, eyeing him before cracking a thin smile.

"The treated water makes me sick, I think. I have the—well, the runs." She watched him levelly now, coming to a stop. "I have to get back, we got word we'll be getting casualties all day. It will be a long couple of days, I think."

They reversed course, with Don, in one of the few instances of his life at a loss for words.

"One of those Aussies," Katie said quietly, her green eyes on Don's, "is a dead ringer for my Uncle Ted, one of my favorites when I was a kid. I was actually afraid of horses until he got me to ride with him. In my family that would have been death, being afraid of damned horses. The Aussie is the same kind of man, sure looks like him. Big and strong, afraid of nothing I suspect. My family is full of men like that. I love them and I hate them at the same time. But I loved Uncle Ted because he never told me I couldn't do something because I was a girl. He just told me I was a McCutcheon and there were horses waiting for me to ride, so I needed to get a move on."

Don nodded, not really knowing how to respond. They reached the ambulance as the last litter was latched in place and the doors were closing. Overhead to the north they heard the throbbing engines of a pair of staggered C-47s turning base before lining up on the runway. Right on cue, another set of ambulances pulled up from the 153rd.

"Gotta' go, more customers!" Katie said lightly. She smiled, her face quizzical as she turned to go. "Nothing to say, Lieutenant Crenshaw?" She teased. Don stuck his hands in his pockets, his foot pawing the ground like a little boy.

"Maybe I'll see you before you go," he mumbled. Katie stared at him as if he had just sprouted some horns. She lifted her wrist, pointing towards her wristwatch.

51

"I think we'll be doing this all day, so I might be able to wrangle another trip out here with a triage team later on this evening. From what I'm hearing, it's a mess out there so this could go on for weeks. I think you'll be going out and coming back with another load of wounded today, so maybe I'll see you." She peered over his shoulder at his transport. "402. I'll look for it." She paused before walking over to the jeep with waiting nurses, all casually trying to look somewhere else. "That is, if you want to see me."

"I'd like that. I'll be looking for you. Maybe—maybe sometime before you leave we can get something eat at the messhall, or something." It was all he could think of to say, which seemed to satisfy her. She beamed a big, beautiful smile before giving him a snappy salute. He saluted back, smiling as the three other nurses in the jeep grinned and saluted too.

CHAPTER 5

December 2, 1942, 153rd Station Hospital, Port Moresby

Vaughn (Vic) Hickey awoke with a start, his brain flashing and popping like a flash bulb. He felt a searing pain on the lower right side of his body. It was dim, twilight, almost like the jungle. Fearful at first he was confused until he heard voices; calm, normal voices. Not combat voices. The smell of raw alcohol, mildew, sweat and some indescribable sweet stink assaulted his senses. *Oh God, that hurts, Jesus!* He instinctively moved his right leg, pinned or bound somehow all wrong. Cursing, he tried to shift his upper body to see what was going on only to receive a poker hot stab in the chest for the effort. There was some kind of restraint squeezing the air out of his lungs. Groggy, lying partially on his left side, his right leg and hip were pulled and twisted away. It was so hot and muggy his bed sheets were soaked through. He was stuck to everything. It was very uncomfortable, his right shoulder and right leg tied or pinned in opposite directions. *What the hell? What have they done to me?*

"Take it easy, buddy, you don't want to pop out your catheter or pull out an IV." The voice, an American male, sounded tired from the foot of the bed. Vic laid his head back, turning so he could see over his right shoulder. The bed had some kind of suspension system, pulleys and ropes, running back over the top. The entire frame was draped with fine gauze—no—mosquito netting, thick and folded. There was an electric light, subdued, somewhere beyond. Somebody with reddish hair—with a yellow halo in the light, tinkered down there out of sight, resulting in a clinking sound. Vic watched an elbow going up and down like a crank handle, feeling his leg being pulled apart from his hip. His gasp and *STOP* brought a young face up, peering at Vic with alarm. The face wore thick rimless glasses, his eyes huge in the lenses.

"Oh shit, *wrong way! Sorry!*" The clinking resumed but the pressure on Vic's leg immediately eased. "That better? I saw we got your leg suspended to ease the pressure on your hip and your leg fractures. Only they got you twisted all ta' hell keeping you up and elevating your leg. We don't have the proper bed for your wounds here. I thought they had your leg too high, was just gonna' lower it down a bit."

"Thanks, chum," gasped Vic, very grateful for the relief. Speaking was difficult, his tongue thick, his throat raw and sore. He was very thirsty. It hurt to breathe. He was also aware of a dull pain on his left side, remembering vaguely he had been shot in the chest. The orderly with red hair came around to the left side of the bed, dropping on his

53

haunches to be at Vic's level. The orderly eyed the extreme angle of the bed before pulling the mosquito net aside to look at his wounds.

"That must not be very comfortable," he chortled, irritating Vic. "With you still under they wanted you sitting up more for your lung. I can't believe they had you twisted this way and that way, damn!" The orderly eased Vic back a little bit, stuffing a couple of thick pillows behind him.

"I'll check with the nurse on the angle, but I don't think they mind me letting you lay back a bit now you're awake." The young man disappeared but Vic didn't notice, dozing off the instant the pillows warmed his back.

Vic could remember two times in his life other than the Army, ever having to stay in hospital. He was born at home in Bombala, New South Wales. If kids got hurt or sick the local doctor came to the house or you just got better on your own. He did get really sick when he was about fifteen, luckily right after returning from a week in the mountains six hours from anywhere moving sheep. He threw up with cramps so painful he could not stand, so his dad hauled him off to the little surgery in Bombala, the same doc who fixed his broken arm years before. It turned out to be appendicitis, the infection after the surgery laying him up for three weeks. No one could explain it. It wasn't a real hospital, more like a two-bed clinic, but Vic didn't like it in any case. There was talk about moving him up to Cooma but his father balked at the cost.

This was the year, 1933, his dad decided there was no future in sheep ranching. The family kept most of the land for a time, Vic and his brothers continuing to raise the sheep. His father's plan was to rent a room from one of his brothers in Geelong, 70 odd kilometers across the bay from Melbourne, and find work at the expanding Ford Motor Company plant in nearby Norlane. He was convinced the future labor for smart Australians would be industrial machinery, not ranching. He would keep his expenses down and come home when he could. When the time was right he would move the whole family to Geelong, buy a house and sell the Bombala homestead. Vic's father's older brothers already made the change, abandoning their land for manufacturing jobs at Ford years before. There were fewer and fewer Hickeys working the sheep or cattle in New South Wales. Those who migrated to the city never came back.

Two years later, Vic, as the oldest boy in that branch of the Hickey family, joined his father to become an apprentice machinist at Ford. The Ford factory transitioned a few years earlier from making Model T Ford cars to Model A's, B's and 18's with good pay and benefits for the workers. One afternoon, pushing a cart of parts across the huge main shop floor, a flathead V8 short block slipped from a block and tackle chain suspended from an overhead crane. The engine dropped a meter in a heartbeat before the safety chain locked under the oil pan, the swinging pan clipping Vic a glancing blow and fractured his skull. The lightweight metal safety helmet he was wearing saved his life. The accident still cost him three weeks in the hospital and reduced pay from his union for six more. *Damn, what a hardhead,* his Dad and his mates had said when he returned to full duty. He had dizzy spells periodically for a few months but they eventually went away. Vic followed his Dad's advice and never complained to his supervisors or discussed it with the company doctors. *You can't trust em', lad. You keep your mouth shut if ya' want to keep your job.*

So Vic was naturally suspicious of anything to do with medicine. It was all about loss, somehow, always yours. It was painful, restrictive and the medical professionals clipped *your status at the bleedin' door.* You suddenly become a bloody child again. He groaned as he slowly woke up, remembering where he was, painfully aware he was hurting all up and down his right lower side, his chest stabbing him when he tried to breathe. And damned if they didn't have a *thing up his bloody pecker.*

He was turned towards a wall or a divider, about a meter away. The first thing he could see once his eyes focused beyond the IV inserted and taped to the top part of his left wrist, were the six or seven big nasty insects crawling on the wall. Instinctively, he started to examine the bed sheets around him, but he couldn't see any. They had him all doped up no doubt about it, but *bloody hell,* his leg and hip were hurting. Twisting slightly to the right eased the pressure on his hip, but he could see his right leg, now only suspended a couple of inches off the bed was partially plaster casted. The lower leg, from about six inches under his knee was casted right to his foot. He could feel something, something hot and heavy around his right thigh with thick bandages, especially on his hip. He remembered vaguely what his thigh looked like when the Nambu burst tore big chunks away.

His chest burned but no matter what, his lung was shot through and through, he knew that much. *Jeez, what a bloody mess I am,* he thought. His angst only lasted a few seconds as his father's face floated in his memory. Never one to show much empathy when young Vic and his brothers whined about a situation or a hurt, physical or otherwise, his dad simply crossed his arms. *Things could be bloomin' worse, laddie!* So true, Vic thought guiltily, as he considered where he was. He was now dreamingly conscious of other voices, the odd, flat accent of the Americans. His mind, narrow focused for only a fraction of time before spinning into confusion, tried to brush aside the throbbing pain and clouds of mist surrounding his thoughts. The narcotics slapped him down efficiently, cloaking his eyes with gathering darkness, silencing his muddled thoughts to extinguish his lights into a tunnel as black as pitch.

Bombala, New South Wales in the 20s and early 30s was reminiscent of those small towns of the American West and Midwest Vic saw in the Hollywood movies. Having seen Tom Mix and Hoppalong Cassidy and the vistas of desert southwest depicted occasionally at the Friday night cinema, he could say he knew what they were like. He didn't know at the time most Hollywood movies were shot in southern California. If he did, he would have said the California desert reminded him of New South Wales. Bombala was about 200 kilometers from Canberra, the capitol of Australia, yet anyone who ever travelled the distance to get to either of those places would agree they were worlds apart. To leave the city limits of Canberra and head south was not to just leave, but to leave for *the hinterlands*.

Some citizens of Bombala would take offense to this almost *outback* characterization referring, with some pride, to a little known bit of history. Bombala was situated almost exactly equidistance between Sydney and Melbourne, about 480 kilometers from both. There was a constant rivalry between the two most populous cities in the country, with Melbourne the largest and Sydney racing to catch up. The two coastal cities were in separate states, Victoria and New South Wales, respectively, each wrestling politically to be declared the official capitol of Australia. Around the turn of the century the Australian Royals, attempting to create neutral ground, suggested Bombala as the home for the new capitol. Developed on rolling hills between the high Snowy Mountains to the west and the lower coastal plain, Bombala didn't even have a railway connection yet. A single dusty wagon trail served to connect it with Cooma, 80 kilometers to the north and then continue south down to the Tasman Sea. Bombalans, upon hearing the proposal, probably discussed it over a pint at the Imperial with considerable merriment, if not with downright alarm if it was taken seriously. *Hunnerds' of bloody politicos an' their lackeys descendin' on Bombala? Are they out of their bloomin' minds?*

In either case Bombala failed to satisfy the requirements for anyone, forcing the development of a completely separate and new city and territory altogether. Out of it came the city of Canberra in the tiny Australian Capitol Territory (ACT), following the American model of the District of Columbia. Bombalans sighed in considerable relief, returning to their quiet, rural lives. As in America, the very nature of Canberra's existence and the type of people drawn to politics ensured most Australians ignored it from the onset. Bombala, home to a thousand people plus or minus a few hundred depending how far out you chose to

56

point, continued to grow on its own, gaining telephone lines, a railway line in 1921 and even a few motorcars.

For Vic being born and raised there, it was a love-hate relationship. He knew his story was no different than two hundred thousand other country lads, rural boys raised hundreds, sometimes a thousand kilometers from anything resembling real civilization. Like most of Australia, it took two to three times the land to raise the same number of cattle or sheep as in other countries with better soil and more rain. Land holdings were vast, the distances between towns and villages equally enormous, requiring long hard days to simply move stock around for decent grazing.

He grew up watching his parents work from dawn to dusk, pinching out a living raising sheep for wool and meat, knowing there would be few opportunities for himself and his brothers to do much else. There was no money for a motorcar or trips to the coast, or even sending Vic or his brothers to secondary school. What cash his parents saved was invested in more stock, feed, planking, corrugated metal or shingles for a new roof for the house. The economic depression meant everyone suffered, he knew, but he could not see himself doing what his parents were doing for the rest of his life. Before his dad made the decision in 33' to find work in Geelong, Vic considered his options and planned his own escape route.

After he completed grammar school Vic planned to get his Wool Classer's Certificate. He certainly had the hours and sheep wool experience required, but there were still a few classes and exams he needed to take and prepare for. Once he gained an Intermediate Certificate he knew of young lads, rural bumpkins just a few years older than him, working at Loan and Mercantile establishments. These firms were wool, stock and station companies in Melbourne paying good wages. These lads wore business clothing and traveled some to the sheep stations about Victoria with expense accounts. They made real money to spend and had time to spend it. No more saddle sores living on a horse or shearing sheep until his back and arms were so spent he could hardly lift them, the work never ending despite brain-broiling heat or snow on the ground. Only to come home dead clapped out to a place 200 kilometers from anywhere.

Instead of his Wool Classer's Certificate when he graduated grammar school, Vic joined Ford to learn tool and die work as an apprentice machinist. At first he found the work interesting because there was a lot of satisfaction in doing precision tasks. After awhile the repetitive jobs, sometimes under strong supervisory pressure to do it faster, began to be less interesting. Geelong, despite its young work force living with the novelty of having dozens of eateries and places to

57

spend money in, was an industrial factory town. True quality housing was very hard to find, as was any semblance of the far-as-the-eye-can-see beauty and peace and quiet of Bombala. As soon as Vic joined his father, his dad signed a lease for a small clapboard row house indistinguishable from those around it, on a narrow, noisy street not six blocks from the factory gate. There was no front yard, simply a door to the street. You could hear the shift change horns around the clock doors and windows closed or not, corresponding with the noise of neighbors coming and going to work.

Vic missed his dad during his first two years in Geelong, envying him his new life in the city, not realizing how hard it must have been for his father to adjust. Despite his age and experience his father started at essentially the same job as Vic, an apprentice machinist, at 35 years of age. You start out an all-out gofer for journeymen as a rookie, not an easy role for a proud man long used to calling his own shots. His father wasn't alone in this role of course, Ford only began hiring again after a long slump when he came on in 1933. His brothers had told him about the opportunity and who to talk to, and for whatever reason it worked. His dad knew he was damned lucky to get the job, any job, as they only hired new men as sales began to pick up and only a handful at that. All of them were older men like him, mostly from rural farm or ranching backgrounds looking for a new life. Two years later he became a journeyman, earning a pay raise. His supervisors asked if there were more like him at home and if so, to send them along.

Vic's dad pumped him for information about the family and the ranch, since he only made the 500 kilometer journey home four times in two years, they couldn't afford it. Every shilling he made after expenses went into savings for a new home. There was a telephone at the Imperial Hotel in Bombala, so his dad arranged a weekly phone call on Friday night. Vic and his brothers hitched up the wagon for the ride into Bombala, his mother decked out in her second best dress (the best was saved for Sunday morning services), sitting next to Vic and his youngest brother, Norman. Vic's next younger brother, Bill, who didn't get along all that well with Vic, sat far to the right on the seat.

If the family made good that week selling wool or meat with a tad profit, his mother took them to the cinema the same evening. They never knew what was showing, it didn't matter. They enjoyed the newsreels, with the cinema showing at least one American western, sometimes two. They had to eat an early supper at home as they couldn't afford a meal in town, but their mum always let the boys have a bit of candy at the general store. Before the cinema they all went over to the Imperial Hotel to wait for the incoming call from their father. They all took a turn

58

talking to their dad, their mum taking the first and last minutes of the conversation. It was always a bit sad, Vic felt when they hung up, as their mother gripped the now dead ear piece for a long moment before carefully putting it away. The proprietors of the Imperial knew Vic's mom well, knowing the situation with their dad, always offering to bring her some tea while they waited for the connection to be made, occasionally springing for soda pop for Vic and his brothers. Vic's mom offered to pay and it was always refused.

Just before Vic came to Geelong his dad came home briefly to begin leasing part of the sheep operation since without Vic, his mother and his brothers couldn't handle the entire operation anymore. One of his dad's younger brothers wanted to remain in Bombala, feeling he could do better with a larger herd. His dad leased both land and animals to his brother, with the understanding of sharing profits until his dad was ready to sell the entire operation. Vic noticed his father spent a lot of time walking around slowly and staring out over the blue-hilled countryside on that last visit, a sad smile on his face. He scratched the ears of their old bay mare, Sundown, her snickering like the purr of a cat, as he unhooked her harness and brushed her down. At the time, Vic, who couldn't wait to pack his meager bags for the train ride to Geelong, worried at first his father might change his mind. He seemed to waiver somehow.

Three years later, in 1938, now a journeyman machinist living in a two-room flat a full two kilometers away from his parents new house in Geelong, Vic believed he understood how his father felt. It was a major change, the consequences not yet realized. The land was gone, all of it, to his dad's younger brother. The past, whatever it may have meant, slipped away and was history. There was nothing to go back to belonging to them. Both of Vic's younger brothers, Norman and Bill, were working at the Ford plant. His dad bought a used Model A sedan, teaching Vic how to drive. With everyone working with good wages and Vic and his dad with enough seniority to take a little time off every now and then, they broke away from Geelong and the two-block long slab sides of the Ford plant to head for the beach.

In all their years living in Bombala, about 80 kilometers from the sea on the south coast, the Hickeys never once went there. They just didn't. So at first they piled into the Model A to head due east straight out of town to Queenscliff, a pretty little village of Victorian homes on a pointy promontory of the lower mouth of Port Phillip, the wide, deep bay leading up to Melbourne. Built around an old Army fort protecting the bay, Queenscliff was the weekend playground for the well-heeled in the south bay. The family rented a small cottage, walking the short beaches and breakwaters as they nibbled at the strange seafood, staring at the colorful sailboats darting about in the sun-shimmering bay, and commenting on how much richer their lives were now they lived in Geelong.

It was true to a point, depending on how one looked at it. Monetarily the family had more money to buy things, both as a group and individually. Even Vic, living apart in his flat was expected to contribute to the family, mostly to help acquire modern household appliances for their mother. The first lesson you learned living in a city is that people seemed to be very interested in the things you had. So interested in fact, they determined whether or not you were someone worth knowing based on those things. The years of economic decline seemed to be over, folks more than willing to believe better times were in the bag. They wanted to have things, didn't want to be denied anymore. Vic's mom seemed appalled of her poverty regarding these appliances and certain household items, so the family men all chipped in to get her what she wanted.

In the year and a half since the big move the new house was filled with gadgets that whirred, buzzed, hummed and throbbed going about their business. Vic's mom loved it, proud to bring her new lady friends over to chat about the machinery. His father, he noticed, was signing up for every bit of overtime work he could find. He was used to working long hours, still a relatively young man, so he went about it cheerfully, always wrapping up anyone's complaint about working conditions with his blanket conversation ender: *It could be a whole lot bloomin'worse, lads!*

There wasn't any electricity at the old ranch house in Bombala, so cooking and heating were done with wood year round. There was a manual water pump in the kitchen, but no plumbing or facilities, the loo being a small shed outside. Nobody much thought about it when they lived there as their neighbors, many kilometers away, had similar situations. If you lived in town you might have electricity and maybe even gas, but only the well-off had indoor plumbing. A man came once a week to empty the pan. It was a chore in the winter, with frost or the infrequent snow on the ground making the hike an adventure. It was an embarrassment now to admit they used to live that way.

The houses in Geelong had electricity and even gas, power to drive overhead and table lamps, small stoves and ovens, and even heat water. A few of the older row houses in Geelong, those neighborhoods built in the years after the Great War, didn't have indoor plumbing. Vic's little flat was one of those, the rent still relatively high, considering. All of the newer homes had it, with Vic hearing but not really believing, there were some larger homes with two or more flush toilets. It seemed very wasteful of space to him for such a minor function.

The more people crowded together he observed, the more irritated or suspicious they became that someone had more of something than they had. There was no other way to explain it, this strange drive to simply acquire things whether you needed them or not. He remembered riding the wagon over to a neighbor's property with his dad in his youth, looking at the worn patches darned on his father's shirt. He was never embarrassed over it, simply considered it part of his dad, part of that life. Most of the clothes his mom and dad wore then were the same ones they wore when he was a baby. He couldn't remember his father getting a new shirt, the half dozen he did own just getting more worn as the years passed. It might have happened, but he was sure he would have noticed.

He still had one of his dad's old coats, a good waxed cotton one from England he inherited when he got big enough. Slightly torn, slick smooth from wear in some places, he would never give it up. The coat meant something to Vic, it was part of his dad. Those neighbors were the same way. They certainly looked the same, shared the same misery of drought, low prices for stock, meat and wool, or long, cold winters. Like sailors serving together on a ship they rode the same storms. It made a difference somehow on how you perceived one another. Vic remembered always looking forward to visiting neighbors, always friendly, always glad to see you and give you news. The distances had something to do with it, the loneliness of the life, but it was the shared experience. They were like family.

Vic couldn't quite put his finger on it at first, realizing on one of his solitary excursions to his flat he really hadn't adjusted or accepted to a life filled with people who were so different from himself. Or maybe, he thought ruefully, it was not so much they were different as the new world gave them opportunities to be different. Maybe that was it. Most of the men on the shop floor, certainly the older ones somewhere between Vic's age and his father's, came here from the same background, all tired of scratching out a living from dirt or animals. None particularly skilled in a trade, just men with strong backs and hands willing to learn, willing to give up their freedom on the land to be chained to a machine, hour after hour, day after day, for a good wage and a steady paycheck.

But that didn't mean they would be happy. One February weekend when all three sons were available for a change and the summer heat made Geelong unbearable, Vic's dad loaded the family into the Model A to make the journey south from Geelong down to Torquay. Torquay was a little village right at some of the very best beaches in Australia, with long rows of tall, charging pipelines of white curling waves racing in a quarter of a mile before pounding to the sand. The Hickeys had never

61

seen anything like it, marveling at the brilliant blue water and incredible power and noise. The Great Ocean Road was just completed a few years earlier, a small ribbon of asphalt and dirt winding around the coast from Torquay to the old whaling town of Warrnambool, over 80 kilometers away to the west. Small coastal villages were beginning to pop up with the new connection, so Australians with cars and time began to hear about and plan the cruise along the coast.

It was unnerving to the Hickeys, not being coast people, to drive on such a tiny road with the roaring ocean straight down, driving sometimes almost right on the beach or a few hundred feet above. Vic's dad, used to driving four or five miles around town, was nervous as was his mum. Vic eventually took over to everyone's relief, driving very slowly, pulling over often and ignoring the honks and shouts from other drivers, all apparently in a much greater hurry than the 20 kilometers per hour the Model A—and the Hickeys, were comfortable with. It was a long drive, the family finally stopping a few kilometers past Cape Otway to walk down to the high white chalk cliffs for a late picnic. There was nobody about as they shook out a blanket. A cluster of lonely sentinels, spires of rock and limestone standing fifty meters high a quarter of a kilometer out to sea, strung out in a line as far as you could see. All that was left, apparently, of a ribbon of shore long washed away, eons in the past.

The wind was strong here but the air balmy, the late sun over their shoulders warm and friendly. Their mum looked peaceful and happy, her face glowing from the long day in the sun. Her brown hair, just tinged with grey, curled around her like a little girl. Vic felt she looked prettier than she had in years. She noticed Vic turned her way, smiling at him as she dished out plates of cold chicken and potatoes. His brothers, Bill and Norman, ate their food quickly before laying out on the blanket. *Ere' we are*, their dad said irritably, *on some of the moost 'scenic land in all o' Australia, an' you blokes 'ant ta' sleep? No appreciation of beauty, mother, might as well hav' left da' clods at home!*

His brothers were snoring in minutes. After picking up a bit, Vic's mum leaned back on her hands, stretched out her legs, rolling her head back before closing her eyes. The breeze continued to swirl around her, moving her curls this way and that, a sensation so obviously pleasurable she smiled to herself and sighed. Vic's dad patted her affectionately on the shoulder as he came to his feet, nodding to Vic to follow him. They walked a short distance away to the land's end, the sea fifty meters below them crashing and thudding against the limestone.

"Won't be long this lot will join them' soljers' out there," his dad noted quietly, pulling out his pipe. It took a few seconds for Vic to realize what he meant. The rock sentinels did look like soldiers, spaced in a row like they did. Vic nodded when he saw his dad was watching him closely, carefully packing his pipe with the dark, navy cut tobacco he liked. He lit the pipe slowly, expertly cupping the flame against the wind.

"You know, Vonnie, we're just not sea people." He said this conversationally but as a known fact, like he would to another man at work or in church. It unnerved Vic a bit, sensing his father wanted to say something to him, but unlike other times, Vic had no idea what it was about. His father puffed his pipe, the bitter smoke visible in wisps then gone instantly with the breeze. He eyed Vic before leaning in a bit.

"Eve' got a good life 'ere," his glance spread over his shoulder to where Vic's mum and brothers were, than back to Vic, "an' your mum 'as never been happier." His dad turned his head, his eyes now far away over the horizon. Vic thought he heard a long sigh, but he wasn't sure.

"Eve' got solid futures, all of us, now. They's rumor 'bout on war, but they's no tellin how such things work out." Vic's dad, who served three years in the trenches during the Great War, would not talk much about the potential threats of another one. "No matter though, they's no going back." Vic could only nod, clueless to what his father was trying to get at. After a long pause his dad pointed out to sea, waving his pipe slowly across from one side of the horizon to the other.

"All of this, this so-called beauty everybody yaks about down ere' by the water," he snorted contemptuously, stuffing his pipe back in his teeth, "Torquay, 'is Great Ocean Road bit," glancing over his shoulder again at Vic's mother, whose eyes were still dreamily closed. "Ayed' trade *the whole lot* for some of them little valleys 'oop in the hill country climbin' 'oop in ta' da' Snowy's—know what aye' mean?" He leaned in close to Vic, placing his arm, hesitatingly at first, on Vic's shoulder, the conspiratorial grin broad and friendly.

"Aye' mean, Vonnie, *aye' really miss* being on a 'orse sometimes, just myself or with you or one of your brothers, out there *days away* from anything resemblin' what we have ere'." His sad smile said it all as Vic put his arm around his father to give him a strong hug.

In the city you are rarely alone. You could certainly be lonely, but rarely alone. On the shop floor, in the street, you were conscious of other people nearby, some watching or monitoring your work, other's oblivious to your existence. Vic, generally an affable sort who liked the company of others at times, also valued his solitude more than he ever thought he would. He was comfortable in his own skin, was confident in his abilities for the things he knew and had some skill. Like his father he found out, he believed in a man's inherent right to do these things you are good at your own way. *More an' one way ta' shear bleedin' sheep!*

63

A lifetime of working hard, but having the freedom to approach the work as you see fit as long as the work gets done, would not change overnight. The Ford Motor Company, in fact all new manufacturing companies founded their business model on uniform production processes. Efficiencies were to be had, which means predictable productivity and profitability by doing things exactly the same way, at the right time, every time. The people using the machines produced products that fed other machines, so production facilitators—*pokers*, the machine operators called them, were there to ensure no one plant *process* was creating a bottleneck.

A process was a step in manufacturing, something bent, stamped, drilled, cut, rolled, bathed or painted to name a few. Because it was part of a production process, the facilitators had graphs specifying how long a particular process should take. No one asked *when will you be done?* In the old days when the family was ranching sheep, buyers of meat or wool would always inquire when you could deliver. It was your business with many things to consider, so the buyers respected your right to determine when the product would be available. The new industrial production line allowed for no such individuality. *When will you be done* was replaced with a flat demand: *These (fill in the blank) need to be done in an hour, be quick about it.* Union representation for any floor disputes happen after the fact. Production must come first and foremost, get the job done, unless the demand is *unreasonable.* Production facilitators, armed with their production graphs dully signed off by the union, rarely lose. Machine operators unable to meet production requirements on a regular basis always lose.

This grim understanding of their new life spawned a special closeness between Vic and his Dad he thought he had lost years before. There was no going back, Vic's father was correct in his mournful way on the Great Ocean Road. They were uprooted, the land, the life gone. The two of them mourned alone however, as it appeared his two younger brothers and certainly their mother, cheerfully embraced the new life. Norman and Bill never spoke of Bombala, except perhaps in the cool tones reserved for the passing of a not-so-popular relative. They might not have loved the new factory work but it was a trade with a future. They did love the money and the spare time, with a city and attractions to vacuum up both. The family didn't see much of them at home as time passed. They were home for some meals, always home before they were scheduled to work, but even their mother complained it appeared their beds hadn't been slept in. *They's out o'school an'workin', mother,* Vic's father would say. *They's young an'want ta'enjoy life. What's ta'harm in that?*

Vic didn't understand it, this strange divide between what should be the same generation. His brothers were only two and four years younger than himself, yet Vic felt he had little in common with them, being more aligned in the thinking of his father. He admitted he liked the money too, the pretty girls who seemed to live in beehives down certain blocks, with the freedom to do as he pleased once he was off shift. Raising Merino sheep was a 24 hour, 7 day a week reality, always with chores or things to do. For the first time in his life he had to think about how to fill his spare time. Friendships didn't come all that easy to Vic, though he had them, mates on the shop floor and the numerous new pubs popping about all around the plant. The new life left him uneasy, strangely unsettled.

The smell of machine oil and the constant whine of heavy motors in the plant were neither familiar nor particularly pleasant to him. It made him feel divorced and separated from what he did like. Many of his coworkers were openly fascinated and enamored with their machines, vocally proud of their skill and productivity. Vic was a good, competent machine operator but when the horns of the end of shift sounded, he finished what he was working on if he was almost done, or cleared the billets immediately from the grinding blades, shutting down and walking away without another thought. His laconic style but steady, efficient production impressed his bosses however, who moved him around to different machines before promoting him to assistant lead operator, than lead operator by the early part of 1939. Although he never had much to say to his supervisors, his ability to guide and train his operators to the same level of efficiency as himself saw him promoted to shift supervisor the same summer with full union backing. He was 22 years old.

This development did nothing but stir more misgivings and discontent in Vic's soul, although he never breathed a word of it in conversation. Being a new shift supervisor placed him in frequent contact with second level Ford management and union officials, at least at first. Although sometimes 10 or even 15 years younger than his shift operators, Vic's quiet competence and steady, even-handed leadership gained him the nickname of "Snowy". Even some of the management called him that, a respectful reference to his former life in the lower eastern corner of New South Wales, and the beautiful, million year old snow-covered mountain range formed by the Kosciusko Uplift stretching from New Guinea to Tasmania. He appreciated the respect from his machine operators, many who came from very similar backgrounds, some with as much life experience as his dad. He went out of his way to treat them as they expected to be treated. They were former sheep shearers, cattle hands, even a few lumbermen. Some were

65

sundowners who worked for men like Vic's dad, others former owners and bosses in their own right. Tough, stubborn, hard-working men who arrived at work in silence, always on time, never complaining.

He sensed in these older men, the ones who had lived outdoors all of their lives 40 or 50 kilometers from their little townships and 10 from their nearest neighbor, scrapping out an existence from a hard land, the same confusion and uneasiness he had with the new work and confinement. They all heard the stories from their grandparents about the great eight year drought from the turn of the century, a vast slaughter of over half of the animals grazed and pastured in Australia. This sobering history placed their sheep, cattle and very livelihood in perspective every season. It hung over the families for decades, the subtle, nibbling fear of every fall when the rain fell late, or not at all. It placed everything you owned and believed in at incredible risk, this nature song and dance, barring the intervention of the Almighty. However to Vic's mind, these men traded one ethereal unknown for another one, the far distant cluster of corporate board members who bought and sold plants and divisions like gods hurling thunderbolts of lightning. The noise and light could be seen and heard far away, but no one on the shop floor will ever know what was going to happen until it happened, that he knew.

Vic felt foolish and selfish at times when he considered his situation, especially since his responsibilities exceeded his father's, a lead machine operator working a different shift and part of the plant, per company regulations. His father, justifiably proud of Vic, spoke about his own feelings about the change only the one time, on the cliffs by the Great Ocean Road. Vic had tried on a few occasions to at least discuss his sense of discontent in conversation with his dad, but each time he backed away, sensing his father's displeasure of his even broaching the subject. Vic knew his dad thought essentially the same way he did. He showed it in many ways, usually when alone and he was not aware anyone was looking. The same sadness would appear in his eyes, a faraway look placing his father in another time. Apparently his dad's comment, *there's no going back*, was the final curtain of any remembrances of their former life. Vic got the hint, keeping his thoughts and dreams to himself.

The dreams were not really dreams, certainly not the nocturnal type Vic would quickly disavow. More like day dreams when he was not walking the shop floor, production report in hand, discussing problems and concerns with his operators or plant management. His day dreams were behind his desk in his office, a small cubicle shoved between a tool and die cage and the maintenance closet. The office did have a door and a large sliding window above his desk so he could see across the plant floor. Rows and rows of machines were visible, as were their operators toiling away. The lathes, presses, benders and grinders spewed sparks, noise and vibration felt as a steady rumble on their feet. Vic would close the door whenever he was in the office, turning away from the machines. Engines and large parts were delivered in huge wooden crates, the squealing, splitting sound as they were pried apart stabbing into Vic's ears. The crates themselves, light softwoods, once fractured open spewed out a brief scent of real wood. Crossing the floor Vic stopped, mesmerized by the odors, smelling in the split pine in his mind's eye the aromatic oils from gum trees, the scent of grass, wattle and bark.

He could not believe how homesick he could feel for a place that didn't exist anymore, or certainly not in the same way. His uncle still operated the old ranch in Bombala, sometimes making a profit, sometimes not. Vic had made the trip back to the ranch only once, in 1938. His father refused to go, which didn't surprise Vic. He didn't know what he would find or how it would affect him, but he felt he had to go. The old house was still there, although his uncle rented it to a young couple trying to make a go of the day-to-day management of the sheep. Vic borrowed a horse to make a tour of the property, homesick at once when he saw the rabbit skin stretchers leaning against the barn. He and his father had made every one of them. He watched the young husband, his ragged moleskin trousers hung with tattered suspenders, move some of the rams and ewes into the woolshed. The young man's loud humming accompanied by the snip of the shears the only sound in the afternoon sun.

Riding down by the Bombala River and the feeder creeks where he and his brothers used to fish for trout, perch and eels, Vic was struck by the peacefulness of the setting, the light greenness of the shallow hills even though it was late summer. Normally the hills were yellow by this time of year, only the gums and the ring-barked eucalypts would be trimmed with green. He assumed late summer thunderstorms were to blame, or credit. Looking west towards the Snowy Mountains the hills began to rise, shedding their pale greenness to dark to blend with the rock, creating the blueness so characteristic of the terrain on the east side of the Kosciusko Uplift. It was in these hidden little valleys and hummocks his father referred to so fondly on the Great Ocean Road. There were little hollows of green paradise, cool and firm, beautiful in their secretive flowering only discovered on horseback, coming over a rise. The meadows, even with sheep on them, seemed unworldly in their quiet. Loneliness, when it came, crept in at night when you couldn't see anything anymore. The crackling of the fire and the bleating of the sheep were all that could be heard, a hushing of the day for this land from eternity.

CHAPTER 6

December 3, 1942, 153rd Station Hospital

Narcotics, penicillin and some nutritional chemical soup dripped through the large gauge needle inserted in Vic's wrist. He stared at his wrist, which hurt, bound by a short tether to the rail. It took him a minute or two to focus his eyes, trying hard to make sense of what he was seeing. *Hospital. Hot and muggy as hell, still in New Guinea.* As awareness surfaced from the murk, he vaguely recalled having a conversation with someone. *Was it here? Have I been moved?*

As his eyes focused farther out he recognized the wall, the gritty texture and the bugs. He smiled, a little acknowledgement he at least knew where he was. *Port Moresby. Yank hospital.* It was uncomfortable as hell, but at least it looked like they had propped his right leg up with more pillow supports underneath and less reliance on the traction system. He was still a trussed chicken, the tape, pulley ropes and firm pillows pinning him in position. Vic was going nowhere.

His leg, thigh and hip throbbed with dull pain, more so every minute he was awake. Vic was aware he instinctively took shallow breaths. Bigger breaths hurt, a lot. He did remember his lung, grimly touching the bandage. He could feel another bandage plastered to his back. The short breaths probably weren't the right thing to do. Somebody said he needed to take slow, full breaths to properly inflate his lungs, pain or no. Otherwise the injured lung might fill with fluid again. *What's a bloke ta do, bloody hell.* Despite the confusion he felt and the pain, there was no denying he was hungry. His stomach not only growled it gripped with sharp, painful contractions. He glanced around hoping to attract some attention. The room was brighter than before, the mosquito net missing, with natural light coming in somewhere. Daylight. He tried to absorb and understand it all, only lasting a minute before his eyelids grew leaden.

Potty stood before him in some semblance of parade ease, his cheeks fuller from good grub and sleep, his face and arms scrubbed free of the grit and stink of the mangroves. The shrapnel wounds on his neck were neatly covered with three small bandages. His tattered khaki drills were replaced by the new jungle greens, so new the wrinkles from the packing boxes had not relaxed yet. His eyes were as glowing and feverish as ever, his bushy eyebrows knitted in a frown from some inexplicable concern or problem known only to him. He rolled his slouch hat around and around in his hands, gripping it nervously. Unsmiling as usual Vic wished Potty would say something, that way he would know the dream image was not one of his "death contacts" from previous dreams, where former chums, long dead, would come visit silently, to stand before him. As far as he knew Potty was okay, he wasn't wounded, was standing right next to Vic in the medevac transport. Vic tried to reach out with his hand in the dream to touch his old friend, but his hands wouldn't move.

"Dare' we go! Hav' ad' a bloomin' brick comin' outta' ma' arse' worrin' ya' nev' goin' ta' come round', Vic!" The voice boomed in his ears, Vic blinking again and again, leaning back as the scarecrow apparition of Potty came closer, grinning now uncharacteristically from ear to ear. The mosquito netting was rolled up and away with some mechanism as Vic felt hands patting and pumping his right hand, the texture scratchy and gnarled yet warm and seemingly very alive.

"Whas' matta', Vic?" Ye' look like ye' seen a bloody ghost, mate!" Boomed Potty again, shaking his head, still grinning like a lunatic. Someone stood very close to Potty, a nurse, a familiar one with a lovely smile. They both looked very real. Vic was beginning to suspect it really was Potty he was looking at; he wasn't dreaming. He blinked again shaking his head, staring first at Potty then the nurse.

"Alm' aye' dreaming? Alm' not, am aye'." he asked tentatively. This was answered with a roar of laughter as Potty pounded on the bed rails, tears streaming down his face. Vic suddenly felt pretty foolish, grinning sheepishly at Potty. He couldn't express how glad he was to see him, but he hadn't expected it. It was—surreal. For the life of him he thought for sure he was dreaming. *How can you be dreaming one second and awake the next?* He gripped Potty's hands weakly in his own. The nurse, Katie McCutcheon came around Potty, leaning across Vic to prop his back with pillows to keep him up and gently turned him to the left. Potty stepped back to stay out of her way, glancing at Katie approvingly, winking at Vic. Although she was wearing unstarched olive drab cotton overalls there was a hint of perfume as she moved around Vic. Even with Potty standing there like a bloody stuffed horse, Vic couldn't take his eyes off of her at first.

"Oh jeez, Vic! Alm' gonna' pop me a gasket! 'On't believe ave' ever seen ya' so bonkers!" Embarrassed, Vic rolled his eyes closed and laid his head back. He *was* confused, no bloody doubt about it. Potty stepped in closer again laying his slouch hat on Vic's good leg, stopping to take in Vic's casts, bandages and pulley system with a critical eye. He walked to the foot of the bed, dropping down on his haunches to peer up under Vic's wounds as Vic opened his eyes, watching him.

"Aye," Potty grunted, shaking his head, "you're ah' mess, chum!" He pointed under Vic's right thigh, slightly suspended between two pillows, his face a grimace. "Watchin' fur' the gas gangrene, aye' see.

Keepin' the wounds open. That holes' big enough ta' stuff ma' fist n'. Aye' know'd the slugs plowed through both sides, they carved ya' up, chum! Aye' can see da' bloomin' bone!"

Katie McCutcheon who stepped away for a moment, arrived in time to listen to Potty's assessment with clear irritation in her eyes. She glanced at Vic's look of dismay as she slid around the foot of the bed, signaling Potty to get to his feet.

"They'll be no more of that, Sergeant!" she scolded Potty, guiding him to Vic's left side with a solid grip on his elbow. "Sergeant Hickey is just now coming out of several days of recovery from his surgery, and he doesn't need *you* to tell him how hurt he is! As a medic you know very well we DPC all large wounds because of the climate and heat here. No wound looks good exposed to the air. But it's to ensure healing. Gas gangrene! I'm ashamed of you!"

Potty, his mouth hanging open, was thoroughly cowed. He blinked, nodded and shook his head at virtually the same time, confusing Katie McCutcheon at first.

"'Erribly 'orry, miss," Potty stammered, "aye' didn't mean ta' mess with da' patient, aye' didn't." He looked so depressed Katie almost relented. "It's Corp'l, miss. Corp'l Johnson. Aye' fixed him up in da' field, just was checkin' ta' see he was doin' well, aye' was." Katie stared at Potty for a long moment, her stern look softened. She smiled as she placed her hand gently on Potty's.

"You know I forgot you treated him and cared for him out there— and on the medevac flight coming over. I apologize, Corporal. You more than anyone saved his life. You have every right to know how your patient is doing." Potty blinked again, looking like he was going to cry. He picked up his slouch hat, crushing it in his grip, slowly nodding. "Yes, miss. Tank' you, miss."

"You Aussies," Katie said, shaking her head, "I am a miss, but I'm a US Army officer. You could call me Lieutenant, Lieutenant McCutcheon." She said this with a wistful smile, disarming Potty completely. He nodded and shuffled his feet his right hand darting to his right eyebrow, flat and open in a casual Australian Forces salute, holding it.

"Yes miss—er, Leftenant'." Katie eyed Potty as he she picked up Vic's chart, bringing up her own right hand in a slow, but formal salute. A movement from the bed caught her eye as Vic brought his free right hand up to salute.

"Leftenant'," he said, looking serious. Katie ignored Vic, studying the chart.

"The only reason I let Corporal Johnson in to see you was because he has to return to your unit. The battle for Gona is going well I understand, but Corporal Johnson, other than an elevated fever from a bout of Malaria—is not seriously injured and has requested to return to the field." She glanced over at Potty, who, looking embarrassed, bobbing his head in agreement. "He'll be returning to your unit straight away, today I think, if he gets over to Seven-Mile and catches the afternoon transport to Dobodura, correct?"

"Yes, miss—er, Leftenant'."

"Well, for both of you," Katie sighed, peering at Vic then Potty, "considering the conditions and the seriousness of your wounds and your—journey out, you were lucky to survive, Sergeant Hickey. With your chest wound the old protocol would have been to keep you at a field hospital for at least four or five days. The new protocol is to transport out of the field because the field surgical hospitals are overwhelmed by the casualties in this campaign. Besides the bullet wound through your lung, you also received bullet wounds in your hip that fractured your femur. Just by chance the bullets missed your femora artery, so you didn't bleed to death in the field." Katie stated this in a matter of fact fashion, but her eyes were wide and empathetic as they met Vic's.

"You also have a very nasty compound fracture down there near your ankle, multiple fragmentation wounds in both legs from a, ah," she examined the chart, not finding what she wanted.

"Grenade," said Potty and Vic at the same time. Vic didn't mention it was a Mills Bomb. His. Katie nodded, setting the chart down.

"Just so you know, both of you, the compound fracture alone is getting Sergeant Hickey a ticket home to Australia for a long time. He'll be with us for awhile until we seal up his lung, can't fly six or seven hours in his present condition." Vic didn't like being referred to in the third person, but her report made his brain buzz with questions. He tried to sit up, grimacing immediately as pain stopped him cold. Katie quickly settled him back into his pillows as he gritted his teeth.

"He needs to rest, Corporal. Say your goodbyes. Your friend will be okay, he's in good hands here." Katie turned on her heels and was gone. Vic laid back his eyes closed, trying to ride out the throbbing pain. Potty stared at the departed Katie, blinking.

"G' bye, miss," he muttered. Even though Vic's eyes were closed Potty shuffled around closer to the bed so he could get within a few inches of Vic. He brushed a loose strand of hair from Vic's forehead, a pained look on his face as he watched his friend screw up his eyes. When Vic opened them again Potty drew serious. He began talking quietly, stating the status of the wounded from 9 Platoon as an after action report. Potty didn't get to the scene at the back of the bunkers until Vic was down and the sniper was hunted and destroyed. The bunker turkey shoot did cause enough confusion to let the other pinned down platoon to advance on the bunkers, taking out two on one side which sealed the fate for the remainder. The Japanese were in the process of pulling back, but they stopped their withdrawal when they realized 9 Platoon blocked their escape route.

Scabby and Biscuit—veterans of Palestine, Egypt and the Kokoda Track were dead. Biscuit saved his life. But they were both gone now. Vic knew it because Potty had told him when they were carrying him out of the swamps, but Potty's report finalized it. Link and Rocko were shot by the same sniper that tore up Vic's hip, but both would survive. Link was shot through both shoulders, Rocko shot clean through his neck with another 7.7mm slug tearing a huge chunk of his bicep away. He wouldn't be able to hoist a Bren gun ever again. Vic asked where they were and Potty said they were in an adjacent orthopedic ward about 50 meters away. The Yanks had all the Aussies together if possible, but certain cases like Vic or the neurological patients, the lads with serious head wounds, were kept in the same ward, Yank or Digger. Both Link and Rocko were busted up and couldn't move around much, but promised to come calling before they were transported home.

Vic laid back silently taking it all in. The battle for Gona, after a couple of failed assaults on the bunkers, was going well. The initial assault by 2/14 Battalion cost the battalion over a dozen dead, nearly three dozen wounded. 9 Platoon, down to a section or less, would be folded up with another platoon until they returned home to Australia for a proper refit. The 9 Platoon he had led and served with for over two years no longer existed. Vic stared into space, turning to Potty once he realized Potty had stopped talking. Potty's eyes narrowed, clearing his throat as he glanced to the left and right.

"Iffen' you be wonderin', Vic, aye' got your boys in safe keepin'," he whispered. "These Yanks tried to strip em' from me, but aye' 'fused, on da' grounds they be my weapons, an' aye' was not wounded." Vic's confused look irritated Potty, who winked conspiratorily.

"Da' boys! Tom and Sam! Aye, they got ye' all drugged up, mate!" Potty's frustration reverted to merriment when Vic suddenly lit up in appreciation, finally understanding. Tom and Sam were the names Vic had given, with considerable amusement among his platoon mates, to his personal weapons. Early in the war when Vic was a private serving 9 Platoon as a Bren gunner, there was no naming of your *bloomin' gun*, chum. But later fighting Vichy French as an assistant then full section leader, Vic acquired a .45 caliber Thompson submachinegun for his personal weapon. He then liberated a World War One era Colt 1911 .45

caliber pistol from a Vichy French Foreign Legion officer. The Thompson was a Commonwealth standard infantry weapon acquired from the British, very popular for close combat. Both of these guns, American made, used the same ammunition so unlike other platoon leaders or Australian officers carrying Enfield Mark 2 .38 revolvers or Webley .455 revolvers, Vic carried his Tommy gun and his Samuel Colt .45 automatic.

The distinctive ripping *BOP BOP BOP BOP BOP* of his Thompson gun or his .45 Colt was known to all of 9 Platoon in the dark green of the Kokoda. Some Jap just bought it. It was an enormously reassuring sound, knowing Vic was in the fight. *I'll go after em' with Tom and Sam*, Vic would say, and every Digger knew what he was talking about. Not at all surprising, certainly for 9 Platoon, guns of all types; Bren LMGs, Lee Enfield SMLEs, the few heavy weapon Vickers around and other Thompsons would soon have very personal monikers from their owners. It was comforting, so why not? You had your chums, kit, bully beef, a billy of tea and then rolled yourself a last racehorse before sliding into your fighting pit for the night with *Loretta*.

Unlike many of the American medics the Australians encountered with the 32nd ID, Aussie medics carried personal weapons, so Potty could get away with the guns until he himself was wounded or killed. In the field no one cared what a Digger carried, as long as ammunition was available and you contributed your firepower when it was needed. The Japs, they discovered on the Kokoda, like to use a medic's aid bag as an aiming point. Potty, when he wasn't hovering over a bloke wounded or sick, was an excellent marksman with his Lee Enfield. Potty had to leave his rifle to take Vic's weapons, so Vic was especially appreciative. Not that it mattered anymore for him, he wouldn't need them. It was Potty's concern and mateship that counted.

"Alm' goin' back to the comp'ny, an'ah' hold on to em' until you join us agin', Vic." Potty added sadly, with little conviction. Without realizing it he was looking at Vic's leg, forlorn, milky grey where bare skin was visible. Vic was too. It looked horrible. Vic had seen better looking limbs on dead men.

"All' be up an' about in no time, Pot. Don't let the skipper mess with the bleedin' platoon, keep em' together if you can. Aye' know aye' can count on ya'." Potty leaned over to grip Vic's free hand with both of his. He shook it firmly before carefully placing Vic's hand on the bed, meeting his eyes.

"Best of luck, Vic, we'll be seein' ya soon, chum!" There were tears brimming in his eyes, tired, worn out and sad. He brushed his brow in a casual salute, a man who never knew how to say goodbye. He simply backed away as Vic returned the salute, turning on his heel to disappear from sight.

In the summer of 1939, a new shift supervisor with growing responsibilities, Vic followed the dark news of Europe at arm's length. Like most Australians he had a strong sense of loyalty to what was regarded as the mother country, Great Britain. His father's thin references to the horrific experiences of trench warfare in France during the Great War, cobbled with nasty anecdotes of *bloody piss poor Tommy generalship*—created images heroic, reassuring but confusing somehow. His father had never been to Great Britain before, spending less than a week near a Liverpool dock after arriving by ship, housed in empty, drafty warehouses before being reloaded on transports for the trip to France. He never got into Liverpool proper, it rained hard every day anyway, never speaking to an Englishman except *bloody bloomin' military police* when he was in the country. *Ran into plenty of Tommies in France,* he admitted, *found them good lads, most of them, a bit queer sometimes, but good lads.*

His father was the first of the Hickeys in recent memory to make it to the motherland, so to speak. His grandfather nor his great grandfather had been there, although the family believed his great great grandfather had been born there, arriving in Australia sometime around the turn of the 19th Century. Originally from Cornwall, supposedly, although the Hickeys were fully diluted with migrating Scots and Irish by the time the land was acquired in Bombala. There was some question on whether the original Hickey *migrated* to Australia or was brought there in chains, but there appears to be no records to confirm either. Hickey's people simple reported the *arrival,* sometime in the early 1800s.

When war was declared officially in Europe on September 3, 1939, Vic's father quietly filled his pipe as he walked away from the repeat radio broadcast. *Ere' we go agin',* he said. Vic, who heard about the declaration of war at work, watched his dad grimly glance at their mother before looking at each of his sons. *Well, lads,* he said in a muted, sad voice, *barely 20 years an'we be killin' Jerries agin'.* Now 42 years old, his dad knew there wouldn't be a place for him in active service any longer, but there would be for his three sons. It was hard to tell, at that moment, what his emotions were. He was certainly not happy about it, but his stoic acceptance of *what is* placed his reaction as neutral to Vic and his brothers. They were excited, keenly excited, yet put the lid on the excitement so as not to dispel what was to their parents, a very sobering turn of events. This was not the time or the place to discuss future plans about the war. The fear in their mother's eyes nipped that in the bud.

In the next few weeks the furor, anger and noisy rhetoric regarding Germany's aggression subsided as Australians began to determine what their personal contribution could be. Older Australians, like Vic's parents, remembered the enormous losses sustained by Australian troops during the Great War, losses way out of proportion to the size of the population. *Set us back a hunnerd' years*, said his dad, *we lost the cream of the Australian crop in the mood' o' France.* There were only seven million Australians in the entire country in 1939, but there was already talk of raising *three to five* infantry divisions to fight in Europe. Rumors were immediate and spread like wild fire among the young and not so young men working the plants. The younger lads, already bored and discouraged by mundane, rote repetitive work with the prospect of only more of it for decades to come, began to think a couple of years sowing oats and seeing Europe might not be such a bad idea. A wound stripe and some campaign ribbons in a shadow box would look good on the wall, something to talk a bit with the grandkids someday. Some of the older gents started wearing moth eaten mufti out of dusty train cases, appearing in the local pubs with a new step in their stride. *It's 'ood to be in uniform agin'—a soldjer'. Aye' 'pect the call any bloomin' day!*

Word finally came down from Ford Canada, the owner of the Ford subsidiary in Geelong, the production of automobiles would soon cease to be replaced by war materials work for the duration of the war. Young plant workers started to drift down to the armed forces recruiting offices to discuss options. National service was right around the corner. There were three services to choose from; the Army, the Air Force and the Navy, and an additional choice *currently* for young men not interested in serving overseas. Those choosing the Militia, a form of local National Guard, would be required to attend a brief training program but then be allowed to return to their home and job, with occasional periodic training. In 1939, Militia units were prohibited from serving outside of Australia or its territorial interests.

The other choice was to join the new AIF, or Australian Imperial Forces. These were being formed as new Australian infantry divisions, air squadrons or ships for overseas service, all units serving under the Second AIF. The First AIF was formed to fight the Great War. The assumption, whether a lad was joining the Navy, Army or Air Forces was he would be trained and serve overseas as a Commonwealth country force in direct support of Great Britain for the duration of the war, plus six months. Vic, reassured he would have his job waiting for him when he got back, enlisted in the Australian Army six months after war was declared, in March of 1940. He enlisted up at Ballarat, about 75 kilometers northwest of Geelong, the family home of one his mates at

75

work. They sent them both home for a month, ordering them to report to Puckapunyal, a brand-new Army basic training camp, northwest of Melbourne near the small town of Seymour in April.

Vic and his plant mate joined the newly formed Seventh Division, but were separated almost immediately before being assigned to different battalions in the brigade. Vic found himself on the roster of 9 Platoon, A Company, 14th Battalion, 21st Brigade of the 7th Division. Although almost all of the new recruits for the 7th Division were from the state of Victoria, only a few of them in A Company were from the Geelong area and none were to be found in 9 Platoon. What he did find was a large number of the lads were from Ballarat, which he had to admit was where he had enlisted. Diggers with nicknames like Potty, Scabby and Biscuit were from Ballarat.

When Potty left his bedside Vic was overcome with a wave of heart-heavy emotion, an intense loneliness and homesickness. He dropped his head back to the pillows, closing his eyes. He was homesick for the only family he had known for over two years, not willing to accept most of them were gone, dead or wounded, but gone nonetheless forever from a life they would never share again. He got a little comfort when he thought about the early days, the division forming in Puckapunyal. He was an outsider to the platoon, many of them born and raised in the Ballarat area, mostly country lads like him who knew a world of sheep, cattle and horses. But most of them knew one another all of their lives, their familiarity obvious in their banter, jokes and closeness.

Vic was a large young man and was selected to train as a Bren Light Machine Gunner, as the weapon was relatively heavy. He never fell out of the marches despite the weight of the weapon and his normal infantry kit. He was distant, apart from the fellows who were lifelong mates, yet never hesitated to assist another soldier who stumbled or had difficulty with his load. Private Hickey noticed Private Johnson, soon to be known only as Potty, a recent graduate of the aidsman course on his way to becoming a full-fledged infantry medic, having difficulty on the weekly no-water allowed, long hump marches. Potty's skinny, spindly legs would begin wobbling like gyroscopes at times, especially when the march exceeded 20 or 25 kilometers. Potty was a very conscientious medic-to-be, quick to apply salve on blistering sores or plaster for the raw leather-rubbed feet of his charges. He was always kind to Vic, so Vic, one day simply hoisted the combat pack off of Potty when Potty was having particular gyroscopic difficulties, slinging the load onto his own shoulder. He did it without saying a word, simply dropping back. Their 9 Platoon section leader noticed it immediately, remaining silent until they returned to camp. Vic was punished with additional duties for carrying another man's assigned load, but was rewarded with Potty's friendship and an introduction into the Ballarat mateship.

Vic, who was simply known then as "Hickey" as there was no one who knew of his old nickname of "Snowy" as a shift supervisor, one day had Potty standing by him, roster in hand, asking him questions about which inoculations he had received during his initial military indoctrination. Battalion was making some kind of medical record book for each individual soldier before they shipped overseas. The roster was oddly reversed as the names of the platoon members were listed by the initial of the Christian name followed by the surname. It was obviously typed by Potty, who confused himself since the surnames were not in alphabetical order, initials were. Middle initials were missing, so Potty, searching for Vic's name on the list came across V. HICKEY.

"Dere' ya' ah, Hick," he declared, with frustration. "Aye' gotta' fix this bloomin' list! V Hickey! Sounds like da' way ma' dad calls a bloody motorcar! V Hickey! Get it, eh?" he cackled, before suddenly looking up at Vic.

"Well, dere' ya' ah! V Hickey! VIC! You're Vic from now on, chum! Easy ta' rememba'!" Vic smiled, nodding his head to this odd rail of a fellow. It could be worse. He was *Vonnie* to his dad and mum, *Von* to his brothers, *Snowy* to his plant workers, and now—*Vic*. Why not? He thought to himself.

"What do they call you, Johnson?" A few of the other fellows were sitting on their bunks, cleaning gear, watching Potty with amusement.

"Well, soom' of me mates at 'ome call me Paddy," Potty answered quietly, glancing sidelong at the two soldiers close by. The soldiers, soon to be known forever as Scabby and Biscuit, snorted derisively before making little piggy noises.

"'On't let em'snow ye', Hickey!" hooted Scabby. Potty, his eyes suddenly slits, peered irritably at Scabby before turning his head away.

"Paddy me' arse'!" snorted Biscuit, chiming in, "E' was known as *Patty* in 'is own bloomin' ouse'! Only he started to get in' Dad's whiskey, be in his cups gettin' ta' school! We 'alled him *Potty* after that, as the bloke was half blind a few mornins' or' awhile. Got is' arse' tossed out, he did!" Potty glanced sharply at Biscuit before crossing his arms, not saying anything.

" Is' dad put a stop to the da' drinkin' straight away, but ole' Potty was done, off to his 'irst 'prenticeship. No more schoolin' for 'em!" Biscuit nodded to Potty, not unkindly, grinning as he did so.

"Course' we other lads were just a 'ew months away ourselves, no more grammar school for this lot!" Both Scabby and Biscuit gathered

77

around Potty, leaning in closer. They put their arms around him, squeezing him with obvious affection until Potty relented, nodding his head. They tousled his stringy hair and patted his shoulders for both Potty's and Vic's benefit, winking at him. Vic liked them immediately for it, feeling accepted even more in their midst.

"Aye' felt bloody awful 'bout gettin' kicked out," Potty sighed admittedly, looking at Vic. He cracked his odd, lopsided grin, eyeing them all, forgiving them all transgressions, which was his way, given time. "But mornin' drinkin' was a new way at lookin' at the day! Was fun while it lasted!"

It was fun while it lasted, Vic thought sadly. Potty was going back to the company, but 9 Platoon was finished so the few remaining men, mostly new replacement lads, would be folded up with another platoon in A Company until the battalion reformed after the campaign. The handful of the old lads left; Potty, Jock, Red and Slim—would be blended with fellows they at least knew as their family. *They'll be okay, they can take care of themselves.* As he mulled the image of his old friends, Vic began to worry about them, his responsibilities as a platoon leader rearing its head irrationally.

He served with them, trained with them, lived with them closer than most human beings could ever conceive. In time he led them in innumerable little actions, losing them one by one to disease, injury or death. There was no rationalizing this reality. He tried to do the best he could to protect them, but on this island the fighting was personal, man to man. A bloke lived or died in an action usually alone. On aggressive patrols the firefights come suddenly, death scything through the stinking, choking air in the form of a bayonet or a bullet. Later you'd check in with your mates, finding them in their fighting pits, rolling a racehorse or mending a wound. If you were with them on the patrol, your eyes would meet having a smoko. The cold chill came when mates could not be found. Looking you'd find them in the position they were in during the last moment of their lives. What was left always struck Vic with infinite sadness and confusion. A man was a spirit, warming skin and bones, a communicating creature whose touch could heal or destroy. As a survivor you came to grips with the residue, a sudden empty sack; stiff, cold, already bloating in the heat, virtually nothing left of the living organism once residing inside. All of it, everything once there, was gone in an instant. Simply vanished. He couldn't explain it.

Vic's back stiffened as the muscles around his bones began to shrink, tightening, pulling hard in a painful spasm directly attached to his eyeballs. Within a minute it was on him, his shivering so strong the metal bed rails rattled loudly. His teeth chattered from the icy chill running straight up his lower spine to his fingertips. *Oh, God,* he gasped, *here we go again.* The shivering cold was inexplicably accompanied by burning heat in his forehead. Sweat gushed out of his pores like a stream to sting his eyes, the salt bitter on his lips. His bedding was soaked through in seconds. Mercifully, his broken body reacted to the spasms this time by simply unplugging his senses, rolling his awareness back like a retracting tongue, the sweet blackness complete. Katie McCutcheon, who heard Vic's moans and rattling bedrails half a ward away, gently mopped the sweat from his face as he lost consciousness. She could see and smell the need for all new dressings, as sweat and bodily fluids dripped from his open casts and bandages. They could wait for little bit, but not too long. Once the fluids dried the cotton dressings would stick, be problematic. Some malaria attacks lasted only 10 or 12 hours, some 48 hours. She was concerned about his fractures, so she made a note on the chart to ensure the leg restraints stayed in place for now.

In the Southwest Pacific malaria was a given, the land war fought in a damp, humid, dark natural breeding ground of anopheles mosquitoes. Like biting flies, the insects were such a constant companion for combat soldiers there was no avoidance possible, only grim acceptance and a mild prophylactic, atabrine, offering more symptomatic relief than anything. Everyone eventually succumbed to the disease in varying forms depending on the level of exposure. Infantrymen like Vic were directly exposed to hundreds if not thousands of the insects every single day in the field; active, hungry insects puncturing the skin and engorging themselves with the victim's blood until the insects could barely lift themselves off. The anopheles female was simply a carrier of the disease, drawing blood from an infected animal or human, then transmitting the disease to another animal or human.

For Vic and the rest of the men from 2/14 Battalion, their exposure to the anopheles mosquito came when they first arrived in Port Moresby. They lived in open tents on cleared swamps those first few days before beginning the journey up the Track, and they suffered through the blinding, heavy rains, following by brain-boiling blistering sun before the evening descended like a black carpet on the landscape. With the sinking sun came dense clouds of mosquitoes, so thick it was almost impossible to eat, speak or even breathe without ingesting insects. It was a relief to leave the swamplands to begin the physically punishing climb up into the Owen Stanleys'. There were no mosquitoes up in the upper reaches of the Kokoda Track, especially over 3,000 feet. Once there weeks after exposure, the disease manifested itself as the bone-raking, chill producing fever taking men out of the fight as effectively as shooting them—for a day, sometimes two or three. There was no routine evacuation possible from the Kokoda Track, it was too far and incredibly rugged for stretcher bearers once the Japanese took the Kokoda landing strip in the highlands. Malaria sufferers would be set aside in their fighting pits to ride out their fevers.

Only in the situation where the soldier's temperature reached 103 degrees would he be pulled from the line. Not very far, just to the aid station. There was no treatment anyway for the fever, the victim simply had to ride it out. Sometimes as in Vic's case, sleep descended on the victim, shutting down the senses as the body was racked with muscular contractions and temperature extremes. Huge fluid loss was always a concern, as was regulating body heat. For Katie McCutcheon having only been on New Guinea for five weeks, she knew it was just a matter of time for herself. She certainly recognized the symptoms in Vic. All of the men who came over with the original 153rd Station Hospital had it, with about 40 percent at any one time out of action because of the disease. Like all the new nurses brought over in October she took her atabrine tablets religiously, didn't go outside after dusk unless absolutely necessary, wore long sleeves and full trousers despite the heat, tried to stay in buildings with two or more screened entry layers, and slept with a mosquito net all around her bunk. Despite all of these precautions she and the other nurses were bitten dozens of time every day. It was just a matter of time.

Vic Hickey awoke, his brain alerting him he was cold, yet a comfortable, pleasant damp warmth was placed on his shoulder and back. He opened his eyes to again see the wall, free of large bugs this time, with the refracted light from sunlight casting a shadow of his bed rail.

"Our patient is coming around." A feminine voice said softly. A nurse Vic had not seen before walked around the foot of the bed, putting what looked like a sponge down to dry her hands. She came closer to peer at Vic, smiling as she shook a thermometer before inserting it under his tongue. "Since you're awake, I'll check your temperature the easy way."

"Hello, Sergeant." Vic turned his head to follow a familiar voice. Over his shoulder he could see Katie McCutcheon, smiling, as she squeezed a sponge into a pail before applying it to his back. It was warm and very soothing. With the thermometer in his mouth Vic could only grunt, nodding his head appreciatively. The other nurse gently gripped his right wrist to note his pulse before checking his blood pressure, bringing his head around to the left. She was about Katie's age but taller with blue eyes. She was all business, the blue eyes on her watch and blood pressure gauge.

"I think the sergeant is beside himself waking up to two nurses giving him a sponge bath!"

It was a little surprising, pleasantly so, as he felt Katie's soft warm hand on his shoulder as she scrubbed down his back. If it wasn't for the dull throbbing of his leg and hip, the pain of his chest, the dippy dizziness he felt after this last episode of fever and the bloody cramps in his gut from hunger, he would enjoy it more.

"We're about ready to do a dressing change but you're still pretty dirty from the field. They only scrubbed what was necessary for surgery. We need to change your bedding again anyway, so this is a good time." Vic, confused, wasn't sure which nurse had spoken. The blue eyed nurse pulled the thermometer from his mouth, examining it carefully.

"101. Much better."

She put the thermometer away before making a notation on Vic's chart. The nurses' bathed Vic carefully, the two pans soon filled with dirty, brown water. They dried him off with towels before covering him temporarily with a single sheet. With the ease of true professionals, they worked together rolling or lifting parts of Vic first one way then the other to remove the damp, stained sheets. His gasps and moans slowed them down only a fraction, their eyes on his. A few minutes later they repeated the process to install the new, clean, slightly drier bedding. They went away and returned with a cart filled with dressings. His leg, now devoid of the support pillows was even more pale and sickly, the large craters left after the surgeons had carved out his numerous shrapnel wounds puckered red. He knew the gunshot wounds unseen under the bandages were much worse. The sight of the raw open wounds turned his stomach. He leg looked like a grey and blue slab of sheep thigh he used to view in the meat locker at home, the cleaver cuts clean and red.

For a soldier with numerous open, draining wounds, dressing changes were memorable experiences. Sticky fluids of all kinds dripped from wounds into the cotton dressings, an excellent glue for adhering the dressing to the wounds. No manner of soaking would lift some dried fluids between the two, but the dressing must be removed and changed. Despite his best efforts at gritting his teeth, Vic moaned and cursed as the two nurses carefully peeled off all of his bandages. It wasn't the first time they informed him, but the first time with him awake. They scrubbed the edges of the raw wounds, examining each carefully for any sign of infection before repainting his skin with some awful purple solution. They scrubbed around and just inside his casts before wrapping him up with clean new bandages.

It took nearly an hour to complete the task. Vic was totally drained and exhausted. He was falling asleep as Katie tucked his shoulder to the left with pillows. Gratefully he laid his head down as he closed his eyes, feeling Katie's cool hand on his forehead. He opened his eyes briefly at her touch, aware of her scent. She was looking away, a lock of her brown hair fallen to her shoulder from the knot tied on the back of her head. It highlighted the delicate curve of her nose and chin. *An angel*, he thought, fading.

Vic realized with a start he was sitting up, or propped up just a bit, sucking on a straw. *Good God, I don't even know I'm awake half of the time*. The tall nurse with blue eyes was holding a small cup of water under his chin. He had been dreaming, he was certain of it. But it vanished from his consciousness, swept away in a heartbeat. The nurse looked at him curiously, canting her head to the side.

"So who are Billy Boy and Copper?" she asked. Vic stared at her for a moment, realizing he had been dreaming about them. That was it, he was sure of it. And the storm that claimed them both.

"Did aye' say somethin 'bout Billy Boy an' Copper, miss?"

"Well, you said something about water a couple times as I walked by, so I got some for you. I think you said Billy Boy and Copper, and more about water."

Vic sucked the cup of water dry, confused and a little frightened by these day dream visions he was experiencing. The nurse's prompt about Billy Boy and Copper brought something right up, so there was no doubt they were at his subconscious fingertips while he babbled like an old bloody rummy. *God, he could smell it,* their musky scent was as real as if they were standing right there at the foot of the bed.

Copper, his mare, was a beautiful chestnut colored Thoroughbred whose father was a Brumby, a wild Australian horse Vic's dad had captured years before. Copper was a sweet, incredibly intelligent horse coming naturally to stock range work, taking to Vic at once when Vic's dad gave her to him on his eighth birthday. She delivered two babies, a filly and a few years later, a springy, rambunctious colt named Billy Boy. Billy Boy's father was a golden Palomino, his coloring the marbled swirls of a precious hunk of maple wood. Copper was a very attentive mother so to keep her happy and still working, Vic brought Billy Boy along on the range rides as soon as he was old enough. As long as they weren't going out too far and there was plenty of water, Vic's dad would let him bring Billy Boy. It was a lot of trouble since Billy Boy was a colt and wanted to do things his own way. Copper helped a lot though, being quick to make noise if she didn't like what Billy Boy was doing or was getting into trouble with stubborn rams or other horses.

Moving the sheep to find better grazing was the occupation for an Australian rancher. Good grazing was hard to find because of the lack of rain. When it came it was the darkened violence of afternoon thunderstorms, the deluge racing down hard, bone dry washes like liquid silver. One day as the sun passed over with grey clouds forming the air sticky and metallic, Vic and his brothers cautiously approached a series of gullies between the herd and some promising mottled green meadows a couple of kilometers away. They were moving 500 head to the far edge of their property. They were a long way from home so Vic hitched Copper to the light field wagon carrying supplies for overnight work. He also carried extra water and feed for the horses, since they couldn't be sure they would find any out in the range. Billy Boy was tethered with a long lead so whenever they stopped, he wandered up next to his mother.

Copper nickered as a matter of course, being a vocal female and watchful mother. Every few minutes she would nod her head around looking for Billy Boy. He trotted along making plenty of noise himself, tiring as the day progressed. If he was left to his own devices Vic knew he would run about, kicking his legs and butting his head into empty air, letting free his six-month old soul for about fifteen minutes out of every hour. He would also be completely exhausted looking for a place to nap by one or two in the afternoon, so Vic kept Billy Boy on the tether until the end of the day, conserving his energy.

Blinking lightning followed by thunder marked the early beginning of the storm. The black, oily clouds formed incredibly fast that day, the wind picking up as the first big bolt of lightning, sparking and flashing, fractured along the purple horizon for five or six kilometers. The initial strikes seemed close. Vic watched Billy Boy, whose huge, curious eyes widened with fright as he tottered along, jerking sideways. Vic stopped the wagon to walk over to him, talking, letting the colt nudge in close, burying his snout in Vic's armpit. Static electricity levitated the long hair on his neck like a comb, until the rain came down.

It dumped all at once with a roar, the wind so strong it swirled around lifting Vic's duster and his hat from underneath, soaking him. Vic peered hard through the deluge at the progress of the herd, just barely seeing his brothers and his father with Gerty and Gimpy, the two yellow-eyed cattle dogs right at their heels. They were all bent over from the rain, hard at work pressing the sheep up through the gullies. At the current pace, Vic figured the last of the herd would be out of the gullies and up on the slopes in maybe seven or eight minutes, maybe sooner. He hoped they had that much time.

The storm was hovering directly above when a blinding flash with accompanying thunderclap deafened him. Billy Boy jerked hard against his tether, the stark white light revealing saucer eyes and flared nostrils. Vic couldn't get close to him. Copper turned hard watching Billy Boy, making a lot of noise herself as she thrashed against her harness trying to come around. The wagon yanked sideways, as the brake was on. Water was already coming down the gullies so Vic had no choice. He either crossed now or had to wait out the storm and any runoff coming from it.

"My God, what did you do?" Vic blinked, realizing it was Katie McCutcheon who asked the question. He had no idea when she arrived. She and the tall, blue-eyed nurse were both right next to him on the left side of the bed. The other nurse had her hand to her mouth, her eyes wide. Katie gripped Vic's bedrails hard. He'd been telling them the story, apparently.

"Where was aye'?" he asked sheepishly.

"The storm was right over you, the horses were frightened, and you had to decide whether to cross the gullies right then or wait until the storm was over," said Katie. Vic felt exhausted but the two young faces, rapt with attention, forced him to think and sit up. He sighed, glancing down at his hands as the reality of the story hit him. Tears welled in his eyes, making it difficult to speak.

"Aye' probably gave tha' story away, aye' imagine, but aye' made a bad decision, aye' did. Da' horses were frightened bloomin' outta' their minds, an' when aye' got about 'alf way 'cross, a wall of water came crashin' down. Not that deep, mind ya', but it was unexpected ta' the horses, a foot or so deep, movin' fast, with a big curl to it, like an ocean 'ave." Vic took a deep breath, closing his eyes for a moment.

"The 'ave pushed a wall a mood' 'n fron' of it, forcin' da' wagon oop' an' on its side, then over. Aye' got tossed 'ike a bloody tin can on ma' ear, washed doonstream' for 20 or 30 meters til' aye' grabbed a big stump an' held on. The flood dribbled away after 'bout 'ive minutes or so. When I could work ma' way up to the wagon, aye' found Billy Boy pinned under the wagon, drownt' in a foot a' water an' mood. Copper— poor ole' Copper… she 'ad a compound 'racture of on' of 'er rear legs, from the twisting of the wagon under her." Vic looked up at the nurses, wishing he never brought it up. Both of them were dabbing tears from their eyes.

"How old were you, Sergeant Hickey?" asked Katie gently, "you were a long ways from home, so you had to destroy your mare?"

"Aye' was about 13 years old, aye' 'magine. Copper 'ould 'ave been 'bout eight years old then. Ma' dad shot her with a 30.30 Winchester he carried in a 'abbard 'case we ran into 'ild dogs. We repaired da' wagon, an' one o' me' brothers hitched 'is horse to it."

"I am so sorry, we didn't mean to bring it back and upset you," said the other nurse, glancing over at Katie. "We actually have a little time to listen to stories from our patients for once, now that we're on the way out of here."

"What do ya' mean? Are ya' leaving?"

"We were supposed to have rotated out of here a week ago, but the Buna – Gona business put a temporary stop to it. We're rotating with the 166th, another American Station Hospital in Australia. They're held up with the campaign because there are no transports available. With more of the casualties going direct to Australia these days, the 166th is coming in small groups on the return flights. They took over the incoming casualty triage and surgeries officially today, so us nurses from the 153rd are handling existing patients on the wards, hence you are seeing us a lot more!" Katie McCutcheon's smile seemed to just beam to Vic, he couldn't help grinning back. "It will take a few weeks for them to transition everyone over, but once that's done the word is we're heading down under to your neck of the woods."

"What part o' Australia will they send ya?"

"Southport, same place we were before, near Brisbane. We're right next to a beautiful beach, an old boy's boarding school."

"Is 'at 'ere da' send all the 'asualties, miss?" His eyes twinkled, but Katie didn't miss a beat.

"No—apparently we have excess capacity according to the generals, so we have American hospitals in a number of places on the east coast of Australia. Because of it, we've been accepting Allied casualties wherever we can. I understand they try to send you boys to a hospital close to your home, either an Australian Forces hospital or an American hospital. Where are you from, Sergeant?"

"State o' Victoria, down south, not 'ar from Melbourne." Vic wasn't sure, maybe it was wishful thinking, but he thought he saw a hint of disappointment cross Katie McCutcheon's face, just a flash.

"Well, maybe if you're lucky you'll be sent there to see your family."

"We 'ad a bit o' leave when the division 'ame home from the Mid' East, so I was 'ome fur' a 'eek or two in June, aye' 'elieve. No one 'ome 'cept me mum an' dad. Dad's with the 'ome guard, volunteers with prior 'ervice froom' the Great War. Still workin' at the Ford plant, essential work, ewe' know."

"Your brothers are all in the service?"

"Aye, miss. Don't know when al' see em' agin', Alm' afraid. Norman's a POW in Austria, Bill was 'hot down in Java, still missin'.""

"Oh my God," Katie gasped, "your parents must be beside themselves! And you wounded!" Vic shook his head lightly, a grim, tight smile on his face.

"Havin' ma' brother missin' is 'ard on al' o' us, but 'ere a small country. Everyone 'as 'amily in the Forces. It's the 'ay it is."

"How long since you've heard from them?"

"'Eard from em'? Lemme think, aye' believe Norman was captured in Greece, an' we 'eard he was a POW in Austria from the Red Cross n' February, 1941. There might 'ave been a letter from 'im once, I believe. Bill 'as with the RAAF, a gunner. Volunteered to 'erve with the Dutch Air Force to stay close to 'ome in the Pacific, flyin' your B-25. 'Ot down in September, this year. No 'ord from the Japs or the Red Cross on 'im at all."

There was a growing darkness in his eyes as he spoke, chased by a shadow passing quickly across his face, leaving it pale and lifeless. It was like a door closing. Katie had never seen anything like it, except in the case of terminal patients. Both nurses exchanged concerned glances without saying anything. When he stopped talking he simply lowered his head to his pillow. After a minute or so it was obvious he wasn't going to continue. His eyes were open, deep black pools, but they blinked occasionally. Katie was relieved when he slowly closed them. His slow, regular breathing revealed he had found some peace. Reluctantly, Katie stepped away as her attention was being sought by another nurse halfway across the ward.

CHAPTER 7

December 5, 1942, Seven Mile airfield

It was a rough ride, from the dicey crosswind takeoff at Dobodura into the dark canopy of rain and turbulence over the Stanleys'. They closed the field behind them. On instruments all the way at least fighters were not a problem. The high casualties from the campaign had the squadron transports airborne from dawn until the afternoon squalls made things un-flyable, especially with at least one airplane a day detailed for the direct flight to Townsville, on the Queensland coast. There were only nine patients on this flight, but it was a special one. Jack Cooper flew the leg, his seat lowered so he could concentrate on his instrument scan. He was one of those pilots who flew instruments naturally and instinctively. The control wheel rolled and rocked with the turbulence, but Cooper didn't fight it or chase the needles on the instruments. Don watched appreciatively, as the needles always returned smoothly to their assigned values, the control wheel eased a tad, a slight adjustment to the props or throttle with Cooper's left hand the only movement. He did not *react* to the instruments, he *flew* the instruments.

The young US Army captain sitting in the cramped space of the radio operator – navigator seat directly behind Cooper looked nauseous and uncomfortable. Don offered him the seat since there was no other place to sit down in the cabin. This C-47, although originally outfitted as a paratroop transport, was stripped of the paratrooper pan-style bulkhead seats to create more floor space. Some of the older planes had the seats folded away but still available. This one was a truck. If you rode as a passenger you sat on the floor, like the young military policeman assigned to the prisoner. The eight patients up forward were all American soldiers, but the ninth patient, a Japanese soldier, was alone in his litter near the rear of the cabin. He was the last one loaded and would be the first one off. He was the first Japanese patient Don carried on his medevac flights, his first glimpse of a live Japanese soldier.

The captain, named Cox, introduced himself as an intelligence officer accompanying the prisoner. This apparently was a big deal especially since the prisoner was an officer. *Japs don't surrender,* the captain sniffed, *this one was found in a bunker after we blew it up. He was unconscious. If he'd moved a muscle, I fuckin' guarantee you he'd be a corpse. Our fellas' shoot em' on sight like rattlesnakes. With fuckin' good reason.* Don recalled only a narrow, bony face with stringy, sparse facial hair under the oxygen mask.

Don lifted the headphones off of his head, sliding his seat track back so he could turn enough to speak to Captain Cox. Cox, nervously eyeing the rivulets of water curling along the side windows of the windshield as the transport bounced and rocked, clearly wanted to be somewhere else.

"How badly is the Jap hurt? Are we safe with just the one guard back there?" Cox looked blankly at Don before nodding his head.

"Yes," he said after a long pause. When he didn't say anything else and looked back out the window, Don just wrote him off as a scared ground guy, turning around.

A tap on his shoulder a minute later brought Don around. Out of his seat and kneeling behind Don and Cooper's seats, Cox had his wrists touching, fingers splayed out in the universal sign of handcuffs. Even Cooper glanced over his shoulder briefly at Cox, who gripped the seat backs as the airplane rolled and groaned.

"His arms are cuffed to the side of the litter with his legs shackled to the bottom. The fucker was shot through the lung with enough shrap in em' to sink a rowboat. They pulled out most of the scrap metal, decided he needs time in Moresby before they can fly em' to Australia. He can't put up much of a fight. We'd like to ask him some questions before he heads south." He grinned weakly, his eyes fearful of the whirling dark mist outside the windshield.

Twenty minutes later, in blinding sunshine, Cooper kissed the runway with the wheels feeling the slight tug of resistance as they spun through deep puddles. Steam was rising so much from the runway neither of them could see the end of it. Per their instructions they parked the airplane in a revetment one away from the other transports. Captain Cox picked up his carbine as he waved goodbye, much happier to be on the ground. A single ambulance with three MPs and an MP officer was waiting for them. As soon as the flight engineer opened the door the MPs were in the airplane surrounding the prisoner, talking in quiet tones with Captain Cox.

"Jack," Don turned to Cooper as soon as they shut down, pushing his seat back. "Mind cleaning her up? This is it for us today. I want to see if I can catch a ride with these guys to the hospital. Okay by you?"

Cooper knew why Don wanted to get to the hospital although they had never discussed it. He was already through the shutdown checklist, something Don would never have to double check with Cooper. With a simple wave Cooper stayed where he was, watching Don's back hurriedly retreat down the cabin passageway. Don wanted out of the airplane before the triage team got on board. He knew Katie wouldn't be with them, encountering the new faces of the 166th Station Hospital staff a few days earlier. He was crestfallen until one of the nurses explained the 153rd was still in Port Moresby, helping the new staff transition. Don made up his mind he was going to make the time today. They'd been flying their asses off and once Katie stopped doing triage, he knew he'd never see her again unless he made a move. Cooper would handle the logs and the paperwork.

The MPs didn't have a medic or a nurse with them, so the sole medic from the flight took a couple of minutes to help the MPs load the Japanese prisoner in the ambulance and hook up his oxygen. The medic checked the two IV bottles attached to the prisoner, glanced at his eyes with a penlight and declared him stable. Don approached Captain Cox about getting a ride, formally saluting him now they were outside the transport. The three MPs and the MP Lieutenant, all strapping young fellows as tall as Don, were heavily armed with .45 caliber pistols, one Thompson submachinegun and two .12 gauge pump shotguns. They peered around them suspiciously as if they expected to be attacked at any moment, one MP at each corner of the ambulance, the MP officer standing by the driver door his hand on the butt of his holstered pistol.

Captain Cox conferred quietly with the MP Lieutenant who was not happy with an unplanned passenger. Inside the ambulance there was a low bench seat on each side, exposed if litters were not fitted. The right side was open. Cox invited Don in first, crouched over to slide along the seat. Cox followed, then a single MP carrying the Thompson. The MP Lieutenant, a sour look on his face, glanced around in the ambulance before closing the doors. He climbed into the cab with the remaining MPs and the truck started moving. Don, seated slightly above the prisoner was two feet away from the man's head. The only windows were the ones on the rear doors and two small slit skylights. Even with the poor light Don was struck immediately how wrong his first impression was. He could see through the clear oxygen mask. The man's face was not only lean, it was emaciated to the point of being a skull with paper-thin translucent skin stretched across it. The smeared, caked dirt on his face blended with the stringy, greasy beard, both masking the withered jawline and the scarred and sunken cheeks. The nostrils and closed eyes were shrunken, dark pits. His exposed arm was covered with deep red sores, a bony stick perhaps two inches in diameter, the joint overlarge and out of proportion to the frail forearm. Don never saw a corpse before, but suspected this man was as close to it as you could get and still be breathing.

The prisoner's mouth parted slightly, a slight gasp, his head rolling back as his back arched. The eyes remained closed, the eye sockets quivering as he continued to gasp for air. Horrified Don glanced at Cox, who also stared. He seemed concerned but made no motion. With no medic in the ambulance there wasn't anything any of them could do.

"He's shot through the lung," Cox added, "I hope he makes it." Don noticed the MP, when the prisoner moved, had swung his Thompson away from the door and moved the muzzle towards the prisoner. There was no mistaking the look on his face. There was no doubt in Don's mind the MP would blow the prisoner in half in a heartbeat if the need arose. Cox looked at the young MP, carefully placing his hand on the muzzle of the Thompson. "He's so sedated he can't do shit, Corporal." Uneasy, Don watched with grim fascination the prisoner fight for each breath of air. It was painful to see. All three of them stared.

"What makes this Jap so special?" Don whispered. "He looks like he's fuckin' starving to death, besides his—breathing problems."

"That's what makes him interesting, among other things. The doc's at the field surgical hospital in Buna said this Jap's been suffering from severe malnutrition. He's been eating somewhat regular very recently, but prior to that they felt he hadn't eaten a regular diet for a long time, maybe months. This gave us a clue to where he's been, or rather, where we think he's been.

"He's an infantry officer, a captain, but the troops our division, the 32nd, and the Aussies have encountered in Gona and Buna are fresh troops. They're healthy, well-equipped, well-fed and for damn sure don't look like this guy." Cox reached out and gently lifted the prisoner's forearm, handcuffed to the litter. "See those jungle sores, some of them the size of quarters? This guy had been living in the jungle, not the coastal swamps. We didn't know what to make of these skinny skeletons our troops were encountering in certain pockets of Buna, but our Aussie friends set us straight. Some of the Aussies over in Gona fought the Japs up on the Kokoda Track up there in the Owen Stanley Mountains..."

"I resupplied the Diggers up there by air many times, I'm familiar with it. That's tough country."

"Exactly, then you know what I'm talking about. The Japs they fought up there had a pretty hard time of it. They were a very special regiment with the intention of eventually taking Port Moresby, once they were reinforced. Guadalcanal put the kabosh on the reinforcements. These Japs climbed the Stanleys' on foot and attempted a supply chain for 100 miles. When the reinforcements weren't coming, they withdrew back down the trail. The supply line broke down in the mountains, what with the Aussies on their ass and our bombers killin' anything that moved. These guys lived on nothing for months." Cox nodded towards the prisoner. "The survivors of this Jap regiment appear to be mixed with the troops over there in Buna."

90

Don stared at the prisoner with new interest thinking of those lean, silent Aussies he dropped supplies to, the ones he'd carried back as casualties, and now this Jap. They all lived down there in the cold grey mist hunting each other, 200 feet under the canopy with no sun. *Twilight green, or the green,* they called it. It made him shiver to think about it.

"When they first captured him a few days ago, they couldn't get shit out of him, even when he was conscious. But he started babbling under anesthesia. Nobody knew what the hell he was saying until one of our guys was brought around. He spoke fluent Japanese and since we hardly ever get a live Jap these days and this one was an officer, they sent for him lickity split. It seems our Jap captain here, was possibly a command staff officer for Major General Tomitaro Horii." Cox smiled as he said this, cocking his head questioningly. Don shook his head and shrugged, the name meant nothing to him.

"We know because his name came up on some captured documents and he repeated the name, and also repeated '*Nankai Shitai'*. This means "South Sea Force", which was commanded by General Horii. This force was originally just the 144th Infantry Regiment out of Shikoku, Japan, a very special unit because it was *formed without* a chain of command link to the regular Japanese Imperial Army command structure. *Nankai Shitai* reported directly to the Imperial High Command in Tokyo. That's like saying General Horii reported directly to the President instead of the local regional army commander.

"Anyway, *Nankai Shitai* was charged with crossing the Owen Stanleys' and taking Port Moresby. A critical campaign assigned to a special unit. 5,000 men. Parts of this regiment were in Shanghai and Nanking, the invasion of Guam and Rabaul, and were the guys chosen to kick the Aussies out of New Guinea. They were the varsity, first string. General Horii is dead, so if we can interrogate one of his staff officers we could learn a thing or two about the Japanese Army command structure. And just maybe how the hell they got as far as they did up the Stanleys'."

"I get it, thanks." They could feel the ambulance coming to a stop, then reversing. Out the rear windows the Station Hospital back entrance loading bay came closer.

"Thanks for the ride. I couldn't imagine fighting up in those mountains. It was spooky as hell just to fly close to the triple canopy, looking down in those—dark caverns. You could see the Aussies down there. They lived off that greasy, gummy, canned beef shit. I know because that's all we dropped for them, other than ammo."

"Bully beef, yeah, I tried it, made me want to gag. And that's all they got, that an' biscuits, I understand. Japs didn't have that, didn't have anything much beyond what they brought with them from the coast—

months before." The MP, bored of the conversation jumped out immediately when the MP Lieutenant separated the doors, his Thompson at the ready. No one was waiting for them to take the prisoner. This irritated the MP Lieutenant much more than Captain Cox, who sat on the steps and lit a cigarette. While the MP Lieutenant stormed off to find out what happened to the planned reception, the other MPs resumed their positions surrounding the ambulance, weapons at the ready.

The late afternoon sun was gone, dark ominous clouds forming rapidly overhead. They could feel the moisture in the air. The wind was beginning to pick up. Don retrieved his cap and jacket, rolling his .45 pistol in its holster and web belt away from his crotch, which was more comfortable when they were sitting in the ambulance, to his side. He glanced at the Japanese prisoner for the last time, giving Cox a casual salute.

"What's going to happen to that guy, if he survives? Practically starving to death can't be good for your health." He didn't realize how stupid the statement sounded until Cox laughed, choking on his cigarette. He stopped and returned when Cox waved him back, looking serious. Don realized he might be in trouble, somehow.

"Look, I didn't mean to joke about it. And if you're worried about me talking about this guy…" Cox shook his head, blowing a smoke ring.

"I know most of what I said went in one ear, out the other. For us it will be nice to confirm or deny some information we know or think we know about these guys. This is our enemy, and we really don't understand at all what they are capable of. They come across as supermen sometimes, and I can tell you this regiment had the big "S" on their shirts, for damned sure. The Aussies have tried to tell us about this Kokoda thing, but we weren't listening very well. We think we might have found the chink in their armor, though. It'll be interesting if we can get this guy to talk."

Don straightened up his cap as he walked through the big double doors, wondering how he was going to explain himself. The hospital was built with a series of doorways, mostly heavily screened vestibules designed to stop insects. He was surprised to find a number of bright electric lights burning in the hallways, corridors cleared marked with neatly printed signs designating INTAKE, SURGERY, ADMIN and WARDS. There must be a lull in the activity he decided, because although there were nurses, doctors, technicians and orderlies moving about, there wasn't any particular sense of urgency. He stood still for perhaps three or four minutes looking at the signs when an Army nurse, a tall blond with blue eyes, vaguely familiar, stopped to peer at him. He had his ruse fairly well organized in his mind by now.

"Well, hello there, Lieutenant," she said brightly. "Haven't seen you since you picked us up at Seven Mile—way back then!" Don smiled, not really remembering the nurse, but encouraged she just might know Katie.

"Really? Good seeing you again—uh, Lieutenant. Look—uh, I had a couple of minutes and thought I'd check in on a couple of guys I got to know—uh, during a medevac. Aussies, both of em'. We brought em' over from Dobodura, you know, and—uh, I told em' I'd stop by when I had the chance."

"Okay, look, this isn't a civilian hospital or a stateside military hospital, we really don't have visitor hours." She glanced at her watch. "Do you know their names? We have most of our Aussie patients in the same ward, unless they're burn victims, neurological or critical care patients." She seemed to be saying this a bit more loudly than necessary when Don noticed another nurse, older and most likely a supervisor, stopping to stare at them.

"Of course, I understand completely. I—uh, don't think I remember their names, right off the bat. I—uh, do remember an Army nurse who was taking care of them, perhaps if I could—uh, talk to her." Don detected the twinkle in the nurse's eyes and the slight rise in her eyebrows as she nodded thoughtfully. Her eyes followed his as he watched the nurse supervisor turn away, distracted by a discussion with a doctor.

"And the name of the nurse is?"

It was too late, the nurse supervisor made a beeline for them. The supervisor was a first lieutenant, a serious look on her face. She nodded to Don before turning to the tall nurse.

"Afternoon, Lieutenant. Please excuse us for a moment. Lieutenant Culpepper, you're going to receive a special patient in about ten minutes in your ward once—the arrangements are in place. Since we have all the wards for the time being until the 166th finishes their transition, we're going to accept this special patient. The patient has multiple injuries; a punctured lung, multiple shrapnel fragment wounds and suffering from both malaria and severe malnutrition. Please inform Lieutenant McCutcheon. I'll make sure all the intake information is updated before shift change, clear?"

Once the nurse supervisor left, the tall nurse—Lieutenant Culpepper, grabbed Don gently by the elbow and guided him towards a corridor. "I think I know where your Aussies are, Lieutenant."

Vaughn (Vic) Hickey laid his head back and sighed, content for a change, after having his third serving of rice pudding. He slipped his oxygen mask back over his nose and mouth, inhaling deeply. Katie McCutcheon started him on semi-solid foods for the first time the night before, opening the flood gates. He couldn't eat enough, alarming the nurses when he requested helping after helping of the bland gruels available. He ate watery oatmeal, mashed potatoes or bean paste soup with equal relish, his speed and capacity to spoon it in his mouth attracting the attention of every nurse, medic and orderly on shift in his ward. When he wasn't sleeping or enduring a dressing change Vic was eating, with no desire to stop. The staff was more than accommodating bringing extra servings left over from meal periods, mostly because it was available and other patients didn't want it. Katie was a little worried Vic was going to vomit up all of the food, possibly aspirating his lung. She was also concerned he would impact his bowels with the sudden load of bulk, so she made sure he was drinking gallons of water and fruit juice. Vic requested and received hot tea with every meal, although he complained *this bloody Yank tay' is too bloody weak! An' da' ya' 'ave any 'ilk an' 'ugar?*

The rice pudding was wonderful as far as he was concerned, although he would have preferred they added more sugar. Yanks didn't seem to care for the pudding, so it was easy to get his hands on more helpings. He loved it. In less than 24 hours he felt 200 percent better, all attributable to having some real food in his gut. It wasn't steak but it would do. He noticed the ward nurses, Lieutenants McCutcheon and Culpepper were working at least 12 hours shifts. They came on right before breakfast and leaving, sometimes, an hour or two after supper. It was a long day for them all on their feet, especially since every bed he could see was filled with a wreck like him. There wasn't much noise though, human wrecks didn't say much.

He lifted his head to watch Lieutenant Culpepper and an orderly wheel three portable visual screens through the ward. A nurse supervisor and a tall, dour-looking American MP Lieutenant followed them, talking in low tones. A minute later a gurney with a patient and a portable oxygen tank was wheeled in the same direction, the orderly pushing the gurney flanked by two huge American MPs with shotguns. *What the hell? A prisoner?* He tried to see who was on the gurney but it was already out of his sight. Katie McCutcheon came into view slowly pushing a cart full of bottles, medical utensils and equipment. She was talking quietly with a tall American officer, both grinning and attentive to each other. He was significantly taller than she was so he stooped way forward. He shuffled along to keep pace with Katie, his cap clutched in his hand. Vic didn't like this Yank right off the bat, talking to the lieutenant like that.

"Leftenant'," he wheezed, "what's goin' on o'er en' da' corner?" Katie stopped when he called, turning her head his way, her bright smile a beacon of warmth.

"Hello, Sergeant. I trust you got enough to eat?" She nodded when the American officer said something, mouthing what Vic saw as a question forming the word *Aussie?*

"Aye' did, Leftenant! Aye' luv' yur' 'rice puddin', I do!" He propped himself up slowly a few inches with his elbow, bobbing his head towards the end of the ward where all the commotion was. "Ya' 'ave a prisoner doon' there, hav' ya?" Katie glanced down towards the end of the ward before turning the cart in Vic's direction. She stopped at the foot of his bed, leaning forward secretively as Don Crenshaw sauntered up, nodding his head towards Vic. Vic raised his right hand to his brow.

"Suh'."

"We have a *very special* patient down there," said Katie quietly. "Shot through the lung like you, with other injuries. He's going into surgery and spend a little more time with us. Don't mind the MPs, he's no risk to anybody." She said this with finality, turning the cart as Don leaned in towards Vic.

"He's special all right!" Don whispered. "I flew em' in this afternoon from Dobodura. A Jap officer!" The reaction was instantaneous, no mistaking his error. The icy glare from Katie could cut steel. Her anger spun away when she saw Vic, the blood draining from his face as the statement sank in.

"Yew 'ave a Jap officer in 'ere?" Vic gasped. He had bolted up as far as possible, his eyes wide, his body rigid. He was breathing in short gasps, his head darting from side to side. *"Air' is he?"* Vic struggled with the various restraints hooking him to the bed, clearly intending to pull himself out. He'd flung the oxygen mask off and was reaching for his IV. Katie was on the right side of the bed in a second, attempting to grip Vic's flailing arm with her left hand and push him back down on the bed with her right.

"Help me, dammit!" Don came around on the left side and pressed his bulk against Vic's upper body, pinning him back. Vic was a big man himself, his strength surprising considering his condition. His struggle was too much for his lung breathing capacity, however. Don could hear him gasping in deep draughts of air as his head rolled back, his back arched. It reminded him immediately of the Jap officer's struggle for air on the airplane. Don lifted himself from Vic carefully, trying not to put any pressure on his chest. He could see Vic's face, pasty white, as his eyes rolled back in his head. He had passed out. One of the MPs walked cautiously up the ward, shotgun at port arms, until Katie signaled all was well. He nodded and turned back. The MP Lieutenant also took a few steps in their direction, stopping to stare at them intently.

95

"That was damned BRILLIANT, Don!" Katie scolded under her breath, working her away around Vic, checking his leg restraints, reattaching his wrist tether and oxygen mask. She fluffed his pillows, padded them carefully around his back, and leaned over to listen to his breathing as she took his pulse. Vic, unconscious, breathed noisily with his mouth open.

"Couldn't you tell I was trying to down play the prisoner thing?" She glanced warily over near the end of the ward, but the MP Lieutenant was not visible. "No one was supposed to know we have a Jap prisoner in the ward," she whispered. "Once he's out of surgery and stable he's going to some special ward where there is better security. This is goddamn hush hush! You could be arrested for doing something like this!"

"I'm sorry, that was pretty stupid of me. Maybe I should go." Before Katie could answer the nursing supervisor walked over with the MP Lieutenant. He scowled at Vic before glaring at Don.

"Lieutenant McCutcheon, this is Lieutenant Barrow, who's in charge of the security of our—special patient. Is everything okay over here? We heard a commotion."

"Uh—Lieutenant Crenshaw was visiting this Australian non-commissioned officer, a man—uh, he knew and medevacked out of Buna. The sergeant seemed to be fine but seeing Lieutenant Crenshaw upset him somehow. He's fine now, and asleep." The nursing supervisor looked at Katie with level eyes before turning to Don.

"Perhaps you should leave, Lieutenant. Come again another time, our patients have gone through a lot and are easily upset. Don't take it so hard, it probably had nothing to do with you. "She turned on her heel, waving Katie McCutcheon along with a raised finger.

"If you're done here, McCutcheon, Lieutenant Culpepper needs your assistance in doing a body bath and dressing change for our special patient. She'll need the cart."

Don had no choice but to wave casually to Katie, thanking her formally for her assistance as the nursing supervisor and the MP Lieutenant walked away, still in ear shot. He was standing in the central hallway of the back entrance five minutes later, wondering what to do next when he felt a hand on his arm. He turned to find Lieutenant Culpepper's blue eyes watching his.

"Hi again, Lieutenant."

"Don, please."

"Okay, Don, I'm Sue. Katie couldn't come, since the supervisor seems to be watching her. She sent me out here to get more dressings— and a contact number if you were still around. I figured you might be.

96

You looked like a lost puppy when you left the ward. I have to get back so we can give that damned Jap a bath. I can't believe it. So how about it?" She held a chart in her hand and carefully slipped a blank envelope under the spring.

"About all I have is my squadron operations number. We can't use it to call out or anything, but it is a way to get a message to a pilot—to me. Problem is I don't know what it is off the top of my head. We keep it with our flying charts and stuff, if we get held up by weather someplace and have to call the squadron. "

"Okay, I've dealt with pilots before. We'll get it, there's a directory listing of all squadron admin numbers. What's your squadron?"

"21st Air Transport." Sue Culpepper wrote this down on the envelope and smiled.

"You guys leaving for Australia soon?"

"Any day now. I understand there's a plane flying down to Townsville, then to Brisbane every day. You need to volunteer to fly that mission, Don, maybe you'll see us more!"

Sue Culpepper's blond hair, tied up in loose knots at the back of her head, was unravelling as she bounded back down the hallway. Don watched her reach up with one hand to pat the knot, then let go. She made a sharp turn and was gone. Don looked down at his hands, realizing it was long time since a girl had asked for his number. He grinned, shoving his cap on the back of his head at a jaunty angle, wondering how he was going to get back to the squadron if there were no more ambulances running out to Seven Mile airfield today.

Katie McCutcheon came back to do her rounds after they served supper. She glanced over at Sergeant Hickey's bed, noting Vic's head angle. After she and Sue Culpepper had bathed the Japanese prisoner and changed his dressings, Katie came back over to see how Vic was doing. He was breathing with difficulty, shallow and painful, you could hear the hesitation so she increased the oxygen flow. They aspirated him once when he first arrived, and there was always the chance the fluid was building again. He needed to be rolled around soon. She was very worried about him, admittedly surprised at how violent his reaction was to hearing about the Japanese officer. She really didn't have any idea she decided, on how much these men hated their enemy. She checked with the doctor and increased Vic's sedation to keep him sleeping a bit longer.

She stopped by the prisoner, sequestered away from the other patients, generally blocked visually by a wall and three dividers. The single MP guard, standing at parade rest by the small entrance formed between two dividers, nodded to her respectfully. When no one approached he was authorized to sit in a folding chair. They agreed there was no need for the MPs to come to attention and salute every time a

97

nurse came around during rounds.

Katie checked his IV connections, volumes and catheter. She noted the MP guard was now standing next to her, watching her every movement. She understood, as the nurse supervisor spoke with the MP Lieutenant, the primary purpose of the security team was the protection of the patient, a high-value subject, not the protection of other American soldiers from the patient. She lifted his eyelids, peered at his pupils before checked his pulse and blood pressure. She had mixed feelings caring for such people, knowing ones like this officer created most of the injuries she and the other medical staff treated day in and day out. This enemy didn't look like much though, certainly not much of a threat. Both wrists were strapped to the bed rails, as were his ankles. He looked wore out, years maybe decades older than his calendar age. He had come, just like herself, Sergeant Hickey and Don Crenshaw, thousands of miles from his homeland to fight and almost starve to death. *A stranger to this place, just like us.*

TWO YEARS EARLIER

CHAPTER 8

December 5, 1940, HDQ 44th Infantry Regiment, Asakura, Kochi Prefecture, Shikoku Island, Japan

The promotion ceremony was so brief Hiroshi Takahashi tried hard not to be disappointed. The regimental commander was away and the only senior officer present was his battalion commander. Hiroshi was introduced to the man when he first reported to the 44th Regiment with two other officers four months earlier. The lieutenant colonel was cool and distant to Hiroshi at the time, the meeting short and so perfunctory Hiroshi remembered nothing about it at all. Two battalion staff officers, both majors, were also in attendance for the promotion ceremony. They carried the warrants and shoulder boards for the five junior officers being promoted. The actual pinning for Hiroshi was done by his company commander, Captain Ichiro Hashimoto. Captain Hashimoto studied the shoulder boards with the single star of a second lieutenant intently before lifting his eyes to meet Hiroshi's. He gave Hiroshi a thin smile before unbuttoning the epaulets from his formal dress uniform so he could slide the shoulder boards on each side.

"May I be the first to congratulate you, Second Lieutenant Takahashi!" His right hand extended to Hiroshi as he offered a slight bow. Hiroshi beamed as he saluted, returning the bow and handshake.

"Thank you, sir!" It was over in five minutes. The five officers were promoted, handed their badges of rank and warrants, congratulated by their commanding officers and led to the door. Hiroshi accompanied Captain Hashimoto and the two newly promoted first lieutenants back to their company area. It was something, he decided, he would just have to get used to. This apparently is the *real* army. He spent four and a half years at the Imperial Japanese Army Academy. Prior to this he endured three years at *Rikugun Yonen Gakko*, the military prep school in Osaka. Cadet promotions at both institutions were always elaborate, drawn-out affairs, with Hiroshi proudly earning his share in the limelight. It was a safe assumption for a cadet this was the institutional way it was done.

The first two years at the IJA Academy was the junior course at Asaka in Saitama, followed by an eight month assignment with a line infantry regiment to learn leadership and how to run an infantry platoon. This experience, for Hiroshi, was with a regiment stationed with occupational forces in Shanghai, China. It was the first time in his life he left the islands of Japan. The war, as far as Hiroshi was concerned, was somewhere else. There were 600,000 Japanese troops in China at the time, some heavily involved in combat operations. Hiroshi was briefed his unit was participating in counter-insurgency operations. His assigned battalion did nothing of the sort, establishing schedules to rotate infantry companies to spend time in well-guarded outposts near remote borders. They were told to not wander outside the wire and secure walls of the outposts. The Chinese, that is, the insurgents, apparently owned the countryside.

The experience was a disappointment in all respects. As a cadet officer-candidate and a very junior one at that, there was a concerted effort on the part of the regimental officers and non-commissioned officers responsible for his training to either ignore him, or give him lukewarm, non-essential tasks to do so he wouldn't get himself or anyone else in trouble. He certainly was never placed in harm's way either deliberately or accidently. He was frustrated enough to consider quitting, but not seriously. Despite the disappointments he did his duties the best he could and given high marks. He returned to the IJA Academy after his training tour to matriculate into the senior course at Sagamihara. He finished the one year, eight-month course to graduate near the top of his class. Per Army protocol Hiroshi started his career at the rank of Sergeant Major, although treated as an officer. Born and raised on large land holdings outside of Kochi City, Shikoku, Hiroshi received his orders to the unit formed from the officers and conscripts of Shikoku, the 44th Infantry Regiment.

Hiroshi was fortunate the 44th returned home from a three-year tour in China one month before he arrived in September of 1940. Some of his classmates had to join their home units still in China, or wait a few months in a career-wasting holding pattern before receiving orders. New graduates from IJA Academy remained probationary officers for a minimum of four months before becoming eligible for commissioning as second lieutenants. As a probationary officer Hiroshi was assigned to a platoon commander and a platoon sergeant to receive his final mentoring. His platoon commander, one of the second lieutenants promoted to first lieutenant, had served with Captain Hashimoto for over a year and a half in China. He never smiled, not to anyone. He seemed angry and agitated, although he never raised his voice to Hiroshi.

The first 6 months or so this officer served with Captain Hashimoto the Regiment was still heavily engaged in counter-insurgency operations. The experience seemed to affect the man a great deal. Hiroshi, who shared a small dormitory room with his platoon commander, was scared half out of his wits several times when the man, suffering from horrifying nightmares and insomnia, would awake screaming to hurl himself out of his bunk, glancing around like a madman in absolute terror. Other times he would not wake or get out of bed, but moan and writhe around while sobbing like a child, babbling with what sounded like *NO NO NO* repeatedly. Hiroshi didn't know what to do when this happened, so he did nothing. He'd clutch his bed covers around him, pretending to be asleep while keeping a wary eye on his roommate. The man would eventually settle down, his moaning reduced to steady snoring or noisy breathing. Hiroshi just recently purchasing a Nambu 8mm pistol from the approved officer's store for his personal firearm. After a couple of these night episodes, he began keeping the holstered weapon on the side of his bed out of sight.

Hiroshi developed a negative opinion of his platoon commander early in his probationary period, basing his perception on the two other platoon commanders in the company. By the end of his probation the opinion was solidified. One officer was a second lieutenant only a year out of IJA Academy, a young man not unlike Hiroshi. He served his probationary period in China and seemed unaffected by the experience, although the officer admitted the battalion was a garrison force by the time he arrived there, seeing no combat action. He was reasonably friendly but standoffish in the universal military ritual of establishing peer rank: He was commissioned six months prior and spent 10 months in China, so he would forever be ahead of Hiroshi in his own mind. Hiroshi accepted it and they got along.

The other officer was another one promoted to first lieutenant like Hiroshi's platoon commander. Hiroshi had to assume this officer had the same amount of experience as his own platoon commander in China, did his own six months fighting the insurgency. He seemed older than his years would lead you to believe, but he seemed to have a normal affect. With these two men to compare Hiroshi drew the conclusion his platoon commander was a weak officer, not strong enough for the infantry. What other conclusion could he make? He had reviewed the regimental casualty reports. Officers and men lost their lives or were seriously wounded during the three year tour, especially the first year and a half. But these weren't particularly heavy casualties. What happened to his platoon commander to make him this way? Hiroshi was not afraid of dying, no Japanese soldier should be. Killing Chinese insurgents is part of the soldier's contract, so what was it? Hiroshi felt the answer would be found with Captain Hashimoto. At some point he hoped, he and Captain Hashimoto could have a conversation. He would understand. Captain Ichiro Hashimoto came from Samurai.

To Hiroshi and the other young men who wanted to be professional soldiers, to be bred from Samurai stock was the highest expression of the warrior caste. Although they no longer existed, the historical shadow of the Samurai leaned far into the Japanese psyche. The Meiji period bled the power away from the Samurai, taking away

102

privileges assumed since the 12th Century. Their social power, like the power granted to knights on the European continent, was based on their personal code of conduct and professional skill with weapons. Traditionally for Samurai this meant the *daisho,* the pairing of a larger sword, the *katana,* with a shorter sword, a *wakizashi.* No other social class could wear the *daisho*, the ultimate badge of power and honor. The Haitorei Edict of 1876 outlawed the wearing of swords in public for anyone except *daimyo,* former Samurai lords, police officers and the military. Despite the formal, official removal from the social class structure, the Samurai clans, families with distinct Samurai bloodlines extending back 700 years, still remained. Their social standing could not be artificially removed so simply.

The social caste system had not disappeared because Japan was a closed country steeped in cultural traditions and mysticism. The Samurai were so interwoven into those traditions and the social fabric of the culture and art there was no *elimination* possible, or even desired. It was simply time for the role to change. The power ebbed away not because a centralized authority wanted to unite the country and compete in the new world, even though this was the primary political reason. It ebbed away because of social change, the desire of the population for more opportunities beyond their villages once they realized it was available to them.

The Samurai depended on the independent feudal land owner, his role to defend and enforce order over the territory and inhabitants. It was in all reality, a small world. Time had marched on, fiefdoms had become obsolete. Governments were stronger and offered the population more stability and safety. Although the Samurai were gone, the symbols of their power and mysticism had not because their value system remained. The Samurai code of honor to young men like Hiroshi, was Japan. Martial codes established by the Samurai were embraced by the military, even though only about 20 percent of the graduates of the IJA Academy were from Samurai families. The martial spirit of the Samurai warrior, the honor code of the *Bushido*, were popularized and simplified. A subjective, ethereal warrior code of conduct established for 12th Century feudal knights became the mantra of the modern Imperial Japanese military, and by extension the Japanese people.

Hiroshi knew Captain Hashimoto was Samurai because other officers told him. Such declarations of blue blood heritage were not taken lightly by anyone, especially in the Imperial Japanese Army. His family name and Samurai heritage followed him as easily as the noble trail from royalty. Other Samurai knew who he was. As the son of a prosperous land owner, Hiroshi recognized where he personally stood on such a tier system. Land owners were near the bottom. He was fortunate young men like himself were given the opportunity to become professional military officers. It was not always the case, the selection process was purely hereditary until fairly recently. Young men who wanted to be military professionals had to be the sons of military professionals, or the sons of soldiers who gave their lives on the battlefield. The traditions, ethics, code of conduct and value system were bred from infancy. A life long journey to the first entrance examinations of the IJA Academy began when a father, a professional soldier, began instructing his toddler son. He would learn to control fear, pain, hunger and thirst. To never complain, to never accept defeat, and prove to himself he was stronger, faster, smarter and tougher than anyone else, because if necessary his Japanese spirit, the spirit of Bushido alone would take him there.

Envy was not an emotion Hiroshi would characterize for himself, mostly because he understood he was raised as a child of considerable privilege, and he had nothing to be envious about. But he did recognize with some embarrassment he came from a very rural, sheltered background. Of all of the Japanese home islands Shikoku was the smallest, most remote and in many ways, most backward. His desire to become an army officer came fairly early, a decision allowing him the opportunity to prepare for the examinations for the *Rikugun Yonen Gakko*. The military prep school was a three year course in Osaka, a big coastal city on the main home island of Honshu. *Rikugun Yonen Gakko* was designed to prepare candidates but also weed out those unsuitable for the IJA Academy. It was here he encountered the sons with Samurai heritage and the sons of professional military officers. Until he had demonstrated his intelligence, strength and physical endurance to be the superior of most of the other cadets, he was shunned by those who considered themselves the only rightful candidates for the IJA Academy.

The experience was hard for him, especially when he began to believe the hereditary cadets were correct. Either from the fear of failure or some other unseen motivation, Hiroshi found the Samurai family cadets absolutely *driven t*o succeed. Not that it helped them avoid punishment or demerits. He could not detect any hint of favoritism from the instructors toward these cadets. In reality, he felt the instructors were even more prone to pick on these candidates specifically, screaming at them for some minor offense or even striking them with their fists or pointers. The Samurai cadets, and everyone knew exactly who they were; never cried, complained, whined or gave any sense they felt singled out, or felt sorry for themselves in any way. And they never quit. Some of the sons of the military officers were no different than the sons of farmers in this regard. Not the Samurai cadets. Hiroshi found he could

104

not help but admire them and wish he had the background, character and preparation he assumed they experienced all their lives. They were *noble,* there was no other way to describe it.

Once Hiroshi and the other provisional officers were promoted, they were returned to their line companies with the expectation they would soon take over their respective infantry platoons. The war with China was a training ground they were told, preparation for the real battles in the future. The Imperial Japanese Army would be meeting and destroying the enemies who chose to stand in the way of Japan's legacy, its rightful place as the leader in the Pacific. In the winter of 1940 conscription was in full force to acquire the manpower to face these adversaries. The IJA was laying the framework for a massive professional force to assault and garrison territories soon to be under Japanese rule. In the IJA there were no conscripted infantry officers, all were professionals and graduates of the IJA Academy. Hiroshi could not help but feel pride and wonderment at his good fortune and timing. After a brief period of leave after so many years in China, the men of the 44th Infantry Regiment would start an entirely new training program. Hiroshi would train with his platoon for this new campaign, leading them personally to victory.

Hiroshi's platoon commander remained with the platoon as his mentor for three additional weeks. Hiroshi was in tentative command, his former commander an advisor soon to be posted as a battalion staff officer. His guidance for Hiroshi was direct because there was so much to do. Both he and Captain Hashimoto were surprised and impressed with the rapidity of change. Their new mission, what could be gleaned between the lines from orders given to junior officers, seemed very strategic in scope. The training schedule was very intense and densely packed with many components, including a razor focus on jungle fighting and large scale amphibious landing operations at night, requiring detailed organization and planning. The 44th Infantry Regiment was reorganized as the 144th under the direct control of Imperial Japanese Headquarters in Tokyo, not within the command structure of any Imperial Japanese Army infantry division. This in itself was a very unusual reporting structure, leading to rumors the regiment was training to be a self-contained special amphibious assault force outside the politically charged leadership of the Army.

With his time as the direct leader of the platoon over, Hiroshi's former commander seemed to lower his guard with Hiroshi, treating him less as a fledgling student cadet and more as a brother officer, a peer. He remained watchful and humorless but he no longer stood aside, coldly and critically observing a training evolution without involvement. Hiroshi was surprised more than once to find his former commander coming directly to the aid of a soldier, assisting in clearing a weapon jam or adjusting a poorly loaded transport pack. He would do it without criticism or raising his voice. Now that he was leaving the platoon he had led for nearly two years, he seemed intensely interested, especially with the newer conscripts who were clumsy and ineffective, in teaching them skills so they would succeed. So they would *stay alive*, Hiroshi would hear him say. Hiroshi still didn't trust the man because the nights in the dormitory were still the same, with much interrupted sleep due to the nightmares. He did listen however, when the platoon sergeant, a very short but muscular man who served all three years in China, noted one day with a true sadness in his voice, he would miss the platoon commander.

This was not what Hiroshi expected from the platoon sergeant, a man who was firm but understanding with Hiroshi and other fledgling soldiers, to a point. He didn't suffer fools at all, with no tolerance for those he felt did not work as hard as they should. After nearly eight years of military schools Hiroshi had endured innumerable physical assaults under the hands of the instructor cadre. The slaps, cuffs to the head or chin, kicks or shoulders hurling cadets to the ground were daily, normal occurrences for discipline and good order. What he witnessed when he was a cadet officer in China and what happened on the parade ground at Asakura or in the field took his breath away. This is *the real* Army, he thought then and now.

The platoon sergeant would take a running leap and kick a slow moving soldier in the side so hard the man's helmet would snap off from the impact. The grunt of pain as the overloaded soldier rolled over and over on the ground would be followed with a gasp and whimpering, because the platoon sergeant had followed up with another kick in the man's side as he lay on the ground.

"DO NOT FALL BEHIND! OUR SAFETY IS IN TIGHT FORMATIONS!" The platoon sergeant would stand over the fallen man, yanking his head up by his collar, their faces half an arm's length apart. "THE ENEMY WILL PICK YOU OFF, CUT YOUR THROAT LIKE A PIG!" The platoon sergeant would drop the soldier's head, pick up the man's rifle and hand it to him. "GET IN FORMATION." He would glare around at the other men, scurrying about, avoiding the platoon sergeant's stare. Hiroshi, witnessing this, never said anything because he noticed other officers did not intervene. He had to assume they condoned it. The platoon sergeant was a combat veteran as were most of the other officers. Hiroshi watched carefully though, never seeing any of the officers in the company striking the men.

The platoon sergeant, who never spoke casually to Hiroshi before, looked hard at Hiroshi when Hiroshi commented *I wouldn't think you would care that much for the platoon commander.*

"Why would you say that, sir?" The sergeant's tone was icy, and Hiroshi realized he had made a mistake. The platoon sergeant was respectful but clearly irritated, narrowing his eyes in thoughtful consideration of Hiroshi.

"You share a room with him, don't you, sir?" Hiroshi nodded, trying hard to maintain eye contact with the man. His gaze had not left Hiroshi's face for one second. The man finally broke it off, looking down at their boots for a moment before raising his head again, his eyes softer.

"Does the Lieutenant still have his nightmares, sir?"

"Yes he does." The platoon sergeant looked across the parade deck at the man they were talking about, nodding slowly. He turned back to Hiroshi, his eyes examining Hiroshi's carefully.

"Lieutenant Shamada is a very good man, Lieutenant Takahashi. A very good man and a very good officer. One of the best I've met in my time in the army."

"I understand, Sergeant. At least I understand your loyalty." The platoon sergeant smiled thinly at this, his eyes back across the parade ground.

"Lieutenant Shamada served with me in China. The first years or so were very bad. Lieutenant Shamada joined us the second year, I believe. Insurgencies are difficult, sir, you're in the city, in the villages where the people are. The fighting—it's not what you expect or how we trained. Lieutenant Shamada kept me from going mad. His—way, gave me faith in our leaders if we have leaders like him."

Hiroshi didn't know what to say to this, nodding thoughtfully to the man. The platoon sergeant came to attention. "Will that be all, sir?" Hiroshi dismissed him, wishing the man had said more. He found very few of the experienced officers would speak about the China experience in detail to him. They either disregarded large parts of the deployment as a garrison force, or spoke carefully about the "difficult" early years. All Hiroshi did know was what he overheard from some of the non-commissioned officers when they discussed the differences between the departure from Kochi City for China in 1937, and the return three years later.

Huge parades, banners, our families, crowds of cheering people lining both sides of the streets as we marched off to the ships, one older sergeant said. *They masked off all the windows on the trains so no one could see us on the return,* said another. *They closed all the windows of the shops, it was so quiet. How could we forget? With the white boxes on our chests filled with the bones and ashes of our fallen comrades to*

107

march down the silent streets. The townspeople lining the road were solemn and sad, there was no cheering, as if we all felt shame.

When Lieutenant Shamada left, the mystery remained because despite Hiroshi's carefully crafted attempts to draw the man out after hours, Shamada never said a word about his experiences in China. One day his bags were packed and taken away, his bunk mattress rolled up. Hiroshi was returning from breakfast when Shamada approached him and stuck out his hand after returned Hiroshi's salute. His eyes, always sad and dark, blinked slowly as they gazed at Hiroshi. Shamada bowed slightly as he silently turned way. He stopped after a few steps and turned around, calling to Hiroshi.

"Lieutenant Takahashi," he said quietly, "the men will follow you, you understand? You are their officer now, their leader. What you do is what they will do."

"I understand, sir. I will protect them the best way I can." This was the wrong thing to say, Shamada's eyes narrowed as he walked back to Hiroshi, shaking his head.

"You cannot protect them, Lieutenant. It's not in your power. You can't protect what happens to them, understand?" He seemed frustrated, peeved, as if he was talking to an errant child. "All you can do is to provide leadership, guidance, in doing what is right." He sighed, his eyes softening. "Or—let them think what you're leading them to do is right. They don't know any better in some cases. They will want confirmation from you. They will ask you, believe me. That is your job, Lieutenant. Make them believe you. That is your most important job in the days that are coming." He spun around and walked away without another word. More baffled than ever, Hiroshi turned to find his platoon. He shivered for a moment realizing this time, this day, it really was his platoon.

The training schedule, once the program was fully established, ran nonstop at breakneck speed. Hiroshi felt overwhelmed trying to stay on top of where his men needed to be at any given hour, let alone a day. His platoon sergeant was patient with him and a godsend, ready and able to implement once Hiroshi established what needed to happen. Hiroshi knew he shouldn't rely on the man so much, but he rationalized his role was management and leadership, not details. He tried to get an audience with Captain Hashimoto to discuss his concerns and problems but Hashimoto seemed to be everywhere at once. Hashimoto's officers' call was scheduled every morning right after breakfast and was lightning fast. His rapid fire delivery of orders came without reference to notes. These orders weren't given until each of the company officers gave a quick report on the status of personnel, equipment or training issues in the platoons. Hashimoto had no tolerance for long-winded explanations.

He asked sharp questions, cut off any statement off point to encourage a succinct report.

When he did deliver his orders, individually, he would usually ask *will you be able to do this?* This was unusual in Hiroshi's experience, causing him to hesitate the first time he was asked. He began to understand, after listening to the other officers, Hashimoto's style of being direct and specific. There was no doubt what he was asking. The other officers usually said *yes sir*, but sometimes they would explain what they could not do because of a lack of equipment or manpower. Hashimoto never challenged an officer who explained his situation well. He would amend the orders or make suggestions, nothing more. It demanded a commitment based on an officer's assessment of his platoon's capabilities, a responsibility Hiroshi was not sure he could perform. Nonetheless he swelled with pride when he made his daily commitments like the other officers, knowing Hashimoto believed he was capable. One thing was evident though, Hashimoto made it clear through this process each of his company officers would do anything the men would be doing. *You* will lead your men, Hashimoto pointed out, by *your* example. When he heard this the first time, Hiroshi could not help but think about his last conversation with Lieutenant Shamada.

The training was hard and endless, so physically demanding Hiroshi would collapse into his bunk at the end of the long days totally exhausted in mind and body. He would be asleep instantly and dreamlessly, a dark empty cavern closing behind him like entering a long train tunnel. He would awaken with a start seemingly minutes after lying down on his bunk, shook by his platoon sergeant or a soldier from Captain Hashimoto's orderly room. There was always something needing his attention, or Captain Hashimoto was calling all officers early for a special briefing. *At 2:30 in the morning? Is he out of his mind?* He would dress quickly, aware Hashimoto did not tolerate his officers not in complete uniform, even in the middle of the night. Hiroshi would follow the platoon sergeant to deal with the immediate problem, or if he was summoned by Hashimoto go directly to the company office.

He was amazed the first time this happened to see Hashimoto and ALL the company officers in full uniform, hovering over Hashimoto's desk as if it were an afternoon conference. What was equally surprising was to find the other company offices lit up, men scurrying about with files and purpose. He noticed the huge two story brick headquarters of the 144th Regiment at Asakura never dimmed its lights. The grand entrance with lanterns on brick piers was lit like a ballroom, guiding visitors to the gigantic, square parade ground built in the middle of the complex. All of the offices seem lit and busy. *Does anybody sleep around this madhouse?*

Not much, he found out. At the IJA Academy Hiroshi learned to thrive on about five hours of sleep. Sleep deprivation was a given in the military, he understood this to a certain extent. Soldiers and officer cadets in training learned quickly *lights out* were simply extra hours for learning new skills, study, or cleaning equipment and barracks for inspection. Hiroshi had done all three after hours with great success, but thought those days were behind him. It was done on purpose, for a specific reason. He expected it to end, for his rise in position and authority to negate such requirements. I'm an officer now he had reasoned, with privileges and men to do my bidding. *How naïve I was,* he thought with despair. He finally understood while standing outside the company offices at three in the morning sleep was *a luxury* in the Japanese army. A luxury relegated apparently to officers of considerably more rank than anyone he associated with. Day or night, Captain Hashimoto could be found in the company office. Planning, writing or meeting with other company or battalion officers. *NO ONE said you could not sleep in the Army,* he thought, *they just woke you up and sent you on your way.*

The other two platoon commanders were China veterans, up and about at all hours like Captain Hashimoto. Hiroshi resigned himself to learn how to work without sleep. The other second lieutenant was moved over to share the room with Hiroshi. The other platoon commander, recently promoted to first lieutenant, now had a room all to himself. The company was waiting for a new platoon commander, another second lieutenant from another battalion to be transferred over. Once that happened the new first lieutenant would move to a position at battalion, like Lieutenant Shamada, to learn staff officer duties. To Hiroshi this was all part of the Army's way of giving the appropriate responsibility to officers as they gained rank. The other second lieutenant's name was Nishikawa. His gear was moved over by a soldier from Nishikawa's platoon one morning, but it was two days before Hiroshi saw the man other than a fleeting glimpse of his back as they lined up in formation, preparing for the morning's hike to a field classroom.

Hiroshi felt lonely at times, finding absolutely no one he could talk to. He slept fitfully, catnapping when riding in vehicles or whenever there was a pause in the training evolution waiting for transport. Exhaustion was a creature of opportunity. He watched the men line up neatly in squads and platoons on the side of the road, then ordered to sit down directly on their equipment waiting for trucks, either coming or going to the field. The platoon sergeants did not say a thing when the men promptly fell asleep. If Captain Hashimoto was not visible and everyone knew what they were doing (waiting for transport), it was clear this was one of those times. His platoon sergeant only had to prod him once, pointing to a soft mound of fresh dirt under a shady tree nearby. *I'll wake you up in about 20 minutes, Lieutenant. The trucks will be awhile.*

When Hiroshi finally saw Lieutenant Nishikawa in the room neither of them were in much of a mood for talking. The training evolution moved on from constant physical training to build up their body strength to long runs with full equipment. These runs stretched out to half day marathons, the pace speeding up, set by Captain Hashimoto in the front. For the first time Hiroshi found sleep deprivation as a training tool in the syllabus in black and white. The troops to be awakened in the middle of the night to begin a full gear road march to an unknown destination, unknown distance. This evolution was to be repeated twice weekly for nearly a full year. Those soldiers falling out of formation on marches or runs would be beaten and punished severely. Some threatened with dismissal from the army as being unfit for service if it happened again. The threat of such shame, shame for the family at home, was usually enough to bring a soldier around. The *Hohei*, the infantry, was an elite in the Japanese army. Soldiers are recruited or conscripted by region, so all of the soldiers from the 144th Infantry Regiment, formerly the 44th, were from the mountains, towns, villages, farms, cities, factories and universities of Shikoku Island. There was no escaping the shame of failure, everyone would know. No one would bring that on their families, no one.

Weekly the battalions rotated with one another to practice on the 600 meter range. Captain Hashimoto requested and was granted the opportunity to have his infantry company fire *all* the weapons available in the battalion, if he could coordinate the range time with the weapons company. He wanted his men to be able to defend themselves if heavy machinegun positions were overrun and the guns no longer had crews. The weapons were normally manned by machinegun specialists, but battalion liked the idea, so soon all infantry companies were running through abbreviated courses on the Juki heavy machinegun. This idea translated into orientation on mortars beyond the squad 50mm, and even a short course on how to load and fire the 37mm assault gun. Since all of this training was new, Hiroshi recognized he was learning these systems at the same time as his men. He dove into the manuals after requesting them so he could assist the instructors with the slower soldiers, allowing him to become more familiar with his men as individuals. This seemed to please both Captain Hashimoto and his platoon sergeant, especially when they noticed Hiroshi knew what he was talking about.

Hiroshi was an excellent runner and gymnast in his school years, skills and physical conditioning seeing him well as the tempo of the

111

training spooled up. Following Captain Hashimoto's example, he moved from a flank side position by the platoon during long full equipment runs to the front. He was perfectly aware his personal equipment load was significantly lighter than most of his men, some who also carried light machineguns, 50mm grenade launchers and ammunition on top of their personal gear. Army regulations and protocol forbid him to assist his men in carrying such loads in training, but he did not hesitate in suggesting to the platoon sergeant certain loads, such as ammunition, be distributed more evenly among the platoon. The platoon sergeant, resistant at first because he believed gunners and assistants needed to be self-contained in terms of ammunition supply, relented when Hiroshi specified only during approach runs or marches.

As the weeks passed Hiroshi felt more comfortable in his role as a platoon commander, aware his physical presence at the front of the platoon on the runs and marches in and of itself didn't mean too much. It was more important, he realized, for his acceptance among his fellow platoon commanders and his company commander. Being in front and looking the part was very important. He needed to be stronger, faster and adept with the weapons available to his men. Captain Hashimoto already made clear the reason why. His relationship to his men was limited though, by design. He recognized quickly when he had stepped across the boundaries where the platoon sergeant ruled the roost. He learned much of this not-so-delicate protocol when he was a cadet officer in his tour in China near the border, but his current platoon sergeant established the finishing school. Hiroshi did not give orders to the platoon except in general, and always in formation. Troop movements, that is, bringing them together, releasing them, or assigning them individually to their tasks was the responsibility of his platoon sergeant and his junior non-commissioned officers, his squad leaders.

All of this made Hiroshi feel lonely, more isolated at times. The better he got at his job it seemed, the more distant and formal the relationship between himself and his platoon sergeant. The division of labor, responsibility and authority were being finalized in strict terms. Rules, the man said. The more he pressed the platoon sergeant for little changes, the more the man fell back on the so-called rules. He was respectful, but chided Hiroshi while shaking his head. One evening when Lieutenant Nishikawa was in their dorm room and still awake, Hiroshi brought the subject up, including his frustration. Nishikawa laughed as he flopped down on his bunk, pulling off his boots while smoking a cigarette. "You lead the platoon, Hiroshi, your authority is the *katana* you wear on your belt." He sighed heavily, dropping back on his pillow, smoking. "But your platoon sergeant runs it, just like a wife." He dropped the cigarette into the sand can ashtray next to his boots, glancing over at Hiroshi. "Stay out of the kitchen if you know what's good for you."

This seemed good advice on face value, although Hiroshi obviously didn't have a wife. He only had his mother to reflect upon, and his grandmother, both who lived in the house when Hiroshi was growing up. Both women, although formally bowing to Hiroshi's father on most occasions, ruled the kitchen and the household. He never considered his role as a platoon commander in this light before. It was difficult for him to imagine his men, most within a year or two of his own age, or in some cases slightly older, thinking of him as a father figure. Captain Hashimoto maybe, but not Hiroshi. The husband-wife analogy between a platoon commander and platoon sergeant was easier to consider. Command, direct authority was always clearly understood when he was at the IJA Academy. The chain of command was absolute. What was it that makes the relationship between himself, a commissioned officer and a senior non-commissioned officer so hard to understand? Why does the Japanese Imperial Army permit an enlisted man to question his superior officer?

Hiroshi suspected it had something to do with what Lieutenant Shamada was trying to tell him the last time they met. He had some authority, the *katana*, as Lieutenant Nishikawa had stated. He could march and run as fast or as far as his men could, and knew as much or sometimes more than his men did about their weapons. But he had done nothing as of yet to make his men truly trust him, as Shamada intimated, enough they would believe him when he told them they were doing the right thing. *How in the world do you do that?* He was trying to get to know them as individuals, but if he got too close the platoon sergeant led him aside. *I'll take care of this, sir.* He would say. The men would look between the two of them, following in the end the direction and guidance of the platoon sergeant. Hiroshi watched carefully the relationship between the other platoon commanders and their platoon sergeants, even observing the way Captain Hashimoto dealt with the company first sergeant, the senior enlisted man. It was not the same.

A few kilometers from Asakura was Kochi City. In the center of Kochi was Kochi Castle, a 17th Century structure built between two rivers, the Kagami and the Enokuchi, both flowing into the North Pacific Ocean at Urado Bay. It was at the mouth of Urado Bay, the public beach at Katsurahama and along the Niyoda River where the 144th Infantry Regiment practiced their amphibious landing exercises. In the middle of the parade ground at Asakura the Army constructed a ship superstructure for the initial training. Heavy rope cargo nets dropped down inside dry landing barges. They were used to get the troops familiar with climbing over the rail, then down the nets with heavy equipment. Once this was mastered the troops moved to the water locations to learn how to get in and out of small boats, then embarking from ships without landing nets on single rope descents into boats. It was here at Asakura Hiroshi first encountered the private fears of men who could not be forced to do something just because they were ordered to do it.

The distance from rail to landing barge was not particularly far, no more than 15 meters, the approximate hull height above the waterline of a typical medium transport ship used by the Imperial Japanese Navy. The drop over the side was sheer and accurate because of the shape of the phony ship's hull, forcing the net straight down to the landing barge on the parade deck. Most of Hiroshi's men followed the lead of the instructors and their platoon sergeant, dutifully turned around and carefully climbing down the net as they were taught. The ship was not in the water, not swaying from a swell or heavy seas, the barge below staying exactly 15 meters distant from the ship's rail and didn't bob, bounce or dance around one little bit. Even so, one man stepped over the side and promptly missed the net below him with his foot, falling like a stone exactly two meters, right into the helmeted head and shoulders of the soldier directly below him. Luckily the man falling was small and the man he fell into happened to have both hands on the net and held on, even after nearly having his neck broken. The fallen soldier was unhurt, but once he was moved off the other soldier and was gripping the net all by himself, he wanted nothing to do with going down.

The platoon sergeant screamed at the soldier, who ignored him, as two instructors climbed up the rope to be on each side of him. The instructors slapped and punched the soldier until they heard Hiroshi, almost directly above them, order them to stop. The two instructors, both corporals, peered up at Hiroshi in surprise and anger, but immediately stopped striking the soldier.

"He is holding up the training exercises, Lieutenant, we have two more of your platoons to cycle through in the next hour!" The corporal spat the words out as the soldier, a conscript Hiroshi remembered described as a pig farmer, tucked his head in and gripped the net even tighter. The corporal's insolent manner boiled something up in Hiroshi. The net training area grew quiet as men stopped moving, their eyes now on the net and the four men a couple of meters from the deck railing above.

"You touch one of my men again I'll bring charges against both of you," he said coldly. His eyes moved to the corporal on the right who had spoken, whose eyes widened when he saw something in Hiroshi's face. "You, Corporal, open your mouth again I'll have you arrested and

114

court martialed for insubordination. Is that clear?" The two men nodded, not daring to take their eyes off Hiroshi.

"Yes sir," they said almost as one. With a jerk of his head, Hiroshi indicated he wanted the two to get away from his soldier.

"Get off the net," he ordered. The two corporals exchanged glances as they climbed down the net. Hiroshi's platoon sergeant stood below on the deck of the landing barge, his hands on his hips looking up at Hiroshi. He said nothing but Hiroshi noticed Captain Hashimoto, probably curious why the training cycle had stopped, was walking across the parade deck towards the training ship. Hiroshi looked down at the soldier who hung motionless below him.

"Private Yamada," he said quietly, "can you hear me?" Yamada didn't answer but he changed his grip on the rope. "This is Lieutenant Takahashi. *Answer me*." Yamada cleared his throat before lifting his head just enough so he could see Hiroshi's face. He hesitated, then bobbed his head.

"I can hear you, sir." he said faintly. "I—I can't go down."

"You heard those men, we're holding up the training for the whole company, Yamada. I need to clear this net for the rest of the men."

"I can't go down, sir." Hiroshi looked up slightly to see Captain Hashimoto stopping 50 meters away, looking directly at Hiroshi. He wasn't signaling, he was simply observing. Hiroshi slipped his leg over the side of the phony ship and hooked the net with his feet. He climbed down and stopped when he was less than a meter from Yamada, slightly to his right and above.

"You fell and frightened yourself, I understand." Hiroshi said evenly. "You will not hurt yourself if you climb back up and onto the ship." Yamada's eyes widened as he considered this. Hiroshi could hear the soldier's labored, gasping breathing. He was frightened stiff, and still was.

"Can I do that, sir?" Yamada asked. "Can I go up?" Hiroshi nodded affirmatively while reaching out with his left hand, an open palm.

"If you wish, I'll help you up. You can try this rope ladder another day." Yamada peered questioningly at Hiroshi for a moment then bobbed his head again.

"Yes sir," he said, "I'll try it another day." Yamada slowly climbed up level with Hiroshi, who got a firm hold of Yamada's pack, helping him climb up into the arms of two soldiers waiting on the railing. Once Hiroshi was back on the deck he found Yamada, head down, standing at attention.

"I am sorry, sir." Yamada said dejectedly. "I didn't mean to hold the company up." Hiroshi signaled down to the platoon sergeant the landing exercise would continue, directing the next squad to the net. He walked up to Yamada and stood in front of him.

"Stand up straight, Yamada! Eyes front!" he ordered. Yamada did so instantly, bringing his head up. "You trusted me to get you up and on this deck. Now I will trust you will eventually be able to climb down this net, but not today." The relief in Yamada's face turned almost to tears. Hiroshi looked at him evenly.

"Leave the deck, tell the platoon sergeant you are excused from this evolution today and you will try again on another day. Is that clear?"

"Yessir!" He was gone in a heartbeat, hustling past fully loaded troops from another platoon going the other way. Hiroshi returned to the deck rail to look out over the parade ground where Captain Hashimoto had stood. He was gone. He looked down the net, watching the last of his men climb out of the landing barge. His platoon sergeant glanced up at him, nodded and gave him a short, but sharp salute. Hiroshi returned the salute before climbing down the net, the last man down.

CHAPTER 9

January 15, 1941, HDQ 144th Infantry Regiment, Asakura

Hiroshi Takahashi expected repercussions from the net training incident for days. He resolved the problem by removing the soldier from the net so the training evolution could continue. Still Hiroshi second guessed his decision to bring the soldier back up to the deck instead of forcing him to go down, like all the others. He reprimanded the two instructors instead, threatening them with charges for striking one of his men. He felt comfortable with this, no infantry officer or non-commissioned officer should tolerate other officers disciplining their men. This was *his privilege and duty*, not theirs. Hiroshi learned this responsibility and *ownership* as a cadet lowerclassman, when upperclassmen of his company would clash almost to blows with other upperclassmen for perceived infractions of this privilege. It reminded him of beatings he had received in the hands of his mother and father. That was acceptable he was their child, their responsibility. They would kill another adult who touched him.

His guilt was for letting Private Yamada off the hook, for giving him options. He manipulated the soldier to get him out of the way. He would not be able to offer such options if the landing evolution was for real. What would he have done then? For young men of Japan, military service was an obligation assumed for most of their adult lives. Before the forced conscription as Japan prepared for war all young men were obligated for two years, but national need could bring them back at any time. For residents of Shikoku the service began within the walls of the Kochi Asakura fortress when they were called up. There, rain or shine, the new recruits were indoctrinated into the ways of the Imperial Japanese Army on the vast parade ground. It was a brutal, physical transition where any hesitation or challenge of authority is met with corporal punishment. The tough discipline did not go away when the recruits joined their line units after basic training. It bred and ensured soldiers who responded instantly to orders without concern for their physical well-being. They were, as the instructors would suggest, more afraid of their NCOs than the enemy they might face.

The concern was put to rest by his platoon sergeant, Sergeant Kato, after Hiroshi asked if Private Yamada had successfully descended the rope ladder after the incident. The battalion moved temporarily into the high country to train in mountain warfare. The two of them, standing side by side on a small, precarious wooden platform shook by gusting wind and horizontal rain, were waiting for their turn to traverse a three strand rope bridge across a steep gulley. As the temperature dropped, the rain turned into freezing sleet, the rope bridge visibly slick with ice. Sergeant Kato quietly smoked a tiny clay pipe, one hand clamped over the bowl to keep the bowl lit and the other gripping the safety rope of the platform. Behind him the 30 men of the platoon stood on a narrow ledge trail, stretched out along the side of a sheer rock wall. Fully exposed to the wind and sleet their raingear flung about their bodies like flags in a gale, offering little protection. They were soaked through. They could do nothing about it as they needed both hands to hold onto the safety rope, stanchioned every two meters with pitons driven into the rock. Their misery was not visible on their faces tucked down into their hoods, but by their huddled forms, small and bent against the elements.

"Yes he did." Sergeant Kato turned his head away from the wind, leaning in close to Hiroshi. They watched with alarm as a wind gust flung some of the men trying to cross the gulley off the ice-slick single rope on the bottom of the bridge, both saving themselves with their hands gripping the two support rope strands, one on each side. One by one the men pulled themselves back up with just their arms, until their boots crossed the lower strand again. Sergeant Kato returned his attention to Hiroshi.

"Everyone completed the course, including the single rope descent," he said loudly, knowing his voice did not carry. "I didn't think about the ladder rope problem with Yamada, I just forgot about it. The platoon went through every part of the amphibious assault course without a hitch. Every soldier." Hiroshi bobbed his head as he shivered, his eyes on the whipping bridge, his own fear rising.

"Oh," he gasped before he could catch himself. Sergeant Kato gave up trying to smoke his pipe, bouncing the bowl against his leg to shake out the sodden tobacco. He put the pipe away, stretching around the platform to see how many more men were waiting to cross. He brought his head back and glanced up at Hiroshi. Hiroshi knew Kato saw the fear in his face, turning away in shame.

"Before we left for China," Sergeant Kato called out, his eyes back on the rope bridge, "we trained on amphibious tactics for months, just like now." Hiroshi listened carefully, no one ever talked to him about China.

"We drilled and drilled and drilled, building memory so the troops would do the right thing, no matter what was happening. Did you know what happened when we landed on the beaches in Shanghai, Lieutenant?"

"Not really, Sergeant, I read the regimental history, but it only explained when the landings occurred, how many men landed and our

118

casualties. There was very little detail of what it was really like."

"The water was shallow with long approaches so we assaulted with our small boats, the kind you have to roll over the side to get out of. The boats we've been training in, over and over. I was a corporal then, a squad leader and Captain Hashimoto was a platoon commander, just like you. Everything went as planned, or shall I say, as we trained. We came at night, there wasn't much of a swell, the debarkation off the ships and into the small boats went like the exercises. As we approached the shore the Chinese opened up with machineguns and some small bore artillery, all kinds of noise, frightening lights.

"The navy did a great job, especially their small boat coxswains, if those men hadn't of done their jobs we would have been slaughtered right there on the beaches!

"For the Army, it was different. Everybody forgot what to do," he continued, shaking his head. "It was as if we never trained for an amphibious assault. The coxswains would drive the boats right up on the beach, standing up in their cockpits fully exposed to the fire. *And nobody would get out of the boats!* Bullets and shells whizzing and hitting the water, and then you could hear the bullets ripping into the boat.

"GET OUT! GET OUT! YOU'LL DIE IN THE BOAT! I remember our coxswain screamed two or three times until a Chinese machinegun bullet blew part of his head off. I saw it, and decided I didn't want to die in the boat and flopped over the side." Sergeant Kato glanced back at Hiroshi's with eyes sad with the memory. "It was total chaos, bodies everywhere in the water, soldiers doing *exactly the opposite* of what they had been taught for months. They bunched up and died. Ran back towards the boats and died. They would lie down in a huddle on the beach, forgetting this was where all the incoming shells were landing, and died. It was the worse experience in my life up to that time, and I figured I would live maybe one more minute if I could just get off the beach, which I did." He sighed with a thin smile.

"What I'm trying to say, sir, is you just don't know what will happen when the shooting starts. Some men will not do what you expect them to do. They just won't, whether we train them to do it a certain way or not. It's the problem when you're dealing with people. If I may be permitted to speak frankly—sir..." He raised an eyebrow in question as he turned his short, powerful body to face Hiroshi, his chin up. Face to face he had to look up, exposing his eyes to the full brunt of the rain.

"Speak your mind, Sergeant." Without thinking, Hiroshi shielded the man's face with his hand. It was a small gesture, but Hiroshi could see it did not go unnoticed.

"Thank you, sir. I was just going to say, Lieutenant Takahashi, you are being too hard on yourself. You are learning fast. When the time comes—when the time comes when we do what is expected of us, these men will follow you—I will follow you. Some of the men will be confused, frightened and forgetful. Everything we have taught them! When this happens, sir—and it will, we will point them the right way."

Hiroshi remembered Sergeant Kato's words a few nights later, trying to separate those thoughts from his last conversation with Lieutenant Shamada. Both conversations were reassuring in many ways, but he still felt ashamed and inadequate. He appreciated what he perceived was a growing bond between himself and his platoon sergeant. *A marriage*, Lieutenant Nishikawa said, *might even last*. Hiroshi sensed the loyalty and trust, so carefully sheltered at first, becoming more evident every day in Sergeant Kato's words and actions. Hiroshi tried to reciprocate as much as he could, but there was no question of the relative value of Sergeant's Kato to the men compared to himself. The sergeant just knew how to do things to make their world less miserable. That is what is important to the soldiers. Find minimum shelter if available. Repair broken pack straps. Make tent poles from stripped saplings, or reinforce tent awnings in strong wind.

After a week exposed directly to the wind and rain at the mountain warfare school, most of the men were exhausted, sick, their equipment filthy and in some cases, unserviceable. They lived in the field in their tents, the elements finding their way into every piece of equipment. Nothing was dry. Hiroshi, living right among them shivered with fever, losing his strength and will every day from bone chilling damp cold. He knew the next training evolution would be the beginning of jungle warfare. He looked forward to moving out of the mountains into the warmer coastal forests and plains.

He was severely disappointed when Captain Hashimoto informed the platoon leaders that evening the company was not leaving the mountains, not yet. Battalion movement orders had the other two infantry companies and the weapons company proceeding at midnight across a mountain range to prepare for an attack scheduled in 24 hours. They were called Red Force. Those three companies in Red Force would attempt to traverse 15 kilometers on a narrow, unmarked mountain trail to get in position. Hashimoto then outlined what their company's independent mission would be. Unbeknownst to the other companies, their company was going to leave at 0200 hours, two hours later to force march down and across a long valley of pine forest. There was no moon but even if there was one, they wouldn't be seen down in the forest if reconnaissance patrols were watching, it was too dense. Once across the valley, which should take the remainder of the night, they would climb up a rocky, snow and windswept ridgeline to be in position to observe Red Force in transit. Their company unit movement, to be called Orange Force, would remain on the ridgeline fully exposed to the elements while tracking Red Force, unobserved, until the following night.

Their mission was to approach Red Force before it initiated its planned, long-range night attack. Captain Hashimoto was tasked to get Orange Force within 100 meters of Red Force, setting up dozens of unexpected trip wires attached to aerial flares in the projected path of Red Force. If Orange Force remained undetected, the assault elements of Red Force would walk in silent night attack formation right into the trip wires. If Red force triggered any flares, Orange Force was to reveal themselves from their hidden locations using a variety of noisemakers, flares and flash bombs.

Captain Hashimoto explained the mission thoroughly, answering questions, before demanding his officers to memorize the compass courses for each segment of the approach march. There would be no lights of any kind used during the operation. The platoon leader, platoon sergeant and squad leader of any soldier exposing a light would be severely punished, he made that crystal clear. There would be no radios used, only runners and only when the platoon positions were known. This would be, he declared slowly but emphatically, a real mission as far as they were concerned. They could expect rain and wind with some snow flurries up on the ridgeline. It would be very cold. They could expect the forest floor in the valley to be muddy, possibly partially under water to slow their progress through the forest. All movement would be under the cover of night just like a real combat operation, with every piece of equipment taped down and secured to eliminate noise. Silent approach. Silent attack.

"In China before we were turned into a garrison force," Captain Hashimoto said sharply, his eyes on Hiroshi and Lieutenant Nishikawa, "we followed the Army's doctrine to always run attacks at night. It became second nature to us, but it does not come easily. Men get lost. Whole units get lost. It takes time for men to feel comfortable moving towards the enemy in complete darkness, in total silence. It's been over a year since the battalion has engaged the enemy in a night action. Even my China veterans are rusty. But we train the way we will fight! Our enemies, the Chinese, the enemies we will face like the Russians, British, Dutch and possibly the Americans—see the elements of weather as their enemies. They retreat like mice into their bunkers when the sun goes down, or it rains or the wind blows!" Hashimoto looked at his officers with tired, veiled eyes, but yet Hiroshi could see them burn with energy as he spoke. Hashimoto glanced at their uniforms and boots, dark and wet, soaked through with mud and tree sap.

"I know you're miserable, I can see it in your faces as are the men. But know weather is our friend when we learn how to use it. Our enemies slink from it, hide in it, go to ground in it. The Japanese Army, this regiment, this battalion, this company—embraces the weather as some of our ancestors wore armor! It protects us from the enemies' eyes, which means we are less exposed to their aircraft, artillery fire, mortar fire and accurate machinegun and rifle fire! *Don't ever forget this* when you are cold and miserable and marching in the rain. When we combine the night and weather with a silent approach, like a tiger, we can get within touching distance of our enemies. When they discover us it is *too late!*"

Hashimoto brought his hands together parallel to one another, keeping them a short distance apart, but motioning together, in concert, like a pantomime. The demonstration caught his officers' attention, their eyes following his hands, mesmerized.

"Our survival and success depend on silent approach and not being seen. When we practice enough, we will have learned to take advantage of the natural tendency of human senses, the perceptions of the enemy, to focus on *the unusual.* They are afraid and alerted to things that are not natural, not normal, not part of the environment they see and hear. We learn to move with the environment; our bodies swaying with the wind when the wind blows, being shadows where there are shadows in the dark. We become part of the night and therefore part of the forest, of the trees, of the jungle. When we are part of the night, the enemy does not suspect or detect our presence. Understood?"

Hiroshi could not believe how difficult it was to follow these simple rules in practice. If it wasn't for the experienced China veterans in the platoon they would have been completely lost. He found you could not simply walk off with a platoon of soldiers in pitch blackness and expect to stay in the same direction, let alone together in a cohesive group, or online, or—remain silent much farther than 30 or 40 meters. This became evident even after schooling the troops for hours on how to use their other senses, primarily their ears, to follow the soft, barely audible crunch of footsteps in front of them.

Under Captain Hashimoto's and Sergeant Kato's instruction, the platoon practiced before dark with blindfolds, stepping out together, all within touching distance only to collide and lose direction. If someone whispered or made a sound Captain Hashimoto would have Hiroshi stop the exercise, identify and reprimand the offender, and start again. If was like learning to dance, choreographing the synchronized movement of one man, then ten men, finally the entire platoon. They were clumsy, disorganized and tired before they even began the exercise. With so much to learn and do before they even attempted this mission, Hiroshi drove the men harder with little to show for it. He was frustrated and angry, listening finally to the suggestion of Sergeant Kato, the men needed to concentrate and gain confidence in one skill set at a time. Like walking. Silently.

Their feet slowly high stepping, toes forward to carefully clear obstacles before gently feeling the ground in front them, lifted in unison once the rhythm was established. Point the toe, maintain the direction, the body follows the toe. Plant them carefully, silently. Listen. Start over. Lift the rear foot so slowly there was not even the creak of leather. You transferred the weight, finding a new place for the heel of the boot and came down steadily. Hiroshi noticed if taught correctly, a group of men out of sight of one another would continue to lift their feet and place their feet at about the same pace if they stop and start together. The speed and rhythm of silent forest walking was like marching. Hour after hour. There was definitely a tempo to it. The men learned to transfer their weight swiftly, keeping their balance, prepared to stop instantly and transfer the weight back to the rear foot if necessary.

Hiroshi took them out into the field one squad at a time, blindfolding them before leading them, by voice command, into the forest. Once in the forest he would impose silent discipline, the only sound the wind, smacking rain drops and light pressure of boots probing gently down on wet, broken wood debris. When they left the field for the forest Hiroshi knew the luminous, dampened dial of his compass would give him the course headings, the bearings toward his objective. This was of no value if you lose focus and get confused, walking into unseen tree branches or solid trunks. You need to sense them like an insect with your ears, nose and touch with feet and hands. At first it seemed impossible.

This was particularly difficult to do with a standard issue Type 38 Arisaka Japanese Imperial Army infantry rifle. It was long by normal standards for a typical Japanese soldier, made even longer with the Arisaka bayonet, adding nearly 40 centimeters to its length. Japanese infantry tactics and doctrine always kept the bayonet on the rifle for silent killing when necessary on approaches, but also providing the soldier the tradition of an edged weapon encouraging the aggressive closing attack on an enemy position, with or without ammunition in the rifle. In practice especially in the enclosed forest, the rifle was clumsy and snagged everything. The soldiers quickly adapted a trail carry when entering the forest, the rifle held down low, the bayonet slightly forward of the body but not so far as to catch on branches, the rifle butt trailing, their grip down on the muzzle and forearm of the stock. It looked awkward, felt awkward, but the rifle could be brought up quickly if the soldier was clear of the tree branches and practiced.

When the training ended the company was exhausted. It was nearly midnight as they gulped a meal and broke bivouac. They could hear the other companies leaving. Despite the best intentions, the sound of two thirds of the battalion marching away was not silent. Equipment still tinkled with the tramping of the troops distinct and recognizable. This was a not a final phase silent approach walk, but a battalion transit in enemy territory. There was supposed to be noise discipline. Hiroshi heard them too, wondering how well his company would do.

Captain Hashimoto suggested the platoon commanders let the soldiers doze on their equipment until it was time to go. Orange Force was going to be an assault team and the troops would be carrying extra equipment, specifically the trip flares, noisemakers, flash bombs, smoke grenades and some aerial illumination rounds for the light mortars they were bringing. Hashimoto ordered the troops to leave their tents, blankets and other housekeeping gear behind. A transportation company with horses would carry the extra gear back down the mountains. Orange Force packed two days of rations, ammunition, poncho rain gear, overcoat, entrenching shovel and individual weapons, leaving room in their rucksacks for the extra paraphernalia to conduct *a noisy attack*.

Hiroshi was impressed as the China veterans placed pieces of white adhesive tape horizontally near the top at the back of each soldier's pack. The tape, not visible from the front, could be seen if soldiers stayed within a couple of meters of one another, in everything except complete blackness. They discovered as they stepped out at 0200 down into the valley there were places in the forest where it was that dark, spaces the trees were so tall or dense there was no sky. But as soon as there was any sort of clearing or separation in the pines, the moonless clouds above were illuminated, glowing and reflecting a natural light down into the spaces between the trees. If the soldiers kept their separation but maintained visual contact with one another, closing and opening this space as required, they could stay together. The trail discipline was absolute: Everyone looked back occasionally to ensure the men behind them were still there. If it was so dark no visual acquisition was possible without actual physical connection with one another, then everyone was to lightly grab the harness of the man in front.

The forest floor, with the exception of fallen limbs, tree trunks, natural depressions and man sized hunks of granite virtually invisible, was surprisingly clear of debris. It was an alpine valley, with a deceptive but very real gravity-induced slope from one side to the other. Water courses from the higher peaks ran through the floor, some trickling runoff a few inches deep, others almost streams with pools and small waterfalls. By first light the company had crossed the forest even more exhausted; faces, hands and knees were bloodied and bruised from countless nocturnal collisions, but after a quick head count, all were accounted for.

Captain Hashimoto was pleased they made the crossing in the time allotted, but seemed intolerant to their exhaustion. This was the first phase of the mission with 20 or 21 more hours until they were in position. Hashimoto remarked before they started what an honor it was to be chosen for this mission. He was not about to disappoint his superiors in their choice. Hiroshi remembered the intensity in Hashimoto's eyes; a determination, an unremitting will to overcome any obstacle, defeat any opponent, withstand any suffering. Hiroshi submitted to this will without hesitation, believing this force as the spirit of Japan, of *Bushido, of the Emperor*. A spirit he could only hope to develop within himself and master. If Hashimoto knew this mission could be completed as ordered, then he had faith in his officers and his men. He had faith in Hiroshi to lead his platoon across this forest, up the ridgeline, then down the other side to meet the unsuspected battalion attack. *I will not break your faith in me.*

There was a small clearing at the base of the ridgeline. The reaction from the soldiers as they stepped into the clearing was slow because of their fatigue. Most were relieved to be out of the forest, until they looked up. The climb to the ridgeline appeared as sheer rock face. It wasn't, but the impression was immediate and soldiers groaned or gasped when they saw it. The sharp look those soldiers received from Captain Hashimoto quelled most comments at once, because noise discipline was still in force and the only voices heard were murmured whispers confirming headcounts. Hiroshi noticed the look and followed up immediately when he heard whispering among his own men.

"Silence!" He barked as quietly as he could, glaring at the offenders. The men bowed their heads meekly, their shoulders bent with the exhaustion of hours stumbling in the dark. Hiroshi felt a tinge of guilt as he stared at his soldiers, knowing like himself, they had not slept but a few hours in the last 36. Captain Hashimoto ordered Lieutenant Nishikawa to send two teams of men up the rock face on a reconnaissance to find a path. Hashimoto gave them one hour. He called for his officers, ordering the company to dump packs, check equipment and get food and rest. They didn't know how long it would take to get up to the top of the ridgeline, but once it was dark again they would be on the move to get in position to intercept Red Force. If they got up their quickly, they would hide and get additional rest. If not, it would be a very long day.

The climb up was hard and slick with the sleet and snow showers, but there were places to plant their feet and hands. It took three hours to get the company up and in positions behind the peak of the ridgeline. When Hiroshi peered over his shoulder as he neared the top, he couldn't believe how steep the pitch was and how far they had climbed. There was, fortunately, a lot of trees and thick brush on the ridgeline with numerous crevices to drop into to provide some shelter from the weather. The wind howled across the ridgeline, bringing the wet snow down into their holes. Once they stopped moving the cold settled in around them, the frozen granite sucking their body heat away. They were already wet from the tramp across the valley forest, then fully exposed to the weather as they climbed up the rock face. A number of men made the mistake of discarding their winter coats during the night trek through the forest. They suffered the most. Their uniforms were soaked through. Their wet, rubberized rain ponchos offered little insulation.

Hiroshi was ordered to provide a small reconnaissance team and join Captain Hashimoto along the ridgeline a few hundred meters to the north. The mission was to put eyes on the battalion coming across the opposite mountains, and determine their course and speed. Hiroshi, being the junior, least experienced officer, was surprised to be so chosen. He quickly had Sergeant Kato select a small group of soldiers. The group hunkered down, shivering in the wind as Captain Hashimoto reviewed his map and compass to confirm their location. He patted Hiroshi on the back and grunted, turning back towards the peak of the ridgeline staying carefully out of sight. He stopped frequently, referring to his map, finally stopping the group near a tight cluster of brush. Without a word he pointed towards Hiroshi and signaled him to follow. Hashimoto crawled right into the thickest part of the brush, so thick there was no snow underneath. Hiroshi followed him, cursing the sharp rocks and pointed spines of the brush.

Hashimoto stopped, glancing over his shoulder at Hiroshi. A small jerk of his head indicated Hiroshi should join him. Hashimoto carefully wrapped his field glasses with a dark gauze material before bringing it to his eyes. Hiroshi stopped a foot short, realizing Hashimoto was looking down through a crack between large two rocks, gray sky was all he could see. Hashimoto was sweeping the horizon slowly with the field glasses from left to right, then down a few degrees, traversing across now from right to left. After a couple of minutes he set the glasses down and slid back next to Hiroshi. Hiroshi noticed a series of deep scratches on Hashimoto's face, the blood long dried. Hashimoto looked at Hiroshi with bright yet intensely black eyes, the blackest Hiroshi had ever seen in a man. He had not noticed them this way before. It was like he was looking at a different person. Hashimoto had a thin, even smile on his face, but what made it a smile were the eyes. They crinkled up in the corners, a lightness that belied the intensity of his pupils. It frightened Hiroshi just a little. Hashimoto looked mad.

"Whoever planned this mission, Lieutenant, knows this terrain very well. They knew we would have a view of the back slope of three mountain ranges right here on this ridge. It's a remarkable view. The back slopes are hidden from the others because they empty out like a fan. But we are on the opposite side and see the entire gorge. It would take hours to come down from the mountains and cross this gorge. They have to come this way in order to enter the valley forest where they are to attack to the east. There is no one there. We are either early or we have missed them!" Hashimoto said this so casually Hiroshi thought he was joking, although he had never seen Hashimoto joke before.

"What should we do, sir?" Hiroshi tried not to chatter his teeth while attempting to talk, the rocky ground sapping his body heat. He couldn't take his eyes off of Hashimoto who unblinking, held his gaze with the thin smile.

"Our orders are to wait until we see them, track them unobserved, and determine their course and speed before we attempt to intercept them in the forest. I think," Hashimoto scratched his unshaven chin whiskers thoughtfully, "by now the battalion has figured out why we didn't join them. I would think some bright fellow has thought out what we might be trying to do, and the battalion is either hiding out during the daylight hours—which is unlikely as they wouldn't make their night rendezvous, or they are staying up near the ridgelines up there like we are, staying out of the valleys and out of sight until they have to. Maybe waiting until dark before they run down into the valley."

"Why would they do that, sir?"

"Why not? The battalion commander is not leading Red Force, the battalion executive officer is. He was a very aggressive, very effective officer in China against the insurgents. An excellent company commander. My company commander. He will take this little war game very seriously, just like I do. I learned from him. He may know exactly what I would be doing."

"Does that mean he will choose somewhere else to make his attack?"

"No, he has a specific target location he must attack by a specific window of time. Everyone knows this location and time window. How he gets there is up to him. He is supposed to be using a trail over there so they would move faster. He may have chosen a different path. I would have. We have to observe his direction and speed to ensure we intercept him at the *right place* before he gets in position. The game is to know

127

exactly where he is going to be an hour or two before his attack, and set up our—ambush."

Captain Hashimoto left two soldiers at the observation point with instructions to simply watch for movement, any movement on the mountain ridges across or down the gorge. If they spotted anything one man would come north along the ridgeline and inform Hashimoto. The rest of them crept along the ridgeline as Hashimoto established two more observation points, dropping off the remaining four soldiers. Hashimoto and Hiroshi moved along for another hour, staying away from the peak of the ridge as trees and cover disappeared. Hiroshi left his pack back with the platoon. He was hungry, but Hashimoto continued on, methodically inspecting the opposite mountain ridge for sign of the battalion. Hiroshi realized with a shock the company might have missed the battalion completely. They were either in the wrong position or, as Hashimoto had surmised, been outfoxed by the assistant battalion commander. If Hashimoto was concerned, he didn't show it. If anything he seemed even calmer than before. The hours passed slowly, Hiroshi's growling stomach a mere nuisance compared to the numbness he was feeling in his legs and arms. He could not remember ever feeling so cold.

After covering nearly a half of a kilometer the ridgeline narrowed and pitched steeply downward into a connecting saddle with the opposing mountain range. From their position they could see the terrain lowering to the east in the direction of the forest valley to their right. The saddle was fully exposed, so it was not the direction they would go except under the cover of darkness. But the saddle was also extremely narrow, mostly rock scale. Any misstep could be fatal. Hashimoto crept forward, removing his cap and replacing it with a dirty scarf to cover his hair. He wrapped the binoculars with the dark gauze again and edged forward. His concentration was completely on the ridgeline opposite now, his glasses moving very slowly across the top of the mountains. Hiroshi, using the skills he learned in an artillery spotting class at the IJA Academy, glanced at his own map to determine some known distances laid out in his limited view. He estimated the nearest ridgeline was approximately three kilometers away.

Hashimoto grunted happily, his head no longer moving. He made slight adjustments to focus his field glasses and locked his elbows to ensure a more steady view. After several minutes he slid back down next to Hiroshi, his eyes glittering with triumph.

"It is as I thought. They are crossing the ridgeline away from the original trail. It slowed them down, but they stayed so far north observers watching the gorge and the back slopes would have missed

128

them. They are marching on the opposite slope, barely visible until they crossed the northern ridge here." Hashimoto directed Hiroshi to a location on his map, his finger tapping tight, close-together lines indicating the ridge to the north. Hashimoto laid the map down and oriented his compass. He hummed happily as he worked, drawing three lines from the ridge down to a circled dot in the forest valley.

"Is that the location for the battalion attack, sir?" Hiroshi murmured, not knowing why he was whispering. Hashimoto noted compass bearings, both directions on each of the lines he had drawn. He looked up at Hiroshi, the pupils now tiny dots in the gray light.

"Yes. I see three directions they may choose to make their approach from their current location on the north ridge. We need to determine which one they will use as soon as possible so we can be in position for them. If we choose wrong we will miss them completely and fail our mission."

"It would be nice to have radios on this mission. We could position observers on all three of the approaches." Hiroshi blurted, understanding as soon as he said it, exactly why radios were prohibited for the mission. Hashimoto nodded thoughtfully, his eyes moving from Hiroshi's face to his trembling fingers. Hiroshi could not control his shivering, his face reddening with shame.

"Yes." Hashimoto said after a moment. He turned slightly to peer over to the north, although it was not visible in their depression. He returned his attention to Hiroshi, the thin smile, the upturned eyes with a hint of humor evident.

"You are cold, Lieutenant." he said it as a statement. "I have a mission for you. I know you're tired and cold, but I need you to do something, something that will make this mission possible." Hiroshi, a little surprised, stared at Hashimoto before realizing he needed to respond.

"Yes sir." Hashimoto slowly turned his map around so it lay between them, still oriented to the terrain in front. He laid his hand, almost black with dirt, palm up on the map, his knuckle tapping the marked forest valley to their north.

"In your first interview when we received you straight from the academy, when I asked you what your favorite athletic activity was, you said running. I believe you said you could run with the wind, if I'm not mistaken." Hiroshi nodded, watching Hashimoto's pupils grow large and dark again, giving Hiroshi the sensation Hashimoto was leaning closer to him, which he wasn't.

"I believe you were quite proud of that. You have demonstrated to be strong and able, as an Imperial Japanese infantry officer should be." His penetrating eyes gave way momentarily as he glanced down at his

129

watch.

"We have about two hours before darkness sets in. I'm going to stay here as long as possible and observe the battalion so I can get an idea of whether I'm seeing the front end or the back end of the battalion. I need to gauge their speed. They have Weapons Company with them, so they are slowing the column down. I want you to go back and get the rest of your men observing on the ridgeline and take them back to the company. Tell Tomita and the platoon commanders to be ready to move in about an hour. As soon as they are ready, have them move north out of sight from the west, the same way we came here, understood? It will take the company about a half of an hour to get to this position once you start." Hiroshi nodded, picking himself up off the ground, ready to leave when dismissed by Hashimoto. Hashimoto brought him back with a simple motion of his hand.

"I'm not done, Lieutenant. Once the company is here, I'm sending you out ahead with another good fast man, to a position *I think* will be the most likely path of the battalion." Hashimoto tapped the map again, drawing Hiroshi's attention to a particular spot, one of the three lines from the north ridgeline down to the forest valley. "I need time for the company to get in position in front of the battalion, as you know. I am making a calculated guess on these two approaches, here and here, as the most likely choices. And this one, the one I'm counting on, I'm putting you in a position so you will know which one they choose. *Here.*" Hiroshi pulled out his own map, but his eyes noted the location and distances involved. The initial approaches, in very steep terrain, were many kilometers apart. He wanted to scream inside. He was totally exhausted. This was impossible.

"Once you determine their choice, you will retreat unnoticed and get back to this location, *here,* giving us enough time to move into their path and set up our ambush."

Hiroshi stared at the map without seeing it, feeling Hashimoto's eyes on him, ashamed Hashimoto could sense his fear and defeat. He knew what was coming. *It was impossible. It was impossible.*

"Can you do this, Lieutenant Takahashi?" The words were calm, but firm. Something rose in Hiroshi, a heat from his gut, wrenching his stomach. He wanted to vomit. He raised his head from the map to meet Hashimoto's eyes, black, level, now cold. *On the bones of your ancestors, they said.*

CHAPTER 10

January 17, 1941 144th Infantry Regiment, Asakura

The company executive officer, First Lieutenant Tomita had anticipated the movement orders. The company ate their supper rations early and the men were reasonably rested. As Hiroshi approached with his observers the other company officers joined him. Before he reported First Lieutenant Tomita asked him to wait, sending a messenger for someone. A thin, yet round-faced officer Hiroshi had never seen before joined them. Tomita introduced him as a regimental communications officer, a warrant officer named Miyamoto temporarily assigned to the company. Miyamoto saluted the other officers, all who outranked him, stopping just outside their small circle. It was obvious to Hiroshi all of them knew him and none of them were comfortable in his presence. Hiroshi had never seen Miyamoto before so he assumed the officer stayed close to Captain Hashimoto's headquarters staff near the front of the column, joining them as they entered the valley forest last night.

Hiroshi gave his report, repeating Captain Hashimoto's instructions. He answered questions based on what he knew, which was little. Hiroshi sensed Miyamoto watching him carefully, but was more aware of the guarded, wary deference Tomita showed Miyamoto. They broke up to get their platoons on their feet. Miyamoto waited until the other officers left before approaching Hiroshi. Since no one in the battalion carried a radio on this exercise, Hiroshi wondered why a communications officer was necessary. Miyamoto was a warrant officer, entering the army as an enlisted man and becoming a highly-skilled specialist without the benefit of the IJA Academy. Alone, Miyamoto smiled for the first time.

"Lieutenant Takahashi, I believe I will be joining you tonight." Miyamoto appeared to be in his mid-twenties but his eyes were older and hard, like Captain Hashimoto. He moved like an athlete. Hiroshi decided he knew why Hashimoto assigned the two of them together. A junior officer who could at least run hard and long and follow orders, and a communications officer without radios, probably equally fast on his feet. Miyamoto seemed to read his mind as the smile faded, replaced with a thin cold line of a mouth matching the hard eyes.

"Captain Hashimoto and I served in China. He asked me to come along because of certain skills I possess. He anticipated the need for long-range scouting to perform this mission, so your battalion commander authorized my assignment. Captain Hashimoto thinks very highly of you, Lieutenant, and felt you might benefit from our little mission tonight." Hiroshi knew instantly who would be in charge, and was ashamed how relieved he felt. It was frustrating for him to recognize how little authority or control he had in his role as a junior officer, yet he grasped the purpose of his assignment. It was an opportunity to learn. His concern at the moment was hunger and exhaustion. Dead on his feet, he knew Sergeant Kato had the platoon ready to go, of this he had no doubt. He wished he was going with them.

Miyamoto followed Hiroshi and stood aside as Hiroshi gave his instructions to Sergeant Kato. Hiroshi noticed immediately the reaction of Sergeant Kato and some of the China veterans when Miyamoto joined them. Their eyes widened visibly when they recognized him, a reaction he would characterize as guarded and fearful, like First Lieutenant Tomida. They did not make eye contact with Miyamoto once they saw him, turning away or finding interest in their equipment. Hiroshi peered at Miyamoto over his shoulder, thinking Miyamoto had somehow signaled something to his men, but Miyamoto looked calm, his face passive. Their eyes met briefly, Miyamoto nodding his head perceptively.

"I know some of your men." Hiroshi was too tired to consider this for long, going to his pack to get some rations, he had to eat something. Miyamoto dropped down to his haunches next to Hiroshi. There was no time to boil rice or tea, so Hiroshi opened a tin of sardines and a tiny jar of pickled plums his mother had sent him. Rudely, he realized, he was eating in front of Miyamoto without offering him anything. He motioned towards the food but Miyamoto shook his head. He watched Hiroshi for a moment before slinging his light pack around and opening it. He pulled out a tightly rolled bundle of camouflaged canvas which turned out to be a set of coveralls. They were identical to the unusual uniform Miyamoto was wearing, most of it dusted with snow. Miyamoto was not even wearing a coat or a rain poncho.

"For tonight may I suggest you wear this. I think we are about the same size. We may get very close to Red Force." His voice was low and calm, but this was no suggestion. Miyamoto examined Hiroshi's other equipment with a glance before the cold eyes leveled on Hiroshi's face.

"We should leave just before dark. We will move quickly, and stay moving all night. Captain Hashimoto says you are in excellent physical condition, yes?"

"I'm tired, but I can do it." Like Captain Hashimoto, the only movement came from Miyamoto's dark pupils.

"You won't need your overcoat, poncho or cap. Leave your pistol and harness and your combat pack. Give all of it to your platoon sergeant to take care of. There is a large pocket in the back of the

132

coveralls for your canteen, you'll need that. Bring your field glasses, compass and your map. That's it."

Hiroshi removed his overcoat and poncho to put on the camouflaged coveralls, noticing the canvas was water resistant. It was still snowing as the company moved up along the lee side of the ridgeline, ensuring they wouldn't be seen from the mountain ridges to their west. Sergeant Kato was by his side, his face impassive as they climbed steadily towards the north end of the ridgeline. The men seemed glad to be moving again, the temperature dropping as the wind picked up.

"You served with this warrant officer, Miyamoto, Sergeant Kato? Did you serve with him in China?" Sergeant Kato stared straight ahead as he walked not acknowledging the question. He turned his head slowly towards Hiroshi, their eyes meeting. Kato's were wary as he nodded.

"Yes I did, Lieutenant. He was in our regiment." The coolness of the response did not encourage a follow up question. Hiroshi glanced over at Kato, irritated by all the reticence but respectful of his experienced platoon sergeant. It was China, again. Something no one wanted to talk about, certainly not with him. He thought he was accepted by Kato, but whatever this was he was not trusted enough to share the history. Darkly, Hiroshi thought of the mission in front of them, the many hours before they could even find themselves in position to engage their "enemy". He had to find the strength, the reserve to stay with Miyamoto, whoever he is. Deep in thought, he was surprised when Sergeant Kato stepped over next to him, close enough to whisper. Kato looked up at him, his eyes tired but alert. He peered carefully around him before speaking.

"I will say this, Lieutenant Takahashi. You should know, I don't think you do. No matter what they say he is Miyamoto is *Kempeitai* (military police). Secret police to anyone else." Kato stayed close to Hiroshi for a few more steps before casually moving away. Hiroshi stared at Sergeant Kato, who resumed his straight ahead affect. Miyamoto was not wearing the armband or the crisp, well starched uniform of *Kempeitai* he'd seen, but if the information was true it explained the reaction of the other company officers and Sergeant Kato and the other China veterans. *Kempeitai* had enormous power, legally and politically in the Imperial Japanese Army, power over-arching all ranks. To be the subject of a *Kempeitai* investigation was tantamount to a guilty plea for a Japanese soldier or officer. In the IJA Academy the instructors were very careful in their discussions regarding *Kempeitai*, the selection of language left only the space between the lines to be filled by intelligent listeners. They hinted of investigative powers reaching into any aspect of a subject's personal or family life. If

Kempeitai decided you were guilty, you would at some point, plead guilty. Their methods, the instructors stated quietly could be characterized as *medieval*.

When darkness came Miyamoto glanced over at Hiroshi, signaling with a curt nod they were going. Miyamoto covered Hiroshi's face with greasepaint to mimic his own, a mottled brown. He handed Hiroshi a dark scarf, one Hiroshi recognized as identical to Captain Hashimoto's, helping him tie it around his head to cover all of his hair. At the last moment he handed Hiroshi a small pill. *It will help you stay awake.* Hiroshi hesitated only a moment after Miyamoto tossed one into his own throat. Hiroshi swallowed the pill, washing it down with a bit of water from his canteen. He seemed to have caught his second wind, the sight of the gorge to their left and the dark shadows far below them making him shiver. He was frightened, but committed now.

Although they were in snow and the ground was white Miyamoto explained most of the night they would be moving in sheltered forest. Just before it got dark they reviewed their maps and oriented their compasses. Hiroshi discovered Miyamoto carried a different map then his, a more detailed display of the terrain, revealing the location of the battalion attack was, in reality, a mocked up fortification. Captain Hashimoto noted the location the company would be waiting for the word on which path to take. With growing dismay Hiroshi understood the two of them would be covering nearly a dozen kilometers in steep and treacherous terrain in *complete darkness*. They were to find and track the battalion without being discovered themselves, determine which direction the battalion choose to approach the site of the attack, and get that information to Captain Hashimoto so the company could intercept the battalion and set up the trip flare ambush. Hashimoto wanted the information in seven hours, by 0200 hours. *Impossible.*

If Hiroshi had any doubt Miyamoto knew what he was doing it was dispelled. The man moved like a weasel, darting smoothly left or right, around or through obstacles in their path. They slipped over the side of the ridgeline straight across the saddle between the ranges as dusk muted into blackness. The saddle was dusted with white, aiding their navigation as they scampered across the cover-free rocks. The wind blew hard and Hiroshi knew a fall would be fatal, or at the very least result in serious injury. He had no time to think about it, all he could do was stay as close as possible to his companion who rarely looked back. It was dangerous and slippery, with Miyamoto moving so fast Hiroshi had no choice but to follow his footsteps directly, hopping across dark, unknown expanses he never would have attempted on his own. He didn't fall, which built his confidence. Their plan was to sprint across the opposite, east facing ridgeline until they made contact. From there they would follow the battalion to determine the approach path to the fortification. How they were going to move, cross country in the dark to where Captain Hashimoto and the company would be waiting, he had no idea.

When they cleared the rocks of the saddle and transitioned into semi-level open country of sparse timber, the ground was thick with snow, nearly knee deep. Miyamoto instinctively avoided this by dropping down into the dark, treacherous slopes where there were more trees. It was hard to see the ground but there was less snow. Once Miyamoto had a line on the edge of the forest he picked up speed again, almost a sprint. Hiroshi found the camouflaged clothing they wore nearly invisible beyond 15 meters, even when exposed against open snow. He was desperately afraid of losing sight of Miyamoto, pushing himself until he felt like his heart was pressing against his throat. After 45 minutes Hiroshi had no idea where they were. Miyamoto stopped twice to consult his compass. They turned uphill again, a punishing climb through thick snow Hiroshi knew he could not sustain for long. For once he could hear Miyamoto's labored breathing as they pumped their legs higher and higher to compensate for the snow.

When Miyamoto stopped abruptly and froze Hiroshi had his head down and was right behind him. He lunged into Miyamoto, who clamped his hand hard over Hiroshi's mouth, spinning him around silently into the snow. The instant they were down and still Hiroshi could hear the *shush shush shush* of feet tramping through snow, very close. He was lying on his back as Miyamoto slowly lifted his hand from his mouth. Hiroshi could just barely make out his face as Miyamoto brought his finger to his lips. They remained motionless for several minutes as the troops shuffled past, some coming within four or five meters of them.

When the last of the soldiers disappeared, it grew quiet. Hiroshi lifted his head for a cautious peek but Miyamoto pressed him down.

"Rear guard," he whispered. Sure enough after a few minutes, they could hear the quiet crunching of boots of what sounded like a squad of men coming through. After another five minutes Miyamoto tapped Hiroshi and helped him up. Miyamoto consulted his compass before leaning in close to Hiroshi.

"We were lucky, Lieutenant, I misjudged their speed. They were slower than I thought. I expected to come right in behind them, not to their flanks. Fortunately we didn't run into their flank guards. They are tired, not paying attention. We won't make this mistake again."

For the next two hours they tramped swiftly down the same track as the battalion, following the three companies as they pirouetted around the northern ridgeline to begin their steep descent. By staying so far north before they turned, Hiroshi could see Red Force would not be visible to Orange Force when they entered the forest from the west during the light of day. If Captain Hashimoto had not spotted them on the northern ridgeline from his observation point they would have missed them completely. The troops were moving fast but had not committed to one of the three approach routes. As the battalion made the turn, the ground cover became sparse. The troops were hidden from view to the east but Hiroshi and Miyamoto would be easy to spot if the rear guard spent any time looking. Miyamoto faded back, dropping to his knees behind foliage. He decided to stay to the south of the battalion, going cross country through the pines to cut the corner of the turn. This meant they would be climbing and above the battalion, but out of sight.

They moved swiftly through occasional knee deep snow for over a kilometer, climbing steadily before altering their course to turn downhill back towards the battalion. They were in thick forest when Miyamoto signaled to stop. He glanced to his left then slowly to his right, dropping soundlessly to his knees before rolling onto his stomach. Hiroshi did the same, watching in horror as a squad of soldiers walked cautiously into view, stopping 10 meters away.

In the darkness they could hear a non-commissioned officer giving orders to his men to spread out, stay alert, keep an eye out for infiltrators. Hiroshi listened with dismay as two of the soldiers were assigned to the cluster of forest right in front of them. Another two were assigned the space *behind them*. They were trapped.

Hiroshi looked up but Miyamoto signaled to him to lay still as he lifted his head inside the boughs of a pine tree. The two men were still there, standing, 10 minutes later when the NCO returned with several of the men. They were apparently the same rear guard, ensuring no one was following the battalion during the northerly curving turn. The squad retreated, but Hiroshi and Miyamoto waited a full five minutes before moving.

Despite the excitement of near discovery and the cold, Hiroshi found himself dozing on his forearm as the minutes passed.

"Are you all right?" Miyamoto demanded quietly, his eyes glittering like polished black marble. He gripping Hiroshi's shoulders hard, pulling him up. Hiroshi grunted as he brushing off snow. They peeled back the covers on their luminous wrist watches instinctively, noting the time.

"Let's go," Miyamoto whispered, turning straight down the slope in the footsteps of the rear guard.

An hour later they were still shadowing the rear guard. The guards sensed their presence. Every few minutes a couple of them would sweep back around, stopping to examine the slope carefully. It was too dark for field glasses so all they could do is peer nervously into the blackness. The column stopped. Miyamoto believed he knew why. The battalion column was turning east into the thick forest. It was much tougher going in the forest than up here on the side of the ridgeline. They had run out of time so Miyamoto glanced at his compass before backing them up a hundred meters. They turned southeast where Orange Force, Captain Hashimoto and the rest of the company, waited for them.

There were clear signs the battalion was directly to their east heading to their attack martialing point. Twice Hiroshi and Miyamoto almost stumbled into the right wing flank, individual squads of men working very hard through heavy forest to provide security for the column. Similar forces were on the left side. In both encounters the individual soldiers were way farther west than they should have been. Once Miyamoto determined they were past the point elements of the battalion, they turned more easterly. Cautiously, they moved in start-stop fashion, listening for sign of the column before moving forward quickly another 100 meters. It was past midnight when they dashed across a small dark clearing and nearly ran down two soldiers looking in the opposite direction, rummaging through one of their packs.

Hiroshi couldn't believe what happened next. The two of them came silently up on the soldiers before either of the soldiers even looked up. Miyamoto, who was in the lead, spun sideways and kicked one soldier in the head while punching the other one in the face three times with the heel of his open palms, his hands a blur, the *THWACK THWACK THWACK* the only sounds. It was over in seconds, the soldiers falling silently to the snow. Hiroshi, gasping for breath, stared at the soldiers and then Miyamoto, but Miyamoto ignored the look, simply pointing at the men.

"Recognize these men?" Miyamoto demanded, "Not your company?" Before Hiroshi could answer, Miyamoto was tearing up pieces of clothing from the open pack to tie the two men up. He also gagged them.

Hiroshi examined the men closely in the dark but it was hard to see facial features. They appeared to be wearing greasepaint like Miyamoto and himself.

"I can't tell," he said finally.

"It doesn't matter. Help me get them off the trail." Hiroshi was so used to taking orders from Miyamoto he just took an arm and they dragged the man and his companion into the forest. Neither made a sound. Miyamoto looked around after they picked up the pack and hid it. It looked like an unoccupied clearing now.

"They're not dead, are they?" Hiroshi whispered.

"No. They are wearing greasepaint and carrying no weapons. I think they are a battalion reconnaissance team scouting ahead, looking for your company. That means a couple more of these teams are around. This tells me the battalion is coming this way. If we had time, I'd ask them some questions, but we don't." Miyamoto came very close to Hiroshi, Hiroshi could sense his eyes and body heat.

"You are surprised I attacked our own men, Lieutenant?"

"Well, it was—a brutal attack. You hurt those men." Miyamoto came even closer, his marble eyes now visible.

"We are training for war, Lieutenant Takahashi. Right now these men represent the enemy. We train the way we fight."

"I understand." Hiroshi didn't, but he was afraid of this man. The eyes bore into him, like red hot pokers from a kiln. Hiroshi could not help but look away.

"If this was for real, Lieutenant, those men would be dead."

It was almost 0200 when they reported to Captain Hashimoto. If Hashimoto was surprised to see them he didn't reveal it. After the encounter with the two scouts Miyamoto established a very direct route back to the company. Hiroshi knew he could not point to where they were if he had a map in his hand, yet Miyamoto never appeared to waiver. He seemed to know exactly where they were at all times. He didn't have a light so he couldn't refer to his detailed map, but shot bearings from his compass with apparent confidence. At the IJA Academy the instructors spoke of highly trained men who were experts in bush navigation, men who lived far outside the comfort, security and comradeship of a line infantry unit. They were usually reconnaissance or intelligence soldiers, like the two soldiers Miyamoto dispensed in a blink of an eye. He had no idea what he was dealing with in a man like Miyamoto. What they did he would not have believed possible if he had not personally experienced it. It was an amazing performance.

Hiroshi expected to simply listen as Miyamoto gave his report. To his surprise Hashimoto directed his questions to Hiroshi. Miyamoto, suddenly acting like a helpful second in command, interjected details as Hiroshi attempted to summarize their mission. As soon as he had the route the battalion was taking, Hashimoto paused the briefing to issue instructions to his platoon commanders, which included Hiroshi. He could see Sergeant Kato among the other officers. Hashimoto told them to be ready to move in 10 minutes, *silent attack*. The company formed quietly in a small clearing created by a series of large buried boulders. Black forest was all around them. The snow was no longer falling, the wind like a gentle breeze. It was almost pleasant. The cloud cover parted partially above them, revealing deep, carbon sky sprinkled with stars. There was no moon, the only light the stars. Hiroshi could make out the outline of Hashimoto's face, the field officer's cap he was wearing again. The black eyes glinted when Hashimoto moved, rarely blinking. Hiroshi could sense the eyes were appraising him.

"I know you need to get to your platoon, I just have a couple of more questions, Lieutenant Takahashi." He wanted the route they took, how they followed the battalion, when they determined the battalion was taking the very route he had expected them to take. Miyamoto was doing most of the talking, but Hiroshi could sense Hashimoto's eyes remained on him. Miyamoto used "we" constantly, meaning the assessment and decision-making process during the mission was performed as a team, between Hiroshi and Miyamoto. Hiroshi did not remember a single instance where Miyamoto asked his opinion. He was surprised how accurately Miyamoto described their actions, including the numerous near-misses with the rear guard and flank security. He described everything. He detailed the encounter with the battalion scouts and the need to *neutralize them* and *restrict their movements*. If Hashimoto was concerned about the welfare of the two soldiers after the "neutralizing" he didn't show it.

"Do you think they've been discovered?"

"No Captain, as slowly as the battalion is moving they won't be near that location for at least another half an hour. Even when they find them, they won't be able to do anything about it, they will be committed if they want to be in position to attack the compound by 0430."

"But they will know we are around." Hashimoto seemed to be thinking. Hiroshi was so exhausted he was hallucinating. When he glanced up wearily to view the stars they seemed to be moving in all directions. He felt immediate vertigo and nausea. He felt a strong grip on his shoulder, then another arm steadying him upright.

"Are you all right, Lieutenant?" Hiroshi realized with embarrassment he had fallen forward into Captain Hashimoto.

"I'm sorry sir," Hiroshi mumbled in shame, "I lost my footing in the dark." There was a long pause as Hiroshi felt the eyes of both men on him. It was so hard to focus his thoughts.

"I'm fine sir. I need to rejoin my platoon."

"Lieutenant Takahashi did very well tonight, Captain." Miyamoto said quietly. "We moved fast."

Hiroshi felt a hand on his shoulder again, a firm grip, only for a moment. Hashimoto's.

"You did well, Lieutenant, as I expected you would. We have to complete our mission, do we not? In a short while the enemy will know we are here. They will be expecting us. All of our work, our training must focus like a beam of light on this attack. Deploy your men."

Hashimoto took Hiroshi aside and reassured him Sergeant Kato was briefed on what to do with Hiroshi's platoon in his absence. The company had moved carefully across the same saddle Hiroshi and Miyamoto had used, traversing southeast then south to where they were now. The men even had time to practice the night approach in the forest and setting up the trip flares.

"Since the enemy knows we are in the area, they may divide the companies earlier than planned to attack the compound from three directions. Such an attack would be impossible to defend against with what we have. So instead I'm going to divert from our orders a bit and set up our ambush farther down the slope, somewhere the battalion will still be together and we can channel them into our ambush. I was thinking of a place Miyamoto described, a ravine maybe a kilometer up from where the two of you encountered the scouts. This means we must get down there quickly and set up. It must be a location they have to go through. We have to be sure."

Hashimoto was talking in a way that made Hiroshi nervous, suspecting another mission was in the offing. Hiroshi noticed Miyamoto was no longer there. Hashimoto must have sensed Hiroshi's apprehension because he suddenly laughed, a brief muffled cough.

"Relax, Lieutenant. You won't need to go. I've sent Miyamoto back down the valley to scout it out and also warn us about any advance scouts coming our way."

"Warrant Officer Miyamoto is an amazing man, sir. I have no idea how he navigated in the dark so effectively." Hashimoto snorted as he nodded his head in agreement.

"Miyamoto is an amazing man, I agree, Lieutenant. Half poisonous snake, half vampire bat. A very dangerous man. To the enemy!" Hiroshi thought of his own men and their reactions to Miyamoto. And the two scouts he brutally attacked. *Kempeitai.* It would depend, Hiroshi thought carefully, on who Miyamoto considers the enemy.

Hiroshi rejoined his platoon, changing into his winter officer's uniform and overcoat. The company moved downhill under strict orders of complete noise discipline. They approached in two columns until they reached an area about 300 meters above the proposed ambush site, the ravine. There they waited until Miyamoto rejoined the company. Hiroshi huddled with the other company officers as Miyamoto described the ravine. It was a natural, steep granite channel, a slash in the forest about a 150 meters wide and 6-700 meters long. The ravine curved around before pointing straight towards the southern flank of the defensive

140

compound, about two kilometers away. It climbed steeply with little impediments for fast foot travel. Out of sight completely from the ridgelines above on both sides and certainly from the compound, it was a natural alleyway to move a large group of men around the forest, unseen. Hiroshi assumed he climbed it with Miyamoto earlier but he had no recollection. In the dark all they did was climb, so he recalled little of the topographical details around him. Hashimoto agreed there was no way the battalion scouts would miss the ravine. The trick would be to be in position before any scouts spotted them, alerting the battalion to their presence.

Miyamoto estimated the lead elements of the battalion were a kilometer away, but warned battalion scouts could be lurking about. He encountered none during his reconnaissance, but he would go back to the base of the ravine to watch for them. Scouts were a good sign Red Force was close behind. The only danger was if the scouts came across the company as they were setting up the trip flare ambush. If Miyamoto came across any scouts that would compromise the mission, he explained, he would *neutralize* them and *restrict their movements*. Hiroshi could not see the faces of the other officers, but again sensed their coolness to Miyamoto. There was no comradeship with him in company. Hiroshi understood now their wariness of the man, all of them having served with him in China when they confronted a *real* enemy. Whatever he had done there affected their attitudes towards him with the exception of Captain Hashimoto.

Hiroshi rejoined his platoon as they took the lead, impressed how well the men responded to Sergeant Kato's direction as he deployed them, in two columns, the last 300 meters to the ambush site. Once in the forest it was pitch black, the only bearing information for direction the luminous dials of the compasses held by Hiroshi and Sergeant Kato. They stayed within touching distance, 30 men strung out directly behind them followed by the rest of the company. It took a half an hour to cover the distance to the edge of the top of the ravine. Hiroshi could see the light area of the ravine as the snow reflected the light of the cloud cover above. The forest on each side of the ravine appeared menacing and black. They watched, as instructed for five minutes in stillness. Nothing moved below them. Miyamoto was down there somewhere.

The men deployed the trip flares in the darkness between five and ten meters into the forest. NCOs wired the final pull rings to the flare canisters by feel and confirmed they were armed. The company had enough trip flares to cover the entire width of the ravine and thirty meters on each side. Once these were deployed the company backed up into the forest, the men taking extreme caution so no flares were accidently triggered. As planned, the company pulled back 50 meters

141

from the trip flares to wait. NCOs had distributed the noisemakers and flash bombs to the men before they started, instructing them not to trigger them until the lead units of Red Force tripped the flares. Each squad had a small 50mm mortar launcher set up to fire aerial parachute illumination flares if the gunner had a clear view of the sky. These would light up the ravine almost like daylight. Up in the forest the ravine was not visible at all to the soldiers waiting. Hiroshi and Sergeant Kato crept back down, counting their steps to ensure they did not come near the line of trip flares. Between a small cluster of smaller pines, Hiroshi could discern the milky sheen of the ravine through 20 meters of forest. Although cold, he was alert, anticipating the action they came so far to perform.

As the minutes passed Hiroshi began to worry if Miyamoto and Captain Hashimoto erred in assuming the battalion would come up the ravine instead of the forest. First light was now less than two hours away. Red Force's orders were to attack the compound, two kilometers up the valley, just before dawn. If they chose the ravine they would save time and possibly the mission. Hiroshi knew Hashimoto was counting on Red Force recognizing the advantage the ravine offered. But could they even find it in the dark? What happened to the other reconnaissance teams Miyamoto was assuming would be scouting ahead? What if the reconnaissance teams missed the ravine? They were late, unless they chose another route, bypassing Orange Force completely on their way to the compound. The confidence he felt so strong minutes before, evaporated.

What he knew for certain was his platoon, and by extension the rest of the company, adhered to the noise discipline *completely*. Other than the wind whirling up the ravine, a haunting low moan as it carved around the granite channel to spool up into the forest, there was no evidence 178 men were close by. Not even the creak of leather to move a numb leg. It was the sudden movement, a dark shadow darting across the pale snow 75 meters down the ravine that caught his attention. Hiroshi stared so hard where the shadow stopped he lost his focus, the other shadows blending together into muted greyness. He closed his eyes for a moment before opened them again, catching another dark shadow darting across. This had to be a pair of the reconnaissance scouts. How far behind them was the battalion? How far up would they scout? The scouts could see the end of the ravine blending into the blackness of the forest, Hiroshi thought. Will they turn back to report their findings? Or continue to explore? His excitement was so high he could hear his heart pound.

As if to answer his questions, one shadow then another reversed

142

course to dart back down the ravine before disappearing around the gentle curve. Hashimoto expected the scouts to report the width and length of the ravine with a lot of excitement. If Red Force was still struggling through the forest, then the ravine would be about the only option they had to be in position for their attack in time. Hiroshi wanted to believe Hashimoto was right all along. Like Miyamoto, there seemed to be no issue with Hashimoto as to what to do next.

For 20 minutes nothing happened. The snow stopped long ago, the air warmer. Only the wind remained. Hiroshi realized with the warm air any precipitation would have been rain instead of snow, the ravine awash with water, perhaps rushing streams like the runoff coming off the ridgelines into the valleys on the other side of the mountains. It might even be like a river, and Red Force would never have been able to use it. This realization struck him hard. How difficult it was to command, he thought. Captain Hashimoto would have lost this option, but then so would have Red Force. But one had to have information. Red Force had their scouts, Orange Force had—well last night, Hiroshi and Miyamoto. But in all reality, just Miyamoto, he somehow managed to stay in tow, that's all. He was in awe with men like Hashimoto and Miyamoto, but he wanted to believe it was something you learned from experience. He could be as good in time.

The sound coming up the ravine was confusing at first. A throbbing, rhythmic drumbeat coming up the funnel of the ravine, carried along by the wind. Hiroshi cocked his head to one side, then the other trying to identify it. The quick-time *CRUNCH CRUNCH CRUNCH* would be recognizable to any soldier, anywhere. It was the sound of men, several hundred of them, marching rapidly. He could hear no cadence being called but there was no question what it was. A minute later he could barely see the dark shadows outlined against the snow in close formation. In astonishment he realized the battalion—Red Force, was not marching up the ravine, they were *running up the ravine. Uphill.* The assistant battalion commander, if he was the man in charge, was trying to make up for lost time by having the battalion run up the granite. The pace was quick; Hiroshi could imagine what it was like for the end of the columns. Red Force would be stretched out like a thick caterpillar, parts of it speeding up, the rest slowing down. The end of the column took the most punishment for the stop and start action. To catch up, constantly, they would run the hardest. With only an hour left before first light it was a desperate and risky maneuver.

Lead elements slowed down within 50 meters of the top of the ravine before stopping. Hiroshi was impressed how quickly the men reorganized into tight columns prior to penetrating the forest. The rear echelons were out of sight around the bend of the ravine. The only sound now was the wind and barely audible murmurings, quiet commands from NCOs. Red Force did not waste precious minutes once the men were closed up and in proper order. Hiroshi could see the forward columns approach the forest. The first men into the forest entered cautiously, the transition from open air ravine to dark confinement unwanted, a hesitation, then a careful first step. Hiroshi assumed these lead men would be NCOs or officers with compasses, trying to maintain a heading and direction uphill in inky blackness. He felt sorry for them.

The first flare *whooshed* and burst into an orange-yellow sparkling mini sun. A man screamed in fright, his howl overcome a second later as a dozen other flares were tripped in the dark, the flares whooshing and dancing sparklers all around. Within a count of two sudden total chaos took over the blackness of the forest as tossed flash bombs burst with earsplitting *BANGS* and blinding whirling light. Noisemakers whirred, whizzed and honked loudly amidst the screams and yelling. The first of several parachute flares popped open, bathing the ravine with orange and white light, revealing men running around in all directions aimlessly as others screamed to control them. The flares and pyrotechnics ignited innumerable small fires in the forest, creating, to Hiroshi, an image of hellish mayhem. The flames outlined frightened men who had no idea what to do, some frozen still, most literally ran around in circles, some dropping their weapons.

It was, for Hiroshi both frightening and exhilarating. If this was what combat was like it was like nothing he had thought. The unexpected destroyed the unit cohesion of Red Force. The fear and confusion in those men's eyes left no doubt the action was a complete surprise. Hashimoto outfoxed his assistant battalion commander. Hiroshi understood if his company had machineguns instead of noisemakers and flash bombs, they could have effectively slaughtered Red Force. The choice of the ravine as an approach route was a calculated risk to save time. The ravine was wide open, and the choice of their defensive position at the top insured the company had cover, concealment and a complete field of fire. The effective use of the parachute flares meant they could have used mortars on Red Force. As Hashimoto described it later, in a tactical situation he would have placed one of the platoons in a flanking position to provide a blocking force to destroy troops trying to flee into the forest.

Later that morning the battalion marched up to the defensive compound to reorganize. Climbing in the forest during daylight seemed child's play. The battalion followed a narrow horse trail leading them away from the compound and halfway down the mountain where the trail joined a real road. Near a large clearing a field kitchen was set up, the men eating their first hot meal in 10 days. The battalion, reorganized back into their respective companies, lining up on the roadway waiting for trucks to take them back to Asakura. The troops, fed and bone tired, slumped down on their equipment and were asleep in minutes.

Hiroshi sat down and closed his eyes. He had not slept in about 45 hours not counting three or four brief catnaps. Still under the influence of the drug Miyamoto had given him the evening before, his body was numb with exhaustion yet his mind raced off and on. Sergeant Kato, sitting next to him, lit his clay pipe. Hiroshi noticed earlier Miyamoto was nowhere in sight. His last glimpse of the man was when he disappeared down the ravine to watch for battalion scouts.

"I spent the entire night with Warrant Officer Miyamoto, Sergeant," he said quietly, when he heard the scratch of Kato's match. "He is a remarkable man. He ran around in the complete blackness of the forest out there and found the battalion like it was broad daylight. Then we made our way back to the company like we were following street signs." Hiroshi opened his eyes, peering around them. Every man in sight appeared to be asleep. Kato said nothing, but after a moment he nodded his head.

"Miyamoto does all of his work at night. You won't see him coming. If you're lucky you'll never see him because you'll be dead. If you're unlucky, he'll bring you back. You'll die eventually, either way."

"You say he's *Kempeitai*, Sergeant. How do *you know*?" Sergeant Kato's eyes narrowed, his lips compressing to a thin line. Hiroshi realized he had crossed a boundary again. It was tantamount to calling his sergeant a liar. The other men and officers were afraid of Miyamoto, so it was probably true, he was *Kempeitai*. Who was he to question it? He raised his hand, making a *please forget what I just said* motion.

"I'm sorry, Sergeant. I didn't mean that the way it sounded. I know you and the China veterans, including the officers are very careful around Miyamoto. I picked that up pretty quickly." Sergeant Kato tamped the tobacco down on his pipe as his eyes drifted off. After a moment he relit his pipe, looking directly at Hiroshi.

"You need not apologize to me, Lieutenant, you're an officer." Kato sat up straighter, his voice lowering. "You're a good officer, Lieutenant Takahashi, and I respect you. We will be going to war soon, and Captain Hashimoto wants you ready for what is coming. He likes you, you can tell, yes?"

Hiroshi nodded slowly, watching Sergeant Kato's eyes, sad but defiant.

"Be careful around those two, Lieutenant, when they're together, Captain Hashimoto and Miyamoto." Hiroshi's sense of propriety was irritated, the comment was border line. Hashimoto was their

145

commanding officer. He took a breath and chose his words carefully.

"They get things done, Sergeant, you got to admit that. Captain Hashimoto is a great tactician, and used Warrant Officer Miyamoto as his eyes and ears. It worked remarkably well last night." Hiroshi could tell Kato knew he had offended Hiroshi, but he would not back down. His sad eyes flared with anger before slowly softening, retreating back to narrow slits.

"Yes sir, they do," he said evenly. "They get things done, but they get them done through us, Lieutenant." He seemed to hesitate before continuing, his eyes not leaving Hiroshi's face. "Miyamoto is a weapon. He has no soul, no conscious." Kato took his left hand and patted his chest. "I fear for your heart, Lieutenant. They think you are like them."

THE GREEN

CHAPTER 11

August 16, 1942, Uberi, the base of the Kokoda Track, Papua New Guinea

Diggers, like soldiers everywhere demonstrated their morale by complaining in garrison. Vic Hickey knew from experience the constant bitching and in-your-face vocalizations from his fellow Victorians disappeared the minute they moved up to the line. It had something to do with the national character of Australians in general, a severe independence of mind and body borne of individual hardship. In Oz it was a pride and acceptance a man was judged not by what he owned but what he could do, usually with his bare hands. What you worked for was yours, the sense of fairness ingrained so balances were observed. In all situations you were expected to fend for yourself and carry your own weight.

This created and revered fierce individualism, yet the shared background and culture developed natural team players. Leadership therefore was a shared reward, something thrust upon people by common agreement. You were chosen because you would do the best for the group. There was no immediate recognition of authority based merely on bloodline or a paper degree from a university resulting in a fancy suit or pips on the collar of a uniform. This egalitarian perspective often made management of such people, both in industry or in the military, virtually impossible for those who demanded respect based on assigned rank alone. You *earned* an Australian's respect by demonstrating superior skills in whatever you do. But it was a two-way arrangement as the respect would remain only if the Australian recognized his own skills were respected and valued in return.

Over a year before when the 7th Division was still in Egypt prior to the siege of Tobruk, Vic witnessed several instances of visiting British officers infuriated when they encountered exhausted Australian troops at rest who would neither salute or even stand up in their presence. In some cases these were general officers used to their own troops snapping to attention with smart salutes even in combat areas. Vic, a section leader at the time, watched with dismay as his own battalion commander, a lieutenant colonel, was severely dressed down by a British brigadier in fresh khakis.

Unacceptable lack of discipline. Outrageous lack of respect towards superior officers. Bloody disgusting approach to managing troops supposedly supporting the Crown. Total embarrassment such troops are allied to King and Country. And so on. To give full credit to his battalion commander, who nodded politely during the brigadier's rant, the BC responded respectfully but rather clearly with most of the men in question within earshot. *Yes sir, I understand. They are quite tired after working most of the night on fortifications. However, sir, I might say, if you had said 'hello', most all of them would have said 'hello' back!*

Dumbfounded to such an attitude, the brigadier stared at the BC as his sunburned face stoked red as a tomato. After a moment where the brigadier's jaw seemed to drop lower and lower, the man suddenly closed his mouth, turned on his heels and strode off. The brigadier's aide, a major, starred at 2/14's BC's grinning face and blinked. Without a word he chased after his boss.

The 7th Division returned from the Middle East in late March, arriving in Adelaide after the long sea voyage to cheering crowds welcoming them home. After a short leave they moved from Camp Watsonia near Melbourne to Yandina, in Queensland for months of tough training before some of the division shipped out for Port Moresby, arriving on August 13th. The constant strenuous training during the winter months gave them the physical conditioning they needed for their coming assignment, but the environment of northeastern Australia did little to prepare them for the equatorial jungle of Papua New Guinea.

To Vic it was like trying to live inside of a sauna hut. At first it seemed impossible to breathe in such saturated, heavy air. During the day the sun baked their brains between the torrential rains, creating steam and humidity draining them of strength and energy. Once the sun lowered on the horizon the heat remained, followed by huge dark clouds of insects descended on the men in the open tents hastily set up near the airfield.

The brigade medical officers, the MOs, knew such intense exposure would become a problem in a matter of a week or 10 days, the typical incubation period for malaria. There wasn't much that could be done about it other than flat out avoidance, but the 7th was an infantry division and would be expected to live outdoors in the field. DDT trucks sprayed around the encampment regularly yet the insects still came every evening at dusk.

The MOs made it a point during the mandatory lectures at Yandina on the 'Hazards To Be Found In the Tropics' to note that the extreme part of the Kokoda Track, the part crossing the 8,000 feet high Owen Stanley Range where the Japanese were engaging the 39th Battalion, was free of mosquitoes. This didn't have much impact on the troops at the time sitting in the bleachers in Australia trying to stay awake after a punishing forced march to the training area. After two days in the swamp near Seven Mile airfield, however, the thought of no mosquitoes suddenly made the Kokoda a desirable destination after all. The complaints were constant, with Vic, newly promoted at Yandina to Platoon Sergeant of 9 Platoon, taking the brunt of the grizzling.

The decision to promote him came as a surprise to Vic, mostly because when the division returned from the Middle East, a number of old hands were moved about including 9 Platoon's former platoon sergeant. A retread from the Great War, Sergeant Waller, a slim, simian-armed man with the bellow of an elephant, was posted to division headquarters despite his extremely vocal resistance. The names of a number of brigade NCOs, all experienced men, were bandied about in the rumor mill as Waller's replacement, but Vic was to learn it was Sergeant Waller and 9 Platoon's commander, Lieutenant Edwards, who suggested Vic for the posting to their company commander, Captain Welsh. It reminded Vic of his selection as shift supervisor when he was still building Ford cars. He was the last to hear about it. He did not want or considered the job for himself. At 24 he was not particularly young for the role as most of his platoon mates were plus or minus a couple of years from his own age, but even Potty noted more than once, *you're an' old man inside, Vic, yew don't even know it!*

What Vic had not noticed was how many of the truly older men, men in their late 30s and mid-40s who served during the First World War or the interim year's right after, were being pulled out of line units and posted to administrative positions. These were men who appeared as fit as anyone, training as hard and as long as men half their age. Most all of them had served faithfully and well for two years in the Middle East. The Australian Army seemed to recognize, as the US Army and Marine Corps would realize in their own organizations when their troops encountered the equatorial tropics of the Southwest Pacific, this would be a whole new ball game. Only the youngest, strongest and most fit need apply. The overwhelming demand of the physical environment was so high no amount of pre-conditioning could prepare troops for what it was like. There was nothing like it in Australia. The Australian veterans of the 7th Division of all ages, extremely well-trained, rested and experienced, were brought to their knees in the Owen Stanleys'. But the physical assault of the humidity, insects, disease, incredibly poor hygiene and altitude compounded by the vertical terrain, destroyed the older men, all of them. It was, to Vic, the most punishing environmental conditions he had ever encountered in his life, where despite his excellent physical health and strength, he was pushed to the absolute limit of his endurance two or three times a day.

Early in the morning after breakfast the battalion broke down the tents and stacked them aside, as they would not be coming along on the

Kokoda Track. The relief in the men was palpable. They formed into their companies and platoons waiting for their assigned trucks. 2/14 rode the trucks to Ilolo, where the road disappeared into a narrow path useful only for foot traffic or mules. They loaded up with their personal rucksacks and weapons, beginning the relatively mild climb up to Uberi, the unofficial beginning of the Kokoda Track. The 96 kilometer Track wound treacherously across the southern tail of New Guinea, up and over the cold and shrouded Owen Stanley Range, across roaring, dark waters in twilight canyons, and down to steaming, impenetrable triple canopy jungle before unwinding into the coastal mangrove swamps of Buna and Gona. But here at Uberi they were on the other side, the foot of the Track, where 2/14 viewed for the first time the sheer vertical environment they would be living for weeks, the first of *The Golden Stairs*.

The Golden Stairs were an appropriate introduction to The Track. The battalion viewed the steps in front of them with awe and trepidation. *The Golden Stairs* were hand built laboriously with imbedded logs, many of them half a meter apart in height, climbing straight up until they disappeared into the smoky mist above them. The battalion was briefed about the stairs, the difficulty understated because there was simply no other way of getting into the Stanleys' short of flying into Kokoda, which was now officially in Japanese hands. The stairs was a section of the Track about 12 kilometers in length, and the briefer noted it would take about 11 or 12 hours to complete.

Having never climbed it before, 2/14 was aware of one thing which made the so-called *Golden Stairs* a challenge to be undermined or dismissed. 2/14 was AIF, regular Army, combat experienced with a keen understanding the men who traversed the trail before them, the 39th Battalion, were *militiamen*. To take nothing away from their desperate struggle against the Japs on the Track, the 39th were poorly trained reservists *for God's sake*, home guard fellows who really shouldn't be in this fight at all, as militia was not supposed to leave Australia. Somehow the politicos had decided New Guinea, the home of a dozen provincial colonial administrators and small clusters of coconut and rubber plantations close to the coast, was in fact, Australian territory, and therefore, *Australia*. A bit of a stretch for the average Digger, but what could you do?

2/14 noted with some appreciation hundreds of Papau natives, mostly from the Orokaiva, Binideri and Koiari tribes who apparently had previous employment relationships with the Australian colonial administration, were joining them on the Track. The Papau natives would serve as load bearers carrying rations, ammunition, medical supplies, wounded men and virtually anything necessary to minimally

151

support the battalion in the field. The battalion troops only needed to carry their personal kit and weapon with a limited supply of ammunition on their backs. Lightening their individual combat load was heavily stressed at Port Moresby, so Vic and 9 Platoon, like everyone else in the battalion, left behind their sweaters, poncho liners, blankets and spare clothing. Vic insisted 9 Platoon keep their steel helmets, entrenching shovels and rain ponchos.

The battalion had arrived late in the afternoon at Uberi, so the companies separated into platoons to bivouac for the night. First thing in the morning after breakfast the trail assignments were handed out so the companies would proceed in order up the Track. There was no rushing the stairs apparently, it was single file all the way, so the companies waited their turn. Vic remembered the briefing very well, appalled at the seesaw journey they faced. On the numbers alone, it didn't seem so bad, he figured. The first five kilometers they would climb about 1,200 feet. Then, the briefer noted, the Track dropped over 1,600 feet, almost straight down for a kilometer. Then it turned straight up again, rising over 2,000 feet over the last six kilometers.

What the briefer failed to mention, however, was that even when carrying a lightened rucksack, the damp, slick and muddy log steps were so high and so close together thigh muscles began screaming in protest *within four or five steps. Oh my god,* thought Vic, when he realized his legs were quivering ten minutes after they started. His lungs were gasping in the damp saturated air, his eyes stinging from the virtual stream of sweat pouring from his face. He slung his Thompson across his back and like everybody else, was looking for some kind of walking stick or prop or push his weight up onto the next step. The more vocal fellows who had been talking so loudly about *the bloody chockos* in reference to the 39th Battalion down in Uberi, were silenced. The Papau bearers, men who walked these trails all of their lives, moved faster so they climbed together as groups. The battalion companies, A, B, C and D were spread out between them. By midday the battalion was stretched out over four kilometers.

Since the battalion was not climbing as a group, there were no organized rest stops. When a Digger could not move forward another step, he slid to the side of the Track until he regained his strength to try it again. The man behind him would simply keep on climbing. After several hours, platoons were dispersed all along the line, mixed together, the younger, stronger men always in the front. As they climbed higher the temperature would fluctuate, sometimes cooler, sometimes hotter. The mists drifted through the canopy as thick as fog at times, but without the coolness one would associate with a mountain mist. Every part of the trail was damp or soaking wet, slick as a greased pan, causing exhausted and confused men to lose their footing, sometimes falling backwards a meter or more until they collided with another man or were stopped. Everyone was injured or bruised, there was no talking. No one had the strength.

Ignoring his exhaustion Vic moved up and down the line as necessary to check on his men, especially, as he learned quickly, the older men. No one wanted to be a burden, to be a chump who needed the assistance of other men who barely had the strength to carry their own loads. Despite the protests of some of his older soldiers, Vic lightened their loads by redistributing their equipment with other willing mates. Vic's own rucksack was growing heavier with some of this gear, but Vic was a younger man, bigger and stronger than most, and he refused to look into the eyes of some of his old friends who cried because their bodies had let them down. *Rubbish,* he would say quietly to them, *you're jus' tuckered out, chum, give it a rest!*

The Golden Stairs were surrounded by dark, slimey ooze, the only firmness to be found the incredibly complex tree root systems everywhere. Potty, who surprised Vic in his ability to scramble up and down the Track to check on the other fellows, was the first to notice the smell of the dead nearby. The volcanic soil was thick and gummy, leached of all nutrients, washed away constantly by rain. Near the end of the trail by Efagi hasty burials of the dead, all apparently Japanese, were flushed out leaving nothing but rotting skeletons, mostly bone white picked clean by insects. Other more recent dead revealed themselves visually with tattered remnants of uniforms supported by bony sticks, but more easily found by the smell. 2/14, veterans of desert warfare and the scent of the dead, were both repelled and alerted. This difficult terrain, enveloped in ethereal swirling mists and dark thick canopy was a battleground. Japs died here, as had Aussies. Men clutched their rifles more closely, stopping to examine their actions and bores to ensure they were clear of mud and debris.

As could be expected with the battalion almost stretched out from one end of *The Golden Stairs* to the other, the lead company arrived in Efagi in time for supper. The following companies, with the constant stop-and-start of the snaking column, took much longer with the trail company climbing through pounded slick mush. It was tough going, with the last men coming in way past dark. Vic, who came up the last steps on his hands and knees like all the rest, did not even want to consider ever having to go back down through it again. The Papuan native bearers, he knew, would make the trip day after day to keep the resupply lines going. It was the only way to Port Moresby and the hospital if a soldier was severely wounded, now that the Kokoda airfield

153

was in enemy hands. He was just beginning to understand just how isolated the 39th Battalion had been in their desperate struggle against the Jap so-called *South Sea Force. And now here we are to replace them,* he thought grimly.

CHAPTER 12

August 10, 1942, 1/144th Infantry, Yokohama Advance Party, Kokoda airfield, Papua New Guinea

To Hiroshi it wasn't much to look at; a short, grass airstrip on a plateau above the village of Kokoda. Hiroshi didn't know much about airplanes or aviation, but even to him the runway seemed far too short. His suspicions were confirmed by the half a dozen wreckages visible at the far end of the runway blending into the jungle, some burned almost beyond recognition, the others cannibalized for parts. The Australians used the strip despite the obvious hazards, the mud-brown transports could be heard and even visible sometimes through a hole in the high canopy as they flew over the Owen Stanleys'. Hiroshi's battalion hid when aircraft passed overhead even though they were certain the canopy was too thick. The daily bombings on the Track appeared to be random; the Allies were only guessing where they were.

When the battalion approached the airfield and the Australians decided it was too dangerous for the planes to land, Hiroshi had seen the C-47s fly very slowly over the airstrip and drop supplies. Now the airstrip belonged to *Nankai Shitai*, at the cost of over 100 casualties all told. Without the airstrip Australians were denied the steady resupply of rations and ammunition, and the critical casualty evacuation. With it the complete South Sea Force, the rest at sea coming from Rabaul with two battalions of the 144th Infantry Regiment and the newly attached 41st, would be relieved of the enormous strain of a 100 kilometer supply line back to the coast at Buna. The Australians bombed the airstrip daily now, the bomb craters currently unrepaired and the runway unuseable by either side.

It was the critical first target for the two-part mission, the capturing of the only useful airstrip on the entire Kokoda Track. The second part for the Yokohama Advance Party, comprising of over 900 men of the First Battalion plus 100 Formosans, Koreans and about 400 native carriers indentured at Rabaul, was to evaluate the feasibility of using the Kokoda Track to take Port Moresby. The Australian defenders, the 39th Battalion, was some kind of National Guard unit mixed with some of the native soldiers, the Papuan Infantry Battalion. The defenders put up a fierce defense with a couple of reduced companies but were simply overrun by the size of the assault. Unlike the Chinese in Shanghai however, the Australians did not panic under attack, even when 1/144th encircled them with the standard tactic of attacking the defenders with a small frontal assault as a separate, larger force pressed from the flanks. The Australians held their ground with good discipline and excellent marksmanship, withdrawing troops before they were completely trapped by the flanking force.

The Yokohama Advance Party command was surprised. They had anticipated the Australians to be confused and easily routed with the "noisy attack" tactics, deserting their defensive positions as some of the Papuan Infantry Battalion (PIB) had under heavy assault, running into the jungle and vanishing from the battlefield. This is what the small defensive force of Australians at Vulcan Beach on Rabaul had done. But these men of the 39th Battalion, *the men wearing the hats with the big wide rims*—the slouch hats curved and curled from rain and the elements so much a part of the Australian soldier, used good tactics and were worthy of respect. Especially since the Australians counter-attacked multiple times with fierce assaults, surprising the Advance Party who had not established complete defensive positions once they took the airfield.

Within a day the Advance Party overwhelmed the small Australian assault force once again without destroying it. As before the Australians utilized a fighting retreat, slipping out of the noose. The Kokoda airfield was now in the hands of the Japanese First Battalion and the battalion commander intended to keep it that way, reinforcing all positions and moving up as many of the Juki heavy machineguns from his weapons company as he could. They even brought up a pair of 75mm mountain artillery guns, carrying them in pieces all the way from the beach at Buna. These guns turned out to be a blessing, providing excellent attack and defensive support in the flatter, less canopied Kokoda airfield area. The muzzles were lowered to the horizon for point blank fire, using close range anti-personnel munitions when necessary.

Exhausted and hungry, Hiroshi found shade to complete the daily reports demanded by Captain Hashimoto. Hashimoto expected complete casualty lists, available ammunition and when the men ate. This last request, since it came every day, was met with blank stares from the platoon commanders. They received no rations since leaving the coast. The men scrounged and stole from the gardens of the natives or stripped the bodies of the enemy. *What were they supposed to say to their commander?* They understood his request was a statement of responsibility, theirs and his, but how do you manufacture food from thin air?

Fed or not, once *Nankai Shitai* established the defensive positions to protect the airfield their initial mission was officially over. The so-called evaluation phase, the secondary mission was apparently overshadowed by events. The M.O., the Moresby Operation, was no longer a proposal waiting for an engineering report so a decision could be made. It was now a full-fledged combat operation. The battalion's new assignment was to hold the Kokoda airfield until the rest of the South Sea Force arrived, and then press on to Port Moresby. First Company was given the specific assignment to advance south down the Kokoda Track to Isarava, continuing the pressure on the retreating 39th Battalion.

The current timetable placed the remaining two battalions of the 144th and two battalions of the 41st landing at Buna around August 17th. The engineer who accompanied the scouting battalion for whom the Yokohama Advance Party was named, Colonel Yokohama, no longer had a role. The battalion commander of 1/144th was now officially in charge. Captain Hashimoto was vague in his explanation to Hiroshi and the other company officers, only admitting there was some confusion about the initial mission. Who proposed or who authorized it. They knew they would most likely never know. It no long mattered. As junior company grade officers they were not advised or consulted. At the altitudes of the summit a radio transmitter worked well and the orders from headquarters at Rabaul were clear enough. M.O. was on.

So much had changed in the two years since Hiroshi joined the Regiment he couldn't keep it straight in his head. All he knew for sure was his lifelong desire to become an infantry officer was subdued somehow. He did what he was told to do and apparently did it well enough, yet his goals and dreams were muted and lost. Nothing had prepared him for what he experienced after the landing at Rabaul and the dark, dangerous world on the Kokoda. But even the Kokoda could not bury Rabaul from his thoughts. He awoke most days afraid, trusting his thoughts to no one. What he witnessed and did in the Rabaul campaign wrenched his heart; confused, darkened and poisoned his soul. There was no other way to describe it. He accepted the darkness now, the shame and guilt pressed down to someplace inside. He could speak of it to no one. He didn't even have the occasional consolation of Sergeant Kato anymore, since he lost his platoon command to promotion.

In the beginning he felt at times he was surrounded by mad men. Now he recognized he was as mad as they were. Everyone acted the same. It was difficult to sleep, his dreams much like his high state of alertness during the day, except more frightening and with less control. He couldn't sit still anymore, movement the only comfort. Action, any action, was preferable to lying still, his mind crowded with confusing thoughts. Combat, advancing silently towards the enemy for a night assault, or long-range reconnaissance patrols where the potential for violence a heartbeat away, spun them up to a level of alertness that felt normal, but wasn't. Hiroshi sensed the difference, accepting it only because it felt better.

When they killed sometimes it was pure fury and insanity, as if they lost total control of themselves. It was a blind rage with a level of violence he would have never imagined for these men. He understood he had trained some of them himself. When he tried to think hard, how it was before, his thoughts spun, his ability to focus blurred. The blood and splatter were the residue of a butcher shop, the trembling hands of the killers mutant claws of insects drawn to the chemical lust of their leader's scent trail. They couldn't stop, the rage driving them to hack and stab until they dropped to their knees in complete exhaustion. When it was over the survivors who still could, circled aimlessly.

After the invasion of Rabaul Captain Hashimoto recommended Hiroshi's promotion to first lieutenant, then specifically requested through channels to have Hiroshi as his new Executive Officer, replacing First Lieutenant Tomita, killed in an accident on Rabaul. It was unusual, and required a series of interviews with battalion staff, including the battalion commander. This was a man Hiroshi witnessed killing a captured Australian officer with a sword early in the battle for Kokoda, a Captain who refused to give any information about his men's position. The Australian had laughed in the battalion commander's face. It was an awkward interview.

The normal process of promotion would have a new first lieutenant transitioning to a variety of battalion or regimental staff assignments for a year or two, and then selected officers would be groomed for a company command. It was not a sure thing. Only the best officers were selected for command. Everybody knew how it worked, so when the promotion and assignment were approved anyway, Hiroshi was looked upon differently. His professional leap over several more experienced and capable officers was not received favorably by his peers. He felt like a leper.

The Regiment left Kochi City under the cloak of secrecy in late September, 1941. They were transported across Shikoku to Marugami, training in garrison for two months until one day they were loaded onto transports in Sakaide Harbor. No one knew where they were going, but during a brief stopover at Osaka on the main island of Honshu, they were issued khaki summer uniforms and sunglasses. The rumor mill was busy. *Where are we going? If we go east, it must be to fight the Yankees. Are we sure they will fight us?*

For a week the nine transports rolled with the heavy Pacific swell, the troops sequestered below decks sick and miserable in the foul air. One day the ships dropped anchor and the men of *Nankai Shitai* found themselves 1,000 kilometers south by southwest of Japan in the Bonin

Islands group. Supplies and horses were hoisted aboard on slings during the brief respite from rolling seas, although the combat troops conducted exercises in amphibious night landings. The resupply complete, the task force departed December 4, 1941 bound for Omiya Island—Guam, a place no one ever heard of. All the officers knew was the island belonged to the United States, who gained the territory after the war with Spain in 1898. Guam was nearly 300 square kilometers of flat, malaria-free, semi-tropical with a decent, fully expandable airfield. It was defended by less than 400 US Marines and several hundred native Chamorros. The 5,000 man landing force expected little serious opposition.

While at sea the troops were informed of the decision of the Japanese government to declare war on the United States and the simultaneous attacks on numerous allied bases in Malaysia, the Philippines and the great naval base on the island of Oahu in the Hawaiian Islands. This information was met with both cheers and quiet reflection, as men began to realize their lives and the Japan they knew would never be the same. The United States most of them knew about was a reflection of what they had gleaned from movies and books, and lectures from schools and universities. For many it was a bit confusing because the general impression until very recently was for the most part positive. This was obvious in the civilian fashions and fads Japanese young people wore in the late 30s, from the horned rim glasses on their faces to the saddle buck shoes on their feet.

The more educated among them who understood the geographical significance of the North American continent were the most concerned. Not only did the United States have a large, youthful population to drawn from for a potential army, but it also had vast natural resources and industrial capacity to out-produce Japan 10 to 1. The naysayers of this perspective noted the isolationist tendencies of the American population. They have no stomach for war. They almost didn't participate in the First World War. They followed the European war this time around for over three years, showing no interest in getting involved. Americans come from European heritage yet recognize their continent is buffered by huge oceans on both sides. So why would they care about Asians thousands of miles away from their shores? For the young officers who listened attentively to the briefings from their superiors, there were numerous wagers on whether the Americans would negotiate for peace within 30 days, as rumor had Admiral Yamamoto suggesting.

Hiroshi Takahashi was more skeptical. He believed there would be no negotiating for peace with the Americans. His perspective was that of a professional warrior who plans for war, not peace. He understood, as he was taught at the IJA Academy, Americans were like other westerners of European heritage. They were proud and racist people. The American president, Franklin D. Roosevelt, working hand in hand with the existing colonial western allies, the Dutch, French and the British, cut off and denied the Japanese government the ability to purchase oil, steel and rubber on the open market. Over 70% of the steel necessary for the massive ship building endeavor came from the United States alone. In order to build the Japan of the 20th Century it needed those natural resources. No one had the right to simply deny another country access to what it needed, they were instructed. Japan also needed a large standing Army and Navy to protect those natural resources. To build and support such forces require even more of those resources.

Some land holdings had been acquired during the post-WWI years when Japan allied themselves with the Western Allies and was rewarded with former German territories in a number of strategic locations in the Pacific. Many others, truly mineral-rich and critical for manufacturing, would have to be claimed by force. It was a form of destiny for Japan their instructors declared, no one was going to deny them that. The Western Allies decision to restrict the resources, with the United States the key player in the Pacific, was in itself an act of war as far as Japan was concerned.

The old colonial powers currently controlling key Southwest Pacific resources needed to get out of the way. Their time was in the past. The Dutch, French and British had little ability to resist, this was clear. A providence not unlike the *Devine Wind* protecting Japan in the past. The Japanese expansion followed the blueprint developed and used by the same western powers denying Japan the tools for growth. It seemed unfair for them to do so, yet understandable under one circumstance, race. Japan was not viewed as an equal by the Western Alliance. After the First World War, Theodore Roosevelt worked with the other major western powers in the Pacific to establish agreeable ratios of weapons and warships. Japan, as well as China were not given a seat at the table and informed of the ratio agreed upon after the fact. When the Japanese government protested and demanded a seat and a full voice at the table like any other Western power, it was denied. The humiliation was not forgotten, and the lesson taught at the Japanese and Navy Military Academies ever since, with prejudice.

Six days later Hiroshi Takahashi saw his first American soldiers. They were captured, a small group of them, apparently without weapons and off duty on a beach, seemingly unaware of the declaration of war between their two countries. They were joking, smiling, friendly with the Japanese troops who had captured them. Hiroshi, marching inland

160

with his platoon, stared at the Americans like everybody else. A couple of them were caricatures of the American cowboy from the movies; tall, very tall, blond haired and casual. They had their hands deep in the pockets of their dungarees and smoking cigarettes as if they were home in Texas or Arizona someplace. They even waved at some of the men in Hiroshi's platoon and some of the men waved back—until Sergeant Kato barked at them and put a stop to it. *These men are prisoners, they are not worthy of your respect!* Hiroshi peered over his shoulder at Sergeant Kato when he said this, looking back at the Americans. He saw Warrant Officer Miyamoto approaching the group of prisoners and barking his own orders to the Japanese troops guarding them. His last view was Miyamoto slapping the cigarette out of the mouth of one of the tall Americans and a guard knocking the man down with the butt of his rifle.

The invasion force rolled over the sides of the transports and into the landing barges at dawn of December 10th. High winds and heavy swells made the sea state very dangerous for a night landing so it was cancelled. There was little opposition expected. The small force of American Marines protecting the harbor and seaside town resisted at first until the island Navy governor surrendered. He felt he had no choice once he viewed the size of the invasion force. The troops moved inland and easily occupied the capital, Agana. By mid-morning most of the island was secure, with only a few dozen American and Chamorro casualties from the token fighting.

For Hiroshi and his battalion, arriving in the later waves of barges, there was no combat action at all. What combat they heard was mostly the supporting off shore gunfire, which was very brief, and the scattered, distant rifle and machinegun fire from the lead battalion. Almost all of the dead and wounded were Americans or native soldiers of Guam. Some civilian natives died simply being in the way. Killed out on the roads or sitting in their homes. They appeared, as he would learn to recognize the look wherever they encountered native populations, as harmless, stunned beyond belief and frightened to death.

Once the island was secure *Nankai Shitai* began training immediately in the balmy, comfortable environment of the big, flat island. Their next target was nearly 1,000 kilometers south of Guam at Rabaul. Rabaul was on the eastern tip of the island of New Britain, centrally located and about 750 kilometers east of Port Moresby. Taking Rabaul, currently in the hands of a small contingent of Australian troops and colonial administrators and their families, had two strategic purposes. Both were considered years before on the highest level sand table war games of the mid-30s.

The risk posed to Truk was one of the primary reasons the South Sea Force—*Nankai Shitai* was established. Japan won the Caroline,

161

Mariana and Marshall Island groups as mandated territories after World War One, all former German colonial possessions. Truk, the infamous super-secret island fortress dead-center in the Caroline Islands, was about 1,500 kilometers north of Rabaul, therefore vulnerable from attack from the allied base there. It had to be captured. Taking Rabaul and its airfields would also put Port Moresby in reach of Japanese medium range bombers and their tactical fighter support. An absolute tactical requirement if *Nankai Shitai* was going to capture Port Moresby. If you capture Port Moresby, you contain Australia and block the supply line from the only legitimate and serious threat to Japan's goals, the United States.

For most of the South Sea Force the invasion of Guam was not even a good training exercise since they didn't do the landing at night. Guam was benign, tropical and as pleasant as Hiroshi had envisioned the tropics would be. There were no mosquitoes or jungle, and certainly for First Battalion, no enemy to fight. Some of the men including a few of the junior officers, admitted in casual, private conversation they wished they could ride out the war on Guam. It was an admission Hiroshi was flabbergasted to hear. He didn't understand it at all. The morale of the force seemed extremely high, as it should be. They were for the most part experienced men, very well trained and equipped, with a special mission any Japanese soldier would be very proud of. They were, to Hiroshi, the closest example to the Samurai model in the Imperial Japanese Army he could ever envision. They answered directly to their Lord, their master, the Imperial High Command, which meant ultimately the Emperor himself, not just some Army division commander. They were an elite force, especially chosen and trained. If Hiroshi was not so loyal to his brother officers he would consider submitting their names. But he knew this meant *Kempeitai* and Warrant Officer Miyamoto. This he would not do.

Hiroshi didn't know how serious the men were but knew none would dare voice such comments to Captain Hashimoto. He walked away from the discussions without comment or reaction. The other's martial fervor may have diminished but not Captain Hashimoto. Although Hiroshi would admit some growing fear of Hashimoto, he still believed in his heart Hashimoto's spirit, the spirit of the true Samurai, was pure. His leadership would be needed and there was much Hiroshi could learn from him. The Rabaul invasion was slated for mid-January, so battalion staff and company commanders began publishing new amphibious training schedules as aggressive and extensive as ever. The battalion commander made it very clear the Rabaul assault would be at night, and there would be significant resistance. Intelligence reports had the Australian forces there at the battalion level, with a force of militia made up of local Australian colonials and the native force, the New Guinea Volunteer Rifles.

Intelligence officers, when characterizing Australians, were vague. The Western Allied enemies always included the Americans, British, French and Dutch. Australians were discussed as an aside, a colonial country aligned with Britain, like Ireland, Scotland or South Africa. *But these men are not of the same character as the English,* the briefers would note, *they are, after all, the children of British criminals. It would be safe to assume they are especially cruel and racist. We understand they are excellent marksmen and horsemen.* That would be about it, as no one on the battalion or regimental staff had ever been to Australia or met an Australian. They did know enough to state Australians were equipped with British arms, so the assault troops should anticipate encountering the excellent Lee Enfield rifle, the Vickers heavy machinegun, and at close quarters the highly maneuverable 25 pounder antitank gun. There was some discussion of the Australians possibly using, like the British, a Belgian-designed magazine-fed light machinegun, the Bren, but no one knew for sure. The assumption was any such light machinegun would be used in the infantry squad for assault support, similar to the Nambu 6.5mm LMG

Japanese Army infantry tactics embraced assault and maneuver as core elements. The forward assault, almost always at night, accompanied with carefully orchestrated noise and confusion, worked very well against the Chinese and the Russians. The infantry officers pressed the intelligence officers for any hint of the tactical posture of the Australian Army, but there was little to be gleaned, no one knew for sure. The Australians were equipped by the British, many of their senior officers served during the First World War in Europe under British command. The assumption could be made the Australians were trained by the British at Sandhurst or in other British Army training commands, and their tactics were the same. Three Australian Army divisions, the 6th, 7th and 9th, were currently serving in Africa under British command, fighting the Vichy French, Italians and German Armies. Rumor, well secured, suggested those divisions would be coming home to the Pacific to fight the Japanese Imperial Army.

Hiroshi, sitting in the briefing next to Captain Hashimoto per his Captain's request, was as frustrated as anyone about the lack of information about their enemy. The Americans were not impressive here at Guam, but the US Marines were ordered to surrender before Hiroshi's battalion had even made it to shore, so seeing the captured Marines at a distance didn't reveal too much. The Australians sounded more dangerous, more serious as soldiers. Hiroshi noticed Captain Hashimoto

163

was staring at him intently, although his head was turned towards the briefers. Self-conscious when he realized it, Hiroshi tried to turn towards his company commander as casually as he could. He was met with the same glittering black marble pupils when he accompanied Hashimoto on the mountain months before in Shikoku, on the training exercise.

The man still seemed mad, but Hiroshi forced himself to meet his commander's eyes, nodding and bowing once respectfully. Hashimoto leaned over with the same strange thin smile, coming closer until his lips were close to Hiroshi's ears. His voice was low, almost a whisper.

"Australia, even with their huge continent, is a small country, like Japan. Most Australians are farmers or ranchers, used to working for themselves and with their hands. They are country people, not a warrior race, and will be stubborn and difficult to deal with. I know men like these well, they are never easily subjugated, if ever." Hashimoto paused, his head moving back so Hiroshi could see his eyes, black and unblinking. "We will have to kill most of them." It was a statement of fact. Captain Hashimoto held his gaze as if he expected Hiroshi to respond. Before Hiroshi could Hashimoto turned away, his attention back to the briefers.

Hiroshi took a slow breath, and then another, listening to the pounding of his heart. He sensed eyes on him but didn't dare turn around. He was just given, he believed, important information from a man he deeply respected. The confusion he felt and the churning of his stomach added to his discomfort, because he couldn't understand why he felt the way he did. *What is wrong? Isn't this what I want?* A few minutes later the briefing ended, although Hiroshi didn't realize it until the officers around him jumped to attention as senior officers left the room. Lieutenant Nishikawa helped pull him to attention, the annoyance in his face evaporating into concern as he peered at Hiroshi.

"Are you well, Hiroshi?" Hiroshi stared back at Nishikawa before glanced over his shoulder at the retreating back of Captain Hashimoto. Hashimoto did not look back.

ONE YEAR EARLIER, THE LANDINGS

CHAPTER 13

January 22, 1942, Simpson Harbor, New Britain, Bismarck Archipelago

The assault transports left Guam on January 14, the holds and passageways of each ship jammed full with men, equipment and horses. The sea state was rolling and nauseating as before when the men of *Nankai Shitai* left Osaka for Guam, but as the ships transitioned south towards the equator the broiling sun turned the deck plates into scorching iron. Below decks were virtual steam baths, every surface slick and slimy with moisture. Hiroshi shared very uncomfortable and tight quarters with other junior officers a few levels above his men. After being down there he could not conceive how they survived in the troop bays. At least as an officer he was allowed to step up on the deck after dark for brief periods. The men stayed below for days at a time, coming up only occasionally for abandon ship drills held at night. He joined Captain Hashimoto and the other company officers on a daily marathon trek down into the stinking, dark and airless spaces to check on the men. It took several hours every time. Unable to move in almost any direction, the men laid in their cramped, swinging hammocks piled high with their equipment. Their eyes were closed or listless, their chests rising high as their lungs strove to find breathable air in the furnace heat and rotting sewage.

The men attempted to come to attention in their hammocks as Hashimoto joined their midst on the second day of the voyage. Unlike some senior and middle-grade infantry officers who were casual in their uniform standards on board ship, meeting junior officers shirtless and hatless in the sauna heat, Hashimoto insisted on a full uniform to visit the men. His only concession was eliminating a uniform jacket. The Japanese Imperial Army used a number of tailors and styles for their officer uniforms, so there was always a slight variation among the officers when they stood side by side. But everyone had the white, short sleeve cotton tropical shirt, cavalry-style, jodpour drill trousers, peaked cotton officers cap and high leather cavalry boots. He insisted on all of it, including their sword and belt. Other battalion officers were seen in shorts and sandals without weapons, but Hashimoto would only allow such casual attire on the upper decks out of sight from the men. His formality bothered some of the junior officers, who considered it ridiculous considering the conditions aboard ship. These opinions were never expressed near Hashimoto.

Hiroshi did not have a problem in wearing the badges of his rank. He understood too much informality was detrimental to the exacting discipline, but the shipboard environment was so bad he didn't believe the men noticed. Hashimoto asked each platoon sergeant the status of the toilets, which was horrible, the availability of water and the quality of the meals. He brought along the company officers to the berthing areas, gathering around clusters of men hanging from their hammocks like a medical school don with his senior medical students. Hashimoto had the platoon commanders introduce their men to him the first time, although he knew many of them well. It was tedious, yet Hiroshi noticed men sat up attentively and waited to be formally introduced. In turn, Hashimoto looked intently at each man as they bowed their heads respectfully towards him. Hashimoto's acknowledgment of these men was a barely perceptible nod when they again looked up.

Hiroshi also observed how the men followed Hashimoto with their eyes after he left a berthing space. Although wretched and suffering, their attentive gaze was still watchful. Their miserable affect was palpable, yet Hiroshi could sense their awareness of Hashimoto above any other officer present, including the assistant battalion commander, who toured the berthing area only once. As it should be, he decided. As company commander, Hashimoto had more direct control over their lives than any other man in the regiment. Hiroshi couldn't tell if they followed Hashimoto out of respect, adoration or fear. He began to suspect it no longer mattered because these men were his, completely his. Some of the men had been with the company nearly four years, with Hashimoto their commander nearly three of those years. Hashimoto had, as First Lieutenant Shamada suggested to Hiroshi nearly a year and a half before, the complete trust of First Company to do the right thing. In his own heart Hiroshi wanted to believe it too.

As the days passed the daily trudge down the narrow ladders became a sensory horror. The stink of backed up toilets, urine, vomit and the sour-sweet bile of concentrated human sweat rushed up the ladders with the rising wall of heat to trap into their nostrils. It was all Hiroshi could do to control his gag reflex. He pressed his hand against the bridge of his nose and kept going, counting the minutes until they climbed back up the ladders. It was the only thing to make the journey down bearable, knowing they would leave. He felt guilty and more than a little ashamed, but it could not be helped, he knew, as he didn't control where he would stay on the ship. He wanted to believe the visits were good for the morale of the men, and maybe in the case of Captain Hashimoto it was true. The men wanted to see him. They wanted to believe he would bring them honor and triumph in whatever was to come. Somehow Hashimoto, the Samurai leader, would protect his men under the cloak of his pure will and sword. For Hiroshi he hoped it would be enough.

The last day before they dropped anchor off Rabaul was the relief of a known routine. *Nankai Shitai* was landing all three battalions and at night, exactly as they rehearsed dozens of times off shore of Guam and Osaka. Amphibious landings on hostile shores are incredibly challenging organizational endeavors requiring precision, intelligence, planning, training, practice and absolute timing to pull off. This does not include the game changing elements of weather, tides, sea states and unexpected variables like sea walls appearing where beaches should be, or assault forces landing where they shouldn't or assault forces unable to leave the beach. Sand table miniatures of New Britain filled the last hours as officers examined what would be their first real taste of the jungle.

New Britain was part of Australian-controlled Papau New Guinea. It appeared like a lumpy, curvy-side up crescent on a map, nearly 500 kilometers in length, mountainous with deep valleys carpeted with dense, green impenetrable equatorial rain forest. The rain came down heavily and constantly, flooding the plains near the coasts. Disease was ripe with malaria, dysentery and debilitating tropical fevers ever-present threats for natives and colonials alike.

The Australian administrators built their habitations near the east end of the island around the city of Rabaul, although the coconut and rubber plantations were established on the eastern and southern coasts. The AIF 2/22 Battalion and the New Guinea Volunteer Rifles, the Australian colonials who comprised the militia, were well aware the Japanese were coming. Rabaul received constant aerial bombardment since early January. Most of the pressure was on the two airfields on each side of the city. When Hiroshi snuck his way up on deck in the waning light of the evening before the landing, he saw only Navy Zeros from the carriers *Kaga* and *Akagi* flying over the task force. No antiaircraft guns were firing, the sky pink, beautiful and benign. If there was an Australian air force it was destroyed or hiding.

Hiroshi was mildly disappointed after the intelligence brief of the expected resistance. At first it didn't feel like a combat assault. There wasn't the anticipated noise of ship to shore bombardment. He needed to get below and join in the flurry of activities necessary to prepare his men for the long loading train from berthing area to assault barges. But as the twilight raced into tropical carbon sponging light from the water and the sky, he found the shoreline scene mesmerizing. His eyes were drawn to the eerie, spooky glow of the erupting volcano, Mount Matupi, then beyond to black places he knew the city of Rabaul stood with its lights extinguished. As his eyes got accustomed to the darkness, he recognized the shadowy outlines of buildings revealed from ebbing fires around the city. It was both fascinating and horrific to view, because he knew he was witnessing the destruction of a city, the end of a way of life for the inhabitants. He was part of the destruction, which he felt both pride and sadness. He never met an Australian, didn't feel any particular animosity towards them, but tonight, his country, Japan was taking from these Australians everything they had. It was meant to be, it was their destiny. There are always winners and losers, the infantry tactics instructors emphasized. *Tonight, we win.* The scene was perfect, a moon and windless night, air thick with heavy moisture yet crystal clear for miles.

Once it was fully dark the landing operations began. The constant night drills paid off as men, impatient as any confined like rats in airless, steaming boxes for a week would be, reverted to their training. They did not rush about or move unnecessarily. They reached for their gear, stowed carefully in specific order close to their hammocks, falling quietly in line. It would take hours as they shuffled from space to space, one level to another up endless ladders to the open deck. *Nankai Shitai* had performed the pre-landing evolution so many times it was done in virtual silence. Breathing air was a premium so no one, even the most aggressive NCO, wasted effort in talking. Men saved their emotions until they stepped out on deck, the air warm and humid. To the men coming up from the bilges the air was fresh, cool and life-giving. Like Hiroshi, most of them were awed and fascinated by the scene across Simpson Harbor. They murmured excitedly among themselves once on deck to be quickly hushed by officers and NCOs. *Narabe!* (Line up!). *Chikayore!* (Come forward!). *Kokoe!* (Here!). *Asukoe!* (There!). *Ushiro muke!* (Turn around!). *Atoe sare!* (Move back!). *Utu na!* (Hurry!).

With the troops slithering down a half a dozen ropes the barges filled quickly, each carrying 70 men to their assigned beachheads. The bay was smooth as glass, the barges chugging along like lakeside ferries. The sky grew eerie as Very flares were fired over the landing force, casting orange glows sinking like falling suns with the descending flares. The dull ember of the volcano and the burning buildings guided the barge helmsmen. First Battalion, Hiroshi's battalion, was going to assault Rabaul along a road near the ocean coast. Second Battalion was assigned the Lakunai airstrip on the eastside of town, with the Third Battalion landing at Keravia Bay to take the Vunakanau airstrip, southwest of the city.

The landing force was not certain where the Australian defense would be the strongest, but they found no organized resistance for the beachheads for the First and Second Battalions. Nordup Beach, the assigned beach for First Battalion turned out to be a seawall three meters high. Luckily there were no defenders, so the battalion climbed over the seawall to find solid jungle instead of a shoreline road. There was much

169

confusion until the road was discovered, half an hour later. First Company was assigned the lead assault role, but it wasn't Hiroshi's platoon attacking the former colonial administrator's home, abandoned by all except a small group of Australian soldiers left to defend the property. It was the only combat action for First Company on this beachhead. In the growing dawn, Hiroshi caught a glimpse of the corpses of the defenders, slumped over their light machinegun and rifles as the company quick-marched towards Rabaul.

The Australians evacuated the airfields once their air force was destroyed, sabotaging and cratering the runways. The Royal Australian Air Force, useless without their aircraft, escaped to the east coast of New Britain. At a pre-planned assembly point they were picked up by flying boats. The rest of the Australian forces disappeared. Spy and intelligence reports revealed considerable panic among the Australian population the days before the invasion, explaining why Rabaul was a ghost town to the First Battalion scouting units. Most of the Australians fled to Keravia Bay, south of Rabaul's Simpson Harbor. The civilians, the Australian colonials and families not part of the militia, headed south to the end of New Britain. Vulcan Beach at Keravia Bay was the assigned beachhead for Third Battalion, arriving before dawn. Waiting to challenge them was a reinforced AIF infantry company from 2/22.

Third Battalion was under rifle and machinegun fire the moment they stepped out of the barges. Initial infantry assaults inland from the beach were driven back by the heavy fire, protected behind hastily-constructed coconut log bunkers. The battalion landed and deployed 75mm and 37mm wheeled artillery right behind the troops, quickly digging in to put pressure on the Australian defensive line with accurate, pointblank cannon fire. The Australians, only at company strength, held as long as they could in the pre-dawn darkness. As losses mounted under the devastating cannon fire, it became apparent they would soon be encircled and overrun. The commander of the reinforced company gave the order for a fighting retreat back to Vunakanau airfield by first light.

With an unknown size force facing them, Third Battalion requested assistance. As assault companies were freed up the First and Second Battalions ferried them across Simpson Harbor to Keravia Bay. First Company of First Battalion, held back with their small action at the former administrator's house, was on their way to the city limits of Rabaul when they got the request for assistance by radio. Captain Hashimoto volunteered First Company immediately and was granted approval by his battalion commander. Hashimoto turned the company around towards the beach at double-time as the morning sun rose in the sky.

Hiroshi was frustrated by how little there was to see of the battle as the barges approached Vulcan Beach. Over the rumbling diesels and swells thumping the sides of the flat-bottomed barge, he could hear no active gunfire except distant artillery. As they approached the surf line, equipment could be seen strewn all along the beach, some of it tumbling in the surf. Hiroshi didn't see any bodies at first, but as the barge slowed down for the last 100 meters or so, he realized with horror floating objects he assumed were flotsam or equipment were bodies. He stood up on the gunwale and stared down at the water, recognizing the corpses as Japanese. Dozens of them. At first he thought the barge was going to run over some of the bodies, but like corks, the corpses, the appendages heavier in the water if they were face down, bobbed away from the square bow wave at the last second.

No one greeted them on the beach except the dead. It was eerie, blast furnace hot, without a hint of breeze. A few of the bodies rolled far enough up the surf zone to be partially buried in the sand. Soberly, Hiroshi and Lieutenant Nishikawa led their platoons off the barge and up the beach, gripping their Nambu pistols. There was no sea wall to speak of, only a small, meter high rise in the angled sand of the beach, residue of a storm. The sand was like pulverized black pebbles, volcanic rock returning tide after tide. Vulcan Beach was a steep, rocky slope with a small little rise blending into the tropical jungle.

At high tide the barges bounced and slammed into the slope, before grinding back and away. The jungle was beautiful to look at from half a kilometer off shore, a luminescent romantic green. Close up it was dark, very dark green, blending in three human steps into blackness. It gave nothing away. If there were gun positions directly in front, Hiroshi knew he wouldn't be able to see them. You couldn't see two meters into it. Hiroshi peered to his left and right as his men came up, fascinated like himself at this first real glance at the jungle close up, in daylight.

"What are you doing, Lieutenant!" The shout, clearly from Captain Hashimoto, forced Hiroshi to whirl around, not certain if the admonishment was directed towards him or Lieutenant Nishikawa, ten meters to his right.

"Spread out, men! Don't bunch up!" Hashimoto, who also had his sidearm in his hand, waved it impatiently to each side of the beach as he marched directly towards Hiroshi. "The enemy can be anywhere in front of us, this beach is not secure!" No one moved at first, even Sergeant Kato was silent and still as there was nowhere to go except down the beach, joining other men now arriving from landing barges.

"FIRST PLATOON, MOVE TO YOUR LEFT DOWN THE BEACH! MAINTAIN YOUR INTERVAL, TAKE A KNEE AND STAY ALERT!" Kato's voice boomed and the men jumped, shuffling apart to maintain about a five meter interval down the beach before dropping down to one knee, rifles at the ready. Lieutenant Nishikawa's platoon sergeant quickly followed suit, moving his platoon to the right. Captain Hashimoto nodded with approval, his face sweating from the heat. Without referring to any map, he glanced to the left and pointed towards a small outcropping of rock leading right into the surf line about 100 meters away.

"There are secured bunkers on each side of that—promontory, that lead to a trail we can use to get to the airfield." He said this impatiently, his eyes cold as he turned towards Hiroshi, his chin up. "Get First Platoon over there and confirm this is true. Watch for Australian stragglers. If you find the trail, go in no more than 75 meters. Is that understood? Then return and report to me about everything you see. Be back here in 20 minutes at the latest!"

The bunkers were there, two on one side and three on the other. This was apparently one of the strongpoints of the Australian defenses for this part of the beach, the small rocky promontory creating a natural dividing barrier so the gunners on one side could cover two or three hundred meters of beach, and the gunners on the other side could do the same for their side. All and all, there wasn't much of a defense mounted here. It was violent and over quickly as far as Hiroshi could see. Based on the number of bodies washing ashore, the Australian machine gunners did a good job in their coconut log bunkers. At least for a time, until the assault forces managed to find firm enough beach to dig in the guns and blow one side of the bunkers apart with the field pieces. Once one side was destroyed, the other side could be taken with grenades or mortars.

Hiroshi, like the rest of First Platoon, walked around the destroyed bunkers carefully. On one side the crews were literally blown apart by the artillery munitions. The bunkers were partially dug out of sand and utilized deep holes in the rock formation as pits, the crews exposed from the jungle side and top. There must have been six or seven men in this one, Hiroshi decided, but other than bits of flesh embedded in the rock and fragments of shoes and uniform cloth, there was little sign of the former inhabitants.

The men on the other side however, four men by the count of limbs and heads, were killed by grenades, mortars, small arms fire and bayonets. The amount of blood sprayed about in the pits seemed far in excess of what would be held in four men's bodies. Sergeant Kato, sent forward to find the trail, returned in less than three minutes. He confirmed a large, man-made trail large enough to wheel the 75mm mountain gun through, 20 meters behind the destroyed beach bunkers.

Hiroshi, glad to get away from the bunkers, followed Kato carefully over a small knoll down into a dark tunnel affair. The sudden loss of light blinded him temporarily, until he saw natural light slipping in like beams far to his right.

"This way, sir," Kato guided, his hand firmly pulling on Hiroshi's elbow in the direction of the light. Once out of the tunnel Hiroshi viewed in amazement a path, clearly hacked out by hand, about four meters wide. A 75mm mountain gun MIGHT get through this, he thought. The overhead jungle canopy was much lower here, no more than 20 meters above them, the late morning sun filtering through until they were bathed with semi twilight. At night it would be black as pitch. This was about as much light, noonday sun, as the place got. The Australians fought a running retreat here, it was obvious as they crept forward and found more bodies, both Japanese and Australians, on both sides of the trail. Both men had their pistols out, but Kato had already sent two of his men ahead as scouts. After five minutes of creeping forward, stopping often so Kato could examine some of the dead Australians, they came across their two scouts. They were on the side of the trail, looking at an Australian soldier. Left for dead or abandoned in the heat of the retreat, his eyes, set in a pale face framed with an untrimmed red beard, were both open. The eyes followed the movement of Hiroshi and Sergeant Kato as they carefully approached, showing no fear or particular interest.

One of the scouts, the younger of the two, looked at Hiroshi with confusion.

"What do we do, sir?" The Australian, when the soldier spoke, grunted, as his lips moved. His eyes, vacant and dull, moved slowly from the two soldiers to Hiroshi and Kato.

"Mee zoo. Ah, kooda say… Ah." The Australian spoke slowly, but faintly.

One of the scouts started to lean in to listen but Sergeant Kato pulled him back.

"Get back! Did you check him for weapons?" The two scouts looked up at Kato with blank stares so he grunted and pointed his Nambu pistol at the Australian's head.

"*Ugoku na!*" (Don't move!). He barked firmly when he saw the Australian was looking at him. The prisoner responded by bobbing his head slowly, remaining motionless. Kato, pressing the muzzle of his pistol against the man's chest, examined him quickly. Kato and Hiroshi both noticed the Lee Enfield rifle, about two meters in the bushes, probably dropped when the man was hit.

"Mee zoo, ah kooda say.. ah, nad' sum' wata', mate," the Australian said a little louder.

"Mizu o kudasai." Sergeant Kato said quietly. "He speaks a little

Japanese. He's asked for water." The Australian, a bit more attentive eyed them warily, nodding towards Sergeant Kato.

"Mee zoo, ah kooda say. Ya' got that rot, mate, dyin' for sum' wata." The man groaned suddenly laying his head back, his hands and arms trembling uncontrollably for a few seconds. He seemed to calm down, wheezing noisily as he tried to breathe, the face pale and drawn. He turned his head slightly towards Hiroshi as if he knew it would be his decision.

Hiroshi looked up to find the two soldiers and Sergeant Kato watching him in expectation.

"Give him some water, see if you can get some from *them*," he ordered after a moment, pointing at two dead Australians a few feet away. He expected his own men to hesitate in providing water for the enemy, especially when their own water supply was very limited. The Australian was wounded in several places, including deep sword or bayonet wounds in his thigh and upper chest. It was surprising he was still alive. Hiroshi decided the man had been shot and then bayoneted during the fighting and left for dead. His mind raced as he considered this new problem. *A prisoner. Perhaps he can be useful.*

His men searched the two dead Australians and found no canteens. Hiroshi reached for his own canteen but the youngest soldier had already brought out his own and lifted the Australian's head, pouring a little of the precious water into the man's mouth. The mouth gaped like a fish out of water, sucking the water hungrily. The Australian weakly lifted a hand to grasp the canteen, but the young soldier gently pushed his hand away, continuing to drip a small quantity into his mouth.

Hiroshi left the soldier with the wounded prisoner, bringing the older one along with Sergeant Kato to finish their trail exploration. With the discovery of the wounded Australian they moved cautiously along the trail for another 30 or 40 meters. They found several more bodies, mostly Australians. None were alive. The trail seemed to go on forever, as Captain Hashimoto didn't tell him where it would lead. In any case the defenses had been slim on the beach with no secondary defensive line to fall back to. There certainly wasn't any evidence of bunkers back here in the jungle. Once the Australians retreated from the beach they simply pulled back. Where did they go? He felt he needed to continue the reconnaissance up the trail, but he had his orders. 75 meters inland, back to Hashimoto in 20 minutes. Hiroshi glanced at his watch. He was already late.

Captain Hashimoto had Second and Third Platoons form quickly into staggered columns as they entered the dark trail, following First Platoon. He listened carefully to Hiroshi's report. Hiroshi was

174

disappointed with Hashimoto's reaction to the Australian prisoner.

"He is of little value at this point," Hashimoto said dismissively. "Unless we want to be responsible for carrying an enemy prisoner for the next couple of days until we catch up with the intelligence staff. They're over there in Rabaul, although I believe Miyamoto is here with Third Battalion. Miyamoto would like to interrogate him, I'm sure, but Miyamoto isn't here with us. We left the big radio transmitter with battalion and we're out of communications until we catch up with the Third, some 10 or 15 kilometers in front of us. It's no use. By then, the prisoner would be dead."

Hashimoto asked to see the prisoner, stopping long enough to examine the scene of the small battle. The Australian seemed to sense his presence, his eyes opening and focusing on Hashimoto. Hiroshi whispered it appeared the Australian spoke a little Japanese. Hashimoto nodded, stepping closer. He put his hands on his hips and looked at the man curiously.

"Nihon go o hanashi masu ka?" (Do you speak Japanese?). The Australian didn't seem to understand, so Hashimoto snorted, losing interest. He glanced at Hiroshi, signaling him to follow behind. After a dozen steps Hashimoto stopped to look over his shoulder at the Australian. The young soldier still sat by the prisoner, loosely holding his rifle. Hashimoto turned to Hiroshi, raising his right hand to his cloth cap and touched the brim briefly.

"You understand he's not coming with us. We're leaving immediately." Hashimoto nodded towards the young soldier sitting by the prisoner. "He's not up to this, yet. Besides, you don't ask your men to do something that is your responsibility. Is that clear, Lieutenant?" Hiroshi felt his throat constrict and squeeze off his air supply as he watched the black pupils shrink to dots in Hashimoto's eyes. Hiroshi stared at Hashimoto, waiting for the question that would seal his fate. But it didn't come. Moments passed and Hiroshi blinked hard, realizing Hashimoto had walked away leaving only an image of two cold black dots.

Hashimoto moved Second Platoon to the lead and Third Platoon was already passing on the trail. First Platoon was holding somewhere to Hiroshi's left, waiting for his orders to join the column. He took a deep lungful of air as he walked over to the young soldier and ordered him to rejoin his squad. The youth hesitated only for a second. If there was any confusion he didn't reveal it, although Hiroshi did not look at his face. Hiroshi felt his heart pressing up against his throat, making his throat thick. He turned slowly to look at the Australian, stunned when he saw the man looking directly at him with what appeared to be a grin on his dirty, weary face.

175

"Do what yah' gotta' do, mate," the man said quietly. His eyes softened then slowly closed. Hiroshi could hear the man breathing with difficulty. His hand shook as he pulled the Nambu out of the holster, pointing the muzzle at the center of the khaki tunic.

CHAPTER 14

February 3, 1942, South of Rabaul, New Britain

The assault phase of Operation R, capturing Rabaul, was over by January 24th. Interrogation of prisoners and information from friendly natives confirmed there were about 1,400 Australian soldiers, a mix of AIF, RAAF and militia on the island known as "Lark Force". There were also several hundred Australian colonial administrators who fled Rabaul to the eastern side of New Britain. In mid-January when it was apparent the Japanese task force was inbound from Guam, the Australian government evacuated most of the families of the colonial administrators and other non-essential personnel by ship or air. Once *Nankai Shitai* was solidly on the island, capturing both airfields and overwhelming the resistance on Vulcan Beach at Keravia Bay, the defense of Rabaul collapsed. The AIF and militia were at first ordered to retreat from Keravia Bay and regroup at Vunakanau airfield. The RAAF, the only organization with a fallback, were already gone.

An hour after sunrise on January 22nd the reinforced AIF 2/22 company holding Vulcan Beach pulled away from the beach defenses, withdrawing towards Vanakanau airfield. 3/144th of *Nankai Shitai* was fast on their heels, potting HE rounds into the retreating troops, killing or wounding several. By mid-morning the commander of Lark Force, confirming reports of the loss of both airfields and the retreat of the forces holding Vulcan Bay, had run out of options. He ordered all units to disperse independently into the jungle in small groups no larger than company size. As Captain Hashimoto pointed out a couple of weeks later in an officers' call, this was a pointless option for the Australians because there were no pre-arranged meeting areas, food and weapons caches, or escape routes to pick up points. There was no real escape possible, even the novice jungle fighters of *Nankai Shitai* knew this. Only disease, starvation and death waited there.

Lark Force followed its orders, slipping away to the north and south coasts. Combat action was over. *Nankai Shitai* engineers refilled the holes on the sabotaged runways by the morning of the 24th. Navy Zeros were the first to use them to rearm and refuel. The engineers promised the runways would be repaired enough to handle transports and bombers within two weeks. The long range plan to turn Rabaul and its deep water harbor and airfields into a major hub for the Southwest Pacific was underway. *Nankai Shitai* now faced the prospect of mopping up operations for the next several weeks, hunting down the Australian soldiers and civilians hiding in the jungle. *Close the chapter, then the sights would shift to Port Moresby.* The commander of *Nankai Shitai*, Major General Horii, made this clear. The three battalions of the 144th divided New Britain into three search areas before sweeping inland.

Leaflets were dropped by aircraft or distributed by troops to nail to trees. The leaflets explained to the escaped soldiers they would find no food or a way off the island. They faced only eventual starvation and death. The leaflet also left no doubt what would happen to the Australians if they did not surrender. Those captured who had not surrendered by their own free will would be executed.

Captain Hashimoto handed a copy of the leaflet to his officers. Hiroshi stared at the English characters on one side, flipping it over to find, inexplicably, the leaflet printed in Japanese.

"Our soldiers wouldn't distribute it if they didn't know what it said." Hashimoto explained, as if reading Hiroshi's mind.

Hiroshi, like the rest of First Company, was exhausted, hungry and filthy. They covered on foot, in Hiroshi's rough estimation, some 150 kilometers in 10 or 11 days since they stepped off the barges on Vulcan Bay. This distance was often in thick jungle. The company had at first believed, while independent and chasing Third Battalion, combat action was imminent. First Company arrived on Vulcan Beach without any extra rations, the last meal provided on board the assault ships. They were eventually fed after 40 hours on the march when they found Third Battalion. Two other companies sent over responding to Third Battalion's call for assistance were not so lucky. Hiroshi heard these men were raiding gardens and killing livestock in the old plantation compounds to get something to eat.

By January 25th First Company was reunited with First Battalion. Hiroshi ignored the inaccuracy of his friend, Lieutenant Nishikawa, who complained the company never fired a shot during the Vulcan Beach support mission. Hiroshi was aware he was the only man in the company to fire his weapon and kill an Australian soldier that long day. Three other men knew this fact, but he assumed they weren't going to talk about it. Why would they? He didn't want to talk about it either. It wasn't a case of not knowing how he felt. He knew exactly. It didn't feel good, it didn't feel right, the best option was to not think about it at all.

The business of hunting the Australians was first priority, but it was more of a nuisance to the senior commanders. The battalion commanders wanted the patrol quadrants swept and done with. It was as if the regiment was sent to rid the island of pests. This final phase of the operation was simply something that had to be done. The sooner they finished the regiment could move on.

After nearly 10 days Australian soldiers were coming out of

hiding, their rifles held high with white cloths attached to the bayonets. Some of them read the leaflets, rushing out of the jungle when a patrol approached, first calling out loudly and waving their white flags before exposing themselves. Sometimes the Australians moved too quickly, and were shot dead dashing out of hiding. Others still out of sight would call out repeatedly, waiting a few minutes before tentatively sticking out their white flags. Most of these men survived their initial encounter with *Nankai Shitai*.

The hunting patrols were at least company size in the beginning to ensure survivability against a large enemy force. As the days passed *Nankai Shitai* discovered no organized resistance existed. The Australians seemed to be running without direction, satisfied to stay out of sight of Japanese formations. A few native volunteers, perhaps sensing a change of hands in the wind, were coming forward to offer assistance in finding the Australians.

Intelligence officers were wary of these native volunteers, not believing the loyalty of these individuals could shift so quickly. But they realized after their initial dealings there were a multitude of tribal issues and conflicts at play. Among natives who worked with the colonial Australian administration, perceived favoritism had formed among certain individuals and tribes. The natives who resented the favorites saw the arrival of the Japanese as a way to get to the new employers first, sticking their thumb in the eyes of their tribal rivals and former employers.

Once the intelligence officers understood the motives, they took advantage of the situation and rewarded the volunteers. For their part, the natives seemed to have no qualms whatsoever pointing out other natives who supported the Australians, and then revealing in great detail the known escape paths of the Australian Army. If they were not aware of the violent consequences of their actions at first, they learned soon enough. Natives they singled out as Australian collaborators, whining and trembling with fear, were taken away by *Kempeitai* and never seen again. Australian soldiers, sick and hungry, were captured in what they thought were secret caves and lairs. It didn't seem to affect the turncoats in the least. This didn't sit well with most of *Nankai Shitai* soldiers, born to loyalty and the tight sense of brotherhood within the rifle companies. They didn't trust these natives at all. They were grown men, tall and lanky with dyed bushy hair yet appeared sly and full of nervous energy, like children. Their mouths, often bloody red from chewing betel nut all day, moved constantly as they chattered away or sang loudly in groups or by themselves.

The native volunteers made the final sweeps for Australian soldiers a targeted affair. It was still not easy. Nothing about getting around New Britain was easy. Third Battalion turned south towards the plantations near the south coast and First Battalion turned northwest to sweep the coastal areas around to the west. The native volunteers revealed most of the escaped Australians would be found in those two areas. After 10 days of constant movement with only six hot meals and light field rations, First Battalion was exhausted. Patrolling the rain forest unprotected insured early cases of malaria and other debilitating diseases. The heat, humidity, poor sanitation and sleeping in the open were taking a heavy toll. Casualties were mounting without a single shot being fired.

Some of the areas the natives pointed to from a small hilltop promontory were 10 or 15 kilometers away, with no known road or trail. Captain Hashimoto, Hiroshi and the rest of the battalion officers looked at the green carpet of the jungle through their binoculars with growing dismay. There were roads carved out in a few key areas on New Britain to support the plantations, but in between there were vast areas of dense, green triple-canopied jungle. The Australians may have run into the bush in their haste to escape, but the *Nankai Shitai* commanders were no longer interested in another week hacking through the jungle to get to the other coast. They were losing too many men.

Orders came quickly, with the companies heading in a variety of directions. First Company was assigned the most remote patrol, requiring the use of small boats to negotiate kilometers of coastline to reach the northwestern swamps and river outfalls. The patrol would take several days. On the narrow road leading to the sea, they met trucks sent from Simpson Harbor and opened crates of provisions. They loaded their rucksacks with rations and ammunition and stood by the boats. Hiroshi noticed a small staff car unloading several soldiers, including Warrant Officer Miyamoto. The sight of Miyamoto made his neck muscles tighten up. Hiroshi had not seen Miyamoto since a few days after the initial invasion. This time Miyamoto wore an officer's tunic clearly displaying the armband of *Kempeitai*. All of the other soldiers with him wore similar armbands.

Hiroshi watched carefully as Miyamoto approached the battalion commander, who greeted him warmly. Miyamoto saluted and was quickly redirected towards First Company. Miyamoto approached Captain Hashimoto with one of his *Kempeitai* NCOs in tow. As he came closer his dark eyes shifted slowly towards Hiroshi, cold but penetrating. He saluted Captain Hashimoto with a perfunctory lift of his hand to his cap while simply nodding to Hiroshi.

"We're coming with you, Captain—if you don't mind?" He said by way of greeting in a quiet voice. Hashimoto, a thin smile on his face, shook his head. The *Kempeitai* NCO stayed a few steps behind Miyamoto, stopping briefly to salute Captain Hashimoto. Unlike Miyamoto, the NCO was a large young man. He seemed extremely fit and was easily a head taller than Miyamoto.

"This just confirms we have an important assignment, glad to have you, old friend!" Hashimoto and Miyamoto shook hands warmly. Miyamoto turned slightly to introduce the large *Kempeitai* NCO, who bowed his head briefly.

"This is Sergeant Inoue. He is my assistant investigator. We've been with Third and Second Battalion as we hunt for the enemy. We haven't captured the Australian force commander yet, but we received information he might be on the west coast to be picked up. Maybe by submarine. General Horii wants to get to him first if we can find him. I'm skeptical, it's very remote and rough country, according to my sources. As we pick up prisoners, we'll get the picture. In any case, we'll try to stay out of your way, Captain." Hashimoto nodded thoughtfully as he digested this information. He reached out to put his hand on Miyamoto's arm, fingering the brightly colored armband.

"No, Miyamoto, we'll stay out of *your* way!" With a self-effacing shrug, Miyamoto seemed pleased before turning his attention towards Hiroshi.

"Lieutenant Takahashi, you look tired but well! Hopefully you're finding this invasion experience interesting?"

"I am, Warrant Officer Miyamoto." Miyamoto's eyes darkened and focused on Hiroshi's face with the same burning intensity of Captain Hashimoto. Miyamoto stared without blinking, totally unnerving to Hiroshi because the sensation was that of a searchlight, probing deep into the recesses of his brain. It took a moment or two for Hiroshi to realize Miyamoto was waiting for him to continue.

"I'm a little disappointed we have missed out on any of the action," he stumbled clumsily, immediately angry with himself. He cleared his throat and spoke clearer and with more authority. "We came to assist Third Battalion when they requested it on Vulcan Beach, but they chased the Australians away so quickly we never had the chance to engage them. We've been hunting them, but it's—it's not really combat. We've captured or shot desperate men, sick and starving." The searchlight seemed to turn off, the eyes retreating somehow. Miyamoto nodded thoughtfully before exchanging glances with Captain Hashimoto.

"What do you think of our enemy, Lieutenant, of the Australians?" Miyamoto continued. Hiroshi could only think of the red-bearded soldier he shot on the trail behind Vulcan Beach. Miyamoto's eyes closed slowly to slits.

"I haven't had a lot of personal contact with them, Warrant Officer. What I've seen of them, as prisoners, they seem very interested in staying alive, like any other man. But beyond that as soldiers, they seem tough and resourceful, and brave. I find them brave men." Hiroshi didn't know what else to say. After a brief pause when Miyamoto didn't respond, Hiroshi stepped back before glancing at Captain Hashimoto, who looked at him evenly. When Miyamoto and Hashimoto were together Hiroshi felt like he had no allies, he was alone. *Why the hell do they look at me like that?* He had to get away from them.

"If you'll excuse me, sir, I have to check on my men. Warrant Officer." Captain Hashimoto nodded his approval with no expression while Miyamoto turned away, dismissively. Hiroshi's face burned as if he were embarrassed or shamed, but felt neither. He felt *angry,* with no idea why. He stalked off as purposely as he could, spotting Sergeant Kato refilling canteens. Kato glanced over at Hiroshi and pointed at a half dozen canteens, soaking wet in their wool carriers.

"Want a couple of spare canteens, sir? Clean water is going to be hard to come by for the next couple of days. The supply truck brought several dozen spare and I took as many as I could before the other platoon sergeants spotted them. Most of the men took a spare." Hiroshi nodded his thanks as he picked up two, stuffing both into his already heavy rucksack. Kato picked up the last of the canteens, peering cautiously over his shoulder before turning to Hiroshi with sudden hard eyes.

"Is *Miyamoto* coming with us, sir?" Hiroshi didn't answer, he didn't have too. His lowered glance gave it away. Kato rose as his face quickly flushed with red. He walked up to Hiroshi, his nose almost touching his Lieutenant's chin.

"We're soldiers, Lieutenant Takahashi, you and me. We do what we have to do as soldiers, but we do it with a purpose. That man— those—are *mad dogs.* This is like China, Lieutenant." He hissed under his breath, spitting the words out with anger and fear in his eyes. Hiroshi simply stared down at him. "Hunting prisoners. You will not believe what is going to happen!"

Kato made his point, retreating backwards a foot or two, his eyes still defiant. Hiroshi sensed the man wanted to say much more but didn't, either out of his own self-discipline or fear he had already revealed too much to Hiroshi. Hiroshi knew Sergeant Kato was aware he shot the Australian soldier on Vulcan Beach. Kato was not present to hear the conversation he had with Captain Hashimoto, so he may not know all of the circumstances. The two of them certainly never had a conversation about it, but Sergeant Kato was waiting with First Platoon

182

on the side of the trail and probably spoke with the soldier guarding the Australian. Everyone heard the pistol shot. Everybody knew what happened in the platoon. The two of them stared at each other until Kato brought himself to attention and bowed slightly. When he looked up at Hiroshi again the anger had vanished.

"The platoon is ready to move, Lieutenant."

"What is going to happen, Sergeant Kato?" asked Hiroshi in a quiet voice. It was more of a statement of fact than a question. His sense of dread and fear churned his bowels over. Kato didn't respond and Hiroshi wasn't sure he spoke the words out loud. All he knew for certain was he heard them in his head.

It took all day to motor the small launches outside the surf zone to get around the 45 or 50 kilometers to the northwestern shore. With no Allied airfields in range, air attacks were not a concern. What looked like a straight visual 10-15 kilometers from high ground was a long curving distance roundabout by sea. The northwestern shore was where the big rivers flushed their deluge from the mountains out to the trade currents, turning the surf brown and dangerous. In the tidal swamps where the rivers broke up the high green canopy there were small islands close to the shoreline. The native turncoats believed the Australian Lark Force soldiers, with possibly the commander and some of his senior staff, were here. In hiding and waiting for a submarine pickup. After a quick evening sweep up the river to ensure there were no enemy lurking about, First Company tied up the boats and bivouacked for the night on two islands close to shore, hoping for breezes to push away insects.

No one got much sleep. Eaten alive by the mosquitoes, the company misjudged the tides and a third of the company was nearly swept away about 0200 in the morning. Most of the men spent the night clinging to and climbing up as high as possible on the island trees, only to discover every crawling insect on the island had climbed up with them, most of them large and capable of painful bites. There was a reported sighting of a crocodile, keeping men even more alert. It was a tough night. Most thought the first 10 days on New Britain were hard and the environment inhospitable. Out on the tidal swamps everything stepped up to a new level of misery.

The humidity and constant exposure to warm, vile brackish water destroyed leather boots, belts and harnesses. Guns, swords, knives—anything made of metal rusted to the point of being inoperable within one day if not meticulously cleaned, dried and oiled. Even bolt-action rifles corroded shut if left alone. Human skin housed in soaking wet leather boots for days at a time suffered the most. The skin, dead white when exposed to sun and air, flayed off to reveal limbs resembling red, raw pulsing sacks of blood, sinew and pain. Captain Hashimoto at first sent the patrols out in full platoon strength, but the environmental casualty rate was so high most platoons had only 10 or 15 men effective any given day. Hashimoto kept the sick and lame on the islands where there was more dry area. They brought along a huge radio and collapsible antennae Hashimoto used to report day search progress, showing less results each day they remained.

The patrols went out in the small boats, motoring against the current of the rivers to explore the river basin. By the end of the second day all of the larger river islands close to the shoreline had been explored, with no sign of Australian soldiers. The two native volunteers who joined the company for this patrol chattered among themselves and managed to convey, to Hashimoto and Miyamoto, they now believed the Australians were farther up the river. This turned out to be correct, as on the morning of the third day a patrol from Third Platoon was fired upon as they were tying up their boats to explore a dry stretch of river beach. This patrol was particularly well armed. A Nambu light machinegun team quickly set up and began delivering a high rate of fire into the forest where the fire has originated. Two grenadiers equipped with small 50mm mortars also set up and lobbed high explosive rounds from the open beach up and into the forest. Some of the mortar rounds were exploding on impact with the high canopy, but shrapnel was still raining down to good effect.

The patrol leader was First Lieutenant Tomita, the company executive officer. After a couple of minutes of furious machinegun fire and a dozen mortar rounds he ordered a cease fire. There was no fire coming from the forest, only dead silence. Tomita was about to send a squad up into the forest to reconnoiter when there was a cry, a man's cry, followed by what sounded like multiple human voices. It was hard to tell in the little cavern of the beach, surrounded by high canopy. The sound echoed. Suddenly at the edge of the beach a rifle poked out behind a tree with a light-colored cloth attached to the bayonet lug. It waved to and fro, accompanied with more human crying or howling. Tomita and the rest of the patrol looked at one another in wonder, because the sound was more like the crying of a rain forest monkey. It was high-pitched, frightened and weak. Every gun turned in that direction.

CHAPTER 15

February 5, 1942, Northwest coast of New Britain

Hiroshi was lucky he saw the hand-fired red flare from the bow of his boat. He ordered the helmsmen of the boats to beach the craft up against the gigantic roots of a hulking, dark monster of a tree when by chance he looked up river. The large, pistol-style flare was designed to shoot its projectile no more than 25 meters into the air. The heavy canopy of rain forest jungle rose anywhere from 30 to 60 meters in height. The flare glowed at the top of its arc at the junction of the river where the canopy was lower, a half of a kilometer away for less than a second.

He ordered his helmsman to stop the boat, which immediately sent it drifting backwards in the strong current, spinning broadside to collide with the other boat. Without waiting for orders the helmsman engaged the throttle and regained steerageway to maintain his distance from the other boat. Hiroshi ignored the confused chatter of his men, never taking his eyes off the river junction as he counted to himself *ichi, ni, san, shi, go* when he saw another flare. He never heard the pop of the flares over the roar of the river.

As a patrol leader Hiroshi carried his own flare gun, with instructions to fire two red flares into the sky five seconds apart if he needed assistance. He quickly opened the box by his seat, loading the single-shot device with a green flare with a spare in his hand, holding it over his head and firing in into the air. Surprised with the powerful recoil, Hiroshi reloaded and fired again, forgetting to count to five. First Lieutenant Tomita was supposed to be patrolling a few kilometers south of Hiroshi's patrol area, so he ordered the boats cautiously upriver, warning his men to check their weapons. Either Tomita was working too far north or Hiroshi had misjudged and drifted too far south. He assumed the error was his.

Tomita was waiting for Hiroshi, directing their boats to a wide and clear beach. Ten meters up from the beach there was a small muddy cove, perfectly rounded out in a semi-circle with a two or three meter high embankment. In the center of the cove sat, or in the case of two of them, lay, four Australian prisoners. Two of Tomita's men were guarding them, but it was very obvious the four men were in no shape to escape. Their uniforms were tattered rags, filthy and mud soaked, indistinguishable from the matted, scraggly beards and hair on their heads. It was hard at first for Hiroshi to recognize the prisoners as white Europeans because of the dirt, mud and grime on their skins. He walked

185

up to them slowly, carefully as one would approach wounded animals. The Australians were covered with raw sores and injuries of all kinds, but made no sound whatsoever. All four men, even the two lying down, had their eyes open, wide open, staring fearfully at Hiroshi and his men as they approached.

"I'm grateful you saw my flare, I didn't figure anyone would see it with the canopy," sighed Tomita, wiping sweat from his face with a dirty handkerchief. "I didn't know what I was going to do, I've got the weapons section with me and I have no room in my boats for these prisoners." He glanced expectedly at Hiroshi, who didn't respond while staring at the prisoners. During the last few days before they were assigned the river patrols First Company had seen hundreds of Australian prisoners, mostly filthy and starving. But these men seemed to have gone through some other level of experience. It could be seen in their eyes. They had not expected to survive. *It wasn't fighting us,* Hiroshi considered, watching them.

"We don't have any food to spare and you can see these poor bastards haven't eaten anything in 10 or 12 days, maybe since the invasion," continued Tomita. "We almost shot one who came rushing out of the jungle after we ordered a couple of them to stop. He just stood up and started walking towards us. My Nambu gunner just about stitched him right then and there until I ordered everyone to hold their fire. You could see the wretch was half out of his mind. You should have heard them, they didn't sound human. They just babbled and carried on, saying anything that came into their heads, like madmen. They seemed glad to see us, but then the next minute they would scream like frightened monkeys, or rats!" *That is exactly what they look like,* thought Hiroshi, *rats. Starving rats.*

"I don't think any of them understand Japanese, but they are so messed up I doubt they would recognize their own language if they heard it right now. In fact, I'm not even sure they understand who we are. They just want something to eat." Tomita sighed again, frustrated. He turned to examine Hiroshi's face carefully before leading Hiroshi a few meters away from the prisoners. Tomita brought his arm completely around Hiroshi's shoulders to bring their faces closer together, but it wasn't a bond of friendship, it was to keep the conversation private. Hiroshi thought he knew what Tomita wanted to talk about.

Tomita ordered Hiroshi to take the four prisoners down the river personally, instead of assigning the task to Sergeant Kato or some other subordinate. One of the prisoners was an officer, Tomita said, and Warrant Officer Miyamoto would want to interrogate him. Hiroshi noted Tomita watched for Hiroshi's reaction over this bit of information, but

Hiroshi again did not respond. Sergeant Kato and the rest of Hiroshi's patrol would stay with Tomita's men and return with them in their own boat. With Hiroshi, a helmsman and two riflemen, there would be just enough room for the four Australian prisoners in one boat.

"I doubt any of these poor bastards is the Lark Force commander, but we have our orders," Tomita said quietly. "In the case of prisoners, it's always good to have them accompanied by an officer if possible when you approach the lines, so there will be no—incidents." Tomita said this matter-of-factly while his eyes searched Hiroshi's intently. After a moment Tomita let his gaze drift down the river before returning his attention to Hiroshi.

"Do you know who Warrant Officer Miyamoto is, Lieutenant? I know you've trained with him back in Japan during our field exercises, but do you know what his real role is?" Hiroshi was wary, having never worked that closely with First Lieutenant Tomita in the past since Captain Hashimoto had taken upon himself to personally guide Hiroshi's professional development. Hiroshi didn't know how much he could trust him.

"Yes sir," Hiroshi answered after a pause. "I knew he was *Kempeitai* before we left Japan, he had previous dealing with some of my men. They told me. I mean, sir, it's kind of out of in the open now since the invasion. He wears the armband openly."

Tomita nodded, watching Hiroshi thoughtfully as he stepped back. Now it seemed it was Tomita's turn to be wary. Hiroshi sensed, like the discussion he had with Sergeant Kato a few days before they started the river delta patrols, a realization on the part of Tomita that Hiroshi did not quite understand something. It frustrated and flared in a rush of heat to his face, a flash of anger he was barely able to contain. Tomita just watched him and said nothing.

"What is it about Miyamoto *I don't understand?*" Hiroshi spat out, with more acrimony than he meant to convey. If there was a reaction from Tomita from the outburst, it revealed itself in the slightest crinkling around his eyes, nothing more. Hiroshi, who prided himself on his self-discipline, immediately regretted the words and his tone. He bowed his head towards Tomita and held it there for several seconds. As his head came back up, he straightened his back and sharply saluted.

"Forgive me, First Lieutenant Tomita," he said humbly, "I spoke out of turn, and—rashly." Their eyes met, but unlike Hashimoto and Miyamoto, Hiroshi did not see Tomita's eyes flash black with menace or aggression. They stayed brown and intense, but Hiroshi felt no predatory sweep across his skin.

"You do not have the experience of serving in China with us, Lieutenant Takahashi," Tomita said in a low voice. "I think I can understand your frustration of how certain things are—left unsaid. I will say this, Lieutenant, for you to consider. The rest you will find out on your own soon enough. There are certain operational tactics used by *Kempeitai* many of us do not agree with. There is no real protection from them, not even those officer tabs you wear on your collar." As if to emphasize this point, Tomita clutched his own insignia on his khaki blouse.

"Remember that, Lieutenant. No protection." He stepped in closer to Hiroshi, lifting an arm toward the high canopy behind him. "Here in the bush, power is fleeting. You must not give it up! You are a Japanese Imperial Army officer, and you have your duties and responsibilities. There are those who will try to take that power away from you when we are in the field. *Don't let them do it!*" This time Tomita's eyes did flash with intensity, but Hiroshi did not feel threatened in any way, only challenged.

"Deliver the prisoners to Captain Hashimoto directly, reporting that I believe one of the prisoners to be an officer, based on his identity papers. I'll point him out to you. Please ensure our commander sees the prisoners with his own eyes so he understands their physical condition. Is that understood? Not to Warrant Officer Miyamoto or any *Kempeitai*. Don't let them have these prisoners unless Hashimoto turns them over to them. Remember, these are my prisoners, and I'm directing you to deliver them to our commanding officer, and to no one else. You outrank Warrant Officer Miyamoto and I outrank you. You are only following orders."

Going downstream with the rushing river was much faster in parts, although more hazardous. Heavy rains in the mountains sent a deluge of fresh water into the delta swamps, overflowing the banks of what was high ground in the morning. Logs, disintegrated and whole, rushed downstream to clog and jam up narrow passages once clear, creating difficult and dangerous obstacles blocking the boat and anything else floating downstream. What should have been a half an hour boat ride turned into a high speed maze taking three times longer. One moment the boat was moving 15 kilometers per hour, the next it was jammed tight against a stack of thick logs blocking the passage. Men had to get out of the boat, no easy task in the turbulent stream, to kick or push the logs and debris downstream. Several bodies, bloated and gray-brown and presumably Australian, were spotted pinned up against river banks or distant tree branches. If the four Australian prisoners in the boat noticed the bodies, they gave no sign. They sat or laid in the bottom of the boat as before, silent and wide-eyed, their ability to process any additional misery mercifully long departed.

It was apparent as soon as they beached the boat the third patrol sent out in the morning had already returned. Their boats were secured with captured prisoners visible up on the dry island. As one of Lieutenant Nishikawa's NCOs explained, one boat was still being used to ferry prisoners. The Second Platoon patrol went up a different river tributary where they had discovered over 30 Australians stranded in the middle of the river. The Australians were sitting on a long, narrow island just two kilometers up river. The NCO believed the Australians were crossing the river as the river was rising and were trapped when the banks overflowed and they had nowhere to go. They were waiting for the stream to eventually subside when the two patrol boats appeared. They didn't seem surprised since they could hear the boats coming, but they didn't put up a struggle as there was no cover or place to hide. It didn't matter since only a couple of the soldiers possessed weapons, which were surrendered at once. Unlike the four men First Lieutenant Tomita captured and turned over to Hiroshi, the Australians in this stranded group seemed more alert and healthy.

Hiroshi could see the new prisoners were bound with ropes behind their backs and forced to sit down in two small groups about 10 meters apart. He counted six in one group, eight in another. They seemed aware of their surroundings but moved cautiously. The Australians were very interested in the prisoners in his boat, craning their necks until their guards barked at them, ordering them to lower their heads. This was demonstrated by directly pointing a bayonet-tipped rifle at them, then slowly bringing the muzzle to the ground. It was effective communications as the heads went down immediately as a group. Hiroshi's prisoners, bound by their hands but in the front, were both carried and led off the boat. They didn't seem to have any idea where they were, or particularly cared. Hiroshi's men took them up the beach where he had them sit or lie down until he could find Captain Hashimoto. He remembered his orders and First Lieutenant Tomita's warning, sending one of his NCOs as a runner to find Hashimoto while he remained with the prisoners.

Captain Hashimoto arrived a few minutes later, his face dark, fatigued and preoccupied. Hiroshi felt his temples throb with sharp pain when he saw Warrant Officer Miyamoto a few steps behind. Miyamoto glanced over at the prisoners, his face revealing nothing. The black eyes flashed before they turned towards Hiroshi. Miyamoto was wearing an ordinary tropical officer's short-sleeve khaki shirt, but it was opened two buttons down, revealing his ropey, thickly muscled neck and chest. His exposed skin, repulsive somehow, was coated slick and slimy with sweat. As he drew closer the khaki was dotted darkly with what could only be blood. Once he recognized what it was, Hiroshi could clearly see the blood droplets and powerful spray pattern up the khaki shirt and across Miyamoto's face. It instantly sickened him, the nausea welling up in this throat.

"You asked for me, Lieutenant Takahashi?" asked Hashimoto, his words edged with exhaustion and irritation. "Your runner stated you personally brought these prisoners and one of them is an officer? Are these it? Just these four?"

After seeing the other groups of prisoners reportedly up to 30, Hiroshi felt a little shame and embarrassment. Nonetheless he conveyed his orders from First Lieutenant Tomita to release the prisoners only to Hashimoto, pointing out the prisoner Tomita believed to be an officer. Hiroshi stated his report while keeping his eyes focused on Hashimoto, agonizingly aware Miyamoto was standing right next to him, blood-sprayed shirt and all, staring hard.

Hashimoto grunted, casting his eyes towards Miyamoto before reached out and touching Hiroshi on the arm with a fatherly pat. He stepped back, sighing loudly and placing his hands on his hips. Hiroshi felt better, but sensed something had changed. The Australian First Lieutenant Tomita identified as an officer was one of the two soldiers too weak to sit up. Hiroshi noticed one of the other soldiers who could sit up recovered enough from his stupor to pull the other man's head into his lap, placing his bound arms around the other's neck protectively. Hashimoto followed Hiroshi's eyes and looked at the men for a moment, then nodded at Miyamoto.

"Do you want them?" he asked Miyamoto. Miyamoto didn't even look back at the Australians, his eyes were on Hiroshi.

"No, Captain," Miyamoto said quietly, "We've found out what we needed to know. In fact, sir, in my opinion we've essentially completely our mission. There is no longer a reason to explore this area. The men that are here will be useless as soldiers, and most will be dead within another week."

Captain Hashimoto nodded his head, looking around slowly before turning his attention back to Hiroshi. "What Warrant Officer Miyamoto says is true, Lieutenant, our mission is complete. He interrogated a number of prisoners from this large group Nishikawa stumbled across, and we learned that Lark Force, when they split up, tried to give out some misleading information. The commander of Lark Force went south instead of north, and there never was any plan to have anybody picked up by submarine. Not here on the western side, anyway. They just weren't that organized. There are hundreds of Australians out there somewhere, and they're going to be in as bad a shape as these men we've found here. They are starving and diseased, half out of their minds from the swamp water and heat. In a week or two they will all be dead. The jungle will do the job for us!" Hashimoto flashed his strange half-smile, scratching his armpits before picking an insect off of his arm. He examined it for a moment before crushing it between his fingernails, flicking the corpse out into the sand. Hashimoto stepped in closer to Hiroshi again, placing his hand on his shoulder. His eyes flashed black and shining.

"Lieutenant, I'm going to transmit our report based on what we know, and recommend we load up the company and head east up the coast and out of these swamps before we become just as sick and as dead as these Australians!" He slowly turned his back on the Australian prisoners, his face close to Hiroshi's. He looked up and waved Lieutenant Nishikawa over as Nishikawa came up the beach with five more Australian prisoners.

"Have your men take your new prisoners up over there with the other prisoners. Is that the last of them?"

"Yes sir. We found one of the prisoners had died while we were preparing them for transport, so we just left him there."

"Very good. We'll still report 30, plus the four Takahashi brought from Lieutenant Tomita. Tomita may bring down some others, but I doubt it. Not live ones anyway, since he has no ability to transport them." With that statement, Hashimoto stepped back and looked at his two young lieutenants. Miyamoto had remained exactly where he was, silent and watchful.

"Our mission is over," Hashimoto repeated, smiling at each in turn. "Something to celebrate, if the conditions weren't so horrific and not a bottle of sake to be found within a 100 kilometers!" Turning serious, he hiked up his wide leather belt harness to rest both hands on the grip of his *katana*.

"We have, I believe, 23 prisoners. 34—correction, 33 live prisoners in total until maybe a half an hour ago. Warrant Officer Miyamoto has interrogated and taken care of 10 of the prisoners. That leaves us 23. We cannot take them with us, we have sick and lame soldiers who will require more space than normal in our small boats, and we will be severely overloaded with our own men. There is no question they will be left behind. We are under no obligation therefore to extend any particular welfare to these enemy soldiers. These prisoners, these Australians, if left exactly where they are right now, alive, would be dead in a week. There is nothing to eat, no sanitary water to drink, and they have nothing to look forward to except a slow, miserable death." Hashimoto let his words sink in for a few moments before his face slowly spread into his half smile.

"We are going to take advantage of this opportunity to do some

191

training. Many of our men have joined the company since China, such as you, Lieutenant Takahashi. Others served in China but after combat operations ceased and we became a garrison force, like you, Lieutenant Nishikawa."

Hashimoto stepped closer to both of them as he spoke, but Hiroshi noticed when Hashimoto addressed Nishikawa, the color completely drained from Nishikawa's face, his eyes sudden saucers of fear. If Captain Hashimoto was aware of the effect on Nishikawa he didn't show it. Instead he rested his eyes on Hiroshi, unblinking black hard dots completely disconnected to the fixed, almost sneering half smile as the eyes, always watchful, locked on.

"Warrant Officer Miyamoto will assist you in setting up your training evolution," Hashimoto continued, watching Hiroshi for a long moment before turning to include Lieutenant Nishikawa.

"Take one of the larger groups of prisoners, Lieutenant Takahashi, and all of the men from your platoon who are physically fit enough to do some exercise. Lieutenant Nishikawa, join Lieutenant Takahashi with any available men from your platoon. They will need their rifles and bayonets. We'll do this training evolution in two phases. The second phase will be this evening when First Lieutenant Tomita returns from his patrol. He has some of your men, Lieutenant Takahashi, and Tomita will also want to have his inexperienced men to participate."

Hashimoto placed his hand firmly on Lieutenant Nishikawa's shoulder in a fatherly gesture. Nishikawa's fearful affect was subdued slightly, his color returning and his eyes less afraid, although he would not directly look at Hashimoto, his head slightly bowed.

"You are an infantry officer, Lieutenant," Hashimoto said slowly and quietly. "You will do fine." The grip tightened, Hashimoto's powerful arm gently shaking Nishikawa to and fro until Nishikawa looked up into Hashimoto's eyes. There was still fear in Nishikawa but he stood up straighter.

"I will do my duty, sir," he gasped, breathing hard, "I will not let you down." Hashimoto stared hard at Nishikawa, his face turning colder like his eyes, the smile vanished. He nodded to Nishikawa, acknowledging him before returning to Hiroshi.

Hiroshi forced himself to meet Hashimoto's eyes, still frightening and invasive. In his mind he could only suspect what the *training evolution* involved, but he was paying attention when Hashimoto so casually noted the 10 men interrogated by Miyamoto were *taken care of* by Miyamoto. To be *taken care of* was to be removed from the list of live prisoners, so it didn't require much imagination to understand what this meant. The prisoners on this river island wouldn't be coming with them. He heard this before from Captain Hashimoto on the backside of Vulcan Beach. *We can't take him with us.* For Hiroshi, who followed his orders and took the life of the unarmed and wounded Australian soldier, the prospect of the immediate future clutched at his intestines. When Hashimoto left Hiroshi glanced over at Lieutenant Nishikawa then quickly looked away. There were no tears on Nishikawa's face, but the man's eyes, unfocused and looking in Hiroshi's direction, were full of misery and confusion.

The prisoners knew something was wrong and were very afraid. The Australians had nothing to eat of any real substance since the invasion two weeks before. They simply ran into the jungle in small groups hoping to find some subsistence. What fresh water was available could be found in the hollow vines running down from the tropical canopy 30 to 60 meters above them. The water was there but it required climbing as the vines were rarely within easy reach of a man. As men weakened, their ability to climb or even think clearly lessened every day. The ground, leeched of nutrients from constant rain, grew no life-giving fruits or grain. Because of it, the jungle had no edible small mammals or large mammal predators to follow up the food chain. There were birds, millions of birds, but they inhabited the upper reaches of the canopy and were rarely seen, only heard.

As far as Hiroshi could tell the prisoners received no food or water since they were captured. They were quiet because their guards would not let them talk. Infractions were severely dealt with, as some of the prisoners lying still next to the others appeared to have recent, fresh injuries. The official leaders, presumably some officers and non-commissioned officers who protested or demanded food or water for the prisoners were the first led off to be interrogated. None of those 10 came back. Hiroshi didn't know if Miyamoto shot the prisoners or not, but if he had the other prisoners would have heard it. In any case the men were fearful when Hiroshi's group approached, rising to visible, shaking terror when they realized they were being ordered to their feet and the man giving the orders was Miyamoto.

The prisoners, five men who could walk and three who were either carried by the others or by Hiroshi's men, were led off the river island and crossed a rickety log bridge over to another island. The second island was much more wooded and dark, which made it less habitable but more suitable for interrogations. Most of it could not be seen by the other island. Miyamoto, whose mere presence created such fear among the prisoners, moved the group quickly across the island into a small, flat area of exposed rock ringed by tall trees. Clearly visible once inside the open area was a small amphitheatre 20 meters away, stepped down from the clearing. In the center of the amphitheatre was a row of bodies, the other prisoners who were interrogated. The bodies were decapitated, their bloody heads visible in an untidy pile a few meters away from the bodies. Even from the distance above, the amount of blood was appalling, huge red-brown pools, not completely absorbed by the earth or the heat of the sun on the large flat rock.

Miyamoto's man, Sergeant Inoue, opened a large canvas sack and handed two meter-long lengths of manila rope to Hiroshi's and Lieutenant Nishikawa's men. Miyamoto asked Hiroshi and Nishikawa to have their men take the prisoners and tie them one each to a tree, facing inward to the clearing, creating a semi-circle. The feet and hands were tightly bound to the trees, Miyamoto specified that. The weaker prisoners, unable to prop their heads up, had their foreheads tied back firmly to their trees. The Australians began to talk, and in some cases cry and moan, but Miyamoto and Sergeant Inoue were quick to beat the men making noise with a truncheon and a short riding crop. The men cried out in pain and terror, going silent or simply whimpering. The other Australians, fully aware of what was going to happen to them, grew silent and wooden. Their filthy bearded faces, full of fear, anguish and hate, watched their tormentors now with flashing eyes, struggling with the knowledge of their coming end, minutes away.

Captain Hashimoto wasn't there and Hiroshi did not expect the officer with seniority, Lieutenant Nishikawa, to be much use. Nishikawa stood aside, his eyes glazed over with his mouth open, almost catatonic. Hiroshi motioned Miyamoto to come to him, and Miyamoto on seeing the signal, stared at Hiroshi very hard before responding a few moments later. At first Hiroshi thought he was going to ignore him. Miyamoto walked over slowly, his black eyes glittering, his mouth a sneering slash across his face.

"Yes Lieutenant?" he asked. Hiroshi noticed Miyamoto was not wearing a sidearm, but his harness was carrying two swords, the larger katana with an elaborate grip. Miyamoto missed nothing, his eyes flickered as he noted Hiroshi's glance at his weapons.

"I don't presume to know your business, Warrant Officer, but have you already interrogated these eight prisoners?"

"No—I don't have to." Miyamoto said this with more than a hint of annoyance. "I have everything I need to know from these prisoners." Hiroshi felt the searchlight sweep up his face into his eyes, into his brain.

"So what are we doing here?" Hiroshi's voice dropped to a whisper, conscious some of the Australians were staring at the two of them. "Are we going to execute these prisoners? Are we providing a firing squad?" Miyamoto's lower face cracked into a wide grin, almost a

194

laugh, but the only sound was a low grunt.

"Yes and no, Lieutenant," he said patiently, as if talking to an errant child, "These men are dead, either way. Your men are going to dispose of these enemy soldiers with edged weapons."

Hiroshi brought along eight of his men, the three from his boat and five who stayed behind from the patrol due to the poor condition of their feet, but were deemed healthy enough for this training. These five were only wearing lightweight open-toed sandals instead of their boots, their painful sores and discomfort obvious in their slow, waddling gait. Miyamoto glanced at them with contempt, moving on to the nine men Lieutenant Nishikawa was able to muster. Like Hiroshi's platoon, at least half of the men were semi-invalids wearing sandals. The men clustered behind their respective officers as if they offered some protection, their rifles and bayonets held vertically close to their chests while nervously eyeing the prisoners they tied to the trees. The Australians, fearful and nervous themselves, began looking at one another and making noise again. When neither Hiroshi or Lieutenant Nishikawa moved, Miyamoto stepped forward, pulling his larger *katana* from the scabbard in one smooth, fluid motion, gripping it in his right hand at full arm's length, the tip of the blade pointed straight up. The flash of the polished steel blade turned every head, Japanese and Australian. After a moment of absolute silence, some of the Australians moaned in outright terror, their eyes huge as they wriggled futilely against their tight rope bindings. With his free hand, Miyamoto motioned towards one half of the prisoners before pointing towards the other half.

"Lieutenant Takahashi, your men have these four men. Lieutenant Nishikawa, these four men on this side."

Miyamoto, his eyes even harder and colder than before, turned and faced the two officers and their men, 19 sets of saucer eyes whose attention rolled back and forth between Miyamoto and the prisoners. Miyamoto was joined by the hulking Sergeant Inoue carrying strips of cloth. Miyamoto turned towards Inoue and simply nodded. Inoue bowed slightly before walking over to the first of the prisoners, gripped him roughly by the hair to tie a blindfold on him. The second prisoner shook his head wildly, screaming *NO! NO! NO!* when Inoue approached. He spat in Inoue's face. In one swift motion Inoue clubbed the man hard across the nose with a short wooden club and yanked his head back. The *thwack*, a sickening hollow sound not unlike a coconut hit with an axe, was accompanied by ruptured flesh and splattered blood. Inoue tied the blindfold on and dropped the head of the prisoner, now unconscious.

"This will make it a little easier for your men the first time," Miyamoto stated casually as Inoue methodically went from prisoner to

195

prisoner.

Despite the immediate threat of a severe beating, several of the Australians resisted Inoue and each in turn was clubbed. One man, Hiroshi watched in horror, had his front teeth knocked out when Inoue swung his club too low and hit the prisoner square in the mouth. The Australian, a large bear of a man, roared with pain and spit teeth and blood into Inoue's face. Inoue stepped back on the balls of his feet like a boxer, cocking the club way up before clubbing the man again directly across the ear. It was a skull-cracking blow that obliterated the ear, the blood spraying all over Inoue, who calmly stepped in close to examine the man, now motionless. Inoue turned his head to look at Miyamoto almost apologetically. Miyamoto simply nodded.

Inoue stepped aside when he was finished. The Australians, their eyes bound, were now visibly shaking with fear. A few moaned, but Hiroshi could also hear others who talking in calm voices, apparently trying to settle some of the more frightened men down.

Hiroshi found Miyamoto staring directly at him. Miyamoto lowered his *Katana,* his legs now flexed in what Hiroshi recognized as an on-guard *Kendo* stance.

"We must not inflict *killing* blows until the end," Miyamoto spoke now like a weapons instructor, his voice louder to be heard by all of the men. "Practice with your bayonet on different parts of the body, and you will learn what it feels like. Remember, in night attack you often *will not be able to fire your weapon!* Your bayonet is your primary weapon! Learn where to put the blade! The body resists the blade. Some parts of the body are to be avoided, like the ribs as you learned in infantry school. But unlike a straw dummy," Miyamoto pointed over his shoulders at the prisoners, "these targets are *alive.* They will SCREAM when you thrust your blade in. You need to understand what inflicts the most pain on your enemy. Don't be afraid to make it hurt! These soldiers are ENEMY soldiers who have SURRENDERED. They are not worthy of your respect, and not worthy of your empathy! Treat them like pigs in a farmyard!"

Miyamoto stared hard at all of the men, pausing especially for Hiroshi and Lieutenant Nishikawa. He suddenly lifted his right leg to spin around on his left and charge screaming directly at the center of the prisoners, impaling one of the Australians in the lower abdomen with his *katana.* True to his word it wasn't a killing blow, the prisoner gasping in agony as Miyamoto withdrew his blade, watching segments of gray intestines fall from the slashing wound. He cleaned his blade on the prisoner's trousers, taking his time before turning around to face the men who watched his every move, their eyes horrified and incredulous.

196

"Officers first!" Miyamoto roared, his finger pointed at Hiroshi.

Hiroshi knew as he drew his *katana* from its scabbard, he had no choice. This training evolution was ordered by Captain Hashimoto. He heard Lieutenant Nishikawa's moan and gasp to his right, but did not look in his direction. Hiroshi turned his back on Miyamoto to confront his men, completely confused and frightened. The only NCO in the group was an assistant squad leader, so Hiroshi spoke directly to them, bringing them around instantly with what was familiar and ingrained.

"Narabe!" (Line up!). By habit they quickly formed two tight lines straight back, freezing at attention. He pointed at the two men in the front of each line, his fingers guiding them to a spot next to him.

"Chikayore!" (Come forward!) The two men hesitated only for a second before advancing and stopping just short of Hiroshi. He glared at them for a moment before nodding towards them, making sure they each made eye contact with him. He raised his *katana* and began to turn around.

"Tsuite koi!" (Follow me!). He barked, charging forward towards the prisoners on the left side, his *katana* coming down, the point of the saber level when he reached the Australians. He could hear the sound of running men, breathing hard, right behind him.

Later, when they were back on the other island Hiroshi vomited up everything in his stomach. He was able to control himself long enough to dismiss his men. Most of them vomited when he ordered them to bayonet the dying Australians a second and third time. The sheer butchery was too much for some of them, they stared and slobbered, crying and falling back, not willing or able to withstand the shock of such controlled slaughter. The prisoners cried and moaned, some shrieking in terror and fright as they realized they would be stabbed again and again. The mercy of a killing blow would come later, after untold suffering was inflicted upon them.

Hiroshi knew no English words but he understood quite clearly all of the Australians were begging for mercy, begging for them to simply kill them, not torture them to death. He realized why Miyamoto had blindfolded the prisoners, there was no way he or most of his men could have done what they did to men who could see them, could look them in the eyes as they were being bayoneted. In the end it was Hiroshi who ended it for them, as Lieutenant Nishikawa and the rest of the men stood by in awed silence and shock, trembling and blood splattered. The prisoners were silent and still, tied and reduced to slumping bags of slashed apart sinew and bone. Without a word or glance towards Miyamoto who stood aside and simply watched, Hiroshi drew his Nambu 8mm pistol, charged the chamber and quickly went up to each Australian, dispatching the dead or dying men with a single bullet in the

197

temple.

Hiroshi could hear a loud argument somewhere behind him but it was nearly a minute before he could gather and focus his thoughts. First Lieutenant Tomita returned with his patrol and the extra boat with Sergeant Kato and the rest of Hiroshi's men. Hiroshi could not hear all of the words as the two men, Captain Hashimoto and Tomita, argued vehemently, but *China* and *criminal* was used more than once. Hiroshi never heard any of the officers raise their voice against Captain Hashimoto before. Once he realized what was being said and who he believed was saying it, he snapped out of his stupor.

By the time Hiroshi got there the voices were subsided. He approached cautiously and stopped outside of Captain Hashimoto's temporary orderly room, a huge, hollowed out tree trunk. Lieutenant Tomita was staring in anger at Warrant Officer Miyamoto who was talking quietly. Hashimoto stood slightly aside, his arms crossed, a very dark look in his face. Everyone stopped talking when they noticed Hiroshi standing there.

"Did our argument attract some attention, Lieutenant Takahashi?" Hashimoto asked casually. Miyamoto glanced over at Hiroshi with, for him, almost a friendly look. Miyamoto's eyes dropped to Hiroshi's chin and shirt, drawing the attention of both Captain Hashimoto and First Lieutenant Tomita. Tomita's eyes grew wide with first surprise then disgust. He turned to Hashimoto with renewed anger in his eyes. Hashimoto simply revealed his half smile towards Hiroshi. Hiroshi glanced down at his tropical shirt, realizing it was spotted and sprayed with blood. It made him instantly woozy, and he almost lost his footing.

"You have blood on your blouse, Lieutenant Takahashi. As I would expect." Hashimoto walked towards Hiroshi and led him to a stump to sit down on.

"There is a change of plans, we won't be continuing our training this evening after all. I think for the sake of the exercise, the mission was accomplished." Hashimoto sat down himself on another stump, sighing heavily. He looked up at Tomita and Miyamoto like a father dealing with two bickering children, weary but knowing there was no immediate resolution possible.

"Lieutenant Tomita, get your patrol fed and join me after dinner so we can plan our departure tomorrow." Tomita, still angry, stared at Hashimoto only for a second before coming to attention and snapping a quick salute. Hashimoto dismissed him with a curt nod, turning to Miyamoto.

"No more threats, please, Warrant Officer. I don't consider First Lieutenant Tomita insubordinate for refusing to participate in the training. His accusations are those of a very tired young man." It was obvious to Hiroshi, even in his reduced state, the conversation was stilted and for his benefit. Miyamoto said nothing, then after a slow glance towards Hiroshi he turned to depart. He stopped to point over to the river, where the remaining prisoners were.

"And the prisoners, Captain?" Hashimoto lowered his head and rubbing his face as he pondered the question. He glanced at Miyamoto before shrugging his shoulders.

"Take care of them."

Miyamoto simply disappeared. Hashimoto closed his eyes and lowered his head again, sighing loudly as his powerful shoulders slowly slumped with fatigue. Hiroshi sat for several minutes, motionless as he watched his commander, realizing from the gentle rising and falling rhythm of the back, the man had fallen asleep. Hiroshi was forgotten. Peering around in the damp corners of the large tree trunk, Hiroshi felt entirely alone. The bile from his stomach was in his mouth, but he recognized immediately the sickly sweet smell of the blood on his arms, shirt and face. He was certain the scent would not go away by washing, not any more than the cries of fear and last gasping agonies of the Australians who died from his hands would leave his memory.

More than anything he needed to talk to Hashimoto, to understand what he was supposed to have learned by slaughtering helpless men. Hiroshi watched his hands shake, twitching like the twitching of those men tied to the trees who knew they would be butchered with razor sharp bayonets and sabers. Now he, an executioner, was the one who was shaking with fear and shame. Like his men Hiroshi needed someone to tell him he did the right thing. He wanted to wake Hashimoto, to shake him from his deep slumber to ask—to demand the confirmation he needed. But Hiroshi just sat where he was as darkness descended on him, heavily on his shoulders and back. The shadows closed around his peripheral vision even as sunlight vented through the trees. He knew there was no going back now, no escape for him. It was like entering a dark tunnel and leaving a candle behind, watching the light ebb away as he drifted farther and farther from the flame.

ON THE TRACK

CHAPTER 16

August 11, 1942, Seven-Mile airfield, Port Moresby

He figured his general malaise was a combination of the heat, humidity, lack of sleep and the stress of the constant flying. His head pounded as he tried to focus his eyes. He had no energy, his brain sluggish and slow. The nausea didn't help either, but he wasn't quite ready to turn himself in to the flight surgeon. He could keep the airplane in the air and right now they needed every ship turning around as quickly as they could.

It was bound to happen, but he was blessed with a strong constitution since he was a baby, routinely staying healthy when other young men became sick. Don Crenshaw calculated he had been flying out of Port Moresby for just about 10 weeks now, and as far as he knew he was the only squadron pilot who hadn't been grounded at least once for some disease-related malady. He was secretly pretty proud of that fact, but recognized Port Moresby was a tropical cesspool of disease just waiting to get inside of his bloodstream. The airfield itself was on a plain, a swamp plain. The dark hordes of mosquitoes were ever present morning and evening.

Don was a quick study and a good pilot, promoted to aircraft commander after only five weeks as a co-pilot. They were starting to get more pilots and airplanes so that might have sped up the process a bit, but he flew the airplane well and he knew his size and easy-going manner made people like him. If it somehow implied more experience and wisdom than he actually possessed, well he hoped his own innate sense of self-preservation would keep him from stepping across that line separating good judgment and inflated ego. It was a very fine line with pilots, he recognized that well enough. It made the difference when the transports departed, usually alone, to perform their missions in some of the worst weather and terrain on the planet. Some pilots turned around when they couldn't get through, flying out away from the mountains and towards the sea and the clear, safe air below them. With plenty of gas, they waited it out and tried again when the weather changed. For those other pilots who didn't listen to the small voices of caution there was sometimes a permanent consequence. Their missions ended abruptly, reported as a small flash in the jungle, or more likely, *Missing, Failed to Return*, never to be seen again as if they vanished from the earth.

So it was both fate and the luck of the draw his first assigned co-pilot, a nice enough kid from Ohio who couldn't chew gum and fly the airplane at a constant airspeed and altitude, came down with malaria so bad they had to ship him back to Australia. The kid had only been flying with Don for three weeks when one night he started the sweats, quickly advancing to convulsions and unconsciousness. This happened in the middle-late days of July, just when it was reported a large Japanese infantry force was landing on the eastern side of New Guinea at Gona and Buna. There was no other target since the marginal defeat of the Japanese Navy at the Battle for The Coral Sea, forcing the invasion force bound to Port Moresby to turn around. This was the back door. These troops at Gona and Buna were headed for the Kokoda Track, the only remaining route to Port Moresby.

On July 18th and 20th Seven Mile airfield and the auxiliary fields were hit by Japanese bombers trying to catch the C-47s and the few B-17s, B-25s and P-40s on the ground. The bombers, twin-engine *Betty's*, arrived with fighter escort but the weather intervened both times. Little damage was sustained since the bomb aimers couldn't see the ground. However the real blessing was not the exquisite timing of the nasty squalls during the raids. On both raids the bombers came when nearly all of the transports were in the air delivering equipment to the Kokoda airstrip, 50 kilometers away. To be caught helplessly on the ground was one thing, but what frightened Don and other transport pilots most were the fighter escorts. *Zeros*. Port Moresby had few operational fighters of their own, so it was not uncommon for the *Zero* escorts to temporarily abandon their bombers to go transport hunting. It was a bus drivers' nightmare for once spotted, especially with no clouds close by to hide in, a C-47 was a clay pigeon.

As usual, the radio range at Port Moresby was turned off during the raids after the native observers on the northern side of the Owen Stanleys' called to report unknown inbound aircraft. It seemed sometimes they would forget to turn it back on. If the weather was bad the radio range was the only navigation aid to point an aircraft, including enemy aircraft, at an operational airfield. The Automatic Direction Finder, or ADF, was a small, compass like dial divided into 360 increments like a directional gyro. It was the primary navigation instrument in the C-47. Any radio station signal in range, including commercial stations, could be dialed in by frequency and the ADF needle would point directly to the station. Of course any strong source of electricity, including an electrical storm, would be pointed to also. At Port Moresby, when the radio range was working and the signal was received, there were published procedures established so aircraft could approach and land in under less than good visual conditions. A number of aircraft could approach the airfield, talk to other aircraft to determine each other's position, and work themselves down to a point they could attempt a visual landing approach safely without hitting each other.

Don heard the stories of Japanese pilots listening in on the frequencies, and simply followed the Allied aircraft down to the runway. Some aircraft were shot down apparently, but mostly an odd, harassing crater or two suddenly appeared on the airfield out of the blue. The raider was rarely seen. It was a legend thing but no one disputed it as not true. It was a strange way to fight a war, but this was New Guinea; primitive, backwards, other-worldly and here at the outer limits of the participants supply lines, fought anyway that worked.

At Kokoda on a nominal blocking position no one considered would actually be used, was one company of Australian militiamen from the 39th Battalion. Once allied aircraft reconnaissance confirmed the Japanese invasion force's direction, now estimated to be due southwest directly over the Owen Stanleys' at battalion strength with native bearers and mountain artillery units, reinforcements were quickly organized at Port Moresby. The other remaining companies of the 39th battalion were to be flown to the Kokoda airfield immediately. Don, who was flying missions into the incredibly short Kokoda runway with his almost useless co-pilot, was pleased and thankful when his squadron CO assigned him Jack Cooper as his new right-seater. Don only had a couple of days and a half a dozen missions to break in his new co-pilot, but based on Cooper's extensive experience as a commercial pilot, Don felt confident Cooper would be an immense improvement.

The triple canopy at the base of the Owen Stanley's swallowed up the Japanese invasion force, now noted in intelligence briefs as *Nankai Shitai* – The South Sea Force. The intelligence photo interpreters could only track *Nankai Shitai* on the 30-40 kilometers from the coast to the Owen Stanleys'. The remaining 50-60 kilometers of the Track to the Kokoda airfield was mostly out of sight. This didn't stop Allied bombers from bombing the Track or every visible bridge crossing streams and rivers. Japanese Army engineers attached to *Nankai Shitai* were very busy indeed.

The Australians who knew the Kokoda Track were quick to point out how rugged the terrain was. Some of the Aussie intelligence officers even suggested the invasion force would never make it to Kokoda. The terrain was simply impossible for heavily armed infantry. They were aware of the mountain artillery units attached to *Nankai Shitai*, a fact guaranteed to impede the advance. There were even intelligence photos showing troops approaching bridges on bicycles, like the Japanese used to cover large distances in China. *The bastards will never make it.*

So they were stunned when ground reconnaissance units reported *Nankai Shitai* halfway up the Track to Kokoda on July 23rd. The company commander of the militia unit holding Kokoda immediately sent two of his platoons down the Track to meet *Nankai Shitai* at Awala. On July 24th Don Crenshaw, with Jack Cooper flying right seat, flew numerous taxi missions into the Kokoda airfield. The airlift required all flyable transports in the squadron to haul the two remaining 39th Battalion companies from Port Moresby. The grass airstrip, demanding a very precise and slow approach to land at the absolute end of the airstrip and immediate braking thereafter, was a location aircrews and passengers never forgot. It was frightening to the uninitiated, simply scary to those who knew what to expect. Don and Cooper got to know it very well, as it was apparent over the next few weeks three companies of militia would not be able to contain *Nankai Shitai*. The squadron flew in stores and ammunition several times a day, while flying out planeload after planeload of wounded.

The men on the ground were growing desperate. At times Don was not certain the airfield was secure, especially when they could not raise the airstrip on the radio for the all clear to land. More than once they advanced the throttles and pulled up the gear and flaps for a go around because Don was not sure what was going on. Sometimes a green flare, *cleared for landing,* would be fired just as he started his climb out, but it was too late. It made the landings tense, the initial ground contact nerve-racking if no one could be seen, and they waited until Diggers came out of the bush to assist in the off-loading. There were clear preparations to abandon the airstrip near the end of July as *Nankai Shitai* grew closer. The current ground situation was not always passed along to the air crews, so the mission brief sometimes bore no resemblance to what they found. Rumors would fly like wildfire for anything affecting air crews. *Jap reconnaissance troops infiltrated the airfield and snipers were in the trees to shoot pilots as they approached to land. Jap troops in Australian uniforms would approach the planes and instead of loading wounded men, toss in explosive devices to blow up the transports.* All rumors were considered seriously.

The village of Kokoda was abandoned by the commander of the 39th Battalion on July 26th, but he brought them back the next day, the beginning of several days of changing possession of Kokoda and the airstrip above it. In the distance of a week *Nankai Shitai* left the coast at Gona, climbed up the Track and was within reach of Kokoda. The Japanese commander, now high enough to use his radio, informed Japanese Imperial Command Headquarters at Rabaul Advance Force was ready to take the airfield on July 28th.

Several missions for Don and his transport squadron were scrubbed when it appeared the Japanese were about to take the airstrip.

Now instead of landing at the grass strip at Kokoda, the transports were directed to deliver their supplies from the air, pushing the cargo out the door on the outskirts of the plains of Kokoda still held by the Australians. Even this was temporarily abandoned at the end of July when it was reported, officially, on July 30th Japanese troops had taken the village of Kokoda and captured the grass airstrip. At this point, with the airstrip no longer in Australian hands the 39th Battalion casualties were trapped, with no other method of evacuation except the 50 kilometer stretcher ride back down the Kokoda Track.

Don and Cooper, peripheral participants in one sense, very direct participants in another, wanted to believe the situation was actually improving. Not necessarily right there on the Kokoda, but this was a desperate battle of which they were playing a very real part. To Don, it seemed they were feeding equipment to ghosts, and the mysterious South Sea Force the intelligence officers talked about seemed unstoppable.

It didn't take much imagination to recognize if the Japs took Port Moresby, and that possibly was raised constantly as even air crews were ordered to stay armed at all times, most of the troops stationed at Port Moresby would not get out in time. Even Don and Cooper talked about it. If they were flying support between Kokoda and Port Moresby and Seven Mile was captured, what were their options? At the closest point Australia was 300 miles away. If their mission at the time was nearly over and they were low on fuel, they would have no option but to land at Port Moresby and surrender. Or should they start carrying parachutes like normal transport crews and keep them on board, jumping when they ran out of gas? To where and to do what? They knew what the jungle canopy on the Kokoda and the swamps surrounding Port Moresby offered. Nothing. There was no safety down there, no escape. They would jump from the frying pan into the fire. They knew neither of them would survive very long. From what the briefers explained and the Air Force Escape and Evasion guys stated, there was nothing to eat and all kinds of things to kill you.

The overall picture of the Pacific war seemed brighter. The Battle for The Coral Sea was the first time the Japanese Navy had been stopped, cold. It turned around the first direct invasion threat to Port Moresby. On August 7th, US Marines from the First Marine Division landed to the east of New Guinea in the Solomon Islands, a place called Guadalcanal. This forced the Japs to divide their overstretched forces even further. The timing of the Guadalcanal invasion couldn't have been better. If the 39th Battalion could hang out a few more weeks, the briefers concluded, three battalions from the Australian Army's 7th Division, freshly trained and refitted after returning from two years in the Middle

East, would replace the 39th on the Kokoda. The bad news was the report the Advance Party currently fighting the 39th Battalion was believed to be only one part of the special force assigned to take Port Moresby. They didn't know the exact size of the entire invasion force, but estimates suggested a regiment, due to land at Buna and Gona by mid-August. They didn't say how they got the information.

The incredible speed the Advance Force maintained up the Track despite the rains, vertical terrain and incessant aerial bombings of critical bridges across the Kumusi River, stunned and fascinated Allied intelligence. They began to believe they were witnessing the operational prowess of a highly trained special forces unit. The Australians, intimately familiar with the Track, simply shook their heads in disbelief. *Nankai Shitai* moved at the rate of the Papua natives, men who lived on the Track and traversed it daily. *These are very special troops,* they suggested.

The first week and a half of August was frustrating and confusing for the Allied air crews. They loaded their transports for a mission, taxied out only to be called back on indefinite holds. Sometimes the missions were cancelled outright, but rarely. Mostly they were ordered to stand by for hours, occasionally extending to the next day. The risk of a Japanese bombing raid was always there, so the crews dispersed the airplanes as prudently as they could. They knew the ground situation at Kokoda was touch and go. The briefers explained the 39th lost the airstrip and the village three times over the course of a week. Then they would counterattack and retake sometimes just the village. Then the Japs would counterattack and ground would change hands. The commander of the 39th Battalion, who Don himself had flown over on July 24th so he could take charge on the ground, was killed by a sniper on July 29th. The battalion XO took over, but communications with the latest situation became spottier. Then the word would come the airfield was retaken. Once confirmed there would be instant urgency and crews ordered to their aircraft.

August 8th through 10th was a particularly nasty time for both sides taking turns owning Kokoda. Heavy rain with thunderstorms ripped through the mountain passes, flooding roads and streams. On the morning of the 8th Australians charged through with three companies on the latest counterattack only to be repulsed. At the same time another company managed to sneak into the village, temporarily abandoned by the Japanese. *Nankai Shitai*, realizing the situation, counterattacked in the rain on the 9th. The attacking unit was too small and driven away with heavy machinegun fire. Reinforcing the attacking force, *Nankai Shitai* charged the village again and failed, then counterattacked once

206

more at dusk on August 10th. This time they overwhelmed the Australian positions and retook the village and strengthened their positions at the airstrip.

This latest development of who owned Kokoda didn't make it to the 21st Air Transport Squadron. Their information had the airstrip still in Australian hands, so on August 11th the C-47 transports were loaded with bully beef, biscuits, canned milk, cigarettes, grenades and ammunition to replace the dwindling supplies for what remained of the 39th Battalion. The mission had the transports pushing their loads out directly over the airstrip instead the plains, which placed the aircraft even closer to the Japanese positions. The squadron CO, who was going to lead the mission, was told this was the best way to get the rations and ammunition directly into the hands of the defenders, who needed it immediately. The airstrip was where they were, and this was where he was ordered to push out his loads.

Following the accepted airdrop procedure at the time, the CO led the flight in high and kept them high until the last minute. They dodged around weather and mountain rocks on each side as he led them in loose trail formation through the high passes, before radioing ship to ship, *here we go, keep your interval, and keep up your speed.* Unlike the usual landing approach to the Kokoda airstrip, there was no careful, slow as molasses descent as if you were trying to land on somebody's backyard. Here they stayed high overhead, the little strip and flat plain far below them, flying a pattern far out of range of any potential antiaircraft guns. As the number three ship in trail, Don watched the Skipper's C-47 do a steep diving turn to the left, nosing sharply down. A few seconds later number two began his steep diving turn to the left, and then it was Don's turn, *one thousand one, one thousand two, one thousand three here we go!*

The Skipper's idea was to keep the sweeping and diving turn continuous as the transports circled and descended towards the airstrip. Observers on the ground and certainly any antiaircraft gunners, would have a difficult time determining exactly where the aircraft were headed. They could track them, but the heading could change at any time by the lead aircraft leveling his wings. The steep but diving turn kept the aircraft speed up as the altimeter unwound rapidly. The mountain peaks drawing closer were seven to nine thousand feet in height, but Don's job, like the other pilots in trail, was not to worry about the terrain as they descended, this was the Skipper's responsibility. Their concern was to maintain their interval so they didn't close the gap with the aircraft in front, and to maintain the necessary 300 feet off the surface of the airstrip, wings level, as they made their drop.

Don watched in admiration as the Skipper's ship smoothly lined up with the airstrip heading and leveled his wings about four miles out. He was still about 1,000 feet high. A few seconds later, number two lined up and leveled his wings. The nose of the Skipper's ship suddenly dropped like a downhill sled, and Don could see half the bottom of the fuselage of the C-47 as it seemed to point almost straight down. *Jesus Christ!* Cooper exclaimed, glancing at Don wide-eyed. Don was too busy to respond as he leveled his wings, again counting to himself to maintain the interval before gently pushing the wheel forward, way forward. He could not see number two under his nose so he pushed harder, easing the throttles back as the negative G lifted him from his seat and the airframe howled in protest. He didn't have time to warn the loadmaster and crew, praying they were holding on and the load wouldn't shift.

They knew the elevation of the airstrip, so to make Don's job easier, Cooper watched the altimeter and did the math, subtracting the known elevation from the altimeter and only reported the last hundreds of feet. The Skipper wanted 300 feet Above Ground Level, and by God that's what they were going to fly, 300 AGL. Don, feeling like he was flying an out-of-control box car, watched the airspeed roll into the 170s as the number two ship slid up the windscreen as it began its level off. *Six hundred feet,* Cooper called out. *Five hundred fifty feet. Five hundred feet.*

Throttles still off, Don slowly muscled the big yoke back with both hands, feeling the strain in his shoulders. *Easy now,* but he had to level off and give the guys in back time to unstrap the load and move it to the door. *Four hundred feet, Don! Three hundred and fifty feet. You're gonna' overshoot!* Don already knew it but he'd never had a C-47 moving so fast. *Easy does it.*

Three hundred feet. Two hundred fifty feet, Don!

Don could see the number two ship was slightly higher than his and was starting to slow down, getting larger in the windscreen. He kept his hand off the throttles, watching the airspeed bleed off once he leveled, slightly nose high. As he eased the yoke back to regain his altitude, he smoothly added power and was rewarded with his target, 150 MPH. *Three hundred feet, right on the button.* Cooper smiled giving him a thumbs up. Don keyed his intercom to check in with his flight engineer, warning him they would be over the drop zone in about one minute.

They could see bundles falling out of the Skipper's ship. At 300 feet and 150 MPH the packages were tumbling and spinning before hitting hard on the pock-marked airstrip. It was bombed by B-25s a week earlier on August 2nd and currently unusable by either side. Don keyed his intercom and told his flight engineer to standby, 30 seconds to drop. Ship number two was now pushing out its load, but Don watched the Skipper's ship, climbing hard to the west away from the Jap positions. The Skipper turned airspeed into altitude, the suddenly lighter airplane up and through 1,000 feet AGL, continuing his climb away from potential guns.

Number two was empty and now pulling up and away. Don keyed his intercom as the selected ground marker came up. *Push it out! Push it out!* He called into the mike. He kept his airspeed and altitude constant, the wings level as the men in the back shoved the packages into the slipstream. Don glanced down at the runway, noting most of the bundles wrapped in burlap by the Australians exploded on impact, hurling the stores far apart. Dozens of men rushed forward to grab the gear as others waved up at the air crews. Don stuck his left hand out his slider window and waved back. He only had a momentary image of the men on the ground, realizing with quiet alarm they didn't look like Australians at all. He swore they wore the darker khaki and peaked caps of Jap infantry.

Their suspicions were confirmed five minutes after all of the transports were safely out of Kokoda airspace. Once clear of the mountain peaks and in radio range, the Skipper reported what they saw, all of them listening with dismay when Port Moresby passed on the latest reports. They dropped precious food and ammunition right into the hands of the enemy. They would have to fly the mission again, but drop their supplies a half a mile to the west at the edge of the Kokoda plain. While they were reloading and refueling their aircraft to try again, Port Moresby would organize a bombing mission and strike the airstrip.

After a long silence after this radioed report, a pilot queried the Skipper on the ship-to-ship frequency on why the Japs didn't just shoot them all down. *Jesus, you dumb ass,* drawled one of the other pilots, *them Japs are just as hungry as them Aussies. They wasn't about to shoot down their first real meal in days! Why the hell do ya' think they was waving' at us? They was so damn glad they woulda' kissed our asses!* Another pilot guffawed into the radio and suddenly the frequency was jammed with chatter until the Skipper told them to knock it off and shut up. It was pretty depressing, but Don had to admit the incident kind of humanized the Japs in a way he hadn't considered before. The bottom line was all six crews flew within 300 feet of about 1,000 Japs and everybody spent the time waving at each other. It was kind of funny as he thought about it.

A week later on August 17th the Japanese returned the favor and bombed Seven Mile airfield. Nobody was laughing this time, as the sky cleared long enough for the *Betty's* to lay a short string of 500 pounders right down the side of the runway where the transports were loading.

The *Betty's* had hugged the clouds and stayed in the weather. The native air watchers could only report the sound of aircraft engines overhead, number and direction unknown. It was raining hard, off and on all day, the air raid klaxon sounding non-stop when aircraft were reported again at 15 miles northeast of Port Moresby. Three P-40s took off in strong gusting rain and wind, hoping to intercept the raiders. Two C-47s were loading equipment for a quick resupply drop, including Don and Jack Cooper's. The weather was so bad Don was certain they wouldn't be able to launch their resupply mission for at least a half an hour. Any inbound bombers would never see the ground either. At least that was the hope. Both ships continued to load, Don and Cooper hovering under the wing to glance at the sky nervously.

It was a very hectic, exhausting week, the sense of desperation barely contained in the daily operations. The Australian troops from the 7th Division sent to relieve the 39th Battalion unloaded from the port on the 13th and bivouacked right on the plains of the airfield. They were only there a few days, chewed alive by the mosquitoes on the swampy plain as Don and the other crews flew over them several times a day. The original plan was to fly the troops directly to the Kokoda airstrip, but this was no longer an option. If they were airborne troops, paratroopers, they could have been dropped on the Kokoda plain, but they weren't. They were going to walk in, up the Kokoda Track just like the *Nankai Shitai* had done from the other side of the Owen Stanley's. On the 16th the first group going, the 2/14 Battalion, loaded into trucks on their way to Ilolo, as far as the road would take them.

The 16th was also the day the new American commander of all Allied forces on New Guinea arrived, Lieutenant General Rowell. There was talk at squadron headquarters about preparing for the new General's arrival, but missions had to be planned, aircraft needed maintenance and everyone else was either loading or unloading aircraft or flying the actual missions. Anyone leftover on the personnel roster was on the sick list over at the 153rd Station Hospital, suffering their latest bout of malaria. The new commander's arrival was quickly forgotten.

Don could still hear the klaxons mounted on poles a quarter of a mile away honking when the ground shook under him, jerking him off balance. He slammed hard into the left landing gear tire, rolling on his back. He could see sunshine pouring like a bright yellow searchlight beam right down the center of the runway, the beam moving slowly east towards the line of aircraft he was in. The wind was gusting hard, blowing puddled water horizontally under the wing. It was still raining, but where he lay Don could see the dark grey cloud deck on one side of the runway and much lighter, almost blue sky on the other. There was a hole right over the airfield and the noise of the rain and wind could not cover up the sound roaring right down the runway. The throbbing of high performance piston engines at full power grew louder and louder. Shadows jetted past but suddenly he was deaf, the noise muted and only his body sensed movement.

WHUMP WHUMP WHUMP WHUMP WHUMP WHUMP. He felt the concussion of rushing air and bright flashes of light rolling towards him. His body bounced an inch or two and barely slammed back down before being bounced up again, hard and painfully. He felt he was being thrown against a hard wall just as the wall itself jerked and moved into him. He rolled away from the big wheel in panic as it bounced away from the tarmac, and for a frightful second he thought he would be crushed by his own airplane. As he scurried from under the wing, a black shadow passed, chased a moment later by a fat, cucumber green smooth fuselage. For just a fraction of a second Don saw a face in the clear plexiglas nose of the Mitsubishi bomber as it flashed past. The bomb doors were open and Don's last thoughts before he lost consciousness, inexplicably, was *that guy is too low his own bombs will kill him.*

Don woke up a few minutes later, rain pelting his face so forcefully he used both hands to protect his eyes and mouth. The latter so he could breath. At first he thought he was underwater, as most of his body was lying in about three inches of—wet. He could smell gasoline, burning rubber and oil. He could clearly smell smoke, except there wasn't any visible because the rain either beat it down or was putting out the fire. *Fire.* Suddenly his brain spun up as he started the process of checking himself for wounds. He kept his eyes closed from the downpour, concerned only for his personal injuries. He hurt everywhere, but as he slowly propped himself up on his elbows, he decided nothing was broken despite the thrashing and ground concussions from the bombs.

The little sky window the *Bettys* had used was gone as quickly as it appeared. The cloud deck was grey and oily and so low you could almost touch it now. Observers over by the squadron offices said the *Bettys* had to *climb* to get high enough to drop their bombs. They came over the north end at 200 feet, some guys estimated, going maybe 250 MPH before the pop-up. They had just a few seconds to drop their bombs. There were three of them, no escorts that were seen, and after they released their loads they punched back into the clouds and were gone. They didn't press their luck and come down to strafe, one pass and history. Everybody felt the crews knew they were too low but they released their bombs anyway, hoping their speed would get them out of the path of most of the fragments. The exploding bombs must have peppered the hell out of them and it was surprising most survived. The tail-end Charlie was the only one that went down. Don listened to the report knowing he saw the one they were talking about.

Each *Betty* released four 500 pounders, hoping to hit the only targets they could see in their brief glimpse of the airfield: the two C-47s on the left side of the runway 100 yards apart. There were sandbag revetments on bomber side of the field, so the gooney birds were separated. Threat Dispersal, the operations officer called it. When the Mitsubishis appeared the guys loading the two C-47s scattered like the wind. Luckily the Japanese pilots had only a second or two to adjust their headings, and the bomb aimers zero time to calculate their bomb releases. Hurtling down the runway with gusting rain and wind all three bomb aimers released their loads early. The pilots had not leveled their wings, so the bombs were tossed, like paper boys delivering their afternoon loads as they turned from one side of the street to the next, in trajectories guaranteed to be left or right of the target.

Both C-47s were riddled by bomb shrapnel, Don's machine taking the worst of it. It was repairable though. His left engine was nearly ripped off its nacelle engine mount from some heavy chunks of curled bomb casings, a total write off on an almost brand-new engine. One of his left wing fuel tanks, fully gassed, received numerous punctures and dribbled fuel all over the tarmac, but no fire. His rudder and vertical stabilizer were peppered like a shotgun blast, but repairable. The Group only had so many C-47s, so they patched them together anyway they could. Not a single person was injured seriously, although some of the men on the loading crew for the other C-47, running as a group to the east, were peppered with shrapnel from two 500 pounders exploding only a couple of hundred feet from them. Jack Cooper, approached Don sheepishly 10 minutes after the raid, admitted he started running when he heard the engines of the *Bettys* and didn't stop running until he was damn near the edge of the jungle, a quarter of a mile away. Don didn't take it to heart, he only laughed. He discovered however, later that night, exploding bombs can reach you even when lying on the ground. As he peeled off his greasy khakis he discovered little holes to go with the other aches and pain. His left arm, face, neck and hip had dozens of tiny little punctures with small hunks of metal and rock imbedded in them. They hurt, and they hurt again when the doctors and corpsmen probed and plucked them out, one by one.

The next day, with no airplane to fly, Don and Jack Cooper took a ride with a couple of other transport pilots to the far end of the field where the *Betty* had crashed. The rain had stopped, the sun boiling hot. It appeared the airplane hit mostly intact, with no debris field. It simply flew into the ground, slid a few hundred feet before burning. The graves registration team had already taken the bodies away, reported to be six crewmen. The *Betty* was totally destroyed either by the crash or the fire afterwards, with only the props and engine blocks the only truly recognizable parts remaining. The other pilots poked around the charred remains of what appeared to be the upper part of the cockpit. Don and Cooper stayed back. One of the pilots pulled out a blackened wire frame, possibly eye glasses, the lenses two charred discs. He held it up by a bent ear piece, pointing towards it with his finger.

"What they always say, huh?" he declared, shaking his head. When Don and Cooper didn't respond he shrugged and tossing the glasses back into the ashes, brushing off his hands. Don could only remember the vivid green of the fuselage, and the small face he had seen for just a moment as the *Betty* roared overhead. *In either case the man and the machine ceased to exist, right here. It happened so fast, like swatting a fly.*

CHAPTER 17

August 12, 1942, First Company, 1/144th Infantry, Advance Party, Isurava

It was no surprise to Hiroshi to find out Captain Hashimoto volunteered First Company for the reconnaissance in force down to Isurava. It reminded him darkly of the mission to the river delta on New Britain. Especially since Miyamoto and Sergeant Inoue were joining them again. First Company was the assault company for the battalion now, leading every night attack and counterattack for the battle of Kokoda and suffering the most casualties. While the other two companies dug in and strengthened the battalion's foothold on Kokoda and the airstrip above it, holding the precious ground until the rest of *Nankai Shitai* arrived, First Company would strike out on the offensive to buy time for 10 to 15 days. Their independent mission was to harass the withdrawing Australians back down the Track some 10 kilometers to Isurava. The terrain at Isurava provided good defensive positions, a natural fallback where the Australians could hold and make a stand. First Company would probe the defenses early, find weaknesses and counter any probing elements from the Australians back up towards Kokoda.

In the three weeks since the battalion arrived in Kokoda they learned lessons about the Australian Army. The Australians did not rattle easily. The noisy attack with the bird cat calls, strange chants and screams accompanied by banging drums and pots, flares and flashing lights so effective in routing Chinese infantry in Shanghai didn't seem to work. Infantry assaults would be met with accurate rifle and machinegun fire, with the Australians holding their positions. Even more perplexing was when the frontal assault forces feinted and withdrew only to be replaced with a charging flank, they found the Australians already pulled back. The Japanese began to accept they were dealing with an army that understood their tactics.

Like the Japanese Army, the Australians also believed in gaining information about their enemy through aggressive patrolling. They did this constantly except at night, and did it well. Other than losses from big attacks on well-defended positions, both sides received most of their casualties from violent encounters on patrols. It was the most effective way of knowing what the enemy was doing in front of you.

The Japanese distinguished themselves by building on their extensive expertise in night operations. Allied armies, the Australians included, did not operate at night in the jungle. The Advance Party owned the landscape at night, taking full advantage of the darkness to maneuver tactically out of observation from regular patrols and aircraft. The Australians, like the British and the Americans, believed in the Fort Apache model, hunkering down in close formations at night. The Allies established defensive perimeters with small listening posts dotted 25 to 40 meters outside of the lines to provide tripwires for the perimeter. Moving around after dark was extremely hazardous if a soldier didn't use the appropriate password. The burst of fire would be brief so as not to give away the shooter's position. If unlucky a night mover, friend or foe, would grunt in pain or surprise, before quiet would return. Both sides understood any noise would draw more fire. There was no empathy or mercy, not at night, certainly not from Diggers. Not with the Japs sneaking up in the dark to cut your throat. The victim of the gunfire, if he didn't survive and crawl away would be examined and buried at daybreak.

Night movement for Japanese infantry included only two primary evolutions, large scale night assault formations, *silent attack*, or small reconnaissance patrols. These usually involved a handful of men assigned the task of determining the strength of the enemy line while taking advantage of the Allies inherent fear of the night to disrupt sleep, create anxiety and fear, and shaking the confidence of the individual Australian soldier.

On the morning of August 11th Hiroshi attempted to find some food in the village of Kokoda for First Company. Most of the soldiers were living on roots and vegetables they foraged from village gardens, supplementing the small supply of tasteless crackers still remaining. With the Australians out of Kokoda Captain Hashimoto sent Hiroshi and his old platoon, now led by a young officer named Tanaka, on a quest for something to nourish First Company before they started their mission down to Isurava. The battalion had nothing to issue them before their special mission. The men were all hungry. They knew from experience there was nothing to eat on the Track. Anything of any nutritional value remained high above them, out of reach in the canopy. No edible vegetation or small animals of any kind would be found down near the jungle floor.

Yokohama Advance Party left the coast with a two week supply of rations crammed into their assault packs or on the backs of their own native bearers. The planning group for the mission anticipated the Advance Party would find ration stores abandoned by the Australians, as was the experience with the defenders on New Britain and with the British in Malaysia. This was not to be the case here on the Kokoda Track. The 39th Battalion, although with a shorter supply line requirement than the Japanese, relied on air transport or native bearers for resupply. There was little surplus to be found. A few of the troops

215

from the Advance Party found abandoned Australian stores after assaults forced the Australians to withdraw hastily, but these were small caches and consumed on the spot. The Japanese still had large quantities of the pep pills given to them when they left Rabaul, a special tablet mixed with green tea known as *Totsugeki-jo*, or *The Storming Tablet*. It was regular issue for them since Guam and the invasion of New Britain. It seemed to perk them up and reduced the hunger somehow, but Hiroshi knew men cannot survive on green tea alone.

Hiroshi and Second Lieutenant Tanaka searched every shed and standing structure in the village. The prospect of patrolling down the Track towards Isurava without any food at all seemed impossible to comprehend. *Who planned this fiasco?* Hiroshi thought to himself. With his old platoon close at hand, Hiroshi felt both comforted and out of place, although Sergeant Kato and his former squad leaders were both respectful and friendly. They all devoted their full energy to the search because individually it was their number one need. All of them thought about food constantly. Hiroshi felt responsible and angry the Japanese Army did not properly prepare for the resupply of his—that is—these men. Frustrated, he knew they were wasting their time. Every unit in the battalion had the same problem, and any of the men passing through the village would have immediately searched and taken anything edible. There was nothing.

He was about to report their failure to Captain Hashimoto when Lieutenant Tanaka seized his arm in alarm. A large formation of aircraft circling far out of the reach of gunners turned towards the airfield. Hiroshi stopped to listen to the droning of multi-engine aircraft coming closer. Their engines and airframes howled as they began to dive towards the earth. *BOMBERS!* Down in the village groves they couldn't see the aircraft yet, but his old platoon didn't need to be told what to do as they scattered like cockroaches into the forest. The bombers sounded like they were coming straight for them, at least a squadron! Hiroshi threw himself down into a shallow ditch, expecting the bombs to land right in the middle of the village. He was bombed before at a distance on the Kokoda Track. These bombers seemed extremely low. Hiroshi stared at his hands in front of his face and watching them tremble uncontrollably. He waited for the shriek of the bombs as they hurled to the ground.

The first aircraft flew slightly to the north of the village at 200 meters height or so, roaring towards the airstrip above them. Hiroshi looked up fearfully as the shadow flashed past, noting the aircraft had US markings. The image presented to his brain was instantly confusing; a huge open cargo door with dark brown bundles falling out in a steady train. *Were they some new form of explosives or poison gas?* When the bundles disappeared from view without erupting a moment later into concussions and mayhem, he realized they were transports delivering provisions for the Australians. The aircraft crews did not know the airstrip was in the hands of the Advance Party!

His suspicions were confirmed as transport after transport, six or seven in total, flew to the exact same altitude and heading while pushing out the brown bundles. Hiroshi could hear cheering and shouting all around him, and despite Lieutenant Tanaka's orders not to move from cover, his old platoon ran in glee and excitement towards the airstrip. *Food! Food at the airstrip!* The more cautious of the men rose carefully, observing others dart around them before screaming themselves as they ran off. Hiroshi was conscious of the implausibility of what he was witnessing. The battalion was being resupplied by the enemy, the event occurring with such normalcy not a single Japanese soldier thought to raise and fire his weapon at the transports.

The bundles exploded like bombs themselves, pushed out of the airplanes at high speed and low altitude, striking the ground so hard small-arms ammunition packed in steel boxes were bent far enough to be useless. The troops had little interest in .303 or .45 ammunition, however. They went straight to the food packages. Much of the food stores were destroyed by the high speed delivery, small tins of milk blown apart and drained before the men could get to it, medium tins of bully beef disintegrating over the grass. But not all of it. To the men of the Advance Party it was manna from heaven, sent directly from the gods. There were still plenty of intact tins of milk, tea, butter, biscuits, jam, bully beef and *tabako,* cigarettes!

It was for many of the men an eye-opener to the high standard of living enjoyed by their enemy. The company commanders quickly contributed men to act as guards as the food stores were hauled away out of sight of the Australians, who totally dismayed, popped mortar rounds out amongst the troops still foraging. The Japanese commanders knew how lucky they were to receive this unexpected resupply. Some of it was immediately stolen and presumably consumed by the men, but the company commanders, Captain Hashimoto in particular, set about an organized distribution so all of his men would get something. He had a long mission ahead and there was no guarantee they would find food at Isurava.

After 20 or 30 minutes the battalion commander determined the airstrip was too dangerous and ordered the men back to the safety of the village. It was a good call as in minutes the first of several flights of B-25 Mitchells flew over to correct the oversight, dropping 250 pound high explosive bombs to distribute hot shrapnel along the perimeter of the

217

airstrip instead of food parcels. The gift was already received and even the battalion commander mentioned to his officers he considered it an omen for their success. For most of the men of the Advance Party it was the first real meal in four or five days. Omen or not, it filled their bellies, even though the food was somewhat strange and bland. Everyone enjoyed a few cigarettes, good ones.

That night First Company moved cautiously out of Kokoda in a light drizzle with a few days of rations in their assault packs. Reconnaissance teams had probed the Kokoda Track to the south and reported the Australians were slowly withdrawing their men out of Kokoda in small groups down to Isurava, leaving two companies holding positions in the perimeter of the Kokoda plains. Imperial Headquarters in Rabaul also noted by radio submarine reports of Australian transport ships with fresh troops bound for Port Moresby, presumably as a relief force for the 39th Battalion. The rest of *Nankai Shitai,* Second and Third Battalions of the 144th and two battalions from the 41st, would be arriving on the coast at Buna in a matter of a week or two. The Advance Party must hold on until they arrived.

Hiroshi, listening to Captain Hashimoto relay these new developments, could not help but wonder why there was no mention of an aerial resupply on the Kokoda airstrip similar to what the Americans inadvertently did for the Advance Party. The weather was horrible but the Americans were successful. Didn't the Japanese Imperial Air Force, who owned virtually the same license-built C-47 type aircraft (with Mitsubishi engines), possess the same capability for resupply? Rabaul had two airstrips with fighters, bombers and transports arriving daily when the Yokohama Advance Party left for Buna. He kept his thoughts to himself, of course, baffled about a strategic plan to feed combat forces based on capturing food from the enemy. It was something you read about the Mongols would do in the First Century after the death of the Christian martyr. Cadets would marvel at the boldness of Khan's forces from the safety and security of the classroom, never imagining their own modern troops would be expected in some future date, *by plan,* to forage for food.

First Company moved at night knowing the Australians never used the Track after dark. With Isurava only 10 kilometers away, Captain Hashimoto gambled the Australians would have only a token force for observation purposes. They used most of the night silently slipping down the trail, stopping often to listen. The trail climbed up into the mountain passes at first before descending down steeply. The mountains were jagged and sharp, the rocks slippery under their hands and boots in the blackness. The drizzle turned into a steady, cool rain. It drew colder as they climbed the forest around them silent and dark. They encountered no enemy forces, arriving undiscovered and exhausted outside of Isurava before daylight on the 12th.

The evening they left Kokoda, Hiroshi came to Captain Hashimoto's company command post to report the readiness of First Company. In the small hut used as a CP, Hiroshi stepped inside without knocking because he was late with his report. He realized his mistake instantly when he saw Warrant Officer Miyamoto in earnest conversation with Captain Hashimoto. They were exchanging something among themselves, both looking up in complete surprise. Miyamoto's eyes hardened with anger, glancing behind Hiroshi. It was Hashimoto who spoke first, his agitation evident with his fierce glance.

"You dare enter my command post without permission?" He hissed, stepping around Miyamoto to confront Hiroshi face to face. Hashimoto's face was beaded with sweat, feverish, his eyes wide and huge in his head. He stared, his pupils dark orbs shrinking slowly to small black dots. Hashimoto never verbally attacked Hiroshi before, but the man who stood inches from Hiroshi's face was a stranger, the skin and eyes reptilian in their coldness. Shocked and embarrassed Hiroshi gasped for air, unable to speak. He bowed deeply to avoid those piercing eyes and began to withdraw from the hut when Hashimoto seized his arm, stopping him. The grip was incredibly strong and painful, the hand trembling with energy. Hiroshi stared down at the hand holding his arm and noticed the other hand gripped a shiny steel cylinder with a needle inserted, a syringe. He glanced up in surprise when he realized what he was looking at, meeting Hashimoto's unblinking stare.

"Watch the door, Miyamoto," Hashimoto whispered, his eyes not leaving Hiroshi's. Miyamoto passed Hiroshi like a shadow. The grip on his arm slowly relaxed until Hiroshi felt Hashimoto's hand release his arm to gently grip his shoulder. This touch was collegial, almost fatherly. The eyes remained the same as Hashimoto perceptively stepped back a few inches, his hand remaining. Hiroshi could still feel the tremor on his shirt as Hashimoto's eyes closed slightly, a wisp of a smile spreading across his face. The eyes finally moved from left to right, brushing Hiroshi's face with a heat ray intensity making his skin crawl. His own sweat ran freely from his pores further burning his eyes, making him blink from the sting. He wanted more than anything to be free of this man, to run away from the hut.

"So, Hiroshi," Hashimoto never addressed Hiroshi by his first name, and the sound of his name struck fear deep in his heart. He began to tremble himself, and he sensed Hashimoto could feel it. Hashimoto nodded his head like an old sage, his eyelids closing to narrow slits before opening wide.

"You have nothing to fear, Hiroshi," he stated quietly. Hashimoto's eyes moved slightly to the right and Hiroshi sensed Miyamoto was right behind him. He could hardly breathe he was so frightened. Hashimoto nodded again, looking behind Hiroshi before handing the syringe out of sight.

"You know our little secret—well, not really a secret, but a secret we would like to keep among ourselves." Hashimoto's eyes softened before he broke the trance to glance away towards the door.

Hashimoto released his grip on Hiroshi's shoulder to wipe the sweat from his face with a handkerchief. When he looked up again he was transformed, his eyes normal in shape, his pupils large and dark in the shadowy hut. He smiled the thin half-smile of the commanding officer Hiroshi respected and revered, the Samurai leader who protected his men in his honor and grace. Hiroshi felt sick at his stomach. He didn't know what to expect, surprised and frightened when Miyamoto silently stepped around to be in Hiroshi's line of sight.

Miyamoto stood slightly behind and to the right of Hashimoto, his face passive after the moment of anger. He held a syringe and injected it vertically into a vial, withdrawing the fluid into the syringe. Once separated, he held the syringe up level with his face and pressed the circular ring of the syringe up with his thumb, squeezing some of the fluid out of the tip of the needle. Hiroshi knew enough from his own experience Miyamoto was removing air from the syringe. Hardly able to breathe, Hiroshi fearfully followed the path of the syringe until Miyamoto swabbed the crook of his own bare arm with alcohol and poked the needle directly into his bulging veins, popped out with the help of surgical tubing.

Miyamoto closed his eyes dreamily before opening them again slowly as he emptied the syringe. He carefully withdrew the syringe, unwrapping the tubing and swabbing the needle puncture site. Hashimoto never took his eyes off Hiroshi, his arms crossed, the patient teacher waiting for the student.

"What is that?" Hiroshi croaked finally, his voice hardly above a whisper. Miyamoto was taking the syringe apart and was placing it a small container of liquid.

"It is a version of what you drink every day in your tea," Hashimoto murmured quietly. "It allows the Japanese soldier to focus on what he needs to be doing, which is to attack the enemy when he is ordered to, even though he may be tired and hungry. Without it, *Nankai Shitai* would have failed long ago, Lieutenant."

"This is the liquid, injectable form of *Totsugeki-jo?*" Hiroshi asked. Hashimoto made it sound like it was similar to taking a vitamin.

He remembered the little pill Miyamoto gave him on Shikoku so he could stay awake so long ago on the night training exercise. He was not able to sleep for days that first time. *They were drinking it in their tea?*

"Yes it is," Hashimoto added gently. "They are forms of *Shabu*—methamphetamine. A wonder drug developed so the Japanese soldier can overcome human weaknesses to conquer any enemy on the face of the planet. It is sanctioned by the Emperor, and therefore a duty for all Japanese soldiers to use it, because with it we cannot fail."

Hashimoto watched Hiroshi for a few moments in silence. He turned away to pull a small box from his leather satchel. Opening the box carefully, he slid open the outer container, like the shell of a matchbox, to reveal the contents to Hiroshi. They appeared to be hundreds of small white tablets.

"*Nekome-jo* (cat-eye tablet), Lieutenant Takahashi. A supplement for First Company. We will need the extra boost tonight. Make sure the *kangohei* (medical corpsman) distribute these. I want each man to have a least one tablet. There may not be much chance for making tea the next couple of weeks. We will distribute more every day. It suppresses hunger, as you know. Keeps our energy level high. Warrant Officer Miyamoto will provide all you need. You need to ensure the men are taking it, understood?"

Hiroshi stared at the box, finally taking it formally from Hashimoto with both hands as he bowed his head.

"Sir, this is *totsugeki-jo?* "

"A form, perhaps a little stronger."

As Hiroshi brought his head back up, he watched Miyamoto finish drying off the syringe kit and close the small wooden box. He handed it back to Hashimoto, his eyes guarded while looking at Hiroshi.

"You've had it, Lieutenant Takahashi, I gave it to you," Miyamoto said slowly. "Remember?"

"Yes, Warrant Officer, I remember." Hiroshi could not help but notice the exchange of glances between Miyamoto and Hashimoto after he spoke. A curt nod, the tiniest gesture, came from Hashimoto and Miyamoto vanished. Hiroshi was alone with Hashimoto. One moment Miyamoto was standing two feet away from him before disappearing like a ghost. This is what the man is, he thought, *a ghost*. Hiroshi turned to meet Hashimoto eyes, realizing with alarm Hashimoto had been speaking to him.

"*Sir?*" He asked meekly, coming to an exaggerated attention.

"Report?" Hashimoto demanded. "You came in, Lieutenant, to report the readiness of the company to move?"

Before First Company headed down the Track Hiroshi distributed the *Nekome-jo*, slipping a single tablet under his own tongue. He

221

regarded Hashimoto's directive as an order for First Company, including himself. He tried not to think about the syringe, realizing he didn't see Captain Hashimoto inject himself, only Miyamoto. Somehow it did not shock him to see Miyamoto use the syringe, at least not as much as he thought, as his own fear at the time was that Miyamoto was going to inject *him*. He wanted to believe Hashimoto was referring to Miyamoto when he stated *you know our little secret*. Yet the madness in Hashimoto's eyes was the same as Miyamoto's. Hashimoto said the pills were the same drug. Did these little pills have anything to do with Hiroshi's personal sense of discomfort and agitation? Something beyond the growing hunger and stress of the landings and combat action they were subjected too? When he tried to think about it his brain buzzed and spun, his thoughts muddled and confused. His only relief was to push it aside.

Hashimoto called for all officers before they started down the Track, describing visually on a clear patch of semi-dry mud what he knew of Isurava. The small reconnaissance team who reconnoitered the area memorized the varied terrain features for their report to the battalion commander. There were no maps, only the visuals drawn on the ground similar to what Hashimoto was doing for his company officers. There were six little communities stretched over four kilometers north to south on both sides of a narrow watercourse known as Eora Creek. The small communities of Kaile, Missima, Asigari and Abuari were on the east side of Eora Creek up on a high escarpment looking down a steep, heavily forested slope. On the west side of the creek the communities of Isurava and Alola resided approximately two kilometers apart. Both of these communities were built on small plateaus on the peak of another steep escarpment. Most of the Australian forces were on this western escarpment. It was expected the Australians would defend the high ground on both sides of the creek; any envelopment would be from the east-west flanks.

The terrain forced all the steep ground towards the creek, with heavy forest covering the slopes. The recon team described waterfalls, log bridges and numerous trails not easily seen snaking through the forest. Hashimoto explained he understood their job was not to attack the Australians at Isurava, at least not yet, but to determine their defenses and potential weaknesses. The recon team did note however, there was high ground to the west of the escarpment where Isurava and Aloha were. They did not explore this area, but they could see it from different angles. It was there. They felt is might provide a natural approach for a flanking envelopment from the west. Hashimoto noted these comments from the recon team and stuck his stick in the mud

222

representing the area to the west of the escarpment. *First Company will determine if there is a path,* he declared. Hiroshi looked up from the dirt map to find Captain Hashimoto looking right at him.

The company moved away from the Track the first hint of graying light. Miyamoto felt they were about a kilometer or less above the settlement and suggested they stop. He wanted to reconnoiter alone, recommending to Hashimoto to fade the men into the forest on both sides of the Track. The forest here was tall and very dense, with the terrain steep on both sides. The trunks of the trees were enormous, black and slick with moisture. The humidity mixed with the high altitude made breathing difficult, the mist thick like dense coastal fog. It was eerily quiet, no chirp of animals or birds, the only sound the steady drumbeat of water, dripping constantly down from above.

Raingear was useless as the rubberized material retained humidity. A soldier was wet on either side. It was very cold as it grew lighter, with no place to sit or lie down not soaked through or pooled with icy water. The men were miserable, trying to stay within sight of one another. They eventually just sat or leaned on trees, moving their frozen limbs when they couldn't stand the cold or wet any longer. Hiroshi, who stayed close to the headquarters group, was totally exhausted from the all-night movement and wanted nothing more than to sleep. Somehow he did just that, lying down on his poncho on wet ground, trying to shut down his racing brain. One moment he was tamping down the buzzing energy in his head, the next he was being shaken awake.

It was Sergeant Inoue, Miyamoto's assistant. Hiroshi brought his head up slowly, with difficulty, his face numb from pressing against the cold mud under the poncho. He heard voices in quiet conversation close by. Inoue crouched on his heels inches away, his round face muddy and impassive. No emotion ever twisted his face in Hiroshi's experience. Remembering New Britain, he thought of the blood spatters on Inoue's cheeks and forehead as he clubbed the Australian prisoners tied to the trees. Hiroshi screwed his eyes tight for a moment to bring him back to the present. The dim light sifting down was the grey twilight as dawn, the earlier mists lower and thicker. Inoue motioned with his hands, offering Hiroshi a cup. It was tea, hot with wisps of steam from the top. *Hot tea? They built a fire?* Hiroshi forced himself up as Inoue pressed the cup in his hand.

"Captain Hashimoto asked me to wake you, Lieutenant," Inoue said impatiently, leaning away from Hiroshi once he took the cup. "We are moving down the trail towards Isurava, there are no Australians near us."

Hiroshi blinked, sipping the scalding brew as his brain slowly cleared. *Totsugeki-jo.* He vaguely recalled the slog in the darkness, concentrating on the dim luminescence of the tree bark tied to the back of the assault pack in front of him. It was hard to see, but with no light at all, the snaking, sudden dropping or rising movement of the pack was all there was in the blackness.

No Australians. It explained why they made tea. No enemy to notice or discover them. Hiroshi nodded his head gratefully for the tea, ignoring his rumbling stomach. He pulled his sleeve back from his wrist, appalled to find his watch covered with mud. As he wiped away the gummy slime he could see the dial was misted over from the inside. At close examination his worst fear was realized, water under the crystal. The hands were stopped and no amount of shaking released the second hand. Waterproof at one time, the humidity and constant exposure to water at New Britain and now New Guinea finally ruined it. Frustrated, he tapped the crystal as the liquid sloshed inside.

"What time is it, Sergeant?" Inoue grunted, not even looking at his watch.

"About 10 o'clock in the morning, Lieutenant." Hiroshi looked up at Inoue with surprise, as the big man easily rose to his feet. It was breaking light when they moved into the trees at dawn. Hiroshi fell asleep as soon as they stopped moving—four, maybe five hours ago? Is that possible? He glanced up into the canopy, following the dark trees as they rose only a few meters before disappearing into the mist. *He slept on his face in the mud for five hours?* He turned to Sergeant Inoue but there was no one there.

It was much easier to walk the Track in the daylight, even in the dim twilight under the canopy. Captain Hashimoto sent scouts 200 meters in front of the column and a security platoon to trail behind. The company stopped less than half a kilometer from the outskirts of the settlement. In his reconnaissance Miyamoto discovered two light machinegun crews on each side of the track about 100 meters out, one staggered about 30 meters higher than the other to cover the northern approach. Each team was supported by riflemen and a single strand cable radio telephone. After skirting around the LMGs, Miyamoto made his way back to the company. He also discovered, quite by accident, a small, flat and reasonably level clearing about 150 meters off the Track hidden from view. It was here they were headed, knowing more Australians would be coming down the Track during the daylight hours as they slipped out of Kokoda.

For the next several days the company maintained a very low profile, suffering constant exposure to the cold and rain without the benefit of physical movement. Captain Hashimoto allowed only small reconnaissance teams to leave the clearing to observe the Australians coming down the Track, while others kept an eye on defensive developments in the settlement. The teams went out before dawn and stayed out of sight all day, with strict orders not to engage except to defend themselves. After four days the movement down the Track trickled to nothing.

Hashimoto deciding most of the Australians had withdrawn from Kokoda and were now in Isurava. He sent a small team led by Lieutenant Tanaka back up to Kokoda to inform his battalion commander of the situation. With the 39th Battalion now in Isurava preparing to make a stand, Hashimoto believed it was time to reveal their presence and false intentions by sending out small aggressive patrols on both sides of Eora Creek, using the known common trails. He wanted the Australians to believe these would be the likely route of any attack. At the same time, he sent Hiroshi and Miyamoto to reconnoiter the high ground to the west with the exact opposite directive: search for hidden approaches for a flank attack on the Isurava plateau, avoid discovery.

Even before First Company began the aggressive patrolling, most of the men had eaten the last of the Australian rations from the airdrop. Since he wanted the Australians to be aware of their presense, Hashimoto authorized the use of fires, mostly for brewing tea. If nothing else, Hashimoto noted sadly to his officers, at least the men were drinking boiled stream water, reducing the risk of dysentery. He did not mention to the other officers as he had to Hiroshi, the point *Totsugeki-jo* reduced the desire for food. It would not have made much difference now, Hiroshi thought, as it was obvious food was on everyone's mind all of the time.

This wasn't a situation of reduced rations or none at all for a day or two during a short-term assault. Yokohama Advance Party arrived on New Guinea July 20th—nearly a month ago. They stretched their initial two-week ration issue into nearly three even under the incredible caloric demand of climbing the Kokoda Track at a relentless pace. All of the men lost at least 20 percent of their body weight coming up to Kokoda. The few days of supplies provided by the unexpected food drop gave the men a chance to staunch the growing hunger, nothing more. It was all gone now. As the days passed, a sense of hopelessness descended on the company. They knew their limited food supply was by design. The Japanese Imperial Army expected them to forage for food where there was no food available. The facts were being ignored by command at Rabaul and the men felt abandoned. Hiroshi sensed it in the way the men withdrew from one another, and how he felt himself.

The aggressive patrolling was brutal on the men, the patrols often mauled with several dead and wounded from brief, violent fire fights.

The patrols were having the desired effect. The Australians appeared to be reinforcing the trails being patrolled. Hiroshi, sitting through some of the debriefing sessions as part of the company headquarters staff, was struck how often the patrol members went on about the smell of cooking fires, food and brewing tea throughout the Isurava settlement.

Captain Hashimoto would press through these comments, patiently redirecting his men to be more specific with their observations on the defensive situation; the strength of the positions and the weapons used. Did the Australians appear to be conserving their ammunition? Did they throw grenades? The damage was done, the exposure was there. The men would return to their platoons to share their impressions to other starving men how well fed the Australians were. As an officer, Hiroshi was also beginning to see a change in the attitudes of the men towards him, the platoon commanders and even Captain Hashimoto. The discipline seemed to be less, the men not as respectful, the growing resentment towards the food situation now directed towards their leadership.

Hiroshi began hallucinating the second night out on the high ground to the west. Up above the settlement the smoke from cooking fires sifted and hung in the forest, like the mist. The delicious odor of stewed meat and tea would not leave them, the scent so strong he felt at times the bully beef was being cooked right around the next tree, instead of a couple of hundred meters down the slope. He had not eaten a meal of any kind for over 48 hours. His stomach gripped in convulsions of explosive gas, the result of tea and more tea, mixed with the bitterness of bits of foliage he nibbled and sampled out of desperation. The rain was constant, or seemed to be as water droplets fell from above in an endless train of cold splotches on his back and face. He coughed up phlegm, fearful he was getting sick, his weakness growing as his mind seemed less and less able to focus on the here and now, whatever he was doing.

The light came from above, a bright yellow light, the warmth glowing like a small sun. He blinked in the steady rain, the brown greyness around him not responding to the light as it should. It confused him, but the attraction, the warmth and sense of dryness was too great. Hiroshi reached out to hold the orb in his hand only to find sudden darkness then excruciating pain when he was bodily thrown to the wet ground on his face. The crushing weight on his back made it impossible to breathe, so he fought back, swinging wildly only to get his arms pinned and a filthy hand clamped hard on his mouth.

"Lieutenant!" the voice hissed in his ear. He hesitated. *"Stop moving! Flares!"* The pressure on his back lifted just enough so he could suck in a lungful air through his nose, the hand remaining on his mouth.

The light above was ebbing as his head was twisted firmly to the right, where Sergeant Inoue's face was inches away. It was Inoue lying on top of Hiroshi and holding him down. The eyes were cold and expressionless. Inoue could have been holding down a small child, considering the lack of physical strain on his face. Hiroshi closed his eyes briefly, opening them again to slowly nod his head.

"Are you all right? Are you sure?" The grip on Hiroshi's face and head remained tight as a vise. He nodded more vigorously as Inoue twisted his face up towards something out of Hiroshi's line of sight.

"Let him up," Hiroshi heard Miyamoto say in a whisper.

The Australians fired flares at night on the Kokoda plain in the open country. Up in the mountain forest mortars were rarely used because of the overhead canopy. Once the mortar bomb left the tube any contact—overhead branches, tree limbs either on the outbound or inbound path of the parabola—would depress the nose plunger and detonate the bomb instantly, showering the ground below with shrapnel. In Isurava the gunners had a few apparent sky windows, using them for night illumination. It was still strange with the ever present mists, as the flares only lit a portion of the sky for a second or two. A layered, shadowy world of veiled sections of tree tops, then smoky glowing soup as the flares descended into mist layers; then sudden blinding brightness as the flares, fully revealed, slipped into a thin wedge of clear air before dropping to the ground in a cluster of sparks.

Hiroshi, even in his spacey state of awareness, was hyper-vigilant to sight and sounds. It seemed when there was momentary light from the flares, he was able to hear and see *everything* crystal clearly at great distances. Down below as the flares descended he viewed, like a telescopic lens, what appeared to be a half a dozen trails snaking through the forest. He could also see, in the momentary vision, small clusters of men in fighting pits scattered among the trees. Then it faded and was gone. He heard Miyamoto cluck his tongue with obvious pleasure; he assumed Miyamoto saw the same thing.

A light machinegun, a Bren, stuttered several short bursts to the east. A rifle fired a single shot, a solid bark like an SMLE .303. A grenade exploded to their east, a dull small flash quickly followed by a flurry of rifle and machinegun fire. *Contact.* Bren, SMLE and the lighter snap of Arisaka 6.5mm rifles crackled like popcorn below them. As quickly as it started it stopped. Another flare popped and sizzled under its white parachute, seemingly right above them, forcing all of them to screw their eyes tight and instinctively lower their heads. Another Bren fired a long burst, shooting at something only the gunner could see, real or imagined.

Hiroshi heard, out of the silence of the forest amidst the steady

227

plops of rain drops or dripping water, voices, human voices trying to mimic animal voices. *Cawing, cackling, warbling* notes like the black and white magpies so common to Shikoku echoed up through the forest. He knew the troops with experience in Shanghai used it to good effect against the Chinese. It confused and frightened them.

To the west they heard the same bird calls coming back, only louder. *It was the Australians!* Hiroshi glanced over at Miyamoto as the flare faded. Miyamoto seemed to be smiling as he shook his head slowly.

Kep it oop, ya' bloody jabberin' monkeys! The voice, strong and measured, carried up easily into the trees. It was followed by a long burst from a Bren, then silence on both sides.

The Australians must have a large supply of flares as they fired a half a dozen more over the next couple of hours. The probing patrols withdrew, apparently, with the Australian fire discipline good enough to ensure there was no more rifle or machinegun fire. During one of the flare descents Miyamoto presented Hiroshi another *Nekome-jo*. At first Hiroshi refused, but Miyamoto pressed it in his hand firmly.

"We're all hungry, are we not, Lieutenant?" he declared quietly. "This will make the pain go away for a time. Make you sharper, and I need you sharper." He motioned Sergeant Inoue to crawl in closer. When he did so, Miyamoto dropped a *Nekome-jo* into the man's hand and patted him on the head. Miyamoto looked at both men, his eyes bright with energy.

"We now know there is a clear path to flank the Australians up here in the forest; that part of our mission is complete. I propose, Lieutenant, we slip down below and use one of these trails to find something to eat. I want to take it personally from the Australians!"

"I thought our orders are not to make contact, Warrant Officer," Hiroshi whispered warily. As the flare died, small sparks reflected on Miyamoto's pupils, like dancing flames. Amused yet unblinking, Miyamoto licked his white teeth as the darkness shrouded his face. Although Hiroshi could no longer see him, the voice was inches away. Hiroshi imagined the eyes.

"I propose then, Lieutenant, we don't make unnecessary *contact*. That implies a fighting encounter of some kind. I don't want to fight any Australians, I plan to steal their food!"

"Won't that give away our intentions to attack from this high ground?" Miyamoto snorted contemptuously in the dark, which Hiroshi found humiliating. His face flushed warm and his hands gripped into fists. He might as well have laughed in Hiroshi's face. His mind raced but he could think of nothing to say. He was too angry to speak anyway.

He almost jumped out of his skin when Miyamoto gripped his arm firmly before releasing it.

"They won't have any idea where we came from. All they will know in the morning is someone stole some of their food. Agreed, Lieutenant Takahashi?"

Following Miyamoto and Sergeant Inoue as closely and quietly as possible, Hiroshi estimated it was about an hour before they stopped moving. They remained motionless next to a large tree trunk for several minutes, the only sound the steady *plop plop plop* of the water drops coming down. As Hiroshi's senses became aware of his surroundings, he noticed the pungent odor of a burning cigarette and the soft, gentle murmur of a human voice. Both seemed very close.

No flares were fired since they slid down the slope, the night a coal bin. Hiroshi could sense his companion's next to him. Miyamoto was suddenly closer, his lips nearly touching Hiroshi's ear.

"*Two of them,* both awake. Stay here and cover us. Don't fire your weapon. Stay put, we'll come back to you. Understand?" Hiroshi mumbled his *yes,* seriously frightened someone could hear them.

They were gone in an instant. Hiroshi turned around to press his back against the tree. He could see nothing around him. The rain drops continued to fall, but the cigarette odor faded and there were no more voices. After a few minutes he heard a brief struggle somewhere close by, more of a muffled scuffling. Hiroshi had no knife, learning long ago to leave his officer's sword on reconnaissance missions. It was too long, requiring excessive space to draw and use. He felt defenseless since he couldn't use his pistol.

He stopped breathing instinctively when a dark form, somehow blacker than the darkness around it, moved across his peripheral vision. He jerked when a hand touched his shoulder from the other side. It was Miyamoto, leaning close to his ear again.

"I have something for you to carry." A bag, some kind of large hemp woven sack similar to one used to carry potatoes, was pressed into his hands. It was heavy, full of metal tins and other things.

"Hold it tight, do not let it rattle," Miyamoto ordered. Miyamoto's hand was on Hiroshi's shoulder, and Hiroshi picked up the scent, familiar and nauseating. It was unmistakable. It was sweet and sour, freshly spilled and damp. The hand, perhaps the entire arm was coated with blood. Hiroshi could sense Miyamoto staring at him but the black, glittering orbs were not visible, only felt. The scent of blood, or his reaction to it was quickly lost and forgotten when he moved the bag. A new scent took over, for in his heightened state he recognized the odor of cheese, meat and bread. His mind and stomach erupted in sensory alarm. *Food!* He started to open the bag but Miyamoto gripped his arm

229

hard, pressing his lips to Hiroshi's ear once more.

"Later! We eat once we get back up on the slope. They are all around us. *Very dangerous.* Follow me exactly." This time Sergeant Inoue fell in to the trail position, staying right behind Hiroshi. More than once, when Hiroshi thought he lost Miyamoto in the darkness, he felt a hand on his back or leg, pointing in a direction. It was humiliating, all of it, but in the end the bag was all he really cared about right now. He needed to eat. Miyamoto found them food; that is all that mattered.

CHAPTER 18

August 24, 1942, First Company, 1/144th Infantry, Advance Party, Isurava

Sometimes it was difficult to distinguish the difference between being in some form of dream state or actually awake. Even reality was questionable in moments of pure confusion when he could not be certain what he was experiencing. He used to always know when he was dreaming. His mother considered him an imaginative boy, laughing at his dreams but often adding *you're just making that up, Hiroshi!* This angered him, as he only occasionally embellished his dreams to make them more interesting to his listeners. The dreams near the end of the night, the short ones flying across his brain like movie picture frames were special and pleasant, like any good experience he wanted to repeat. He looked forward to it with expectation. He knew he was dreaming a scene as moldable as soft clay. He could kick up and fly, hover for long periods high above buildings, fields, people and animals. He had strength and speed, but most of all the freedom and knowledge of doing something with a predictable outcome. If it wasn't, you just pulled the plug on the dream.

In some of his dreams here in the high canopy he could either open or close his eyes and nothing would change. Now he waited awhile before his brain would accept this unchanging state as being a reliable indicator of being awake. What he saw or felt was often excruciatingly clear and tactile. He could taste food with every bit of his sensory ability, feel the texture of the meat, soft, juicy and spicy with herbs on his tongue pressed against his teeth. He could see it at a distance, smell it and eat it at the same time. His endless hunger, with convulsive spasms across his empty gut, sometimes triggered a switch, a toggle of recognition which was getting harder and harder to accept, that if he was awake there would be *no food*. Reality was nothing to eat. This in turn released intense disappointment. This disappointment had a color, dark grey. It would permeate his thoughts, his vision, becoming neutral. The intensity of his dream world would evaporate with the grey tones around him, his sensory reaction dull. It made it easier. This was the reality of being awake. Of being hungry all of the time.

After nearly two weeks hiding and living in the shadows of the forest, First Company was no longer operating like a Japanese Imperial Army Infantry unit any observer would recognize. Except for occasional firefights caused by roving patrols, the daytime—the twilight world obscured by three layers of high canopy and swirling mists when it wasn't raining so hard you couldn't see 10 meters—was eerily quiet. The men kept to themselves when not assigned to patrols or observation duties. They turned inward, speaking in whispers. No one could shave or bathe unless they stripped naked and stood in the icy rain. After a few days the soldiers gave up and stayed in their uniforms, slowly turning the same grey as the earth.

They were never dry in the forest. Even in the heat of the day, dampness and wet ruled anything in contact with their skin. They watched their skin layers fall off and a bone structure appear in startling detail from the lack of nutrition. Captain Hashimoto was rarely seen, although he was close by and didn't go out on any of the patrols. It was as if the world stood still for First Company. A small group of soldiers found the energy to do most of the patrolling, but they secretly kept their energy level up because they were the best fed. Now and then a patrol would go bold and get close, finding taro roots or tiny onion shafts near a hut. Hiroshi learned this quickly, as did a few of the others. The smell of cooking fires or meat was too great. Desperation demanded risk. To move about in the daylight was extremely dangerous, but Isurava settlement had some food available in the abandoned gardens if you looked for it, and the Australians usually carried rations with them on patrol. And tobacco. You had to kill them to get it. Very little of it came back.

The greyness of the daytime twilight was blending, soaking into the skin and darkened souls of the soldiers who stayed behind to hover in the forest. They could feel the encroachment, but they had no power to resist it. The moisture of the mists was soon indistinguishable from the slick slime on the trees and the ground, or in their lungs or mouths. For a few who were so weak from hunger, malaria or other tropical disease the desire to eat was leaving them. They discovered the habit of chewing still hard to break. The green slime and moss around their mouths, no longer wiped off, was a telltale. The men were eating dirt. Hiroshi sensed some of these soldiers felt a powerful desire to lie down in the icy mud and just not get up, like men in the later stages of hypothermia. They wouldn't look at him or any of the other officers. The officers and NCOs left them alone. They were leaving. It was easy. Lay down. Don't move. Not ever.

Hiroshi didn't know how many men succumbed to this temptation. The strict discipline of weeks past was gone for all but a few of the men. Lethargy, hopelessness and weakness slipped into their souls and there was no military solution other than feeding them. There was no category for their passing available except "death by illness". *Starvation* was not a legitimate explanation for grieving relatives. The

232

platoon leaders would report casualties daily as either KIA (killed in action) or WIA (wounded in action). To be ill enough to require evacuation, considering this meant a native bearer stretcher ride nearly *90 kilometers,* was out of the question. Direct removal from the immediate combat area to an aid station was about the only option for the sick or wounded. For First Company down on the front side of the Track, it meant the surgical aid station up at Kokoda.

There wasn't much in the way of serious medical treatment available even there. Second Lieutenant Tanaka, who was often assigned the task of taking information from Captain Hashimoto up to the Advance Party leadership at Kokoda, was brutal in his assessment of the aid station. *There is nothing there, except maybe a quiet place to die*, he said. Men were lying all over the ground, covered with flies. There was little medicine and few supplies, and of course, no food. *A very depressing place. If you get wounded*, Tanaka added quietly, *just stay here. Why suffer the ride all the way up there?* All of them watched the process of wounded men being evacuated. It comforted them, it was a way out. Now they knew. Wounded men who were too injured to heal on the line were carried out by First Company men. They would meet the native bearers a few kilometers up the hill and return. There was always the feeling the wounded men were getting away to a better place. No more.

The combat losses as they waited for the rest of *Nankai Shitai* to arrive were not many, a man here and there shot while on a contact patrol. The Australians were excellent patrollers and marksmen. Sometimes patrols crossed each other's path at almost pointblank range, the result a brief violent firefight as both sides tried to extricate themselves with minimum losses. The Australians, with their short-range but very effective Thompson submachine guns backed up by Bren LMGs, could cut the jungle foliage to ribbons in seconds with 100 bullets and take the biggest bite. The Japanese patrols only carried their Nambu LMGs on the longer range patrols. Their disadvantage with only bolt-action rifles was obvious. They broke even when they surprised the Australians, closing at almost touching range so bayonet and sword could be used to full advantage.

If the Australians spotted a Japanese patrol first losses were not always inevitable, but expected. First Company patrol members not alert and using cover and concealment *all of the time* would rarely be given a second chance. A single .303 rifle shot would bark and echo through the forest as a Japanese soldier dropped like a sack of potatoes, his skull punctured. His colleagues, moving as cautiously as they could so they didn't suffer the same fate, would try to view the body to confirm his death before withdrawing. The body would be left where it fell. The patrol survivors were very conscious the enemy was watching and rarely alone. The dead man's friends would grieve for him, hoping to recover the body once Isurava was taken.

The loss of confidence made Hiroshi question again the planning of the Japanese Imperial Army. Men were willing to die for their country and their Emperor if the need arose, but not for every circumstance and certainly not for a lack of food or equipment. A Japanese medical corpsman, *kangohei,* carried only essential first aid equipment, not even aspirin. Morphiates for pain and medicines to combat infections were only available at surgical aid stations, until even that ran out. Yet Warrant Officer Miyamoto seemed to have an endless supply of the *Nekome-jo* pills for Hiroshi to distribute, and the men were still boiling and drinking the *Totsugeki-jo. You could try to mask the hunger for a few days, but weeks and months at a time? This was insane.*

Hiroshi never went out on contact patrols, which usually involved one or two squads of soldiers led by an experienced NCO or occasionally a junior officer. The job of a contact patrol was just that, probe and seek out the enemy to determine his location and strength. Being a larger force moving through heavy foliage meant a higher likelihood of being seen. At the same token, the force was large enough to sustain and defend itself against most enemy patrol encounters, as the Australians were doing exactly the same thing.

As the Isurava settlement area became more familiar to the First Company patrollers, they realized the true size of the three defensive perimeters established by the Australians, and the relative strength of the defenses for each. In specific areas, especially between Isurava and the Rest House, and the area between the Rest House and Alola, there were huge spaces of thick forest and steep terrain the patrollers found completely open and unguarded. The Australians simply did not have enough men to establish defensive positions out in these areas. This was, as Captain Hashimoto characterized it with his strange thin smile, *no-man's land, or Indian country*. He didn't have to explain himself, most of his officers had seen American westerns and early settler films. It was right out of *The Last of the Mohicans* and *Stagecoach*.

Both sides conducted contact patrols in these open areas. The three settlements were established in the most level, hospitable areas with easy access to water, clear spaces for what passed for buildings, huts and what little ground that could be used for growing food. The areas between the settlements were steep, heavily forested, rocky and dangerous to traverse at night. The gorge carved by Eora Creek was cavernous at some places, falling 80 or 90 meters straight down. Access to the water was impossible here, with constant mist from waterfalls and slick rocks around the gorges an invitation for disaster for the unwary and less sure-footed. From the edge of the gorge the escarpments on both sides climbed abruptly up into thick, almost impenetrable forest.

The contact patrols served their purpose. The men were platoon volunteers for the most part, led by their platoon leaders or platoon NCOs. The camaraderie of the platoons, if there was any for a Japanese officer, excluded Hiroshi now. Warrant Officer Miyamoto and Sergeant Inoue continued their small intelligence-gathering patrols almost every day. Once Hiroshi realized how effective Miyamoto was in finding food while on these patrols he asked if he could join them. Miyamoto didn't seem to mind and Hiroshi knew Captain Hashimoto approved. The small patrols, covering as much as a dozen kilometers every day, discovered many of the little trails leading up from the creek to the escarpment on both sides. These were carefully mapped for the eventual arrival of the rest of *Nankai Shitai*.

As the days passed both sides settled into a predictable routine. The Japanese respect for the Australian's fighting prowess seemed to be mutual. Firefights on contact patrols were over in seconds, each side withdrawing immediately to keep the losses down. They licked their wounds, did not pursue each other, and noted the strength and location of the contact. The Australians were trying to hold onto what they had. They instinctively understood or knew First Company didn't have enough men to pursue the attack and was only there to probe, hold and determine the strength of the Australian defenses. Neither side had the ability to overwhelm the other, so they didn't try. A wary standoff but one where men still died every day for the latter half of the month of August. Both sides, Hiroshi thought, were waiting for reinforcements. The first to receive them would go on the offensive. He tried not to think about what would happen to First Company, reduced to only a few dozen men truly effective as soldiers, if the Australians received their reinforcements first.

After dozing in the mud for an hour or two 30 meters outside of a small cluster of thatch structures in the Rest Area settlement, Hiroshi awoke with a start to the aromatic scent of sweet tea and cooked wheat or barley of some kind. He could see in the growing light the rest of the village 100 meters away, a curl of smoke coming from some of the chimneys. No one was moving around outside yet. The three of them, Hiroshi, Miyamoto and Sergeant Inoue—awoke at the same time. Hiroshi slowly shook his head, blinking hard to confirm he wasn't dreaming. The numbness of his body seemed separate and distant from him, a painless remoteness making his body unimportant somehow.

His mind spun and swirled, finding difficulty in focusing his thoughts. He realized his trust in Miyamoto was now complete in this

235

kind of endeavor. He knew they were in a dangerous place, but these raids right in the villages at first light when people started to cook bore fruit. *Cooking fires meant food.* Most Australian soldiers, unless they were on a defensive position, weren't up. Only a few would be preparing meals. They were at least 50 meters inside the defensive perimeter established for the Rest Area, which meant there were Australian soldiers *in front and behind them.*

Hiroshi couldn't even remember how they got there. It was much darker then. They knew many of the interior trails between the Isurava and the Rest Area settlements by heart now, coming down the same trails night after night once they realized the Australians didn't cover them. The Australians withdrew to their perimeter and the trails were left wide open until daylight, when their own contact patrols became active again. The Australians still fired flares periodically at night, but they understood there was little likelihood of a major attack with the current forces in standoff. They even withdrew most of their listening posts outside of the perimeter line. The Japanese recon teams were able to traverse the trails quickly all night with confidence. That is, men like Hiroshi had complete confidence in men like Miyamoto to get them exactly where they needed to go.

In the beginning Hiroshi was left behind as Miyamoto and Sergeant Inoue crept into the structures on these raids. Hiroshi tried to believe he had a necessary role, covering Miyamoto and Inoue from outside in case Australian soldiers came around. His shame was complete one morning, however, when Sergeant Inoue, his arms and face covered with fresh blood spray, pushed him aside to reach first into a booty bag to select an unopened ration can. Stunned, Hiroshi stepped aside, aware Miyamoto observed the incident and did nothing except to offer Hiroshi food from his own bag. The message was clear: *officer or not, you didn't take this food from the Australians. We did. You wait your turn.*

The same day Hiroshi asked and received instructions on how to kill silently with a knife. Miyamoto taught him, allowing Hiroshi to attack him repeatedly from behind with a short stick until Miyamoto was satisfied Hiroshi would be able to do the job without getting himself killed. Hiroshi was appalled with the brutality in the mechanics of a knife attack, but was determined to get his own food, not rely on the charity of others. His desire to be the equal of his comrades was stronger than the revulsion he felt when he considered what he was doing. It was necessary, he told himself, he had the right to survive any way he could. The Australians were the enemy. They had food. Miyamoto ordered Sergeant Inoue to get Hiroshi a knife. A few hours later Inoue handed

Miyamoto a small sheath knife with a short blade.

Miyamoto handled it approvingly before giving it to Hiroshi. Hiroshi asked why the blade was so short, less than 100 millimeters in length. Miyamoto, his eyes glistening, reached over and touched the blade carefully with his finger. *Razor sharp,* he said soothingly. *You're not stabbing people with this knife, remember. Too much of a chance for noise. You don't need depth to cut a man's throat. Two or three inches of blade is all you need. It just needs to be razor sharp.*

Their boldness was astonishing when he first thought about it. He didn't anymore, because hunger honed his willingness to take such risks and success with Miyamoto was—well, a given. The end justified the means. Miyamoto's cold demeanor, rock solid competence and steel nerves calmed Hiroshi, who was thinking of what they might find in the hut to eat without regard to how many Australians were inside. Every time Miyamoto and Sergeant Inoue crept back outside from a raid, their hands and faces dotted with blood spray and carrying a sack of food, they shrugged their shoulders when Hiroshi asked how many Australians were present. He knew they must've killed the cooks and anyone who was up and potentially able to sound the alarm. What about any others? Were there men sleeping? Sergeant Inoue ignored his questions while Miyamoto would just look at him evenly in silence, as if to say, *why don't you come along and find out?*

Miyamoto tapped Hiroshi's arm to point at the knife in his hand, a quick directive for Hiroshi to arm himself. *Follow along,* Miyamoto whispered, *stay close behind Inoue. Watch what we do. There are rarely more than two awake and cooking this time of morning. It will be dark in the hut, Inoue and I will move quickly. Soon as you are inside, move so your back is to the wall right by the door. No one must escape, understand? Observe and do nothing unless we tell you to. As your eyes get used to the dark, look to the walls for weapons, the Australians tend to lean their rifles on walls or beams.*

Hiroshi's heart was pressing up against his throat and pounding so loud in his head he could hardly hear Miyamoto. It beat and throbbed like a kettle drum. He nodded his head slowly of his understanding, his hands slick with sweat. Miyamoto leaned in so close Hiroshi could feel Miyamoto's lips touching his ear. *Don't do anything, Lieutenant. Is that clear? I don't want you killed.* He leaned back and stared hard at Hiroshi, his eyes unblinking dark brilliant black dots. Inoue crept in on his left, his huge shoulders brushing tight up against Hiroshi. His face, coated with fresh mud like Miyamoto, was alert and impassive. He looked right through Hiroshi.

They watched the open spaces around the three structures for several minutes, seeing or hearing no movement. They were only going to enter the one hut with a cooking fire. No one moved about the other structures in the main village 100 meters away. There were no barking dogs, squealing pigs or livestock of any kind anywhere in the village to call an alarm. If there were when Advance Party arrived many days before, Hiroshi mused, they would have been eaten within a day or two.

As Miyamoto explained to him a few days earlier, about two-thirds of the Australians living in a hut would be out on the defensive perimeter all night, so the ones in the hut were off duty and sleeping. These men were also apparently responsible for preparing meals for the ones returning from perimeter duty. Once the cooking fires were started at first light, the men on the perimeter would start cycling back to the hut to get something to eat and a cup of tea unless the Japanese were so rude as to mount an attack at the same time. Miyamoto knew this procedure from constant observation. Miyamoto also added, with a sly smile, *we're trying to get breakfast before the Australians start coming in and take it all!* There was about a 30 minute interval from first light, the lighting of the cooking fires, and the appearance of the first men coming in for breakfast. The morning raids they conducted so far were never in the same place. The Australians always seemed surprised.

Miyamoto got up in a half crouch and was halfway to the first hut in a heartbeat. Inoue joined him a second later, sprinting silently to the side of the hut with an incredible lightness on his feet considering his size. Hiroshi followed suit, surprised how winded he was once he reached the hut. The three of them hugged the mixed thatch outer wall without actually touching it, listening for a moment before Miyamoto signaled with his hand they were going around to the front. The structure, a surprisingly elaborate wooden framed construction when examined up close, was covered with a mixture of small stripped branches, straw thatch and roughly sawn lumber woven together tight enough you couldn't see inside the hut. Hiroshi glanced over to the structure directly adjoining, noticing the door was closed and there was no smoke coming from the chimney. He also peered nervously across the forest floor and narrow clearing to the next small structure and the village beyond. There wasn't a sound or any movement.

Miyamoto and Inoue made an abrupt turn, pulling a wooden door open and charging inside in one swift motion. Hiroshi, a few feet behind them, didn't hesitate to follow them. He heard the sound of a struggle the instant Miyamoto and Inoue were inside, the muffled grunts and thuds terrifying but Miyamoto had made him even more afraid of something else—a released cry or scream loud enough to awake the sleeping men all around them in the village. Inside Hiroshi could see nothing at all at first. The smell of cooked food, wood smoke and the sour sweet odor of blood and unwashed human beings overwhelmed him. He followed his instructions and immediately backed himself up to the interior wall next to the door, his hand clutching his knife as his eyes searched frantically in the moving shadows. There was no doubt in his mind to the source of a gagging, gurgling sound, as the light shifted in the room revealing a pale man's head nearly severed from his body, suspended in mid-air, until Sergeant Inoue's face appeared above it, pulling the skull back, widening the gaping, carving raw slash of glistening wet from ear to ear.

As his vision improved Hiroshi could see there were at least six men in the small room, one standing, Sergeant Inoue, and one kneeling, Miyamoto. Two bodies were motionless, slumped down next to a portable two burner stove, while Miyamoto and Inoue were slashing, cutting and punching two men so furiously Hiroshi watched motionless in stunned horror. Against the wall stud, as Miyamoto noted earlier, were three or four Lee Enfield rifles propped up vertically. Hiroshi remembered suddenly Miyamoto's brutal attack on the reconnaissance team on their training exercise, months or years before on Shikoku. Hiroshi watched mesmerized until he noticed a face lifting up in surprise from a bunk on the far side of the room. Fearful the man would start screaming, Hiroshi stepped out of the shadows and picked up the closest Lee Enfield, rushing the man as he started to lift up from the bunk. Hiroshi reversed the rifle and attacked the man. The Australian, thin, wiry and heavily bearded, never saw the blows coming.

Hiroshi hit the man again and again, knowing he killed the man with the second or third blow. The heavy rifle and metal butt plate on the end of the stock crushed the skull like a watermelon. The sound was sickening, the skull bones cracking and disintegrating as they mixed with the watery mush of exploding brain tissue. Hiroshi was only aware of his own breathing, or gasping, as the exertion exhausted him, but he kept swinging the rifle. Miyamoto gripped the fore stock of the rifle just as Hiroshi was about to deliver his eighth or ninth blow, stopping the forward motion. Hiroshi whirled around in surprise until he recognized Miyamoto. Miyamoto, soaked in blood like a butcher, held Hiroshi's eyes for a long moment.

"He's dead, Lieutenant. You did a good job. We didn't see him in the darkness. But we made a lot of noise. We need to get what we can and leave immediately." Miyamoto didn't release his grip on the rifle, instead he steadily pulled on it until Hiroshi let go of it.

"Help us gather food, Lieutenant," he ordered.

When Miyamoto felt they ran out of time, he had them gather up their sacks and stand behind the door. He peered outside through the open crack for a moment, before partially closing the door. There were a few Australian soldiers walking about over across the clearing at the village, but they were a 100 meters away. Miyamoto had them each pick up a flat, English Commonwealth issue helmet and a Lee Enfield rifle, after yanking the cloth hair covers off their heads. They stuffed these in their pockets. He glanced at them carefully, shaking his head. Their uniforms were two shades too dark, but the color really didn't matter since they all looked like they just butchered a cow. The drying blood on their uniforms, hands and faces was a bright rust color now.

"There are soldiers across the field, so we walk outside with the helmets on and the rifles in our hands. Walk upright and casual, like you were going out to replace someone on guard duty. Walk straight outside and make the right turn and we'll be mostly out of view. We won't look all that out of the ordinary."

Hiroshi put on the strange helmet and hefted the rifle, waiting his turn. He stepped outside with his rifle and bag of food and simply turned right and then right again. Once out of direct sight of the soldiers milling around by the Rest Area, the three of them crouched down. It was light now and Australian voices could be heard from a distance. Realizing it was just a matter of time before soldiers would be coming in for their breakfast, Miyamoto led them again in a casual saunter for about 30 meters until they were back in the familiar protection of the forest. They removed the helmets and stuffed them with the rifles out of sight in the trees. Their only weapons now were their handguns and knives.

They crept forward in the forest, aware the small trails leading from the defensive perimeter crisscrossed the forest when coming from the east, the direction they wanted to go to escape into the steep, thick growth heading down towards Eora Creek. After about five minutes Miyamoto signaled to Hiroshi and Inoue there were Australians in front of them. Hiroshi knew they were approaching the perimeter.

Miyamoto led them in through a break in the perimeter last night, but Hiroshi had no idea if they were coming up on the same location. In the dark, and admittedly here in the semi-twilight under the triple canopy, the forest all looked the same. Some of the trails, however, especially the ones leading from the creek area they tended to use every night, were becoming familiar. He knew enough to head east towards the creek until he encountered a recognizable trail. He had a compass but relied entirely on Miyamoto for cross country navigation on these recon patrols. Why not? Miyamoto knew exactly where he was and where they were going. He had no map except the one he drew himself, and only occasionally stopped to look at his complicated, radium dial lensatic compass. *The man could see in the dark.*

Miyamoto crept forward, immediately disappearing from sight.

The heat of the day was evident and oppressive even this early, as any sense of night coolness was gone. It had not rained for a couple of hours, but the air was soggy damp and humid with a thin mist up in the trees. Hiroshi turned his head slowly to the right to glance at Sergeant Inoue, not surprised to see him as motionless and fixed as a stone, his narrow, darting eyes the only indication of his watchfulness.

The excitement of his fight with the Australian soldier in the hut, if you could call it that, spun Hiroshi's energies up over the charts. For a short while he felt he could run all night and never tire. He tried to recall what that euphoria felt like. Whatever it was, it was gone now. Hiroshi was completely drained, his eyelids heavy with drowsiness, his brain equally sluggish and depleted. He ran so long on nerves and pills the reservoir was empty. And for a time there was something else. He felt the incredible sense of personal power growing in him as he attacked the Australian, the sleeper who made the mistake of waking up at the wrong time. For a moment he owned the man, given the power to *destroy* the man's face and skull, take away his ability to retaliate, to kill back. The horrors of the hut—of the pale faces, the gaping throats, the blood— everywhere, seemed remote, distant and dreamlike. *But it was him, wasn't it? The energy, the madness to kill like that, that was him. He wasn't dreaming, was he?*

As easily as he vanished Miyamoto appeared between them. Miyamoto was excited himself, his eyes wide open, the pupils tiny specks. A hand darted out from the staring face and Hiroshi felt his jaw gripped in a vise, his head roughly jerked left and right.

"*Wake up*, Lieutenant!" Miyamoto hissed, his grip tightening so hard Hiroshi felt tears coming to his eyes from the pain. "We're a long ways from safety, and we all need each other to survive the next few minutes! Do you hear me?"

Frightened, furious and in pain, Hiroshi shook his head free from Miyamoto's grip while slapping Miyamoto's hand away. Miyamoto didn't appear surprised, but his pupils dilated as his nostrils flared in visible anger himself. Miyamoto held the hand Hiroshi had slapped away in front of him, suspended and motionless. They stared at each other for long seconds, but Hiroshi, emboldened, would not back down this time.

"Don't you ever touch me again like that, Warrant Officer," Hiroshi seethed between his teeth. Miyamoto stared for a heartbeat before his hand came down, a thin smile forming on his face. He nodded, just briefly, acknowledging Hiroshi.

"Forgive me, Lieutenant," Miyamoto murmured, "my mistake." Hiroshi felt his blood boiling even though he heard the apology. There was a growing pressure behind his eyeballs hot and sharp. He was so

241

angry he could hardly speak. He heard his own fast breathing as if he were running up stairs instead of lying quietly on his stomach in the mud. Miyamoto said nothing. The silence between them stretched out for perhaps a minute. Then as if nothing happened, Miyamoto turned to Sergeant Inoue as if to include him in the conversation. He spoke quietly, requiring Hiroshi and Inoue to lean in closer to hear. He described the perimeter defenses along this stretch in front of them facing due east for 200-300 meters.

"The defenses here are the lightest in the perimeter," he explained, "because the Australians know how steep the terrain is from here down to the creek. We came in here last night about 75 meters to the north of this spot. In the dark we slipped in between two positions and they never knew we were there. But I think we can do as well right here." He glanced at his watch before pointing back towards the settlement.

"The bodies will be discovered any minute and they will be looking for us in the perimeter. We need to get past the perimeter guards before they are alerted."

In front of them, he explained, were two fighting pits about 30 meters apart. These appeared to be the most isolated positions on the eastside of the perimeter. The next defensive positions were at least 50 meters on either side of these two. "The pit on the left has two men, both riflemen. The pit on the right has three men, two members of a Bren gun team and a section corporal. Miyamoto looked at Hiroshi carefully.

"I propose we fade left, use the large unprotected area to stay to the ground and crawl away immediately." Miyamoto glanced up questioningly at Hiroshi, who realized Miyamoto was either asking for Hiroshi's approval or his opinion of the plan.

Once down by the creek they started to breathe again. It took only a few minutes to crawl the 30-40 meters through the low brush before they slipped into the forest. Hiroshi thought he would be shot through the head any second. He felt his head, covered with the dirty hair cover cloth was a huge target. They stayed down flat, pulling themselves along a few inches at a time, camouflaging their outlines with foliage tucked into their collars and belts. They kept going down until they crept into the dark, damp and slimy foliage away from the trails, cautiously picking away the biting ants and insects living in the darkness, finding their way into their clothing. They knew the patrolling Australians would avoid such places so they stayed put despite the discomfort, remaining out of sight.

It was a long day waiting for real darkness. They lay flat, listening to the occasional roving Australian patrols above them near the trails. Miyamoto wouldn't let them open the ration tins from their food bags

242

because of the risk of noise and the smell, but he produced a large chunk of a powdered and sweetened cake. He broke this into three equal pieces to share. They washed this down with the few drops of water left in Hiroshi's canteen. It was the one of the best things Hiroshi's ever tasted. After a few hours in the heat, the drowsiness from their exhaustion overwhelmed them to the point they ignored the insects. Hiroshi awoke to the loud snoring from Sergeant Inoue, which alarmed him instantly once he realized where they were. One of them was supposed to stay awake so the other two could sleep, but even Miyamoto was asleep.

Hiroshi placed his hand carefully over Sergeant Inoue's nose, a trick he learned long ago to quiet his snoring father, and it worked. Inoue snorted before turning slightly, returning to a more quiet form of slumber. Hiroshi stopped for a moment to look at his companions in the dim shadows, men he would never characterize as his friends. He stared in astonishment at the amount of dried blood on their uniforms, hands and faces. There was no love for these men, in many ways he feared and detested them, but he understood he trusted them with his life. There was no escaping this point. He was smart enough to recognize it, more so than the men back in the First Company compound waiting to die. These two men had given him life, in a way, in that they took him under their wings, especially Miyamoto, to teach him how to keep living. It was sad, he thought, with more clarity than most days, probably because he had eaten—they lived by killing others and taking their food. He stared at his hands, cracked, bloodied and torn, and closed his eyes to give thanks. If there was guilt to be realized from this, he thought carefully, he didn't feel it. Not yet. The food tasted good.

He examined Miyamoto's sleeping form for several minutes before he understood Miyamoto's entire physiognomy had changed in the year and half he had known him. Lack of proper nutrition during the last six weeks certainly had something to do with it. But the transformation was shocking. His solidness, all muscle and taut bulk for his size, was boiled away, gone. His cheeks were hollowed, his round skull gaunt and fleshless. It explained why his eyes seemed especially large, his eyeballs bulging out of their sockets. Hiroshi watched Miyamoto's body twitch around as if his nervous system was out of control, firing random messages to muscle groups for no purpose. Then Hiroshi noticed his own hands, frail and blood soaked, twitching out of control. *What is wrong with me? What is wrong with us?*

They left at dark, slipping away soundlessly into the forest. Miyamoto found the connecting trails within an hour. They arrived back up in the damp compound around two in the morning. It began to rain. Hiroshi joined Miyamoto at Captain Hashimoto's command post, a simple lean-to with a surprisingly well built small dirt oven. Hashimoto

243

proudly directed their attention to his enlisted aide, who built the oven. He only wished he had a chicken or a pig to bake in it, he said sadly. At night the oven was warm and drying.

Miyamoto and Hiroshi gave their report, both sharing some of their food bounty with Hashimoto and his aide. They were touchingly grateful. They talked frankly about the situation for an hour or two, savoring the heated bully beef and canned milk. Afterwards, after Australian cigarettes, Hiroshi watched Hashimoto then Miyamoto inject themselves with the magic drug, methamphetamine. Miyamoto cleaned the syringe in alcohol once more before offering Hiroshi the syringe and a dark glass vial.

Hiroshi knew now it was made from crushed powder—*Nekome-jo*—heated into liquid form. They must have used a lot of the tablets, he thought. Miyamoto didn't say a word, simply held them up as if he were offering Hiroshi a bottle of fine Scotch whiskey. Hashimoto, a peaceful, satisfied look coming into his face Hiroshi had never seen before, simply nodded.

Japanese, Miyamoto mused aloud as he wrapped the surgical tubing around Hiroshi's upper arm, are blessed with excellent veins. He dabbed a small cotton ball with some alcohol from the cleaning tray and swabbed Hiroshi's arm. The small pain prick was instantly replaced by warmth racing through his veins, accompanied by a glowing yellow light like morning sun, slowly spinning into his brain, changing the colors into a rainbow kaleidoscope. He sat down, mesmerized with the sight and pleasurable warmth. The vision kept changing though. More color than Hiroshi had seen in weeks and weeks, brilliant colors, all blending away until he began to see only the color of red. Bright red, arterial red. This frightened him. He tried to shake his head to clear the vision but lost his balance and fell down. He heard laughter, far away, then someone crying or moaning as if in pain. His stomach churned then heaved. He vomited what he had eaten, and vomited again until nothing came up. Hiroshi started crying, sobbing like a child, asking for forgiveness, apologizing to the voices in pain all around him.

CHAPTER 19

August 26, 1942, A Company, 2/14 Battalion, Templeton's Crossing, Southeast of Isurava

After four days trying to get the battalion organized at Myola, 2/14 was ordered to relieve the 39th Battalion at Isurava on the 25th. The 53rd Battalion was coming up to protect a side track south of Isurava. 2/16 was also arriving up the Track, adding more confusion. Exhausted men coming off the trail wanted nothing more than a warm meal, a cup of tea and a place to sleep for a few hours. Nothing of the kind was available for the leading companies. Crates and boxes were stacked everywhere exactly as the bearers dropped them. Since natives were faster than anyone in 2/14, there was no one waiting for them to receive and organize the distribution. It was a mess as men tried to marry up jumbled piles of stores to the assigned platoon, company and now battalion.

A few hours before the orders came the battalion commander called for officers and platoon sergeants. Vaughn (Vic) Hickey joined Captain Welsh and Lieutenant Edwards in the crowded hut serving as their BC's command post. Ten days earlier before they headed out of Port Moresby, the BC briefed the same group of men. At the time Kokoda and the airstrip had already fallen, the 39th withdrawing in stages down to Isurava. Like cavalry from American western films 2/14 was leaping to the rescue of the beleaguered militiamen. The attacking Japanese force, confirmed to be at least a reinforced infantry battalion, stopped to secure Kokoda and the airstrip. With 2/14 and 2/16 right behind it sufficient forces would soon be in place to stop the Japanese advance.

The current situation 10 days later shocked everyone in attendance. Aerial and ground intelligence confirmed the so-called South Sea Force, *Nankai Shitai* in Japanese, was actually a heavily reinforced independent assault regiment. The battalion-sized force currently holding the Kokoda airstrip was reinforced by sea landings by the remainder of *Nankai Shitai* on the 17th and 18th. Two infantry battalions and a mountain artillery battalion were the first to land. Intelligence believed there was another partial regiment involved, with significant engineering forces attached and thousands of native bearers.

The intentions of the Japanese were obvious now. If the initial battalion was a reconnaissance in force, then the new troops represented a viable assault force. *Nankai Shitai* was targeting Port Moresby. What the Japanese did not know was the Allies had staged over 20,000 men into Port Moresby. This however, was no advantage to the defenders on the Kokoda Track. Sixty kilometers up in the Owen Stanleys' the Japanese would soon have a numerical superiority in manpower. In addition were several 75mm mountain guns to support the ones already pounding Australian positions at Kokoda. Although *Nankai Shitai* was under constant aerial bombardment, especially the few bridges across the primary river, the Kumusi, the regiment was only partially visible for the first 15 kilometers or so before disappearing into the canopy. The size of the entire force, including the battalion currently holding the Kokoda airstrip, was now estimated to be about 6,000. This did not count the thousands of native bearers.

The most important update revealed the fresh battalions of *Nankai Shitai* arrived at Kokoda that morning. They could be expected to come down the Track to attack Isurava at any time, but most likely sometime the following night. That got Vic and Lieutenant Edwards attention, both shaking their heads in disbelief at the turn of events. With only three understrength companies in Isurava, less than 300 men, the 39th would not last long against a reinforced regiment. The aggressiveness of the enemy in night assault was already experienced. The Japanese had no fear of the dark. The *Nankai Shitai* scout battalion routinely slipped up to Aussie positions at Kokoda camouflaged and silent in the complete blackness, charging at first light with bayonets and swords at almost point blank range. Casualties on both sides were always heavy, with the element of surprise giving favor to the attacker.

The experience at Kokoda, the BC highlighted, also demonstrated the Japs would repeat an assault, increasing the troop strength and supporting firepower until an Aussie position was overrun or forced to withdraw. Once the Japanese were engaged, the assaults would continue throughout the day. They seemed to have an endless supply of men and energy to hit a position again and again. Ammunition and other stores were in short supply for the 39th, but the primary immediate need was to get fresh reinforcements to stiffen up the perimeters in Isurava. The 39th reported they had 150 effective soldiers in the three perimeters, with another 100 wounded still able to fire their weapons. If 2/14 and 2/16 could get in soon enough, *Nankai Shitai* might be forced to regroup for a day or two, giving Australian command enough time to get the 25th Brigade up the Track, and to amass more air and ground firepower. The weather, constant pounding rain, made this unlikely for several days. The relieving force would go up with what they had. Of course if they couldn't get up there in time the 39th would be destroyed. Vic could not recall a time when the officers and NCOs of his battalion ever looked so glum. Like himself and Lieutenant Edwards they were totally exhausted, but every one of them wanted the briefing to end so they could get their men moving.

With the disorganized supply situation the battalion commander determined only one company could be fully outfitted at a time and sent to Isurava. Native bearers would be carrying additional supplies of ammunition and rations for the depleted 39th Battalion. Once they unloaded their supplies they would start bringing 39th Battalion casualties down the Track. C Company, the first up the Track and ready to go, was sent directly to Isurava. The other companies of 2/14, A Company included, were ordered to Alola and Templeton's Crossing to hold until they could get a full kit of ammunition and rations. Alola was much closer to Isurava then Templeton's Crossing. Vic and Lieutenant Edwards waited impatiently by the door of the hut for Captain Welsh, who wanted to talk to the battalion commander, trying to sell the BC on the idea of letting A Company go on up to Isurava with what they had in their rucksacks.

Vic knew what his men were carrying, which was the absolute minimum gear so they could negotiate the Track faster. 9 Platoon was carrying no grenades, extra rations, mortar bombs, spare magazines for the Bren gunners from each section, and only about 60 or 70 rounds of small arms ammunition each. They had not expected to engage the Japs until they got here. That was the plan. He couldn't imagine any of the other platoons in A Company carrying much more than that. They wouldn't have made it. The BC would have none of it, of course, explaining to Welsh irritably he wasn't sending any company up without the men stuffing every square inch of their rucksacks with ammunition. *What good are ya' if all kin' do is contribute about eight minutes of firepower 'fore ya' resort ta' bayonets, Welsh! Eh? Think boy! You'll get your bloody chance, mark my words!*

Captain Welsh, his head down, walked past Vic and Edwards without a word. Welsh waited until C Company had taken what they needed from the ration and ammunition stores. The native bearers were concentrating more on ammunition than rations for 39th Battalion per the BC's orders, but still left a few crates of rifle ammunition, a dozen boxes of Mills hand grenades, and the odd box or two of Bren spare magazines in the small clearing. Following their orders B and D Companies left for Alola after a couple of hours. Welsh quickly had the platoon sergeants distribute the remaining rifle ammunition, grenades and spare Bren magazines to the sections. The rifle ammunition was packed in five and 10 round stripper clips in individual pockets of canvas bandoliers. There was enough for 9 Platoon to give each soldier a bandolier of 100 rounds of .303 for the SMLE Lee Enfields, and a few hundred extra for the Brens. There were enough grenades to give most of the men one Mills

Bomb each, and all of the Bren gunners gratefully accepted two or three spare 30-round magazines.

It wasn't much, but it made everybody feel better. Ammunition for Vic's Thompson submachine gun and Colt pistol wasn't available here. He did have seven loaded 20-round magazines for the Thompson and three loaded seven-round magazines for the pistol, so he was okay, for now. Most of the section leaders now carried Thompsons so .45 ACP ammunition would be provided in the next resupply.

B and D Companies were moving up to Alola, southwest of the central perimeter at Isurava known as the Rest House. The actual village of Isurava, another Australian perimeter under siege, was north of the Rest House. Alola was the last Australian perimeter in the Isurava settlement, the Australian Headquarters for Isurava. A Company would remain in a reserve position at Templeton's Crossing about eight kilometers south of Alola until it was resupplied and ordered up. Being too far away to be cable-linked via radio telephone to Alola, A Company had to wait for the word to move up by runner. For 24 hours it rained off and on all day and night. They set up four-hour watches and rotated Bren gun teams north and south of the Track. It was impossible to keep dry, even with their ponchos draped over their shivering bodies at night, so they didn't try. Vic was constantly checking in on the men to make sure they were protecting their weapons from the elements if nothing else. He was getting an odd snatch of sleep every now and then, but the constant stream of native bearers, now impressed as stretcher carriers of Australian wounded, kept waking him up.

Several times Captain Welsh would stop the stretcher carriers to ask the more lucid of the wounded men questions on the conditions up at Isurava. He was usually disappointed as the men were heavily sedated. Most had no idea who he was or what he was talking about. Welsh still stopped a new group every now and then. The native Papuan bearers, who the men were hearing would run away at the first hint of gunfire, were nonetheless very gentle in their handling of the wounded. It was impressive to see and it appeared to Vic evidence of a very empathetic nature in their culture. They simply seemed to be sensitive to human suffering and care more.

The men more familiar with the Papuans said they were called the "fuzzy-wuzzy angels" by the wounded men because of their kindness and their furry, often brightly dyed heads of hair. Unlike Allied stretcher carriers, the Papuan bearers carried the wounded men's stretchers on their shoulders, not down low, close to the ground. It was a much more stable platform, therefore more comfortable for the wounded. The Papuans had more stamina than Australian troops because they were used to the altitude and climate. They fell less often, their bare feet almost prehensile in their ability to grasp wet and slick roots with the toes.

A very expressive and demonstrative people, sometimes too expressive and casual to the naturally tactiturn quality of rural Australians, it was not surprising some Aussies didn't trust them. Papuans cried, argued loudly, laughed and became boisterous at the drop of a hat. Even when assigned to grueling, menial tasks, the Papuans found the energy to sing, chant and dance. To Vic, they reminded him of the Ethiopian troops working with the British Army in Northern Africa. Or in a different way, the Italians. They were fun-loving people, gregarious and social. You couldn't knock this out of a culture. But it also ensured they would not be the best soldiers. Fighting didn't interest them much at all.

Finally on the afternoon of the 27th a staff officer from 2/16 came over from Myola with a message for Captain Welsh. The note was brief but Welsh let out a whoop and waved Vic and the other company officers and NCOs over to his CP. The company had been grimly watching Papuan bearers pass their position all day heading up with orders to take the supplies only to Isurava. The orders were in writing and the lead Papuan made it clear he would follow the orders from the big chief, the BC. More supplies, he said, would be coming today. Myola had a large radio transmitter and was in contact with the 2/14 battalion commander at Alola. A Company was to receive their resupply by the end of the day and they were to proceed at the first opportunity up the Track to Alola. The situation, the staff officer intimated with a slow shake of his head, was getting desperate. *Your C Company is fully engaged and already lost so many men it is nearly combat ineffective. Your B and D Companies, freshly outfitted, have arrived to replace men killed and wounded in action. The bloody Japs keep attacking, day an' night!*

The next resupply train of bearers arrived in the afternoon. The heat and humidity, even with nearly constant rain, kept everyone lethargic and exhausted. Vic had no idea how the Papuans could climb up the Track day after day, the trail itself pounded into a thick sticky glue mixed with slick rocks and roots, virtually impossible to walk on— unless you were Papuan. One group of Papuans dropped the supplies slated for A Company and immediately headed up the trail for Isurava. Even though they had no equipment for the last eight kilometers, they were needed as relief stretcher carriers. Vic noticed the Papuans assigned between six to eight bearers for each stretcher, rotating two at a time periodically all the way back to Port Moresby. He only hoped, as he assumed every other man in A Company did, he wouldn't be wounded bad enough to require this type of evacuation. The trip must take at least a couple of days, he thought, and despite the best efforts on the part of the Papuans, the wounded men were fully exposed to the weather. He wondered how many actually survived the trip.

Captain Welsh decided ammunition would take precedence over rations, ordering his platoon sergeants to restrict the men to a two-day ration supply only. He knew the next eight kilometers up the Track to Alola would be steep and brutal with full rucksacks, but he reminded the usual complainers they could go a week without rations and survive. But ammunition was truly finite. Once it was gone they no longer had offensive capability. The Japs could slip around behind Isuvara and cut-off the resupply line and they would fight with what they had.

How long ya' think you'll live without rifle ammunition, fellows? The 'oonly thing the Jap understands is lead or the steel 'rom your bayonet. Let's 'eep em' at bay with lead, lads! Ya' can't help ya' cobbers by throwin' rooks!

Welsh made his point. Vic and the other platoon sergeants personally checked the men's gear, not only to make sure they were carrying a full load of ammunition and grenades, but they were also sharing the load of extra, fully-loaded Bren light machinegun magazines. The Bren was the attack stopper, it's accurate and lethal carpet of .30 caliber copper-jacketed lead discouraged frontal assaults. *The Japs keep coming until there aren't any left,* the intelligence briefers said, *so make sure the Bren gunners are well protected with riflemen and they have plenty of ammunition.*

Vic also made sure 9 Platoon held onto their steel pots and entrenching shovels. The only safety for an infantryman, especially facing an enemy who has mobile artillery, is to go below ground level. A *funkhole,* or fighting pit, kept a couple of soldiers within arm's reach in the pitch blackness, allowing them to "back to back" and protect one another. The pits would be filthy, half-filled with water and cold at night, but the solid walls and stinking mud did a good job of stopping red hot chunks of steel whizzing around from inbound artillery, mortar rounds or hand-thrown grenades. A man without a helmet and an entrenching shovel in a metal shit storm was a man waiting to die.

A Company took off right after a quick supper, the last cup of hot tea and a *smoko* they might have for a few days. They were led by a Papuan scout, a sergeant in the Papuan Infantry Battalion (PIB). It was raining when they started, the light under the canopy grey and misty for the first hour, then as usual, with no warning, the light disappeared as if someone had thrown a switch. What was vaguely visible faded completely to be replaced by a sensory vacuum of utter blackness. It created instant vertigo for most men. There was no reference point at all, especially on uneven terrain.

Tree limbs and protruding rocks at head height clubbed brutally into men's faces, knocking them down hard on to equally solid but slick rocks or tree roots. Disoriented and stunned senseless, men staggered to their feet only to be stepped on or knocked over again by another man following blindly behind him. After a half an hour of men cursing and calling out in mass confusion, Captain Welsh authorized section leaders to use their torches to light the path periodically. After another half an hour to determine they had not lost anybody to a deep crevasse somewhere in the darkness, Welsh decided they would continue using the electric torches. The trail was more dangerous than the Japs right now anyway.

It was impossible in the ink blackness to maintain any order or spacing. Australian troops rarely moved overland in the dark except on the assault in the Middle East, but there was always some form of ambient light available in the desert, whether it was overhead star shells, burning vehicles or buildings. In the desert the sky was usually clear at night. The stars so bright you could touch them. And the terrain was *flat and solid*. Navigation, if you had a compass or could read the stars, was a piece of cake. Right now even Vic began thinking of the desert with a certain amount of fondness. Maybe you get used to it. *How in the devil did the Japs do it?* As they climbed, it grew colder and the rain finally stopped around midnight.

Any discomfort they felt from walking the Track disappeared as they slowly approached Alola. The sky would erupt in blinding flashes to be followed a second or two later by the long rippling thunder of impacting artillery rounds. They could feel the ground tremble from the concussions, three or four rounds at a time. It sounded like the Japs had a lot of artillery. It was hard to tell if there was any return fire, but they knew the 39th didn't have much beyond a couple of antitank guns, light mortars and one 73mm mortar the Weapons Company brought up. In between the artillery, which was intermittent, they could hear at least two or three different kinds of mortars and the thumps of hand grenades. It was the middle of the night and one hell of a battle was going on.

The machinegun fire was constant, interspersed with clusters of rifle fire, both the deep bark of .303s and the light crack of what they assumed were the Arisaka 6.5mm Jap rifles. They could hear the *whump whump* of mortars, followed by star illumination shells to light up a part of the horizon. *There must be a lot of targets out there,* Vic thought, grimly. Jap targets, as the 39th and 2/14 would be hunkered down behind their guns. A Company was too far away and down the Track to even see over the next rise, but Welsh's insistence on carrying every round of ammunition they could get their hands on seemed pretty flippin' smart right now. The men were quiet around Vic, listening carefully like himself to the growing sounds of battle. Combat infantrymen are not impressed with noise, but were keyed to the sounds of serious threats to their life and limbs. Outgoing artillery, even heavy machinegun fire can become background noise once a man determined it wasn't pointed at him. So the men listened and climbed.

The machinegun fire was a cacophony of four different types as far as he could tell with professional discernment. A couple of Vickers water-cooled heavies; several Brens; a brace of Juki 52s—called *woodpeckers* by the Aussies because of their slow, rat-tat-tat cyclic rate—and fast-firing Nambu LMGs. These were some heavy, tripod-mounted machineguns on both sides, mixed with the two light LMGS the Diggers and Japs used for infantry support. The Juki 52s were heavy, and Vic was surprised the Japs would haul them all the way up the Kokoda Track. But *bloody hell*, they dragged 75mm mountain guns up the same hill, didn't they? It could certainly make the difference. The LMGs on both sides were limited to their box magazines and what the gunners could carry. They also had the tendency to overheat after sustained fire. Not so the Juki 52 *woodpecker,* or the Vickers, both could be fired all day. *These people are serious.*

He shivered as they climbed, not really knowing why. It was cool in the dark, the rain intermittent, his body pouring out heat and sweat with the exertion. The middle of the night attack made it clear A Company would have no time for rest or orientation once they got up there to Alola. They were going straight into the line, wherever that was. Vic knew the general layout of the settlement while viewing a rough drawn map the battalion commander had spread on a wooden artist's easel.

Eora Creek was in a deep gorge carving straight down North to Southeast. Stretched out over 10-12 kilometers were the three Australian perimeters. Isurava was on the top of the western side escarpment; the Rest House two kilometers further south on the same escarpment. Alola was five kilometers south of the Rest House. Aloha, the Australian HQ, linked the eastern side of Eora Creek by road and to a log bridge. The big gaps between the perimeters worried him, knowing the Japs, with their numerical superiority and night fighting skills could be all around them. The road across the log bridge turned north and led to the eastern side escarpment and to the waterfall at Abuari. No one knew what was there as the 39th chose to stay on the western side close to the Track, except for a few lonely communication outposts in the tiny native villages there.

A half a kilometer out of Alola there was a small clearing revealing a cluster of tied and raised tarpaulins and lit kerosene lanterns. With the enemy so close, Vic was surprised to see the kerosene lanterns until he realized they lit up an aid station of some kind. Twenty or thirty wounded men were being attended to by a couple of hospital corpsmen and a single medical officer. The MO, a young captain, kept asking A Company men for the commanding officer until Captain Welsh made it to the clearing. It was here Vic and the rest of the company realized the Papuan stretcher bearers drew their line in the sand. They would go no further towards the gunfire, and no amount of cajoling, yelling or negotiating would change their minds. The MO said this in a matter-of-fact voice, although his face and dull eyes, drawn and exhausted, reflected only a heavy weariness.

"If possible, Captain," he asked Captain Welsh, "if aye' could get a platoon of your men ta' go up ta' Alola an' pick up the fresh wounded at the surgical station there. They've been stacking up boot' da' Japs keep cooming', an' nobody has men ta' spare. Captain Carlson an' 'is staff are handlin' the triage an' initial treatment. Lait' cases stay if they kin' still handle a weapon. *Expectants* stay there, boot' we're transporting everybody else, even those really too injured ta' move. The situation is too fluid an' da' Japs kill wounded men, so we 'ave no choice. The BC said ta' transport, so we are. If they naid' transportin', we have ta' use our own men oop' on' da' line ta' bring 'em down. Papuans won't go oop' there. Ma' team keeps 'em stable during the nait', an' at first lait' the Papuans take 'em down da' Track ta' Moresby."

He explained this as if describing a simple administrative function, but kept his eyes on Captain Welsh and Lieutenant Edwards, soon joined by Vic Hickey. Welsh, already irritated they were the last company in 2/14 to get up to Isurava, grimaced and stared at the MO. Lieutenant Edwards broke the silence by volunteering 9 Platoon.

"Looks like they'll be plenty of fightin' ta' go 'round, suh'! We'll find the compny' an' join ya' as soon as we can." Welsh agreed reluctantly, knowing it would be hard for 9 Platoon to find A Company in the dark once they were assigned a place on the defensive line, *somewhere*. A Company moved out immediately as Vic pulled 9 Platoon aside, ordering them to drop their heavy rucksacks but to separate out their helmets, entrenching shovels, and several bandoliers of ammunition. Carrying wounded men or not, there was no way he was sending them up near Alola without sufficient ammunition to defend themselves, or the means to dig *funkholes* when the Jap artillery started arriving.

Vic listened carefully as the MO described the location of the surgical aid station in Alola. He found out both Isurava and the Rest

253

House had their own wounded, but with the current attacks no one was moving them. There were reports of Japs on both sides of Eora Creek, with new pressure on the east side near the waterfall. If all went well the wounded at Isurava and the Rest House would walk or be carried down to the Alola surgical station in the morning. If the attacks continued and they couldn't push them back, they had to make do where they were.

It took the rest of the night to bring the wounded down from Alola to the lower aid station. When they approached the surgical station at Alola the first time, Vic knew immediately they didn't have enough men to transport them all in one trip. There were easily 60 or 70 casualties being attended to or lying quietly on the ground. The surgeon and his corpsmen worked with flashlights here, as Japanese infantry assaults were occurring almost hourly on the curved perimeter less than a kilometer away.

On one occasion earlier in the day, an assault broke through and 20 or 25 Japanese infantrymen charged straight towards the HQ, which was 200 meters from the surgical station. This happened just as D Company from 2/14 arrived from the Track, looking for their assignment. The Japanese were cut to pieces by D Company Bren and rifle fire, but unfortunately the fusillade of lead also found its way into the HQ building, wounding several officers and men. An hour later two Japanese artillery rounds burst in the treetops above the aid station, hitting high canopy trees 20 meters above them, shattering and hurling wood splinters and shrapnel in all directions. Some wounded men were killed, many received additional wounds, and apparently six men who had been pressed into stretcher duty were all wounded. Hearing all this, Vic and the rest of the men in 9 Platoon were very glad to get away from the surgical station and their humanitarian duties. At the time they thought it was too damned dangerous.

9 Platoon picked up their rucksacks and headed back up to Alola for the fourth and last time. There was a hint of light in the sky, the trail, now familiar, could actually be seen if you knew where to look. They were completely exhausted, but recognized with each trip to the aid station how critical the situation was becoming. Jap artillery had eased off, probably due to ammunition shortages because they had been firing all night. Lieutenant Edwards reported to the battalion commander and asked for the approximate location of A Company. Vic, who accompanied him, listened with growing alarm as the BC explained the level of penetration the Japs managed in the last two days. There were at least six battalions attacking Isurava from three directions, the assaults gaining ground hourly. Reconnaissance reports revealed another battalion or two working the eastern side of Eora Creek, the high

escarpment that led to the waterfall at Abuari and eventually the log bridge linking the road to Alola.

"If the Japs close the gap an' get behind us," The battalion commander sighed wearily, "we are lost. We're withdrawing men doon' the trail an' they'll soon be joining us, especially what's left of 39th Battalion." The BC glanced at Lieutenant Edwards with a thin smile before he rubbed his face and thick mustache.

"B and C Compny' are 'oop near the Rest House. C Compny' was mauled yesterday mornin'. Aye' think the compny' is commanded by one of the platoon sergeants now. Aye've' got D Compny' over by the log bridge on the east side of the creek, and aye' 'ave your A Compny' just south of the waterfall at Abuari. Get 'oop there and join 'em because they'll naid' every man jack they can get if the Japs decide to make another move down the rood'. They hit A Compny' about an hour ago in a probin' attack. Should come back with more strength next time, probably at dawn. They just don't bloody stop comin'. 2/16 should be arriving mid-mornin', once they get 'supplied. Aye'll' see if they cn' spare a compny' to relieve ya', if ya' kin' only hang on! Be sure Welsh understands we have nothin' 'tween us an' 'im other than D Compny' an' they 'ave had their 'ands full with the Japs cooming' doon' the creek. Rait' now, there is nobody else. We have to keep this Track open as our escape route. Understood?"

Lieutenant Edwards and Vic Hickey looked at each other outside the HQ, each holding an RT set and extra size cable reel the battalion signalmen had given them. They had to be careful as they walked, as the cables were already attached and linked to the battalion radio net. They walked and dropped cable as the reels noisily spun.

"As ewe' pass D Compny', suh', give em' one of these radios an' cable reels if ya' kin', dey' loost' an RT ta' an artillery roond', poor 'astards! The other one's a spare for your compny'.'"

When Vic and Lieutenant Edwards returned to 9 Platoon they were not surprised to find most of the men dozing on their rucksacks. They were tapped out from the stretcher duty, oblivious to the pounding and crackling gunfire all around them.

"Oon' your feet, mates!" Vic barked, swinging into his own rucksack, groaning under its load. "Da' soft cops' over! Time ta' join da' compny' earn your flippin' pay!" 9 Platoon moaned and stirred before quickly getting to their feet. Potty, their hospital corpsman, had removed his low-quarter boots and puttees for some reason, and the others were getting some pleasure in watching him dance around trying to get his now-swollen feet into his boots.

"Deres' a bloody fool fer' ya'," cracked Scabby, shaking his head in sad wonder. "Ewe' new ya' feet wood swell, an' ewe' a bloody flippin' coorman!" The others laughed as Potty, his feelings hurt, stomped a few feet away to sit down on a stump, his back to the entire platoon to continue struggling with his boots.

It was getting lighter and Lieutenant Edwards was in no mood for joking. He signaled to Vic to start them out. They were just about a kilometer away from the waterfall where A Company was holding the road leading to Abuari. Edwards took the battalion commander at his word for the anticipated attack from the east side of Eora Creek. Vic directed the 1st Section to take the point, staggered trail formation, each man maintaining about a 10 meter interval.

Check your weapons, fix your bayonets! Make sure your bandoliers are clear of your rucksack straps if ewe 'have ta 'reload your weapon with your 'ack on! 'Eep your bombs handy! Move out, mates!

Some of the men glanced over at Vic with trepidation on his order to fix bayonets, but within a minute there were 24 metallic clicks as the bayonets were attached by the men with Lee Enfields. 2nd and 3rd Sections brought up the rear, each man glancing over his shoulder at Potty as they fell in line. Vic, last man in trail, nodded as Potty hopped into his rucksack and snatched up his Lee Enfield. Vic grinned at his old friend, clapping Potty on the shoulder as he trundled past, grumbling to himself.

As they marched behind the HQ building, which was nothing more than a long rectangular hut, Vic noticed the men sitting and lying in a shady area out of the way. There were only 12 or 15 of them, but you couldn't miss them. In fact, none of 9 Platoon could take their eyes off of them. None of these resting men seemed seriously wounded, although a number had fresh bandages on their faces, arms and hands. Vic knew immediately they were 39th Battalion survivors, pulled off the line as 2/14 arrived. 39th Battalion men were still fighting up at the Isuvara perimeter and the Rest House because they couldn't fall back with Jap forces all around the isolated perimeters. Vic was certain none of these men were going to do anymore fighting, at least not today. Under normal circumstances when relieving other men fresh from campaigns in the Middle East, there was a certain amount of good-hearted banter between the two groups, the passing over of cigarettes from the relieving troops to the ones coming off the line. Always a hand-off on new information. *Scuttlebutt* is everybody's business, whether it was true or not.

Not with this group, there was no recognizing 9 Platoon was even passing by. The 39th Battalion militiamen, filthy, thickly-bearded, thin and scarecrow-like, stared with saucer eyes into nothingness. Their affect was other-worldly; they were seeing or had withdrawn to another place. Although some smoked cigarettes, their silence and remoteness left no opening for conversation. Every one of them clutched their rifles close, yet the rifles seemed less as weapons than simply familiar props to lean on. For Vic, he suddenly felt less the veteran cavalryman coming to the rescue, seeing instead these men as the veterans, survivors of six weeks on the Kokoda, fighting the Japs far on the other side of the Owen Stanleys' before being forced to withdraw again and again, losing men every step of the way. Just coming up the Track from Uberi was physically daunting. 2/14 had only been on the Kokoda for 10 days. Fighting the mountains, the mists, the rains, the mud *and* the Japs for six weeks was difficult to comprehend. He had an idea though. He saw it in the militiamen's faces.

Vic hefted his Thompson and confirmed his makeshift breech cover was in his pocket, not over the gun. His Thompson, a M1928A1 model with Cutts compensator, cooling fins and horizontal forward grip made famous by the American gangster movies, had to be cocked if a magazine was inserted and the breech was closed. The gun fired from an open breech like most submachineguns, and for the first time in months he might need *Tom* at the drop of a hat. The open breech was a perfect catchall sponge pit for debris, dirt, cigarette ashes and insects. So you kept the breech closed or covered it somehow. But it was open now. Like all Thompson owners who wanted their guns to work, his right hand was on the trigger grip and the left rested casually across the open mouth of the breech. The damned thing was heavy—nearly ten pounds before you inserted the magazine—but right now he wouldn't trade it for anything. It began raining, hard, as they approached the bridge and the first fighting pits dug by D Company.

As they came up on D Company they crouched down trying to find some cover as Lieutenant Edwards went looking for the D Company CO to give him the RT. Their positions covered both sides of the creek and the bridge, although the company stayed close together on the west side in their funkholes. Even in the rain 9 Platoon could see dozens of Jap bodies down by the creek bed, which was mostly very large boulders. There were more up on the opposite bank before everything disappeared into thick forest. Vic had to imagine if he got closer, he would see Jap bodies down below in front of the guns. He realized D Company only had about 30 or 40 meters of clear field of fire on three sides of their position. When the Japs appeared they would be almost on top of you in seconds. The Bren gunners on his extreme left were watching the forest intensely directly to the north; dark, dense foliage right down to Eora Creek. He could see another dozen bodies lying right on the side of the creek edge or floating in the eddies next to the bank. His keen eyes noticed at least 100 brass empties all around the one Bren gun in front of him, the smell of cordite and gunpowder very fresh, even in the pouring rain.

Lieutenant Edwards sent the men running across the wooden bridge two at a time. *About a half of a kilometer up the road they would come to the waterfall,* the D Company CO had said, *and somewhere close by was A Company—and a bloody battalion of Japs. He said it with a straight face,* Edwards said, glumly. Not a round was fired until the last two men were dashing across. A single rifle bullet zipped between the two of them, both arguing the round came closer to them than the other once they safely got across. D Company had returned fire on the sound of the shot with a single short burst from a Bren, good discipline, Vic thought. It let the Japs know they were there, but they didn't waste any precious ammunition without a live target to shoot at. Eerily, the road wound around a dark cluster of forest on both sides and disappeared. The column stopped almost immediately, the men maintaining their intervals on each side of the road but crouching lower to the ground or taking a knee. Vic trotted up carefully, Thompson at the ready, joining up with Edwards to look around the corner.

Sprawled in a semi-circle were four Japanese soldiers. All were dead, shot to pieces, it appears by the close stitching of the bullet holes, both entry and exit wounds, by a Bren gun—or two. The bottle green flies were all over the bodies, even in the rain. The blood, pink and purple now, spread wide over the road, the rain drops pelting the deeper pools like pebbles. The soldiers' weapons were stacked over on the side of the road for some reason, the sight unusual or peculiar to Lieutenant Edwards, who stared at them long and hard.

"Our fellows, aye' suppose, aye'?" He whispered to Vic. Vic nodded but his eyes were on the dark forest all around them. The rain was coming down so hard it was very difficult to see much further than about 15-20 meters. He was worried about the men spread out behind them, possibly exposed to view and fire from the other side of the creek.

"We're bloody exposed, suh'—we naid' ta' move oop' into the trays'." Edwards seemed to snap out of his reverie and fascination with the scene to glance sharply at Vic.

"'Pose you're rait', Sergeant! Aye' want some scouts oop' ahead if 'is road continues like this, aye'? There might be bloody Japs 'tween us an' A Compny', aye'?

Vic sent Scabby and Biscuit ahead with hand signals, holding 1st Section until he was certain the scouts were about 30 meters away. He also moved two Bren gunners up forward, figuring if they needed firepower they would need it right quick. Dawn arrived with a whimper. There was a slight lightening of the road surface as visual details became clear even in the downpour. The forest and canopy rose high into the sky on both sides, blotting out any hint of grey except directly above the road. This space, 20 or 30 meters over them, turned into a venturi funnel, propelling icy pellets of water straight down. Their cotton canvas rucksacks, stuffed full with ammunition, were sodden and now a third again heavier. Water poured over their flat steel helmets to run straight down their collars. If the water wasn't so cold it might have been pleasant.

After climbing half the night in the dark then transitioning to the stretcher duty, 9 Platoon hadn't much time to do a thorough job of cleaning their rain-exposed weapons when they arrived at Alola. At least Vic didn't. He thought of his men sleeping on their rucksacks when he woke them up to come here to the waterfall, feeling guilty for his negligence. Sighing, he could only hope the section leaders had the men check their weapons before they dozed off. It was a stupid, amateur oversight *militiamen might do*, exhaustion be damned. But then thinking of the men of the 39th Battalion, he relented and felt even worse. It was part of his responsibility, part of his job. It was too late now. Even with the heavy gun grease Vic had slathered on at Templeton's Crossing the day before, a fine coat of brown rust was evident on every metal surface of his Thompson. He could run some of it away with his finger, but what about what he couldn't see? The thick grease coating was gone. The rain had simply washed everything off. He prayed the grease on the bolt rails and internal mechanisms would allow the Thompson to work when he needed it too. He made a mental note to strip it apart the first lull they got.

Lieutenant Edwards signaled for the RT from the rifleman assigned to carry it, asking the man to crank the handle, which rang a bell on the radio at the battalion CP at the other end of the cable. He stretched the coiled cord and pressed the handset to his ear and mouth as he continued walking. Battalion answered immediately, confirming Captain Welsh was informed 9 Platoon was coming up behind on the road. Vic, who was walking behind Edwards, watched Edwards stiffen from information he was receiving, glancing hard suddenly to the right side of the road. Edwards handed the handset back to the soldier carrying the RT while looking over his shoulder. Seeing Vic coming up, Edwards looked relieved as he waved him to come up faster. He signaled 9 Platoon to call a halt and 1st Section to retrieve the scouts up ahead.

"Just chatted with the BC," Edwards whispered, his eyes still watching the forest on the right side of the road, out to the northeast. "He's in contact with Welsh. A Compny' is dug in a couple hundred meters ta' the east of the waterfall. Welsh says he's got some men watchin' the high ground above the waterfall, an' that the Japs are circlin' 'round an' tryin' a'o flank their position." Vic watched as Edwards took a hard swallow, his adam's apple moving up and down visibly. Edwards turned abruptly to stare at Vic, his eyes wide, unblinking.

"Welsh passed on through Battalion he wants us ta' 'old short an' prepare a defensive line, a blockin' force, 'ack 'ere on the west side of the rood'. He figures da' Japs will be 'ere in about five—ten minutes. It's rough country they're walking through. El' probably break out right 'ere in front of us, headin' down da' rood', showin' 'ere backs to attack A Compny'."

Before saying a word, Vic signaled to the three section leaders to join them immediately.

"Ow' many Japs?" Vic asked, already knowing the answer. He remembered what the battalion commander had said.

"Welsh said 'is men weren't sure—a hunnerd' at least." Edwards' nostrils flared as he took a deep breath. "I think 'ere facin' a compny', mebbe' more." Vic nodded in agreement. There wasn't much else to say. They had their orders. Vic moved quickly, talking to the returning scouts to get an idea what was around the bend. 50 meters further north the road opened and curved gently to the west. It provided an excellent field of fire from the west side if men were stepping out on the road from the east. Lieutenant Edwards agreed with the suggestion. He wished he knew exactly where the A Company positions were in front of him, but if all went well, most of 9 Platoon's shooting would be to the east or northeast. There was also so much forest he wasn't even sure much of anything they shot would penetrate very far. He hoped not.

The platoon jogged quickly down to the spot, slipping into the darkness and safety of the forest about three meters, just far enough in to not be seen on the other side of the road. Lying down on the soaked cold ground was uncomfortable under normal circumstances, but the men knew what was coming. They flopped down gladly, snuggling up to the slimy trees. 9 Platoon set up one Bren LMG to cover the southern end of the road where they came from, then tasked the remaining two the wide curving turn of the road as it turned northwest. The tree trunks were medium sized near the road and close together. They provided adequate clearance for their weapons while providing decent cover and concealment. The men gladly took off their rucksacks, pulling out a good supply of ammunition and Mills hand grenades. Everyone was glad to hand over some of their loaded Bren magazines to the gunners. They were pure dead weight in their packs. The gunners were pleased, stacking them in neat piles next to their guns.

Artillery could be heard now, the impacts somewhere north of them, possibly in the Isurava area, Vic thought. Machinegun fire erupted directly behind them, perhaps a half a kilometer, which placed it on Eora Creek near the D Company positions. This was joined almost immediately with multiple reports from all kinds of small arms; rifles, Tommyguns, Brens, Nambus, *woodpeckers* and Arisaka 6.5 Japs. Over the noise of the gunfire and the thumps and whumps of grenades and mortars, they could hear a roar, a rolling noise of human voices moving somehow. Singing, screaming, shouting, yelling, crying and howling. All of this seemed to be behind them or somewhere far over to the north. Vic glanced around and watched the men start to peer around nervously, trying to determine where the gunfire and noise was coming from. All of a sudden the cacophony of noise shifted to their left, *much much closer* now, as gunfire and the same roar of human noise started to shift and seemingly roll directly to their north—where the A Company positions were.

Most of 9 Platoon shifted their attention to their left, to the north, wiggling around their trees in the sticky icy mud, trying to keep their weapons clean and their ammunition supply dry and instantly available. Vic, however, stared straight ahead across the road into the dark foliage 20 meters away from where he lay. A humming sound was growing, separate from the constant pelting rain and the incredible racket of the firefight a couple of hundred meters away from them. He could feel it, but none of the other men around him seemed to notice, their attention solidly to the north, which was understandable. The feeling lifted the hair straight off his head, so stiff he was certain it was lifting his helmet liner. For the others who didn't hear or feel it, there was absolutely no reason not to believe that any second 200 screaming Japs, fresh from stabbing and chopping to pieces what was once A Company, would break out of the forest and run straight up the road at 9 Platoon. No reason at all.

The Bren gun pointed to the south opened up with two long flashing bursts, the noise in the tight confines of the forest absolutely deafening. The section supporting the Bren in a tight semi-circle opened up with rapid rifle and Thompson submachinegun fire and did not stop. Vic spun to the right to peek between two trees to see Japanese soldiers, at least a dozen still standing, coming out of the forest 30 or 40 meters to his south, the soldiers clearly confused as some of their colleagues were being shot at close range. Vic could see another dozen Japanese soldiers, already down, some still and not moving, while others were trying to crawl back into the forest on the east side.

Vic was baffled why no one else in 9 Platoon was shooting, until he realized most of the men had instinctively shifted all their weapons and their use of cover to align to the north. Both Bren gunners were pulling their weapons back to shift them to different positions, as were most of the riflemen, when the humming sound Vic had temporarily forgotten about spun into the center of his brain, a growing whirring, buzzing directly in front of him across the road. He had to look up as most of 9 Platoon did also. The foliage was moving, faster and faster, not from the rain but some unseen forces right behind it. Suddenly like a herd of panicked sheep erupting over a hilltop spilling out in all directions, dark khaki clad Jap infantry, bayonets glistening on the muzzles of their Arisakas, stomped through the forest on a front at least 50 meters wide.

For a moment the soldiers looked relieved, free of the dense jungle. Either confused by the direction the gunfire was coming from, which was both north and south, or oblivious to it in the forest, most of the soldiers were immediately turning to the north, where A Company was. Only a few glanced to the south in obvious confusion, realizing the firefight occurring directly to their south. Vic spotted a Jap officer, his peaked cap and officer's sword separating him from his helmeted infantrymen, stepping out on the road, turning his back to Vic and 9 Platoon 15 meters away. The man was pointing silently towards the north, guiding his men like a military policeman when his head turned right. He suddenly barked an order in alarm, reaching for the pistol at his belt as Vic and at least two other members of 9 Platoon blew the back of his head away.

CHAPTER 20

August 26, 1942, First Company, 1/144th Infantry, Kokoda village

General Horii arrived on the 25th with the rest of the battalions and the mountain artillery. He met with the First Battalion Commander and Colonel Yokohama before assuming command. The Advance Party dissolved and *Nankai Shitai* was whole again. Upon hearing of First Company's reconnaissance role down the Track outside Isurava, General Horii ordered it relieved and Captain Hashimoto sent for.

There was a flurry of activity after the messenger met with Hashimoto. After nearly two weeks in the forest First Company's mission was over. Normally, when holding orders to report directly to the Task Force Commander and movement orders, Hashimoto would leave Hiroshi in command as the executive officer. There was much to do and the company was in bad shape, but Hashimoto insisted Hiroshi and Miyamoto accompany him. Hashimoto knew General Horii well enough to expect direct questions regarding the terrain and enemy tactical situation in Isurava. Having no desire to disappoint Horii, Hashimoto was bringing the two men who knew the defenses better than anyone. Besides, First Company couldn't leave until their contact patrols returned in the evening. He put Lieutenant Nishikawa in temporary command with specific instructions to maintain their defensive posture until they were formally relieved.

The three of them did not possess presentable uniforms. Like all of the men in First Company their leather gear was rotting away, including their officer cavalry boots. They hooked the broken parts together with whatever they had. Hiroshi found his sword, which he didn't wear in Isurava, rusty and pitted. He was deeply ashamed of its condition but there was no time to clean it. Like Hashimoto and Miyamoto he was unshaven and filthy. They were wet, smelled like animals and rotting earth, and would report to their commanding general in the same condition. Hashimoto called them together for a few minutes explaining what they could expect from General Horii. *The questions*, he said carefully, his eyes on Hiroshi, *will come after you give your report. It might be a minute or two as the General thinks about it, but then they will come. Be direct and honest. Answer every question and be thorough. Give no opinions or guesses. Understand?*

The climb back up to Kokoda was exhausting with no time to rest. Hashimoto led them directly to their battalion commander who used his RT to contact General Horii's headquarters. They were told to report immediately. On seeing their appearance the battalion commander wanted to get them clean uniforms, but his orders were succinct.

Horii was a muscular, vigorous man in his fifties. He seemed fatigued, his eyes red-rimmed and hooded, but they still conveyed energy and interest. Hiroshi had only seen the man at a distance on Guam and Rabaul. He was always surrounded by a large entourage of staff officers. Here in this small building the General sat in an old wicker chair by himself. An aide, a major, stood at attention in the shadows. Hiroshi and Miyamoto followed Captain Hashimoto's instructions to remain completely formal, letting their battalion commander introduce Captain Hashimoto while they stood stiffly at attention. The battalion commander made a point to note the physical conditions down near Isurava were *primitive* and there was no facility for bathing. Horii, his uniform immaculate because he changed on arrival, nodded his understanding. Hashimoto introduced Hiroshi and Miyamoto to the General, explaining their daily reconnaissance patrols all over the settlement of Isurava.

General Horii's eyes examined their uniforms before his attention seemed to rivet on their faces, moving methodically from one to the other. Blood stains were very visible. His eyes opened wider in apparent growing anger, now directed towards the battalion commander. The General started to speak to the BC then turned suddenly to his aide, bringing him quickly to his side with the wave of his hand. He spoke in low tones, motioning towards the men standing in front of him. The aide rushed outside, calling for other officers. Horii turned back towards Captain Hashimoto with what seemed genuine fatherly concern.

"Forgive me, Captain! When have you and your men last eaten?" Before Hashimoto could answer, Horii stood up and searched his pockets. He pulled out a box of English Players, walking over and offering Hashimoto a cigarette. They were still at attention so Horii waved his hands. "Please, relax. At ease. Have a cigarette! I've ordered some food delivered for you men, you must be starving! Let's get you something to eat, and then we can talk."

Captain Hashimoto guided General Horii to Hiroshi after giving a brief overview of the patrol activities in Isarava. Miyamoto produced the detailed maps of the settlement they had drawn in the field, letting Hiroshi explain the significance of the numerous trails in the forest on both sides of the western escarpment down to Eora Creek. These were carefully received by Horii as if they were precious scrolls. The aide accepted them from Horii after the General examined them himself. Hiroshi did the best he could in answering the General's pointed questions, although his attention was often divided with the amazing repast being offered them on a table brought into the room. There was actual china and silverware. Hiroshi could not imagine how or who carried all of this up the same mountain Track he climbed only weeks before. Nothing on the table resembled the rations they ate or even the food they stole from the Australians. Everything came from cans, of course, but they weren't served in cans. There was excellent succulent fish, steamed rice and even pickled plums. Sake was poured, heated, into small porcelain cups. It roared through his body like fire. He knew he would be sick but he ate everything he could get into his mouth as General Horii digested what he said, patiently waited for Hiroshi to swallow his food and continue.

In the end it was a bittersweet meeting, certainly for Captain Hashimoto. General Horii asked Hashimoto directly what rations First Company ate while down in Isurava. Hashimoto was truthful in noting the men saved some rations from the mistaken Australian airdrop, but also foraged from the gardens in the Isurava settlement and stole from the Australians. Horii seemed to find a great deal of pleasure from this last admission, asking a few quick questions on how this was done. After Horii asked Hashimoto if Australian soldiers were present during these raids and Hashimoto simply answered *yes sir*, there were no further questions.

Hashimoto loyally attempted to protect the battalion commander when he sensed Horii's growing irritation. Hashimoto added he understood the BC was having difficulty supplying Second and Third Companies up in Kokoda, so First Company was not going to add to his burden. Horii, watching his young officers wolf the bowls clean on the table, seemed to appreciate what they experienced and was pleased he could feed them. He glanced over at the BC with barely concealed anger still in his eyes. When he began speaking, he spoke clearly and authoritatively, directives without room for discussion for anyone present, especially the BC.

"These men need a rest. We are attacking Isurava this afternoon as planned, but First Battalion will go without First Company. These men will stay here in Kokoda as part of the reserve force, but I don't want them coming in with Third Battalion on the 27th. The 41st Regiment should be arriving tomorrow, and we'll let First Company recover."

Horii turned his attention to the three younger men, now standing again once the table and empty bowls were quietly whisked away. Hiroshi's stomach growled but he ignored it, sensitive to Hashimoto's immediate distress on being told First Company was not part of the assault. Hashimoto's hands shook visibly, not unnoticed by General Horii.

"You have performed well, Captain, as all of your men. Your company needs a rest. Food, dry clean clothing and new equipment. In a

265

few days you can rejoin First Battalion."

"*But sir*," Hashimoto couldn't contain himself, his eyes pleading with General Horii until Horii slowly rose to his feet. He was not a small man.

"Yes, Captain?" There was no room for argument with this man, it was painted across his face. Cross no lines, watch what you say.

"We explored the high western approaches, sir. My men," Hashimoto turned to include Miyamoto and Hiroshi with a small wave of his hand, "know these trails intimately, sir." He stopped abruptly, recognizing the hooded eyes of his commander were growing remote. Hashimoto stiffened, drawing himself up sharply.

"Forgive me, sir. First Company will stand down as ordered."

Their battalion commander sent other officers looking for clean uniforms as soon as General Horii dismissed them. They were also summoned by the commander of the 144th Regiment who asked them to attend the final assault briefing in 30 minutes time, and to be prepared to answer questions. They had not seen him in over six weeks, since they left Rabaul. He congratulated them individually on the completion of their mission, but shook his head at their personal appearance.

The regimental commander, a full colonel, led the three officers to a small clearing behind his tent. He offered them the use of his private commode and wash basin. Three enlisted men appeared with water cans, standing by as they stripped off their ragged uniforms. A staff captain handed them soap, clean towels and scrub brushes. He also laid out a small selection of officer breeches, shirts and tunics. They were all used but clean. The staff captain stripped their old uniforms of collar tabs and insignia, apologizing he didn't have time to find them new boots. *Hurry,* he said. *The briefing begins in 15 minutes and General Horii insists they start on time. Late arrivals are not allowed in.*

Unshaven, they still felt 100 percent better as they were hustled into the large storeroom with 80 other officers shoulder to shoulder. It was very hot and stuffy in the room. Captain Hashimoto nodded to a few of the others, who nodded back hesitatingly but in all cases could not take their eyes off of him or his companions. They were beginning to realize how much they changed in the six weeks since landing on New Guinea. All three lost so much weight they looked like scarecrows in their new uniforms. General Horii arrived a few minutes later, stopping all conversations as the group was called to attention. He strode to the small space in front of the room without saying a word, waving impatiently for his staff intelligence officer to begin. Looking to the front of the room, Hiroshi recognized Miyamoto's maps had been reproduced on much larger butcher paper and stretched on wooden frames. Kerosene lanterns were hung from the rafters in front of the maps revealing their details. *How did they do all this in the scope of an hour or two?* The main landmarks of the Isurava settlement were all present; the creek, the east and west escarpments, the thick forest areas—*the no-man's land*, the main and subsidiary trails, and the three defensive perimeters of Isurava, the Rest House and Alola.

Hiroshi was impressed on how well the intelligence staff interpreted Miyamoto's symbols for weapons, enemy troops and his detailed trail notes until it occurred to him, rather sheepishly, Miyamoto knew exactly what he was doing and communicated in such a way the intelligence people understood him. Miyamoto was an intelligence officer in that regard, *kempeitai* or not. Hiroshi glanced over at Miyamoto with new respect. Miyamoto's lowered eyelids suggested he was dozing or nearly asleep. Hiroshi knew better. He listened carefully to the briefing, but not with the same rapt attention as Captain Hashimoto as the briefer methodically outlined the attack plan. The regiment would move down the Track and into position tonight to assault the first defensive perimeter, Isurava, at first light. The plan had First Battalion of the 144th, minus First Company, attacking the Isurava perimeter directly with one company in a frontal assault, and another company attacking from the western flank.

Third Battalion, which was to be held in reserve for one day, would work down the western escarpment and also attack the Isurava perimeter from the west, but well above Eora Creek and farther south. Hiroshi sighed, aware this was the route he and Miyamoto and Sergeant Inoue used many nights in a row to get below the Australian perimeters. Second Battalion was to quietly slip around the eastern escarpment on the other side of Eora Creek, working their way south towards Abuari and the waterfall on the road to Alola. This would take an extra day or two, and Hiroshi immediately noticed a small thin smile crease across Hashimoto's face. Hiroshi already knew what Hashimoto must be thinking, but was also aware he and Miyamoto had spent very little of their time on the eastern side of the creek. They couldn't help Hashimoto because they didn't know it. The escarpment on the eastern side was lightly defended and the forest extremely steep and thick. That was the report. Other recon teams had explored that side, finding it a very long way to get around to Alola. But if a sizeable force got there before the Australians slipped down the Track, which was their style under continued pressure, they could trap them.

The regimental commander spoke a few minutes on logistical problems, specifically rations. After sampling General Horii's bountiful feast Hiroshi assumed the rest of the regiment was equally supplied. There seemed to be hundreds of native bearers around, some preparing to carry wounded men apparently all the way back to Buna. That seemed impossible. The RC stressed his commanders to ensure men were careful with their rations, because the Allied attacks on the Track had increased three-fold and native bearers were deserting in droves. Many of the supplies were destroyed by early air attacks or abandoned by the native bearers. When possible what the bearers didn't carry Japanese soldiers would have to carry. There were shortages, 3,500 men use a lot of materials. If necessary, he warned, he would have to institute a reduction of daily rations until the food supply situation improved. The supply train was too long and the human carriers insufficient to maintain *Nankai Shitai.* Ammunition was the first priority, rations the second, but in either case they didn't have enough. As it was, he estimated the regiment would see serious food shortages *in less than a week.*

All of this surprised Hiroshi, because there were thousands of men now in Kokoda, the entire 144th Regiment. If anything he wondered how they would find a way to hide them all from the inevitable air attacks. The only safety net was the weather, the boiling skies overhead grounded Allied over flights for days, but how much longer could they count on that? Horii understood the urgency of keeping the momentum going, moving *Nankai Shitai* while no Allied observation was possible. The mountain artillery battalion was coming through Kokoda, their 75mm guns still broke down into moveable pieces, to be set up once in position outside of Isurava. He watched these exhausted crews struggle with their incredible loads on the uneven ground. *These men and their now dead horses, carried these guns 90 kilometers!* He was most grateful he was not an artillery officer.

Without warning, Hiroshi found himself guided to the front of the room by Captain Hashimoto, who handed him to the regimental commander. General Horii stepped up next to him, beaming, placing a large hand on Hiroshi's shoulder in a fatherly gesture, explaining to the officers in attendance First Lieutenant Takahashi had led dozens of reconnaissance patrols down in the forest south of Isurava and the Rest House. *Here's an officer who can tell us exactly what we are up against when we penetrate the perimeters in Isurava. Here's a soldier so bold he slips inside Australian living quarters and steals their food from under their noses!* The officers in the front row, most of them majors and lieutenant colonels, grinned and murmured at General Horii's joke, but when their eyes finally rested on Hiroshi they stared. They stared as if they were examining a large insect pinned to a board.

The questions stopped coming after five or six minutes. Hiroshi tried to be honest and as truthful as he could, describing Australian defensive fighting pits in the Isurava settlement, how they were manned, how far apart they were on the eastern side, and how they used star shell flares at night. The Australians used hand grenades sparingly, he answered to a question, and almost always in more open terrain. They were dangerous in close quarters in the forest as the bomb could deflect off a tree branch or trunk and bounce back to kill or injure the thrower.

Only one officer asked the question about their experience entering the Australian sleeping quarters, looking for food. *What weapons did Hiroshi use, personally?* Hiroshi looked at the man closely, a young major, deciding he was sincere and deserved an honest answer. So Hiroshi told him. *I carry a short-bladed knife, sir,* he said quietly, *which I've seen used to great effect. But to kill an Australian who was preparing to call the alarm, I used an enemy rifle butt.* That shut them up right quick. Perhaps as Japanese officers they had not considered how they would defend themselves against an enemy when they could not make noise. Or they considered crushing a man's skull with a rifle butt too crude for an officer. The officers would not meet his eyes for long after this and General Horii ended the briefing. Horii, for his part, seemed pleased with Hiroshi's performance, patting him on his back and offering his hand, wishing him good luck. Hiroshi came to attention and bowed, wishing General Horii the best of luck in return on his soon to be great victory.

CHAPTER 21

August 28, 1942, First Company, 1/144th Infantry, Abuari waterfall

Hiroshi listened with growing hopelessness as Captain Hashimoto went through his list of what needed to be done. Hashimoto, his face unusually bronzed with an orange cast seemed feverish, his skin visibly moist and damp. His cheekbones, hollow and bony, were drawn tight under his skin. His teeth seemed to have deteriorated to the point he hid them and often kept his mouth shut, his lips tight together. His eyes appeared huge in the sockets. In the past they stared unblinking and uncompromising; a steady, fierce confidence and will few men would challenge. The stare remained but there was movement now, a nervous darting Hiroshi never seen before. Hashimoto still had the capacity for great focus, but his eyes and parts of his body moved constantly. There was no stillness, no peace. He didn't seem conscious of it. Down in the twilight world of Isurava his appearance was lost in the shadows, everyone looked the same. In the sunlight of the Kokoda plains it was as if Hashimoto's body was boiled dry then reconstituted. He was a different man.

Besides the normal housekeeping chores of finding a safe place for the men to bivouac, Hashimoto wanted an immediate list from the platoon commanders of the men fit for a combat assignment within 24 hours. This was the top priority, above and yet including the other priorities such as getting the company fed, issued new equipment, cleaned up and medically evaluated. Hiroshi met with the officers, two as ill as their men, to update the company roster to reflect losses to death, wounds or illness. *What does he want?* They demanded in frustration. Hiroshi would rarely hear this. The others knew he had Hashimoto's ear and was loyal to his commander. They also understood Hiroshi never turned on his fellow officers if a discussion was done in confidence. *The men are sick and starving, Hiroshi! They should send all of us home to Japan to recuperate, the company is finished. Why is he asking about fitness for a combat assignment? Has Hashimoto gone mad?*

Second Battalion slipped out early in the morning of the 26th heading down the eastern escarpment on their mission to cutoff the Australians at Alola. Hashimoto watched them depart, his eyes bright with anticipation because he was going to join them within 36 hours. Once he determined there were 40 men fit for duty including two officers, Hashimoto carefully approached the regimental commander

270

with his plan. The RC wasn't aware of the conversation between General Horii and the First Battalion Commander on standing down First Company until Hashimoto informed him of it. The RC knew intelligence reported few Australians on the eastern escarpment, but the unknown factor bothered him. Two battalions were attacking the western escarpment, and there was only one available for the eastern side of Eora Creek. The 41st Regiment was still climbing up the Kokoda Track and not expected until the 29th.

Hashimoto proposed sending the functional part of his company, slightly more than a single platoon, to be provisionally attached to the Second Battalion. They could be used for reconnaissance, or simply another platoon to supplement the prime assault company of Second Battalion. The RC could see Captain Hashimoto was rail thin from poor nutrition and stress, and appeared to be, in some ways, quite mad. The situation was not desperate on the eastern escarpment by any means, not yet, but numbers mattered in combat operations. The Australians could be reinforced from Port Moresby any day and *Nankai Shitai*, stretched critically thin on a way too long supply train, could lose its momentum and tentative advantage. The eastern escarpment could be key to the success of the Japanese attack; it could also very well be part of the Australian plan.

The RC considered Hashimoto's offer for a roving reconnaissance unit for a moment and dismissed it, when a thought came into his head. He wouldn't have even seen Hashimoto under normal circumstances, but the First Battalion and their commander were already in Isurava. Hashimoto had no chain of command to submit his request, he was no fool. He had to apply directly to Regiment. Hashimoto threw himself at the RC's mercy knowing he was risking a rebuke and at worst, a court martial. The RC knew Hashimoto personally from years of experience, fully aware of his reputation as an aggressive, effective leader. He also understood General Horii relieved Hashimoto's company because the forest, Australians, malaria, typhus and starvation nearly destroyed them. But here the man stood, offering himself and a handful of his men because he considered it his duty. Or was mad. The RC stared hard at Hashimoto, a little concerned about the look of desperation in the man's eyes.

He reached for a single sheet warning order outlining the units staged for the Isurava assault and studied it carefully. What stuck out was what wasn't on the list. The regimental reconnaissance and intelligence platoon, comprised of mostly *Kempeitai,* translators and intelligence specialists did not currently have a mission, since the First Battalion Advance Party had performed this mission for Isurava. These 30 or 40 men were cooling their heels in Kokoda, waiting for a mission, as they often worked in small teams assigned temporarily to individual battalions. Combining the two units, a true provisional company, would add close to 80 men to the mix. The RC smiled and called for his communications aide. He could explain this to General Horii somehow, he was sure. Horii wanted results and victory.

Although the eastern escarpment was a rough trail, it was better than trying to work through the heavy forest and the steep, rocky slopes. Hashimoto, given command of the provisional company, was extremely pleased to have Miyamoto and the rest of the R and I Platoon under his command. It started to rain hard as soon as they reached the outskirts of the Isurava settlement and never let up. The two units hooked up surprisingly well, especially since First Company worked with some of them before. Hiroshi wasn't aware previously that Warrant Officer Miyamoto was the commanding officer of the regimental R and I Platoon. It surprised him because Miyamoto never seemed to be concerned about anyone else except himself and perhaps Sergeant Inoue. There wasn't an administrative bone in his body. Hiroshi couldn't imagine Miyamoto working up equipment rosters or sick lists. He did notice, however, men would approach Miyamoto frequently for some problem or another, and Miyamoto would listen carefully and either issue instructions or follow his men to deal with the problem. It was a side of the man he would have never suspected.

Second Battalion moved fast, completely surprising and sweeping aside the few groups of Australian communication units stationed in the small villages down the back of the escarpment. Apparently these units did not expect *Nankai Shitai* to attack the eastern escarpment in force. These teams had no infantry support. Second Battalion came through quietly and swiftly, fully camouflaged with foliage tied to their helmets, rucksacks and uniforms. A few of the Australians ran into the jungle and escaped, the rest were shot dead or bayoneted while still transmitting on the radio. Second Battalion, knowing the R and I Platoon was coming up behind them, left everything and moved on. The R and I Platoon sifted through the abandoned communication gear looking for code books. Unfortunately Second Battalion was in a hurry so there were no live prisoners to question.

Second Lieutenant Nishikawa was left in command of what remained of First Company in Kokoda. Both he and Second Lieutenant Tanaka were quite ill but remained on duty. At least they could eat regularly and stay reasonably dry. Hiroshi didn't know why he volunteered to accompany Hashimoto back down to Isurava, he certainly didn't want to go back. He was weak, ill and despite recent regular meals found he needed the *Nekome-jo* tablets several times a day so he could feel better. He felt best when he injected the warm liquid in his veins with Hashimoto. Hashimoto casually admitted to injecting twice a day because he said it would take too many tablets to keep him well. Hiroshi understood that now. No number of tablets could replicate the warmth and pleasure of the liquid rushing through his veins once that method was introduced to him. It must have been the same for Miyamoto. They all craved it now, the pills took too long. During the day Hiroshi had no choice, but found himself taking the tablets two at a time, often only four or five hours apart. He hungered for the evening when Hashimoto would call him to his CP and Miyamoto would cook up an evening dose. He didn't like not feeling well.

The provisional company caught up with the Second Battalion late in the afternoon of the 27th outside of the village of Abuari. The mountain artillery units firing constantly all day, and Second Battalion, bringing their own RTs and cables, was linked on the artillery net and with Regiment in Kokoda. Captain Hashimoto listened carefully as the Second Battalion Commander reported the latest intelligence based on captured Australians and message traffic passed on by First and Third battalions on the western side of Eora Creek. The Australians not only reported 20,000 men staging in Port Moresby, there were fresh Australian units coming up the Kokoda. Some units, reportedly the 2/14 Battalion of the AIF, were already in the Isurava area and another Battalion, the 2/16 was on the way. Of particular interest was what was in front of the Second Battalion on the other side of the waterfall. The road from Abuari led southwest down beyond the waterfall to the log bridge crossing Eora Creek. On the other side of the log bridge was Alola, the Australian headquarters for the settlement, the last stronghold.

In the morning, the Second Battalion Commander said quietly, *we will assault the Australians holding the ground by the waterfall, reported as an infantry company. Another company is holding the area around the log bridge. In both cases they have excellent fields of fire on the creek, the banks and the open roadway. We will assault the company on the other side of the waterfall from three sides.* He looked up and nodded towards Captain Hashimoto. *I want your men to go up over the ridge and come in behind the Australians and attack their positions just as we hit them again in the morning. There is a large gap between the unit holding the log bridge and the unit holding the waterfall. You should be in perfect position and virtually unseen. Hold by the road until you hear our attack from the North, then you attack from the South, their rear. They will have nowhere to go, no direction to withdraw, which is such a large part of their strategy. We will then destroy them.*

It was very rough going climbing through the forest. It was raining hard, the visibility only a few meters in the twilight. The mist

273

was heavy up in the trees; they knew they were back down in Isurava. It was like ascending into a cloud, making breathing difficult as men sucked in moisture, not oxygen. Hiroshi felt like he was drowning. The soil was mostly washed away on the slopes and there were few handholds. They slipped and fell constantly. He knew they needed to get down and behind Abuari before dawn but the distance to go around, only a couple of kilometers, seemed to grow not shorten. There were no trails so the provisional company rotated men every five minutes on the machetes necessary to cut through the foliage. It was brutal, exhausting work but there was no other way to get to the ridgeline. Hashimoto and Miyamoto conferred frequently, referring to their compasses. No one questioned Miyamoto's navigation skills under the canopy. His brain sensed direction from some innate gyroscope as if he was an albatross. If he felt they needed to go in a certain direction, they went. He was always right.

The remnants of First Company quickly fell behind on the steady, brutal climb. Miyamoto set the pace and Hiroshi knew what to expect. The men in the R and I Platoon were personally selected by Miyamoto so they stayed up with him on missions or were reassigned. There were frequent stops to wait for First Company to catch up. Once they reached the ridgeline the going was a bit better because it was rocky with fewer trees, but the steep rock drops were dangerous in the waning light because they were smooth and slick with wetness. Once it became completely dark they stopped, making themselves as comfortable as possible in the driving rain. Miyamoto estimated they were less than a third of a kilometer to the east of Abuari, which was confirmed a few minutes later when the first flares of the night were fired by the Australians. There were easily three mist layers visible down below them, the small village of Abuari, abandoned by the Australians, was a shadowy cluster barely visible. The flare, dampened by mist and heavy rain, fluttered and spit sparks on a quick fall into darkness and oblivion.

Hiroshi, who looked down and watched like everyone else, searched the shadows to their south for the road and the waterfall, only to witness the blackness envelop the scene like a dropped blanket as the flare fell. The men dug out rations and huddled together. He was conscious of growing cramps and a nervous tension but no one moved around, it was too dangerous. What his body craved he couldn't have tonight, not here among the men. There was no CP, no privacy possible. Hiroshi pulled out his box of *Nekome-jo,* protecting it from the rain, swallowing two tablets with water from his canteen. All of the men tonight were given a half a dozen of the tablets, above and beyond the *Totsugeki-jo* in their tea earlier in the afternoon. At least they had something to eat with it for the time being. He tried hard to think of something else as he waited. The tablets would start to work soon to calm his agitation, slowing his racing brain so he could focus. *Hurry, please hurry.*

Hiroshi didn't dream at all, a most unusual thing. He knew he was exhausted from the climbing, yet surprised the downpour of icy cold water on his body didn't wake him as he lay tucked against a slab of rock. He slept like a dead man. He opened his eyes to a world only a fraction less dark then before. He sensed the dawn, knowing the blackness was fading, although there were no recognizable shapes just yet. He rubbed his eyes hard with the palms of his hands, shaking his head to try to clear the murkiness of his brain. He jumped as a body dropped down next to him, the movement as light as a cat. A sudden hand on his shoulder was firm and steady. Hiroshi knew it was Miyamoto before he could see his face.

"Time to go, Lieutenant," Miyamoto whispered. "Hashimoto wants to meet before we start down."

The most difficult part of the approach left was the small subsidiary creek that fed the waterfall on its way to Eora Creek. They had to cross it to get into the forest on the south side of the road behind the waterfall. The torrential rains made the creek deep, fast and dangerous. With just enough light to get around, Miyamoto and Sergeant Inoue were going ahead to reconnoiter. The provisional company was to get down to the bank of the creek and wait. There was little time left, perhaps 20 minutes before the attack began.

The twilight was fading when Miyamoto returned. Captain Hashimoto was relieved, Hiroshi could tell, but Hashimoto said nothing while they waited. Miyamoto reported they found a spot where the men could cross safely. Inoue had swum the strong current and made it to the other side. He brought along a coil of rope for just this purpose, stringing a life line above a series of large rocks just barely exposed by the current.

The creek was not wide at the selected point, only four or five meters, but the rocks were actually the top edges of a small waterfall. Water poured over the tops of the rocks keeping them slick and wet, but those were the only footholds. The water thundered down below them creating a deafening roar flushing away all conversation. The drop was only a few meters, but the water churned and raced away like a dam sluice. To fall would be to be swept away, that was apparent. How Sergeant Inoue crossed the creek Hiroshi could not imagine. It must have been above this point. They were out of time and Second Battalion would begin their attack at first light, literally minutes away. Two of the strongest men were placed on the opposite sides of the rope line, keeping it taunt for the men crossing over. After a few close calls, another man was stationed to hold the rope in the center of the creek, one hand on the rope and the other on a swaying branch overhead. His position was absolutely precarious. Hiroshi found it was almost impossible to hang on to the rope with only one hand and not lose his balance.

Once across men pulled the rifles from their rucksacks and followed the directions from Miyamoto to run down along the edge of a small clearing to form into their squad units. In front of them was a dense, dark forest, menacing in its thick, low foliage. Despite this, Hashimoto insisted the men fix bayonets. Miyamoto estimated the road was less than a quarter of a kilometer away to the direct west. The instructions were clear; once they came to the road they were to immediately turn to the right, to the north. They would be a few hundred meters behind the Australian positions, and once they were on the road, they would reform and quickly rush behind the Australians, forming two skirmish lines before they attacked. The troops lined up behind Miyamoto in one line and Hiroshi leading the other.

They heard the artillery fire first, 75mm mountain guns, the rounds landing somewhere to the far north. Machinegun and rifle fire to their west chattered about with the strange moving echoes of the forest, the drifting *poc poc poc poc* sifting away before stopping abruptly. A moment later a dozen machineguns opened up into a cacophony roar of noise, blending with artillery, mortar fire and the whumps of hand grenades to signal the beginning of the attack. It all sounded far away, closer to Isurava and Alola, but everything carried strangely in the forest.

As Hiroshi swerved and swooped around trees he could see the darkness of the forest thinning out, getting lighter. Miyamoto, 10 meters to his right noticed it too. They eventually made eye contact and signaled the columns to stop. Hashimoto came up at once pleased to see the road in front of them. Hiroshi asked if Hashimoto wanted to send a patrol forward to check out the road before proceeding. Hashimoto shook his head, frantically waving the men in both columns forward. *Get on the road! We need to get in position to attack immediately!* Hiroshi turned to signal to the men behind him but they were already passing on both sides, responding to Hashimoto's arm movements. The men, sensing the freedom of the road coming up, spread out rushing forward. Some turned to the left and the others to the right.

Hiroshi noticed it was much lighter to the left, deciding to follow the men heading there as the most direct path to the road. At least once out in the open they could see where they were going. He understood one group of the Australians was at least a half a kilometer to their southwest near Alola, and another, their target, was only a few hundred

276

meters to their north by the waterfall. The gunfire was growing louder, especially to the north, but it could be heard in all directions. It was unnerving and a bit confusing, especially since the roar of the constant pounding rain was increasing as they approached the road. Anticipating the road excited him, to be temporarily free of the jungle and away from the confinement. The imminent combat drove him forward as he tried to catch up with his men. He gripped his sword by the handle, loosening the blade an inch, ready to withdraw it from its scabbard once he was clear of the trees. 20 or 30 of the men were in front of him now, rushing the road at almost a run. *He was furious, he was supposed to be in the lead!*

The first line of men broke through the trees joyfully, although they almost disappeared from sight in the torrential downpour landing on the road, unencumbered by canopy above. They stopped in wonder, incredulous at how hard it was raining, before remembered their instructions to immediately turn right, to the north. There was a tremendous clatter of gunfire to the right somewhere, a machinegun. Hiroshi could see the men on the road suddenly turn, some starting to point their rifles when nearly all of them started falling down as if swept aside with a giant invisible scythe. Men directly behind the first line were stepping out onto the road, not yet recognizing what was happening until they too were shot. Hiroshi stopped in his tracks, fear clutching at his heart. He instinctively stared to his right across the road, picking up the dozen dim yellow sparkles of muzzle flashes in the forest on the other side. There were no tracers visible, just noise, the sound of zipping bees and snapping whips all around him, disturbing the air, making him suddenly deaf. As Hiroshi turned a tree trunk to his left exploded inches from his head, spraying his face with dozens of splinters to pierce his flesh and blind him. A second later another missile punched through his cheek, blasting through his teeth and out through his jaw on the other side. Gagging on his own blood, he stumbled before his head slammed against something very hard, the stars and numbing pain a mere flash before blackness.

Hiroshi awoke sometime later, cold rain on his face. When he opened his eyes there was only blurriness and pain on the right side of his face. One eye didn't work at all. He felt something cold, metallic and hard brush along his jaw before it settled hard against his throat. It was round, like a gun barrel. The pressure made him gag, forcing his eyes wider. He raised his hands instinctively to his throat only to have them gripped hard and twisted down, painfully. A figure moved above him, accompanied by murmuring voices in a language he didn't understand. English. A rifle report exploded to his right so close and loud he was instantly deafened, bits of foliage and mud splattering on his face. He thought he had been shot, but despite the numb ringing in his ears, his panic subsided as he realized he still felt the cold metal pressed against his throat. A few seconds later another deafening rifle report sounded, making him jerk involuntarily. *They are shooting the wounded.* In panic again he fought against the unseen forces pressing down on his arms, but the effort was too much. He faded away again.

Hiroshi blinked in the rain as the vision returned in his left eye. It was cloudy but he could make out figures above him now, one leaning much closer. A hand fingered his collar for a moment before being replaced by others roughly searching his body. His belt harness was unstrapped from his waist, his pistol and sword removed. The murmuring continued but one voice, closer than the others, stood out as he heard a word he understood. *Shoko.* Officer.

CHAPTER 22

August 28, 1942, A Company, 2/14 Battalion, Abuari waterfall

Vic Hickey slowly stood up, releasing the magazine from his Thompson as he reached for another. Somehow he fired three full 20-round stick magazines in the span—of what, 30 seconds—and it was over. The only sound he was conscious of was the incessant rain pounding down onto the road. After the ear-numbing, close-in gunfire here in the grove of trees, now silent, the battle 200 meters to the north didn't even register. Even with the rain the cloud of smoke from all the shooting hadn't dissipated. It hung on the road and in the trees, an ethereal ghostly mist. The grey of the mud swirled pink and purple, the life drained and washed away from torn bodies. The Japs ran out on the road fully expecting a straight shot up to the waterfall. They would have attacked A Company from the rear just as their comrades were charging from the front. It would have been a slaughter. *He saw it in their faces, the bastards.*

"Sergeant!" Vic turned to his right, spotting Lieutenant Edwards signaling towards the road. Vic glanced down around him, noticing one of his Bren gunners was bleeding from his face and forearms.

"Right, suh!" he called out, looking for Potty. "Aidsman! Potty! 'Eve got a wounded gooner' 'ere!" He noticed men starting to stand up, so he barked his instructions quickly.

"Aye' put, gents! Section Leaders! Check your men! Gooners'! 'Coover us as we check the 'oad! First Section, on 'our 'eet!" The Bren gunners changed magazines and re-shouldered their LMGs as Vic and the First Section cautiously stepped out on the road.

He waved to get the attention of the section covering the road to the south, and it was here out in the open he realized how many of the Japanese they caught. Easily 35 or 40 men just on the road, stretched out over 50 meters. He could see another ten or so bodies in the first couple of meters into the forest on the other side. He knew they didn't kill them all, in the middle of the shooting some of the Japs finally realized what was happening and turned on their heels. Some of them were shot but many just disappeared back into the forest.

Some of the Japanese were still alive but no one asked Vic what to do with them. They bayoneted all the bodies to be sure. If a body moved the Aussie bayoneted him twice or shot him point blank and then bayoneted him. Everyone was scared the Japs would come again so there was no wasting time. They tossed the weapons in a pile on the road and moved on. Vic walked over to the captain he had shot first. The blows from the rear toppled the man onto his face. The entire back of his head was gone, flushed clean. The skull deflated and scrubbed away by the heavy rain. He was a large man for a Japanese yet appeared frail somehow. His uniform hung on his tall frame. Vic stepped over the body to pick up the Nambu pistol in the man's grip, putting it in his belt. He noticed the weapon was rusty. His eyes lifted to the forest in front of him as he brought his Thompson up to his shoulder. Link, Scabby and Biscuit joined him as he entered the forest on the other side as if it were a minefield.

Once in the trees it instantly became dark. Many of the bodies here were shot in the back, having turned away trying to avoid the slaughter on the road. You only needed to go about three or four meters in before you became invisible in the green twilight. These Japs, Vic mused, were mostly unlucky, hit by machinegun and rifle fire that somehow got past the tight cluster of tree trunks near the road, finding a home in their bodies forever. He sensed danger for him and his men if they went too far, so he signaled to Link on one side and Biscuit on the other to stop. Biscuit waved to Scabby, and they looked cautiously into the murk of the forest. This was as far in as they wanted to go. They faded to the south a few meters and found another cluster of bodies. Some were still alive. These men were the first on the road, shot up by the section covering the road to the south.

Vic approached a body cautiously, his Thompson pointed at the man's head. The Japanese seemed unhurt except for a head wound. Vic could see the man was shot through the jaw and his face was peppered with tree splinters, most still stuck in his face. One eye was encrusted with blood. Scabby joined him and so did Lieutenant Edwards. Vic pressed the bore of his Thompson against the man's throat, waking him up, the eyes opening wide as he reached out with his arms. Vic was a millisecond from pulling the trigger when Scabby dropped to wrestle the man's arms down.

"Aye' got un' alive, here," Vic heard Link slowly, but as Vic turned his head slightly in that direction, he jerked from the sudden loud report of Link's rifle.

"Off ta' yur' ancestors, mate!" Link ejected his empty with a flick of his bolt, reloading and moving to another body Biscuit was standing over. A second rifle report came a moment later. Vic raised the muzzle of his Thompson to his man's forehead, making sure he was clear of Scabby's arms and started to press the trigger.

"Hold it, Sergeant!" Annoyed, Vic glanced at Lieutenant Edwards, following his hands as Edwards leaned close to the Japanese soldier. Edwards grabbed the man's collar and brushed some of the mud off the insignia.

"Aye' think we should 'old on ta' 'is man, Sergeant, aye? He's a bloody Shoko! An officer! Aye' think we mite' 'earn somethin' 'om 'is man, aye?" Vic peered down at the prisoner and found the man was staring up at him with one good eye. He called Link over to give a hand and they searched the prisoner for weapons, taking his pistol and sword. It took a few minutes, but Potty tore up strips of uniforms from dead Japanese to tie the prisoner's hands and make a makeshift blindfold. Other than the head injuries he seemed unhurt.

By the time First Section was back on the other side of the road the attack on A Company subsided. Artillery fire, all Japanese, continued periodically. They could hear it landing somewhere else, mostly on the western side around Isurava and the Rest Area. The machinegun and rifle fire was only an occasional burst or cluster of single shots. They were definitely in a lull. When Vic sat in on the briefing earlier they were told they could expect the Japs to attack every hour until they overwhelmed a position. This was how *Nankai Shitai* operated. The BC said intelligence believed the Japs would have over 5,000 men in the Isurava area within 48 hours. They were facing about 3,500 right now. With 2/16 arriving sometime today the Australians would have maybe 1,800 men available, the total probably less with casualties the last day or two. There was no *winning* this battle, there was only holding on as long as they could before they were surrounded, withdrawing down the Track to find another place to make a brief stand. They had to hold on until help came or until they were destroyed.

In either case Vic was feeling the fortunes favored 9 Platoon so far. Lieutenant Edwards called Battalion to keep them informed and to check on the status of A Company. He also reported the prisoner, the Jap officer. What did Battalion want them to do with him? Send him back to Alola? Did Captain Welsh want 9 Platoon to stay put or come up and join them at the waterfall? The answers came back in less than a minute, in fact Battalion patched Captain Welsh through directly to Lieutenant Edwards. Vic, sitting just a short distance away, could guess what Welsh was saying to Edwards.

When Edwards rang off the RT he repeated the conversation to Vic. Welsh asked Edwards some questions about the prisoner before telling Edwards to just hold onto him, Battalion would send someone to pick him up once the situation stabilized. D Company was hit very hard at the log bridge and almost lost it. 2/16 was only an hour or two away, reportedly, but everyone expected the Japs to attack again before 2/16 arrived. The 39th Battalion remnants and both C and B Companies were barely holding on in Isurava village and the Rest House. They were catching the brunt of the artillery fire and planned to start withdrawing

281

tonight if they could. Their problem was casualty evacuation. There were lots of casualties and if necessary 9 Platoon might be asked to take on that task again. This time most likely under fire.

9 Platoon saved A Company's bacon, but A Company, even in their good defensive positions was almost overrun by the Japs in the last attack. Casualties were high, but they couldn't evacuate. The Japs were coming back. There were just too many of them to withstand repeated assaults. In the thick forest near the waterfall the Japs came within 20-30 meters of the A Company lines before they were first seen. With no artillery support and limited ammunition supplies, Welsh had no choice but to fall back to the log bridge and the D Company's positions after dark. They would try to hold on during the afternoon and evening. So 9 Platoon was to stay put until dark, providing security and a blocking force if the Japs try to attack from the rear again, or broke through C Company and were coming down the road for the log bridge. Once it got dark, 9 Platoon would come up and assist in removing the wounded.

Despite the toll on the Japanese in the morning battle on the road, 9 Platoon had only four casualties, none serious enough to require evacuation. All of the injuries were caused by Bren gunners pivoting their weapons too far in the forest, shooting through tree trunks and limbs on this side of the road. 9 Platoon riflemen, only a meter or less from the muzzles of the LMGs, were hit by exploding splinters of wood, some imbedding themselves deeply and painfully into soft tissue. In the middle of the shooting no one cared, but when it was over the Bren gunners were the brunt of considerable criticism because of it. In the end the man who got the most complaints was Potty, who had the job of removing the foreign splinters out of the wounded men's hands, faces, forearms and necks. It was slow work, and it hurt. To criticize Potty at a critical moment guaranteed it would hurt even more.

The Japanese prisoner, tied hand and foot horizontally to a tree, was temporarily ignored. He seemed to be suffering far beyond what would be expected from his visible physical wounds. He moaned and groaned constantly, and was wracked by powerful muscular contractions jerking him about. At first the men assigned to guard him thought he was trying to escape and he was almost shot a couple of times, but finally Potty, after plucking out all the splinters for the unfortunate in 9 Platoon, stopped by and observed him. He finally injected the prisoner with a shot of morphine. After a few minutes the man calmed down and became quiet.

Potty sat down and examined the man carefully for unseen wounds to explain his odd behavior. Not finding any, he examined the prisoner's jaw where the gunshot wound entered and exited. He also noted the wooden splinters all around the man's face and right eye. Potty swabbed out the jaw wound, plucking out bits of torn gum and broken teeth. The best he could do was insert small compresses on each side and wrap the jaw. There was still a big hole. The battalion surgeon would have to fix that. The man needed stitches, lots of them. Potty removed the blindfold carefully. Although the man seemed awake he was groggy, his good eye fully dilated in the twilight of the forest. Potty set to work and carefully plucked out the splinters and cleaned the wounds. Lucky Jap, he thought, as he discovered none of the splinters had actually penetrated the right eye. The inflammation, bleeding and draining fluids from many punctures around the eye closed it solid, but once the splinters were removed and the tissue was cleaned up, the eyelid moved normally.

Potty's gentle movement around the prisoner's eyes seemed to awaken the man, for suddenly he opened both eyes. He stared at Potty for a long moment before blinking his eyes repeatedly, realizing he could see again. Tears came to the man's eyes. He watched Potty gratefully before nodding his head weakly towards him, holding it for a moment. It was an attempt at a bow, Potty was sure of it.

"*Arigato,*" the prisoner said very slowly, his word inarticulate, muffled by the gauze in his cheeks. "*Arigato.*" His face suddenly crimped with pain as he bent over as far as the straps would allow, his knees coming up towards his chest until stopped by the restraints. His hands shook as beads of sweat poured out of his face. The Jap was in bloody poor shape, Potty observed, this looked like malaria to him. Although he couldn't explain the severe stomach cramps. Nothing else pulled you up like that. Maybe something the poor bastards were eating was toxic to their systems. Who knows. He knew he shouldn't care, but he did.

"Yew' need wata', mate?" Potty inquired. "Is 'at what ya' sayin', chum?"

Slim, the man guarding the prisoner for the moment, sniggered and snorted loudly as he watched Potty try to communicate with the enemy prisoner. Slim shook his head slowly in pure contempt, knowing there wasn't a bloody thing he could do about it. Like all of the other men in 9 Platoon Slim would do anything for Potty, but the bloody fool was such a soft touch for the aches and pains of his fellow man. He was always being taken advantage of. And now he was tripping all over himself to fix a bloody bleeding Jap! Slim couldn't stand it anymore, picking up and throwing a gooey mud clod at Potty, hitting him on the side of his arm.

"Crimey, Pot! Ewe' makin' me bloody gag ova' ya' nursin' a bleedin' bloody Jap! 'Ave 'ewe lost your bloody mine', bloke? 'Aye can't stan' listenin' ta' his bleedin' jibberish, an' 'ewe blibberin' like a nursemade' fixin' ta' treat 'is every bleedin' 'urt—is that it, Pot? Are 'ewe outta' your bleedin' mine'?"

Vic, listening to the exchange, smiled and made his way over to the prisoner. The prisoner looked pretty quiet now. His eyes were closed, the splinters removed and bandages were in place. The jaw wound was covered with a large compress bandage tied to the top of his head. Potty and Slim exchanged more insults before Potty picked up his kit bag and shuffled off. Slim tipped his head towards Vic, accepting the proffered cigarette Vic held shielded under his hand, palm downward. Dry cigarettes were hard to come by. Vic bent his head so the rim of his helmet covered his own smoke. He offered it over to Slim, who butt-lit his and handed Vic's cigarette back. Most of the men were down to a few tailormades remaining from their last ration resupply. *It would be back to roll-your-owns in a day or two, if you were still alive in this cock-up.*

Neither said anything, they didn't have to. Slim and Vic and the rest of the boys from 9 Platoon had been together since the beginning, since they raised the division back in Victoria. Slim and Vic served as a Bren team once. Vic the gunner, Slim the A-gunner. When Vic was promoted to section leader, Slim was still an A-gunner. Now that Vic was the platoon sergeant, Slim was still an A-gunner. Attempts to promote him, to move him behind the gun were met with a *thanks, but no thanks.* He liked his job, was good at it and would take over as gunner if necessary, but felt he was a natural assistant. His eyes weren't good enough, he said. Good enough it was, as far as Vic was concerned.

They were both indifferent to the Jap prisoner under the best of circumstances, and these were not the best. They bloody well knew they were facing a superior force, most likely a battalion, less than an eighth of a kilometer away directly to the north, and at least two more battalions somewhere out there to the northwest. They both heard what happened to Australians when they were prisoners of the Japs. This was a time when things could happen fast. It was not the time to be keeping prisoners, slowing men down or tying them to babysitting duties. They expected no quarter from the Japs and gave none themselves.

Lieutenant Edwards moved the platoon 50 meters north down the road, deeper in the forest. The three sections, a Bren gun team in the center of each, protected three different zones facing north, east and south. Edwards had some of the men pull the dead Japanese and their weapons into the forest where they couldn't be easily seen. If some of the Jap troops who survived the firefight came through again they would not immediately recognize the location without the bodies. The rain washed most of the blood away by early afternoon. Vic was amazed how quickly the forest and mud simply healed itself as if the morning carnage never happened.

Sitting in the forest, listening to the rain and the raging battles around them made them nervous. It was like being in the eye of a tropical storm, knowing any minute the calm eye would pass over and the storm would return as strong as ever. It was very apparent A Company was under attack again, as was D company behind them to the southwest by the log bridge. Lieutenant Edwards, checking in with battalion and trying to hook up with Captain Welsh, was told the Japs overran a number of A Company positions and Welsh was prepared to counterattack to regain the ground. Edwards pleaded with Battalion for permission to move 9 Platoon to A Company's aid, but was told to hold their positions. *If the Japs break through again,* the battalion executive officer told him drolly, *they'll be about 600 of em' in your damn lap, laddie, so sit tight!*

Edwards passed on the word. 9 Platoon, lying in the rain, counted their magazines, stripper clips and Mills bombs. *If the Japs come up the road in force, we can hold em'fer' 'bout 'ive minutes. They'll swarm us like bees, chums, like bees.*

Twenty minutes later they got the call that 2/16, like the bloody Yank cavalry, arrived and was sending two companies up the road from Alola to relieve 2/14's A Company at the waterfall and D Company at the log bridge. *Sit tight.* Edwards, about ready to explode, again requested permission to move 9 Platoon forward to assist A Company at the waterfall. It was denied, the battalion executive officer was clear: *Once the 2/16 companies pass your position, fall in behind them and report to Captain Welsh. 9 Platoon will assist in moving A Company wounded to the surgical hospital at Alola. Bring your prisoner at the same time.*

285

CHAPTER 23

August 30, 1942, Alola Surgical Hospital, Isurava settlement

The last thing he remembered was being strapped down to a stretcher and carried onto a wooden table with a brilliant light. It was incredibly hot. There was pain, remote yet present in his face. A bearded Australian leaned inches from his eyes with a blinding hot light, a gauze mask moving just below huge blue eyes behind refracted glass. Hiroshi tried to move his head to get away from the light but found his head firmly held in someone's hands. There was a prick in his arm as a mask dropped over his nose and mouth. The scent was overwhelming, he couldn't place it. He wanted to vomit but he was losing control, drifting away. It felt heavy on his chest, drifting down on his lungs like a thick dark blanket, filling every corner until he forgot to breathe and the blackness closed in.

He awoke, hours later, he wasn't sure. It was dark. Mosquito netting clouded his sight until he realized what it was as someone walked past carrying a kerosene lantern. He seemed to be off the ground, on a cot. Even so he could feel the upheavals and air displacement from artillery rounds landing close by. There was small arms fire, rifle and machinegun, some of it very close. Hiroshi didn't feel frightened, the gunfire was nearby yet he couldn't register what it meant. There was a dull, throbbing sensation just at some comfortable threshold around his face. His cheeks felt as if they were stuffed with cotton. He wanted to reach up and touch them because they itched, but his hands were still restrained, as were his legs. He closed his eyes and drifted off.

When he awoke again he was being moved, carried by stretcher in darkness. There was a lot of movement around him, many men, Australians, talking quietly but urgently. Artillery and small arms fire was still present, but distant. His face, especially around his cheeks and jaw, now throbbed with pain. He could feel the stomach cramps coming on and wanted to curl up his legs to his chest but couldn't. His feet were tied to the stretcher as were his hands, forcing him to lie on his right side so his mouth could drain. He moaned and cried out to no avail as whoever was carrying his stretcher ignored him.

An electric torch flicked on, the lens shielded with tape so only a thin beam of yellow light could be seen. The mosquito netting was removed and insects were biting him around the head and neck. The light moved to his face, forcing him to turn his eyes. A hand brushed the insects away as a man's face, another Australian half in shadow, leaned in close to examine his face. The light moved away so Hiroshi could see

286

the man's face more clearly. It was familiar. From the fog in his brain he finally recognized it. This was the man who pulled the splinters out of his eyes after the forest firefight. He was certain of it. When both eyes were working the man was the first thing he saw. Now in the poor light of the torch he could see the buggy eyes and stringy hair. This was the man who swabbed his eyes kindly, with gentleness. He could not forget. Hiroshi wanted to say something but his mouth didn't work. He groaned. The Australian watched him for a second, before swabbing his arm with something wet. Hiroshi felt the prick of a needle. The warmth came slower but it was working. Morphine. It was almost as good as *shabu*. The man with the buggy eyes was replaced by a big man with a submachine gun. The two Australians talked in low tones as the electric torch went out. Hiroshi started to drift back to sleep. The stretcher was lifted, the movement making him dizzy. He could feel the heavy rain drops pummel his face until even this sensation faded away.

The pain was intense, reaching far into his subdued consciousness to jerk him to the surface before he was ready. His head spun, his eyes opening to opaque whiteness he could not understand. *Silk shrouds? Was he dead?* He moaned before crying out in fear and pain once he was semi-conscious. Something was very wrong. The hurt in his jaw and his mouth stabbed deeply, followed by a strange burning sensation. Hiroshi shook his head back and forth, unable to reach his face with his restrained hands. He couldn't breathe. He gagged on something hard in his mouth, yet something—was *moving*. Groggy but more aware every second, Hiroshi felt something crawling in the tube and in his mouth—insects, hundreds of biting insects, *biting him*. He gagged and coughed and spit the drain tube out of his mouth, feeling the ants pouring out over his cheek. He panicked and screamed again. Hiroshi had no awareness of the men who were suddenly all around him until they put their hands on him. They cut his restraint straps and turned his body over. After frantic discussion they started pouring water over his head and into his mouth. He choked but they kept at it, talking loudly he finally processed, *in Japanese*.

Hiroshi sat up in his cot as the medical officer applied salve to the swollen insect bites all over his face. He was back in the Alola Surgical Hospital, the opaque whiteness he had seen was the mosquito netting the Australians draped over him before they abandoned the hospital. They left a single kerosene lantern burning close to Hiroshi to apparently mark his location. The Australians pulled out with all of their own wounded, leaving only their dead. Hiroshi was the only living person left in Alola discovered by the lead units of the 41st Regiment. The 41st used the trails above the western escarpment discovered by Hiroshi and Miyamoto two weeks before, bringing two battalions all the way around in an attempt to cut off the Australians north of Alola. The 41st, alerted by Hiroshi's screams, found him instead.

The Australians pulled out less than an hour before the 41st charged down through the trees in the pouring rain. General Horii was furious. The withdrawal was masterfully done, with 2/14 and 2/16 continued to engage all three battalions of the 144th in a fighting withdrawal right down through the Rest Area. The First and Third Battalions attacked the front and flanks repeatedly with bayonet charges. Only a few Australian units held the ground as the rest streamed south down the Track right past Alola. Once darkness set in, the last Australian units pulled out, abandoning, uncharacteristically, a considerable stockpile of stores and some ammunition. Hiroshi, his torn cheeks sewed up by an Australian surgeon, was sedated and left alone with a drain tube in his mouth so he wouldn't drown in his own secretions. The Australians also covered him with mosquito netting so he wouldn't be bitten alive. The ants found him all on their own.

The medical officer noted the Aussie stitching was workmanlike but more than adequate. Hiroshi would have two starfish-shaped scars on each side of his face once it healed; one small, the entry wound, and one quite large—the exist wound. The medical officer was frankly astonished, as were Hiroshi's battalion commander and the regimental commander that the Australians treated him so well. Even General Horii, who came to visit him briefly after hearing of his story, was surprised.

Were you interrogated? they asked. When Hiroshi explained the Australians did nothing but offer medical treatment, they couldn't believe it. He couldn't even answer their questions of why they captured him in the first place. *They killed everybody else who was wounded around me,* Hiroshi added quietly. How could he forget the rifle reports just a meter or two away. He thought his fate was the same. What he did remember, finally, was one of the Australians looking at his collar tabs and calling him a *Shoko*, an officer. Whatever their intentions might have been, the Australians were too busy with a fighting withdrawal and no one had the time to interrogate him. *They could have taken him with them, with all their other wounded men,* the battalion commander said, shaking his head. *I would have put a bullet in your head myself.* The BC, who Hiroshi recognized was fairly drunk, smiled in a friendly way before pushing himself onto his feet. He patted Hiroshi's leg before turning serious.

"Lieutenant, I thought I would have to promote Nishikawa to Company Commander when I heard we lost Hashimoto and you on that fiasco at the waterfall. He's not my first choice but the Regiment is short experienced company officers. Isurava was hard on us the last couple of days, we lost five officers in the battalion, not counting the sick and injured like yourself. Sergeant Kato has First Platoon now, as I've moved Tanaka to Second Platoon. If we can get a replacement for Third I'll move Nishikawa to Executive Officer to give you a hand. As it is, the battalion is down to less than 300 men, with about 250 ready to fight. I still have First Company available as a reserve only. We lost 30 over there by the waterfall, and Regiment lost another 15 or 20 from the Reconnaissance Platoon. So I thank my fortunes you survived. The doctors say you can return to light duty in a day or so, providing they can figure out how to get food down to your stomach!"

Hiroshi stared, finally understanding Captain Hashimoto was dead. The BC stepped in closer and offered his hand. His eyes, although slightly glazed from drinking and bloodshot from fatigue, watched Hiroshi with anticipation. Hiroshi sat up more erect and tried to shake his hand. His arms weren't restrained anymore, but both hands were quivering uncontrollably. He couldn't stop it. The BC took his right hand firmly and held it.

"You've had quite an experience, Hiroshi," he said. "You've done well as an executive officer and I have no fear you will not do well as a company commander. Captain Hashimoto had the highest regard for you."

The BC released his hand and turned to go. He paused to place his cap on his head squarely before glancing over his shoulder at Hiroshi.

"The 144th has been relieved from the attack for a few days. The 41st will take over the chase down the Track. It will give you time to heal. All of us time to regroup. We have a number of companies down to only 50 or 60 men. We have no replacements of course, but I might suggest we consolidate some of our smaller platoons, especially since we're short officers and NCOs. Did you hear about the cache of provisions the 41st discovered here in Alola?"

The lead units of the 41st searched every building and hut in the settlement and discovered the Australians, in their fear of getting cut-off, abandoned a storeroom full of rations. There were floor to ceiling stacks of canned bully beef, corned beef, milk, tea, cheese and butter. There were even sweet biscuits. *Nankai Shitai,* saddled with a 90 kilometer supply line pounded by constant Allied air attacks, native bearer desertions and horrible weather was again touched by fortune. Although the lead units of the 41st assaulted the storeroom with a vengeance to tear everything open in sight, their commanders quickly took control. Guards were placed around the provisions like the 144th during the mistaken Kokoda airdrop, the rations distributed more rationally. *Nankai Shitai* ate well for a few days.

Hiroshi received a number of visitors. He was particularly glad to see Corporal Yasuda, Captain Hashimoto's enlisted aide, and Miyamoto. Yasuda, doomed to join a line platoon as an infantryman with the death of Captain Hashimoto, was relieved to retain his role as aide. Miyamoto, whose men entered the road near the waterfall from the North, withdrew with the remnants of his platoon after the firefight believing Hiroshi perished on the road. Miyamoto, appearing even more haggard than the last time Hiroshi saw him, was recovering from his own gunshot wounds. A burst from a Bren punched a hole through his right forearm and blew off the little finger of his right hand. His hand was swaddled in cotton and his arm was in a sling, but Miyamoto still led his reconnaissance platoon.

At first Hiroshi didn't know how to approach Yasuda about what he was most concerned about, but Yasuda and Miyamoto were ahead of him. Yasuda was not a user, at least not an injectable user, but understood his discreet role of keeping the syringe clean and available for Hashimoto and Miyamoto in the past. He already knew Hiroshi was a user. Morphine was in short supply and the medical officer casually mentioned to Hiroshi they would wean him off of it this very day. Hiroshi, wracked with cramps and nervous energy, was sick at his stomach and very concerned. He wanted to feel well again.

The pain of the torn tissue on his cheeks grew less and less, but without his *Nekome-jo* he hurt everywhere else. The morphine helped but now it was going away. He couldn't think straight or focus on anything except his need to feel better, to feel—normal. He asked Yasuda to come back after dark with a set up. Right after the evening meal Yasuda returned as ordered with Hashimoto's wooden box. There were only a few wounded men kept at Alola, the bulk still up at the hospital at Kokoda. They were left alone. Yasuda held up a small dark vial for Hiroshi to see the moment he was sure no one was looking. *Miyamoto just cooked it, Lieutenant,* Yasuda whispered, *I'll set it up for you while it's still warm.*

Yasuda released the surgical tubing and swabbed Hiroshi's arm. Hiroshi gasped with pleasure as the warmth rushed through his veins, subduing the darkness and panic throttling his heart. Morphine barely touched the surface compared to this delicious alixir. With the warmth came a buzzing lightness, a sense of floating just for a moment above his body. *If only he could feel this way forever, to float high above the canopy, high above the pain, away from Kokoda. Away. Stay up, please stay up—up in the sun, in the blue sky.* It wouldn't last. Like his dreams it would fade and a new day would begin.

CHAPTER 24

September 8, 1942, A Company, 2/14 Battalion, Mission Ridge, Efogi village settlement

In a moment of reflection Vic Hickey accepted how fortunate he was, how his fortune seemed to extend to 9 Platoon—until today. It was Potty who confirmed the day. Despite his slovenly appearance, often pushing the grooming standards of the Australian Army to the limit, Potty was a highly organized record keeper. He kept meticulous medical records on 9 Platoon; dates of inoculations, when the malaria pills were started, and detailed notes on wounds, injuries and deaths. He kept his calendar up to date. *"LT Edwards shot thru neck by Jap sniper at first lite. Punctured carotid art. Died from his wounds."* Vic read it right out of Potty's mildewed 'Platoon Medical Log'. It said nothing about Vic's and then Potty's efforts in trying to staunch the spurting blood from Edwards' neck. Edwards, as tall as Vic but less thickly built, was crouched down and sipping a hot cup of tea right next to Vic when he was hit. He gasped, surprised as if he spilled hot tea on his shirt. *Phhuutt.*

Vic glanced down at his blouse where a distinctive series of brown stains remained. He splashed water on it after they carried Edwards' body five meters behind their positions. They covered him with his poncho with the hope to bury him later. There was no time to even speak any words over him as they prepared for the attack this morning. There was no soap and Vic only used a half of a canteen of water. He washed Edwards off of his shirt, arms, face, hair and hands, but couldn't get the sound out of his brain. They never heard the shot, just the *phhuutt,* the slapping sound of wet clay hitting something.

He knew the bullet, piercing Edwards' neck like a rapier and then gone didn't make the sound. It was the plasma, the moist tissue; muscle and arterial tubing and blood rupturing out of his neck to spray all over Vic. It was not much to signal the end of a man's life. Edwards was with them since they sailed for the Middle East, two years before. He showed up straight from his commissioning, full of piss and vinegar. He grew, in time, into a fine officer for a city boy. Vic would miss him.

The Japs somehow worked up both sides of the steep slopes where the trees were thick and higher than the ridgeline. They moved up in the dark sliding above the Australians between the defensive line and the Brigade Headquarters at the top of the ridge. The little bastards must have shimmied a sniper up where they could look down on the positions and take potshots. There was no other way they could have seen down in the position where Vic and Edwards were squatting. Two Vickers were already working the trees methodically on both sides, putting tracers into the canopies. Vic watched nervously, not really expecting a body to simply drop out of the trees. They wouldn't do it long, he knew, they didn't have the ammunition to waste.

Lieutenant Edwards, who removed his helmet to don his mufti woolen officer's cap the second it became light, was wearing his helmet when he was shot. Vic noticed Edwards' cap on the edge of the funkhole and picked it up. To Edwards the cap was the badge of his authority, of his rank. He always joked wearing the cap was like painting a target on his head. Vic shook his head and put the cap back. *It must have been something else*, he thought. *The Jap chose you over me. Or did he? Vic looked up into the trees apprehensively, then over his shoulder at the ridgeline behind them. On each side of the ridge the forest grew thick, blotting out the skyline. He stared and finally shrugged it off. The bloody Japs would be in their laps in minutes, what the hell was wrong with him? He'd cop his when his time came, whether he worried about it or not.*

It was only a week since their withdrawal from Alola. When 9 Platoon caught up with A Company at the Abuari waterfall on August 29th, they were shocked to see their comrades as they were relieved by 2/16 Battalion. The funkholes and the ground directly in front of the positions were littered with bodies, both Japanese and Australian. A Company, over 180 men strong when they climbed up into Alola just the day before, was down to about 90 effectives. This included the 37 intact men from 9 Platoon. Everyone who served at the waterfall seemed to be wounded at least once. Captain Welsh, despite Lieutenant Edwards' mild protest, sent 9 Platoon to work as stretcher bearers again, toting A Company wounded and the Japanese prisoner back to the Alola Surgical Hospital. Welsh really had no options. The two companies from 2/16 would now bear the brunt of any attacks from the Japanese battalion. A Company was temporarily relieved after being mauled and needed to move their wounded. 9 Platoon was able-bodied, fully-manned and available.

Once the A Company wounded were taken care of Welsh was ordered to provide a platoon to assist moving additional wounded at the Rest House, five kilometers up the Track, back down to Alola. 9 Platoon with two other fresh platoons from 2/16 Battalion companies were called into action. As before, it was grueling, back-breaking and exhausting duty taking the rest of the day and most of the night. There was the constant threat the Japanese would mount a flanking attack behind them near Alola, so the men moved quickly yet cautiously. Artillery fire was landing near the Rest House the entire night, with Japanese probing attacks occurring with more frequency. Despite the threat and attacks all around them, the bearers and their wounded survived the night unscathed.

On the morning of the 30th, exhausted and worn out, 9 Platoon stumbled away from the hospital looking for something to eat and a place to sleep. Rations were distributed and the men were searching for their rucksacks when Captain Welsh called for Edwards and Vic Hickey. They joined Welsh and listened to their battalion commander pass on their orders.

The situation is 'ery grave, gentlen', their BC explained. *The 39th Battalion an' the three 2/14 Battalion companies 'porting the 39th in the Isurava village an' the Rest Area will begin a phased 'ithdrawal down to Alola by this aft'noon. 2/16 was 'oldin Abuari to our eastern flank an' 'as lost it. They 'ave reformed 'alfway back to the waterfall an' will be attemptin' to retake it in about an hour. They only 'ave two companies over there now, both in 'ad shape, so I don't think they will last much longer.*

Vic, dead on his feet, knew what was coming. The BC, his shoulders sagging, glanced at Vic as if he had read his mind.

'Believe the Japs are bringing a 'couple of fresh battalions 'round the western escarpment to come behind Isurava an' the Rest Area, split us up, cut off our 'scape. Not 'oing to 'appen, we'll pull them back 'ere, but at the same time start movin' the wounded out of Alola an' down far enough the natives can take over for the 'acuation back down to Moresby. The rest of us are right behind 'em, pullin' back to Eora Creek. We can expect 'em to give chase, so this will be a 'nother fightin' withdrawal.

There was no more sleeping for 9 Platoon or any able-bodied men in A Company. Throughout the day they carried wounded down the Track to the surgical station where the native bearers were waiting. This was their lot during this action. They carried many of their wounded comrades from A Company for the second time. These men were wounded at the waterfall, treated by the surgeons at Alola and now starting the long journey to Port Moresby. They hoisted men they carried last night from B, C and D Companies. 2/14 took a severe beating. 9 Platoon, intact, could only glance at one another, almost in shame, seeing clusters of wounded representing, in some cases, over half of the men from sister platoons. Vic, who hoisted stretchers all night right along with the rest of his men, felt no shame. It was not their time yet, that's all. He didn't believe in luck, thought men made their own. He knew, however, things had a way of balancing out.

He sensed it would be today whatever was due, with Lieutenant

Edwards' death the forerunner. The Japs were coming and Brigade Command passed the word they needed to hold the ridgeline as long as possible. Right. The Japs who chased them down the Track from Isurava were different from the ones they had fought at the waterfall and the Rest House. They were fresher troops, they moved fast but they were not as aggressive in action or tactically as experienced. Carrying the wounded 9 Platoon moved slower, finding they were going up and down the Track passing men ordered to withdraw. Most of them were in bad shape, especially the 39th Battalion troops, so Vic was not surprised when 9 Platoon, one of the last Australian units to leave Alola, was ordered to withdraw down the Track in stages. A fighting withdrawal. They leapfrogged with two other platoons from 2/16, setting up trailside ambushes directly up the Track with flanking attacks from the steep sides.

Descending down the Track from Isurava the mountain passes closed in again, like the Track from Kokoda to Isurava. It was claustrophobic. The mists were thicker, the humidity stifling. It rained constantly, but even when it didn't, the sun never found its way down through the thick canopy. The foliage was dark and dripping with moisture, the trail roots slick and dangerous underfoot. Visibility on the trail was very poor making ambushes at shorter range easy. They watched as the 41st Regiment came down the Track cautiously, aware every dark corner in a turn five meters away could have an Australian Bren gun pointed right at them. That was the idea. The scouts would peer ahead into the forest nervously, pointlessly attempting to wipe the mist away with their hands as if it was smoke. Everything in sight was subdued and dark green. Sometimes this is exactly what they found—a Bren gun, except Vic or another Australian platoon leader would have two other Brens and supporting riflemen on the high side of the trail waiting for them to dash to the flanks. When three or four Japanese soldiers were fully visible the first Bren would open up with a long burst, cutting the soldiers on the trail to pieces. The Japanese behind them would run for cover only to be cut down by a fusillade of Bren LMG and rifle fire at almost point blank range.

One by one the Aussies would pull back until all the flanking attackers slipped away, leaving only the first Bren covering the trail. When no one moved down the Track they too pulled back, jogging under the protective cover of a few Aussie riflemen. It took time for the 41st to recover from these ambushes, giving the attackers time to move down the Track a few hundred meters until they reached the next ambushing platoon's position. They slipped through, leap-frogging past this position and the next before looking for a suitable place for their next ambush.

This went on for a couple of days and the Australians had few casualties. Vic and Lieutenant Edwards marveled at the inability of these Jap troops to adapt to the ambushes. Time and time again variations of the same ambush were applied with the Japs responding the same way and losing a number of men. It was as if the Japs understood there really was no true defense against it, so they simply pushed through.

The terrain was on the side of the ambushers, going farther than a few meters from the Track was to encounter very steep and rocky vertical slabs. The 41st had to work their way down the Track one way or the other, as it was the only viable route down. Their leaders could read a terrain map as well as the Australians, counting on the Aussies to move most of their men to the next suitable area for defense, Eora Creek, leaving a token force on the Track to buy time.

The Japanese pressed on despite the casualties, their eyes on the next opportunity to destroy the Australian forces once and for all. It made it hard on the lead units, the sacrifice a given. Vic could see it in the faces of the Jap scouts as they passed his position, the fear of the inevitable. The scouts knew they were expendable, would be the first to die. And it would happen. He didn't know if they rotated the point men like the Australians did. It was a strain, and would break a man if he never got a chance to, well—live. Every time 9 Platoon did their leapfrog and shot up another group of Japs they seemed to be different men. But Vic didn't know if it was rotation or the fact the other Australian platoons were killing everyone tasked to the duty.

Vic lit a cigarette very carefully, shielding the glowing end down in his hole. It was still dim enough for a cigarette to be a bloody beacon light and absolutely forbidden, but he needed the smoko badly. Thinking about the doomed Jap scouts on the Track made him remember the Jap prisoner—the officer—they left at the Alola Hospital as they pulled out. They got nothing out of that deal, there were no interpreters or Japanese-speakers in Alola so the man didn't get interrogated. In the end, 9 Platoon pulled out with Jap artillery landing right outside the village. With orders to prepare trail ambushes and delay the enemy with the two 2/16 platoons already down the Track, Lieutenant Edwards made the decision to leave the prisoner behind. Edwards was frustrated, Vic could tell, but Edwards either detailed four of his men to get the prisoner down to Eora Creek, or let him go. He knew he would need every man. HQ pulled out and the major concern was to get the Australian wounded down the Track.

The surgeons even sewed up his face, so the bastard got away clean. If it was up to him, Vic knew the Jap would've never left the grove of trees by the road where they found him. He was more trouble than he was worth, and you can be damned bleedin' certain the Japs

wouldn't be sewing up any Australian faces. *'Aye might cut ur' balls an'*
pecker off an' sew 'em to ur' bleedin' 'ace! Might do 'at fur' ya'!

As it was, there was no such option with Edwards and Potty
around. Potty was protective of the little bastard. Potty said the prisoner
had said *thank you* in Japanese when he first treated him, which was
more than he was getting in appreciation from the undeserving men in 9
Platoon. Link and Slim were all over him as a *bloody bleedin' Jap lover,*
but even they knew the limits of their ribbing with their beloved
corpsman. They shook their heads and left him alone. Edwards gave the
word so Potty went to see the prisoner to ensure he would probably
survive. Potty examined the results of the surgery and even gave the Jap
a final shot of morphine to relieve his pain. Vic could only watch and
sigh. Artillery rounds were landing less than 200 meters away and Potty
was concerned they would soon target the hospital, but it couldn't be
helped.

They left a full, lit kerosene lantern hanging just a couple of
meters away. Without the phony sense of protection the former hospital
used to give them, the light made them feel vulnerable, a solitary visible
target for miles around. It was the best they could do. *Ewe' could only
wish they 'ould do the same fur' ewe', Pot!* Vic chided. There were only
a few men around them now, everyone crouching down, staying to the
shadows. The Japs could show up any minute. No one wanted to be the
last man out, aware of what happens to the missing in the jungle. All
they could see to the north beyond the single glowing lantern was the
shimmering traces of the rain and then blackness. Vic patted his friend
on his shoulder while giving the nod to Edwards they were ready to go.
He'll be okay, Pot. We got to go.

They pulled back to Eora Creek only to find Brigade Command
deciding to withdraw again to Myola. Myola was much like Kokoda, a
flat alpine plain with few trees. Like Kokoda the open plain was used
previously for Allied air drops, but not anymore. With the Japanese 41st
only a day away, Brigade Command changed their mind again when
they realized how easily they could be flanked at Myola. They withdrew
down the Track to the village of Efogi, situated on the Track where it
crossed the river. To the south of Efogi the Track climbed steeply
between two valleys up a long ridgeline. Way up the face of the ridgeline
in and around the high Kunai grass overlooking the valley, they finally
dug in. Brigade HQ dug in a couple of hundred meters above them on
the ridgeline. With the battered 39th set up to the rear of Brigade HQ as a
reserve only, 2/14 and 2/16 dug in their weapons facing the steep gullies
on each side of the ridge. It was known as Mission Ridge.

First Battalion was assigned to the far right of the line, the defensive positions turning northeast to face a different track leading south. Although it meandered and took longer, this smaller track was an escape route if the Japanese flanked them. It did not show up on maps and wasn't visible from the air. It was possible the enemy didn't know about it. The battalion commander assigned A Company to the far right position facing the southern track. Captain Welsh placed 9 Platoon on the extreme right position, digging in with the track less than 50 meters away. There were no other friendly positions to their right, or to the northeast. Nothing in front of them but a steep slope overlooking the gully, leading across the valley towards Efogi and the southern track. The BC, stopping by to inspect their positions, moved one of the Vickers heavy machine guns behind and slightly above them. *You might need their firepower,* he added quietly. Captain Welsh thanked him, Lieutenant Edwards and Vic simply stared.

Up on the ridge it was lighter sooner. The attack came right at the point they could see almost down to the valley floor. Vic heard the rumor the Japs moved mountain guns down the Track from Isurava, and sure enough the shrieking, howling incoming announced the arrival one or two seconds ahead of the 75mm HE. They slammed in hard over the ridgeline where Brigade HQ and the 39th Battalion was holding in reserve. *Poor bastards!* There wasn't a lot of it, not yet. It felt like only one or two guns were working the hill. A couple landed to the north end of the defense line. There was noise below them, so Vic carefully peered over his hole down the slope. It was actually raining harder now. Pulling out his worn glasses, he scoped the gully below them, realizing he wasn't looking at waving foliage dancing in the rain halfway up the gully, but well camouflaged Jap infantry. *A lot of Jap infantry.* The valley floor was clear when he looked out earlier so they must have crossed in the dark. Even with the flares popping most of the night, no one noticed these troops moving across. Not in the rain and mist. *They are very good*, Vic thought, hopping out of his hole to start alerting his platoon. And they really were his platoon now, with Edwards gone. He scrambled over to the RT and rang up Captain Welsh, who alerted Battalion.

Section leaders, platoon sergeants and other leaders were moving about on the line alerting people the enemy were halfway up the gullies. The sudden loud *RAT TAT TAT TAT TAT* of the Juki was jarring and immediately confusing, because it seemed to be coming from *behind them.* It was. The gunner was not using tracers but once Vic turned around, there was no doubt it was a Juki heavy machine gun, firing across the ridge behind their position at a diagonal towards the men of the 2/14 and the 2/16 on their left. He could see the bullet impacts on the dirt around the funkholes, and on one unlucky section leader who didn't get back into his hole fast enough. *How in the bloody hell did the Japs get a woodpecker all the way up here in the dark!?*

Vic called out on the line to alert his men there were Japs behind them now, but there wasn't much they could do about it. 9 Platoon held the flank position and couldn't be running off trying to destroy a Juki. Not yet. The platoon was firing straight down at the troops slowly working their way up the gully. The foliage was thick almost all the way, so the climbing Japs were taking advantage of the natural concealment, although most of it offered little cover. If you could see a Jap you could probably hit him. But there were a lot of the little bastards, hundreds of them, swarming around, disappearing from sight and then a muzzle flash. *That pop was a 6.5 a coupla 'centimeters from yur 'noggin', mate!* He rang up Welsh and gave him the news. The fire was getting much heavier from the ridgeline behind them now, the Juki joined by a chorus of 6.5 Arisaki rifle fire and Nambu LMGs. The only benefit for 9 platoon, tucked away as a flank guard, is the very strong probability the Japs above them didn't see them or know they were there. They weren't getting much fire on their position at all. Once the Japs figured it out, though, they could overrun them in a heartbeat. Vic kept an eye out, but so far they hadn't been discovered.

As the day wore on the rain never let up. The Japanese never charged them from the Ridge. Brigade sent a company down the slope to test the strength of the Japanese positions between the Brigade HQ and the defensive line facing the valley. Few of them made it back. Many of their bodies remained visible on the hillside. It was apparent the infiltrating Japanese unit was close to battalion strength, although no one could explain how such a large unit came up in the heavy forest without being discovered. For the time being the Australians on the far southern ridge remained unseen, the fire they received mostly harassment unless the Diggers were foolish enough to stand up in their funkholes. The three Aussie battalions on the defensive line were essentially trapped. The Japanese unit doing the murderous frontal assault up from the gully was also estimated at battalion strength, although it charged the slope repeatedly only to be beaten back every time with grenades, Bren and rifle fire. It was a strange tactical situation, but the Aussie Brigade Commander understood he could not resupply his men down below on the face of the ridge in the present circumstances, and all three battalions were reporting they were low on ammunition.

At some point in the afternoon the Japanese infiltrators found and cut the Brigade communications lines down the ridge. Captain Welsh and every other commander in the three battalions on the line were cut off from Brigade, although most of the comm lines between individual battalions and companies were still working, since the lines were draped directly on the defensive line and not exposed over the ridgeline to Brigade HQ. Battalion commanders sent several volunteer runners over the ridgeline, with none making it through. Welsh called over his platoon commanders to confer final instructions. They listened as Welsh explained what was happening. One battalion, the one farthest to the north, was going to attempt to break through the Jap line on the ridge and connect up with Brigade HQ. If they were successful in creating a corridor thru the Jap line, the rest of the battalions would attempt a fighting withdrawal up the corridor, leap-frogging up the hill and consolidate at Brigade HQ.

An' if they're not successful, suh?' Vic asked. Welsh peered over at Vic with a thin smile before glancing at his watch.

Well, Sergeant, we 'all back to Plan B. A an' D Companies from First Battalion will 'old this flank open as long as necessary. We 'ope to God the Japs 'aven't discovered the southern track. We take all the 'ounded an' pull out fur 'Menari! When they realized what we 're oop' to, they 'll be on us like flies on ice cream!

By late afternoon 9 Platoon had tossed every Mills bomb they had down the side of the gully, managing not to lose a single man killed, with the exception of Lieutenant Edwards. Half of the platoon had gunshot wounds, although only three were serious and needed immediate attention, according to Potty. Preparing for the defense of the ridgeline, Welsh and his platoon commanders made the men conserve their ammunition. There wasn't much to eat. Most of A Company had over three times their normal ammunition carry load sitting with them in their funkholes when they started. There were only a few mortar tubes so they used their remaining Mills bombs and let gravity do the rest. It was a very prudent precaution as they prepared for yet another assault attempt up the gully. Cut-off from Brigade and an ammunition resupply, men started to count individual rifle rounds. They could not believe how these Japanese troops would continue to climb up the slope even under extremely accurate and lethal rifle and LMG fire. *If there was a battalion down there this morning, they were more like a couple of small companies now.* They would rarely see the Japs until they charged up the last 50 or so meters. None ever made it. But now, ammunition was starting to become a problem.

Vic watched with his glasses in disbelief as four infantry companies walked up the slope to his left, online with bayonets attached, towards the dark forest that hovered between them and Brigade HQ. The last time Vic remembered approaching the enemy standing up, online with bayonets fixed was in the Middle East. There they moved across open country towards Italian positions after a murderous artillery prep. It reminded him of films he had seen from the Great War. Australian and British soldiers coming up over the parapet after the whistle, advancing 'at the ready' to face artillery, machinegun fire and gas through no-man's land. Incredible. Only the Italians fired their machineguns for a few bursts, with scattered rifle fire, then stopped. As the line approached the Italians, the Iti's started to leap up with their arms high over their heads.

The huge firestorm of lead suddenly descending on the advancing four companies was more in line of what he expected. Men were falling, being struck multiple times. The company on the southern side, farthest from the forest, faded to the left and appeared to make it over the ridgeline mostly intact. The companies on the far right, towards the north, were being mowed down like fresh alfalfa. They apparently approached the Japanese stronghold. Men were breaking ranks and diving to the ground, and some, he could see, simply turned around and ran only a few feet to be shot in the back. Vic slowly lowered his glasses and picked up the RT after it buzzed.

It was Welsh. *It's Plan B, Sergeant. 'Ewe called it, Vic. As the men start to withdraw behind your position down the southern track, 'ave your men pick up as much ammunition as they can squeeze from the troops going past. You'll need it more than they will. We'll need every bloody round. 'Ave 'our 'ounded ready to transport. They will go out first.*

CHAPTER 25

September 8, 1942, First Company, 144th Infantry, Mission Ridge

General Horii, frustrated with the cautious approach used by the 41st Regiment as they chased the Australians down the Track towards Myola, ordered the 144th back into the fray. They were to resume the lead assault role by the time *Nankai Shitai* reached Efogi, relieving the 41st. The 144th, still staggering from the heavy losses during the repeated frontal attacks at Isurava village and the Rest House, had no choice but to consolidate their battalions. The decimated First Battalion was in much worse shape than first realized. Men finally pulled from the line totally collapsed. With so many sick and wounded, the battalion could only muster about 200 men by blending all three infantry companies and the remains of their weapons company. Of those only about 150 were ready to resume a combat role. The 144th Regimental Commander stood down First Battalion, transferring the 150 available men, all to be part of First Company, temporarily to Second Battalion.

Hiroshi, the company commander for First Company, was overwhelmed. He was finally up and about by September 4th, but he was still having difficulty chewing food and eating. A large chunk of his jaw and about a quarter of his gums and teeth were gone. He could eat soft food on his opposite side, but the movement of chewing and even talking was very painful. He needed to eat and for a few days there were the Australian rations. The surgeon said that due to the lack of medicine, the wound was becoming septic. There wasn't much he could do, except possibly cut away more of Hiroshi's jaw. Hiroshi walked away in total dismay. He went to see his battalion commander about being relieved but was informed he was the only first lieutenant left in the battalion, and the planned consolidation. There were no captains, one staff non-infantry major, and a handful of inexperienced second lieutenants who weren't ready for a company command. Everyone else was dead, too sick or severely wounded. *You're all we have, Hiroshi.*

Miyamoto and his men were also assigned to Hiroshi, which pleased him since Miyamoto was now his only source for injectable *Shabu*. Without it he would have to eat dozens of the *Nekome-jo*, and only get half of what he wanted, or figure out how to cook it. Dejected, Hiroshi reported to the Commander of the Second Battalion, who integrated First Company into the assault plan for Efogi. Hiroshi breathed a sigh of relief when he learned the Battalion's coming role. Reconnaissance teams shadowed the Australians as they withdrew down the Track; first to Eora Creek, then to Myola and finally to the settlement of Efogi. The Australians chose their defensive line well, high up on the side of a long ridgeline with a commanding view of the valleys to the north. On the actual ridge they established their Brigade HQ. On each side of the ridgeline were thick forests climbing right up to the ridges. Third Battalion was assigned the primary role of frontal assault up the slopes while Second Battalion was to infiltrate into the thick forest on the northern side at night, unseen, establishing a complete containment and separation between the Australian forces on the top of the ridge, the command structure, and the force down the front. The main Australian force on the line would not be able to withdraw. To withdraw they would have to climb up the slope into the hidden Second Battalion guns.

Third Battalion was to traverse the open valley at night in the anticipated steady rain. Even with the frequent use of aerial flares, General Horii believed the rain and mists would be so heavy ridgeline observers would have difficulty seeing the troops down in the low, but thick foliage of the valley. Once across the valley the foliage at the base of the slopes was much denser, easier to conceal a battalion when it became light. The Australians had no artillery to speak of and only a few light mortars. Third Battalion would be in position to assault the Australians on the ridgeline at first light, holding their attention as Second Battalion began interdiction and harassment fire on the rear of the Australian positions. It was known as Mission Ridge because of the small structure, presumably once a mission, visible on clear days. As usual per doctrine, attacking the positions at first light meant any Australian counterattack would be in full daylight, a distinct disadvantage for those trying to retake ground.

The experience gained in Isurava revealed itself as Second Battalion camouflaged their gear expertly with the local foliage. They darkened their faces with mud and tied leaves and branches to their helmets, rucksacks, belts and weapons, breaking up any recognizable outline. They silenced loose gear ruthlessly, responding instantly to hand signals and whispered commands. It reminded Hiroshi of First Company and First Battalion when they moved up the Kokoda. Second Battalion had been on the Kokoda three weeks now; First Battalion as part of the Advance Party had been there over two months. Right now with his 150 men and the 16 from Miyamoto, they were all that was left.

Hiroshi wished more than anything for Captain Hashimoto to appear and take over. He felt hopelessly over his head, although he managed some comfort with Lieutenants Nishikawa and Tanaka, Sergeant Kato and of course Miyamoto as familiar leaders he leaned on. Miyamoto, his forearm still bandaged from the clean-through gunshot wound, favored the arm but was active as ever. You wouldn't know he

302

lost his finger if it wasn't for the small bandage and stump. Hiroshi had not seen Miyamoto for a day or two and assumed he was part of the reconnaissance of the ridgeline slopes. With Miyamoto's platoon assigned to him, Hiroshi wasn't sure exactly how he was going to use them, or how Miyamoto would respond under his command. Miyamoto had no reporting relationship with Captain Hashimoto in the past, his was a regimental command. But it was Regiment who gave him to Hiroshi. No matter what, Miyamoto had a special role in the regiment, and on top of that he was still *Kempeitai. Don't ever forget that, Hiroshi.* Right now First Company didn't have any special mission to perform. They were just an additional infantry company to beef up the firepower and strength of the battalion.

He was wrong on both counts. It was obvious the Second Battalion Commander considered the capabilities of Miyamoto's men, because as Hiroshi suspected, they performed the reconnaissance of the slope and discovered the significant gap behind the Australian HQ and the defensive line on the ridge. They would lead the battalion right up the slope in the pouring rain and pitch blackness—except when the Australians fired their aerial flares. Glowing tree bark was again used as basic guides in the blackness of the forest. First Company, because of their extensive experience in *night approach and night attack*, was given the choice point company role following the guide lights of Miyamoto's men. The BC had chosen First Company over his own best assault company. Hiroshi understood with alarm the Second Battalion Commander had a much higher opinion of Hiroshi and First Company's capabilities than was warranted. He didn't know if it was General Horii's glowing praise or Captain Hashimoto's past performance, but Hiroshi knew it was just a matter of time before he failed and was found out.

It was a strange experience, mostly because they were climbing, in some cases rocks, roots and thick forest in complete darkness. The dim embers of glowing bacteria left by Miyamoto's men helped, but it was very difficult to sense and know what was in front of them. It was also almost impossible to be truly silent. This slope was not an ordinary, earth-rooted forest. Rocks slipped, tree branches creaked and occasionally cracked or broke. Equipment still sighed, a buckle would tinkle.

Hiroshi knew the Australians were, in many cases, less than a few hundred meters away. He knew because he could hear them, even in the rain, the sounds of voices and shovels scratching wet mud right *above them*, or *over there*. He knew the Australians must hear them. It was the first time he moved in the dark with a large enemy force in such lethal range. It made him sick to his stomach. Even after a stop because of some noise, he anticipated the blast of machinegun fire or a grenade. He kept waiting for it all night. They climbed as the voices and noise from the Australians drew closer.

At some point the sounds subsided and moved away. The course turned to the south on the ridgeline. They were now above the Australian positions and below their headquarters. First Company had the farthest to go but the ridge was sparser here, so the men moved cautiously. Luckily with the rain there was no potential for moonlight or shadows. Miyamoto's men led the way and so far encountered no Australians. It was both crazy frightening and exciting to know Australians were directly to the left and right of them—100, 200 meters each way, a trigger pull in either direction, and they were in the middle.

There was little cover up here on the ridge except the thick forests on each end, so Hiroshi ordered his men to start digging fighting pits. He knew the Australians could hear them but they had no choice. If the Aussies charged them, and there was no doubt they would, his men needed cover. They had a small window. The Aussies wouldn't attack in the dark. A Juki heavy machinegun was reassembled and assigned to Hiroshi. He had the crew dig a big pit to face to the north, covering the Aussie defensive line below them.

They could smell cooking fires, apparently burning in the fighting pits so the Aussies could make tea—and smoke cigarettes. Hiroshi was struck by how normal and civilized the Australians were so early in the morning. Amazed really, considering the Aussies faced the prospect of an attack at any time. Hiroshi dutifully felt his way along the line and checked on his men before it was too light to move about. Like himself, his men were quiet once they finished digging their fighting pits, listening to the sounds of the Aussies rattling pots, producing delicious scents of tea and cocoa, wood smoke and cigarettes. He began to realize the Australians were oblivious to their presence. Despite what had to have been sounds of men moving on the hillside and digging in, the Aussies went about their day as if they were on maneuvers. As the sky gradually transitioned from pitch black to varying shades of muted grey at the top edges of the horizon, Hiroshi started to pick out the unique flat curve of the helmeted heads below them.

Second Battalion was given specific instructions once in position on the ridge. No one was to fire until the Third Battalion began its assault, then only assigned individuals, mostly designated marksmen with telescopic sights on their Arisakis', would work the ridge searching for officers, NCOs, RT operators and machine gunners. The Juki heavy machinegun would add to this steady harassment fire, laying down a base of lead across the rear of Australian positions. This would force the Australians to keep their heads down, suppressing some of the defensive fire unleashed on Third Battalion. When the Australians made the decision to begin withdrawing up the ridge from the pressure of the Third Battalion assault, the Aussies would have to turn around and climb up the ridge towards their Brigade HQ. At that point Second Battalion would let their full presence be known.

First Company was miserable. On their position on the far south side of the ridge they were fully exposed to the rain. They were swimming in their fighting holes, trying to keep their bodies below the rims but their weapons clear. It was a losing battle, the water icy cold, their bodies slowly succumbing to hypothermia. Hiroshi could not control his shivering and chattering teeth.

The battle for the ridge changed dramatically in the afternoon when the Australians on the North side stood up from their holes and advanced diagonally up the slope. This was the direct route to the Australian Brigade HQ, and the most heavily defended by Second Battalion. The Australians below First Company on the South side held their positions, but the other companies were ordered on line with fixed bayonets. This kept the attack far to the left of First Company, so Hiroshi had his men hold their fire. This attempt to break through the Second Battalion lines was a failure, although it appeared one company made it over the ridge because they stayed out of the forest. The others, clearly surprised at the intense volume of deadly fire, pulled back down the slope to their original positions, leaving a hundred torn bodies of their comrades on the hillside.

Despite the accurate pressure on the rear of their positions, the Australians on the face of the ridge maintained steady fire down on Third Battalion. Steady and strong enough to force back a half dozen assaults on the slopes. Hiroshi felt very fortunate First Company was assigned to be attached to Second Battalion instead of Third Battalion. He knew by the end of the day Third Battalion would be decimated, it would be up to Second Battalion to swarm the Australians. After watching the Aussie companies tramp up the slope under withering rifle and machinegun fire, he knew this was not going to be an easy task. These were brave men. But at this very moment, slowly freezing to death with half of his body in icy water, to be up and moving seemed to be a better choice.

The mountain guns knew approximately where Second Battalion was supposed to be on the ridge, so they kept their rounds short of the peak, or sent them howling over the ridge towards the Australian HQ. It was harassment fire, only a few rounds at a time, still terrifying as the projectiles screamed inbound. Some landed short, further down the steep slope, possibly on Third Battalion. Hiroshi kept waiting for the RT to buzz signaling Second Battalion to leave their positions and charge down the slope towards the Australians, but it never came. The original plan was to let the Australians come to them, assault up the hill or run out of ammunition, whichever came first and the BC was not wavering.

Once it was dark they heard a lot of movement down near the Australian lines. Hiroshi got out of his hole to check on his men. They were miserable, the noise of the Australians moving around making them nervous and jumpy. *Australians don't attack at night! What are they up to?* Third Battalion, unable to get much closer than 50 meters to the Australian positions on the ridge finally pulled back to the base of the slope to lick their wounds. Aussie flares were popping overhead only occasionally, but they fell, with a blanketing shadow, across a barren landscape. When the flares ignited the Australians were down and out of sight. The valley below was a huge bowl, the rings of light from the descending flares revealing a momentary glimpse of a vast, drizzling cavern then blackness. Whatever they were doing in the dark, the Australians stopped until the flares were out. Then the noise resumed.

The BC called Hiroshi on the RT requesting a reconnaissance patrol to the south end of the ridge. *Something was going on, the Australians appear to be withdrawing to the south. What is to the south of your position we don't know about.* It took a half an hour for Hiroshi to find Miyamoto. They were in no position to cook up some *Shabu* and inject it, so Hiroshi took three *Nekome-jo* tablets with water. Miyamoto seemed to have anticipated the patrol request, as he was dressed and ready. He accepted the direct orders from Hiroshi without question, but Hiroshi pressed why Miyamoto needed to go himself. His injuries were not completely healed, he still favored the arm. Miyamoto did not answer immediately. Hiroshi could sense Miyamoto's eyes burning on his face in the dark.

"Am I not the commander of the Reconnaissance and Intelligence platoon?" It was quiet but carefully stated.

"Of course you are, Warrant Officer. But you are injured, and you have very capable men to do this."

Several seconds passed before Hiroshi realized the dark shape before him was gone. He was alone.

It was close to midnight when there was a sudden firefight far to the right of their position, perhaps 200-300 meters away. It was Australian gunfire; Bren, Tommygun and 30 caliber rifles. It was brief, then quiet. There were no Japanese units anywhere in that direction, it had to be Miyamoto. The BC called on the RT demanding a report. Hiroshi simply stated the patrol had not returned. He couldn't sleep, in the darkness he laid shivering outside of his hole. He couldn't believe how cold he was, numbness was slowly taking over the lower part of his body. The rain stopped briefly around two o'clock in the morning to be replaced with a chilling wind. His jaw ached terribly and he was hungry, but he had no rations. He stood up carefully, clumsily, his legs numb and unable to completely support his weight just yet. The Australians had not fired a flare for several hours so he risked getting to his feet. A hand and arm suddenly clutched his elbow, surprising him completely. He jerked in fright.

"Are you all right, Lieutenant?" It was Miyamoto. Hiroshi never heard him approach. He sensed more than saw a much larger man nearby, Sergeant Inoue.

"Can you walk? I don't have time to explain this twice, we need to talk to the Battalion Commander."

Hiroshi felt it would take too long to traverse the ridge and do a face to face with the BC. If he sent Miyamoto alone he would make it of course, but Hiroshi wanted to hear this information too. Miyamoto wanted to go but Hiroshi insisted he wait. Miyamoto was not pleased yet held up. Hiroshi rang the BC to see if he would accept a report on the RT. He did, once he knew it was Miyamoto who would give the report. Hiroshi was impressed at how Miyamoto was able to compress his report in such a way he was done in a few cryptic sentences.

South there is another track, smaller than the Kokoda, large enough to accommodate the enemy in their escape. It appears southbound, presumably towards the next village on the main Track. In either case, intelligence is not aware of this secondary track, and the enemy is moving wounded and their men down this track as we speak. Why the enemy didn't use it instead of their futile charge up the slope is not clear. Possibly they didn't realize the size of our forces when we infiltrated last night.

Miyamoto paused for a second before continuing. *My report was delayed when the patrol was trapped between several large enemy units passing on both sides. We were almost caught, when spotted just as a flare ignited and fired upon. We escaped one group and went into hiding as the enemy searched for us. We were, in some cases, a meter or two from enemy soldiers and could not move until the enemy was ordered to leave.*

Miyamoto's face was invisible in the darkness, but his weariness was telling in his voice. Hiroshi could hear his fast breathing, and not far away, the deep exhales of Sergeant Inoue.

The BC could not contact General Horii for direction or advice. The RT cables they laid were for the companies on the ridge, they had no contact with Third Battalion. At the same time there was little the battalion could do in the dark. To charge blindly across the ridge in the blackness until they encountered the Australians was tactical suicide. If

307

Nankai Shitai knew where the southern track led they might be able to cut them off, but they didn't. The Australians once again appeared to be slipping out from under their grasp.

Hiroshi stayed close to the RT until it was almost light. Miyamoto returned to his platoon to prepare for the assault orders that never came. He and Sergeant Inoue came back after a couple of hours as the horizon started to turn grey. They could see no Australians moving about below them. The positions seemed deserted. There was none of the noise and carrying on of making tea like the morning before. *What are they waiting for?* Miyamoto hissed, clearly frustrated. *They are getting away!* His eyes glittered, flaring in a rare instance of emotion and anger. In the dim twilight his body was wasted, the ragged uniform hanging on him like a scarecrow. His intensity still remained as strong as ever, a will Hiroshi could feel like a heated iron several feet away. He reminded Hiroshi of Captain Hashimoto in his last weeks, and even Miyamoto could not seem to control his trembling hands or restless legs. His beard, sparse on his cheeks but thick and scruffy on his chin and upper lip, was flecked with grey for such a young man.

The RT buzzed and Hiroshi picked up the handset, pressing the talk button. *First Company,* he whispered. It was the BC. *First Company, prepare to move towards the south and the new track, but hold until you get movement orders. Send a reconnaissance patrol to your south again and determine if the enemy is still withdrawing. I don't want us walking into a trap, understood? Take a radio and cable. Report immediately.*

Hiroshi gave his orders and made his decision to lead the patrol himself. He buzzed Lieutenant Nishikawa, placing Nishikawa in charge of the company. Miyamoto gave no reaction when Hiroshi told him he was going along on the patrol other than his simple statement, *we're looking for them in the daylight, and they will be able to see us too, Lieutenant.* Hiroshi had nothing to say to this. He was the company commander now, he shouldn't be doing any patrolling, but he wanted to go. Hiroshi picked up the RT and cable reel and handed it to Sergeant Inoue. Miyamoto stared at the RT with ill-concealed irritation. *The Battalion Commander's orders,* Hiroshi stated flatly. *If the enemy is still there he wants to know it immediately.* Miyamoto turned on his heel and headed out towards the south. This time both he and Sergeant Inoue were carrying rifles and ammunition pouches besides their knives and pistols.

Miyamoto guided them straight into the forest and out of sight of the Australian positions below them. In minutes the ridgeline was lost from view. It was very dense forest on this side of the ridge, much denser than the Northern side. It was difficult going and hard to determine relative direction. Hiroshi knew Miyamoto and Inoue had slipped through this same area in the complete darkness last night, marveling again at Miyamoto's land navigation skills. They stayed close together and climbed quickly, Hiroshi guessing they were now heading southwest, up over the ridge to find the southern track. He glanced over his shoulder and could see Inoue's hulking shadow only a couple of meters behind him, silently feeding out comm cable. The cable reel wasn't a big one, and Hiroshi was a little worried they would run out of cable before they reached the new track. If they did they would have to leave the RT and come back to it to report their findings and make their escape.

Miyamoto signaled them to stop and to remain silent. They hadn't gone that far up the ridge before it began to descend down. As the forest thinned and light began to filter in, the rain returned with a vengeance. They could hear it pouring down for nearly a minute before the drops slithered their way through the canopy. Icy cold, Hiroshi was startled with the first few drops until it turned into a steady stream of water, running off his cap into his eyes. He watched Miyamoto stop before gradually crouching down, lowering his profile. Over Miyamoto's shoulder, Hiroshi gasped when he spotted a khaki colored shirt moving less than five meters away. He froze, afraid to move a muscle. Behind him Inoue was silent. A second later another knaki shirt slid along the trees before Hiroshi could see a tanned face outlined in an open space. This must be the new track.

The Australians disappeared towards the right, the space quiet for several minutes as Miyamoto, motionless, watched. Hiroshi slowly slunk down onto his heels and did the same. After a few more minutes, Miyamoto glanced over at Hiroshi to signal they would be moving to the left. They walked very cautiously for about ten minutes, staying a little farther away from the track but generally parallel to it. They saw no more Australians. Miyamoto stopped them again, changing directions and moving silently towards the track. Just for a moment Hiroshi felt a burst of fear as he remembered approaching the road behind the waterfall in exactly this same fashion, stepping into thinner and thinner forest until suddenly the gunfire erupted all around them. Two meters from the open space of the track Miyamoto stopped again, crouching down, his head moving very slowly from left to right. Just like the road near the waterfall, the rain came down extra hard directly on the road, the heavy drops bouncing and splattering in all directions. It was raining so hard it was difficult to see the other side of the track, four or five meters away.

Miyamoto was stone still for what seemed an eternity. Hiroshi's thighs ached from the tight crouch but if Miyamoto could freeze like a rock he could too. The minutes passed with no sound or motion except constant, thundering rain.

Carefully pushing his body straight up with his legs, Miyamoto got up and in three or four steps was standing at the side of the track. His attention was entirely to the left, his rifle up into his shoulder. After a moment he seemed satisfied, motioning Hiroshi and Sergeant Inoue to follow. As soon as Hiroshi reached the track the rain stopped, like someone turning off a spigot. It still dripped huge drops from the overhead trees but there was a break open to the sky. The roar of the torrent was gone to be replaced by a light, thickly humid breeze, buzzing through the forest. It was almost pleasant if Hiroshi wasn't so frightened. Miyamoto signaled to Sergeant Inoue to leave the RT and reel just inside the trees. Inoue did this and raised his own rifle. It was apparent to Hiroshi they weren't going to go very far, simply check out the track to ensure the Australians were gone and call it in. They marked the spot with two stacked rocks on the side of the trail and cautiously crept up the track, staying to the inside, close to the trees.

The track climbed up a small rise and dropped down into a trench filled with muddy water. They walked around this carefully and climbed up another rise as an Australian soldier, his helmet off but hung from his neck by a chin strap, struggled right up next to them, his head down. Both of his hands were down by his thighs, the front end of stretcher poles in each. He climbed up the rise and right behind was a soldier on the stretcher and another one carrying the other end. Both men handling the poles looked exhausted and were concentrating on placing their feet. Neither saw Miyamoto, who froze momentarily two arms lengths away.

No shots were fired as the three men were attacked. The lead stretcher bearer was just raising his head when his lower skull was shattered by the steel buttplate of Miyamoto's rifle. The man was still walking over the rise when his face exploded and he dropped the stretcher. The soldier holding the rear of the stretcher was also raising his head when Sergeant Inoue impaled his throat with the bayonet on the end of his rifle. The thrust was so violent and powerful the soldier was pitched up off of his feet. He made a gurgling cough and was silent. The stretcher slid to the mud, rolling the wounded soldier off. He groaned and gasped once as Miyamoto bayoneted him in the back.

Hiroshi stood stunned, not only by the violence of the attack, but because like Miyamoto and Inoue, he could hear others coming right around the bend. Miyamoto dived into the trees to the left as Inoue did the same to the right. Hiroshi, his feet suddenly full of lead, turned and started to run back down the rise and tripped over one of the Australians

310

lying on his back, the pulverized lower jaw filled with mud. The man's face was inches from Hiroshi's, and he watched in horror as bubbles formed from under the mud and there was a gasp of wheezing air. The man was still alive. Hiroshi spun away from him as another stretcher team came into view a few meters away. He was in clear sight, they couldn't miss him. The Australians stopped abruptly when they saw the two dead bodies and the flipped over stretcher. Then both men looked up petrified at Hiroshi.

The stretcher bearer in the front didn't have a rifle but was wearing a revolver in a canvas holster. His helmet hung around his neck, his long stringy black hair partially covering his face. He appeared to be an Australian Army aidsman with a medical satchel kit strapped to his chest. The man at the rear had a Lee Enfield rifle across his back, barrel down to let the water drain out. He blurted out something to the other soldier and was lowered the stretcher to the ground when he was bayoneted through his side by Sergeant Inoue. Even though he was bayoneted, the man turned and grasped Inoue's rifle, the struggle one-sided as Inoue was stronger and had both hands on the rifle. Inoue pulled the rifle and the bayonet back as the man gasped and fell to his knees. Miyamoto pounced on him, bayoneting him in the back. He pulled the bayonet out with difficulty as the man twisted and fell to the side. Miyamoto instantly spun on his heel to attack the stretcher bearer on the front, but the man had dropped the stretcher and ran straight towards Hiroshi in panic, clawing at the snap on his holster.

Hiroshi had gotten to his feet and collided with the Australian because he couldn't get out of the way fast enough. Hiroshi pulled out his Nambu pistol, aiming it at the man as he rolled up trying to get to his feet. Hiroshi looked at the Australian with the shock of recognition. It was him. The buggy eyes, the stringy hair. This was the man who took care of him at the waterfall, who gave him his sight back. The man's eyes widened as Hiroshi pointed his pistol at his face. The man had his own moment of recognition as he stared at Hiroshi's facial scars. He mumbled something, partially lifting his hand as if to point it at Hiroshi. Hiroshi glanced up from the motion of Sergeant Inoue bayoneting the soldier on the stretcher, as Miyamoto walked quickly up to Hiroshi. He shook his head several times.

"*Don't shoot*! The enemy is close by!" Miyamoto hissed, pulled his shoulders up. Hiroshi saw the flash of the bayonet as Miyamoto began his downward thrust.

"*NO!*" Hiroshi gasped before reacting instinctively, grabbing the rifle stock and pushing the bayonet aside. "*This man saved my life, we can't do this!*" Miyamoto stared in disbelief. His eyes flashed black, his anger so palpable Hiroshi could feel the heat. Miyamoto grunted before shoving Hiroshi hard in the chest, pushing him nearly off his feet as Hiroshi stumbled away.

"You don't tell me how to do my job, Lieutenant! How dare you! I told Hashimoto you didn't have the stomach for this, but he didn't believe me. You stand there and stay out of the way!" Miyamoto glanced up the trail for an instant before turning to glare at Hiroshi with contempt. He stepped next to the Australian soldier and kicked the man hard in the side as he again reversed his rifle. Hiroshi shook his head violently.

"*NO!* This is a direct order Warrant Officer! *Kitkanaito utsuko!* (Obey or I'll shoot!)" Miyamoto turned his back on Hiroshi and raised his rifle. Hiroshi, his Nambu still in his hand, brought it up and shot Miyamoto once in the back of the head at two meters. The noise was loud in the confines of the track. Sergeant Inoue, who was walking up while watching the track over his shoulder, spun around with the pistol shot. As Miyamoto fell Hiroshi saw Inoue's rifle coming up in a flash. Hiroshi, already aiming at Inoue's head, pulled the trigger twice. Inoue's head jerked when one of the 8mm bullets found his skull. The Australian looked around him in total confusion, his eyes wide and fearful. Hiroshi stared at Inoue's slumped body before glancing at the Australian, not believing what he had done.

He could hear the shouts of Australian soldiers coming. Fear gripped his heart and he turned to run in the opposite direction, down the track, away from the danger. He barely had the presence of mind to remember the stacked rocks when he saw them. Running back he dashed into the forest, almost abandoning the RT and cable until he realized the cable would lead him back to First Company. He was so confused he had no idea which direction to go. His hands shook violently making the cable reel rattle as he picked it up. He squashed it hard to his body to silence it. Slipping the RT over his shoulder he walked about 15 meters into the forest, following the cable before stopping to listen.

Hiroshi pressed back into the dark shadows when he heard whispered voices. He knew they couldn't see him, but no doubt the aidsman told his comrades which direction he ran. He crouched down further, the only sound in his ears the rattling of his own knees and teeth. They were chattering and beating his gums as if he was frozen, but he wasn't. His jaw, painful and bloody, jerked like the rest of his body in a spasmodic dance, completely out of his personal control. Somehow he had dropped his pistol when he grabbed the RT and reel. There was no way he was going back.

He stared unblinking at the track for several minutes, waiting in terror for the enemy to see the stacked rocks and figure it out. They stuck out like a sign post, how could they miss it? He had no weapon except a knife now. He had no one. Hiroshi could not quite grasp what just happened, or why it happened. It felt like a dream, but this was too real. There was no waking up from this. The rain was real, the patrol was real. He was alone, he was cold. This was real. He was alone because he killed Miyamoto and Inoue. He killed them for the kindness of an enemy soldier. He could not believe it. Killing his men. *Killing Miyamoto*.

Hiroshi felt sick and vomited up a bitter, sandy mash of bile and blood. He coughed it up right onto the back of his hands. The hands, jerking without rhythm or purpose, seemed detached from him, not belonging to his body. He stared at the blood for a long time. When it began to rain again, he stood up slowly while listening. He coiled the cable carefully but it didn't matter, the roar of the rain was so loud the squeaking was drowned out. The Australians weren't coming for him. He was utterly alone.

THE WET

CHAPTER 26

December 7, 1942, Dobodura airfield, 15 miles South of Buna

Unlike Seven Mile airfield by Port Moresby, Dobodura airfield didn't have a working air raid klaxon. The field was rough, the facilities primitive and for the first few days the Japs didn't know about it. Don Crenshaw, like all the other gooney bird pilots, was distressed to hear Jap fighters flew over it yesterday, probably by accident in heavy weather, and strafed a couple of C-47s as they were loading. The crews who lived through it said these Jap pilots were crazy. They didn't have much ammunition left apparently, so it was two quick passes with the last one pretty scary for ground crews because the Japs weren't shooting anymore, they were looking to decapitate. They screamed down the side of the runway at 250 knots ten feet off the deck, putting the bottom of their propeller arcs right at a man's crotch if he was standing up. The Japs bore down on the crews kicking their rudders around, trying to run them down and saw them in half. Nobody got hurt but there was no doubt some dungarees got soiled from the close calls. Men flopped to the deck moments before the three-bladed buzzsaws of the Zeros roared over them, sucking them up off the dirt and mud for terrorizing seconds before dropping them free.

Don and Cooper heard the stories over and over from different crewmen, nervously considering their own odds with every run between Dobodura and Port Moresby. They were strafed and bombed once at Seven Mile themselves which was no picnic, but their real fear was being caught in the air. Zeroes with their cannons and 7.7 machineguns could turn a C-47 into a flaming torch in one two-second pass. *Where the hell are our fighters* protested the gooney bird pilots, their eyes over at the empty fighter revetments. *Out strafing Jap positions at Buna and Gona, my guess,* said some wag and they knew he was probably right.

A P-40 wasn't exactly a perfect close air support airplane just as it wasn't the best fighter against the Zero, but there were only so many B-25s or A-20s to go around, and the P-38s hadn't arrived yet. The Aussie and US Army Air Corps pilots did the best they could to fullfil both missions. Jap fighters and bombers had to fly all the way from Rabaul now that New Guinea airstrips were no longer available, arriving at the extreme edge of their range over targets with little loiter time. With more and more Allied fighters showing up every day to challenge them over Buna or Moresby, the fighters and bombers played a cat and mouse game, dodging in and out of weather, often going for easier targets difficult to defend. *Like transports sitting on the deck, or caught in between clouds.* Without an air raid siren, the best a crew could hope for would be a call on the radio from the makeshift tower telling them Jap airplanes were spotted two miles and thirty seconds away. On the ground you ran like hell from your airplane. In the air you dove for the nearest heavy cloud as fast as you could push those Pratt and Whitneys, but if you get caught in the gun sights you will die in your airplane.

Don was listening to Sue Culpepper when she mentioned the daily flights from New Guinea to Australia. Somebody in the 21st was flying those missions. Culpepper and Katie McCutcheon were going to Australia. It would be great to see them more often. Who said he had to risk his life forever? The medevac missions moving Aussie and US Army wounded from Dobodura to Port Moresby were necessary and saved hundreds of lives every week, but it was a dangerous mission. Don was no coward, but he was in the air upwards to 10-12 hours a day, seven days a week. In between the weather, poor maintenance and the Jap Zeroes, he felt his luck was wearing thin.

He approached the Squadron Executive Officer (XO) and the Operations Officer about getting on the list of pilots who flew the Townsville and Brisbane run. Operations, a major, stared and laughed at him. *That's a choice assignment, Crenshaw. I fly that mission. So does the XO, our two staff admin captains AND the CO. You get the picture, Lieutenant?*

The XO, also a major, was more thoughtful in his response, choosing to smile knowingly at Don as he lit a cigar. *How long you been with us, Crenshaw? How many hours? I know most of you guys are flying 200-250 hours per month. You still flyin' with that odd bird, Cooper, aren't you. I know he has a ton of time pre-war.*

Since May of this year, about seven months. I have over 1700 hours now, sir, all in gooney birds. Don said nothing about Jack Cooper, partly because of a fear of losing him and partly because Cooper might be considered a liability if they saw them only as a team.

The XO nodded noncommittally as Don answered the questions. He stood up from his desk, his eyes searching among a row of clipboards mounted on the wall behind him, each holding thick stacks of carbon copies of typed lists. Don could only imagine there was a list for all the squadron crewmembers and their qualifications under a variety of categories. His curiosity led him to the clipboard closest to him, and he read: *Officers in Southwest Pacific with pilot MOS background and multi-engine or transport experience currently in non-pilot MOS under the rank of Lieutenant Colonel.* Don stared hard at the list, especially since the list was rather short, just eight or nine names and their rank.

They were all majors and none of the names were familiar to him. *Damn,* he thought, *they're scraping the barrel looking for gooney bird pilots.* It sobered him, wondering why he was wasting his time.

We, uh—hopefully, the XO said, *should get some new pilots in the next couple of weeks. We might be able to schedule a couple of runs for you once the new pilots are assigned, some co-pilots move up and so forth. That will lighten up the flight schedule, providing of course, this business in Buna and Gona gets wrapped up. The original plan was to rotate all pilots with the Australian assignment as a sort of breather, but somehow it always seems the same pilots keep flying that mission. I'll let you know, Crenshaw.*

Thanks, asshole. Don walked by Operations because the XO's office was right outside of it. The Operations Officer looked up at Don and winked. Don pretended he didn't see him and fumed his way back to his squadron quarters. He tried. He thought of Sue Culpepper or Katie McCutcheon calling the squadron operations number published in the directory and trying to reach him before they left. They might get the Operations Officer or one of the Admin SOBs. He could imagine the conversation. *I'll pass along this information sweetheart, to this, uh, Lieutenant Crenshaw. By the way, did you say you were with the 153rd? Aren't you all moving back to Oz soon? I'll be there myself. In fact, I might just fly you out of here. What was your name again?* As he thought about that, he got even madder.

As if the Operations Officer wanted to punish him for even suggesting he was worthy enough for the Australian flights, Don discovered he and Cooper were on the schedule board for medevac, resupply and troop hauling missions from dawn to dusk for the sixteenth day in a row. With General MacArthur fully committed to push the Japanese out of New Guinea by the end of the year, the US and Australian Air Forces were using anything flyable to transport men and materials direct from Australia to Port Moresby. Some of the 21st Air Transport Squadron pilots and planes were part of this endless supply train, but most, like Don and Jack Cooper, flew the short, nasty missions hauling troops to Dobodura from Moresby. At some point soon, they were told, the Australian flights would land direct from Australia to Dobodura, but not until security improved. Don couldn't comprehend the difference between flying the troops from Australia to Dobodura in a C-47, to his flight from Port Moresby to Dobodura in a C-47. Neither had escort 80 percent of the time once in New Guinea airspace, and there was almost no warning when the Japs decided to attack the field. The only difference was who the pilots were.

On the morning of December 7th, one year exactly since the war started, Jack Cooper was flying the ship as they climbed slowly out of

Dobodura. It was late in the afternoon and even when they decided not to top off their tanks, the heat and humidity combined with the tired old Pratts of tail number 686 robbed them of any decent climb rate at all. Cooper mushed the Douglas off the runway, pushed the nose down as he ordered wheels up. There weren't any trees or hills to speak of around Dobodura, which was fortunate. The airplane was full of wounded but nowhere near gross weight, especially with only half tanks for the 90 mile trip. It struggled anyway. It took two miles to get the airplane up over 800 feet. Don glanced at the engine gauges before shaking his head in concert with Cooper. 686 flew like she was carrying a couple of Pratt replacement engines instead of a dozen wounded. As the air cooled in their climb out the airplane performed marginally better. Cooper nursed her into a steady 500 FPM climb as they punched into the bottom of the clouds on a direct heading over the Stanleys'.

Twenty minutes later Cooper had no choice but to turn away from the Stanleys' and to continue his climb parallel to the mountains, turning around every five minutes or so working the altitude like a staircase. They were too far away and low to pick up the Port Moresby radio range on the other side of the mountains, so Cooper kept his position by estimated time and distance, hoping any winds aloft were blowing them southward, away from the mountains while they were lower than the peaks. The clouds were dark and thick, moving like soup swirling around in a tureen, never still. They knew they were over the peak when the altimeter topped 11,000 and the greyness grew brighter and brighter until suddenly they burst out into brilliant blue sky and sunshine. As Cooper nosed the airplane slowly over to level Don could see the edge of the sea and the Gulf of Papau beyond. Cooper sighed and grinned, but this disappeared as they both saw the Zero rising dead ahead out of the clouds, pointed directly at their nose. The Zero punched out of the cloud at the same time they had, rising from the opposite direction.

Before either could react the four wing guns sparkled and twinkled yellow as the Zero filled their windshield. *That SOB was tracking us, Don thought, he guessed where we were and guessed right. Had his gunsight on and his guns charged and warmed up. TINK TINK TINK TINK* followed instantly by *POP POP POP* as three holes appeared on the windshield on Don's side from right to left. The Zero was gone as Don felt his body lifting from his seat from negative Gs. Cooper had shoved the yoke forward, HARD, the airplane groaning as it struggled to respond. There was some high-pitched whistling, howling sound right in front of him, appearing out of nowhere. It wouldn't go away.

It was very cold now, cold air swirling around him. In the back of

318

his brain he wondered why the side window was open. This concern faded as Don felt a crushing pressure on his chest followed by the first nibble of pain. His right eye stung, and he couldn't see out of it. It was closed, encrusted with dried fluid, and when he moved his eyes he felt something in the right one. Something hot was burning against his left elbow. He could smell burning flesh, *holy shit*. So much wrong with him. He couldn't breathe right, and that was another source of the pain, but all of these conditions gave rise to a sense of panic he could hardly control. He was hit in several places. *Was he dying?* He tried to lift his left arm to see his elbow but it didn't seem to work. The burning sensation continued, the strange heat and smell, but it was feeling numb and heavier. He couldn't focus on it, his arm, because it drifted from the center of his attention. It was confusing. The blue sky ebbed grey as if the lights were dimming, a voice, far away, called his name.

Don turned his head to the right towards Cooper, trying not to move his eyes. Cooper glanced back at him before returning to the business of flying. It was darker, they were back in the clouds. Cooper seemed to be moving his arms in slow motion. The instrument panel didn't look right, but mostly Don noticed Cooper's left arm was hanging straight down from his shoulder, like it was too heavy. Normally it would rest casually near the center console with the dual throttles, mixtures and propeller controls. There was blood on his arm, lots of it, and as Don's eyes lifted to Cooper's face, there was blood there too. He would need help, Don thought idly. But Cooper was flying the airplane.

Don kept coming in and out and could taste blood in his mouth. This frightened him even more but he was distracted trying to breathe lightly enough to control the sharp pain in his chest. It wasn't working. He would get a sharp stab and take a deep breathe instinctively, which hurt like hell and he would cough and breathe some more. One of the medics on the flight was stuffing something under his shirt which hurt him, so when he tried to push the hands away he found Sergeant Larson, his flight engineer gripping his hands and telling him to *quit fightin' me, sir, gawddam' it*. The medic pressed Don's crew oxygen mask over his face, and Don had to admit this made him feel a bit better, but he breathed in more and it hurt. It was the old style bladder mask, the inhale and exhale filled and emptied the bladder, sometimes slipping the bladder under the jacket they had laying across his chest. This folded the bladder and he couldn't breathe. He could hear them arguing as the medic wanted to pull Don out of the cockpit seat so they could lay him down, but Larson made it clear *Lieutenant Crenshaw's too gawddam big, he kin' hardly get in the fuckin' seat all by hisself!* He felt the prick of something in his arm before he simply faded away.

He woke again as turbulence or something bounced old 686 hard

319

and Sergeant Larson, kneeling between the cockpit seats, slammed against the side of Don's seat before being lifted off his feet and tossed against the top of the cockpit. It was full of switches and sharp edges. Larson wasn't wearing any leather helmet, never did, just his tattered ball cap. He cracked his head pretty good, opening up a gash. The blood dripped from his forehead but he ignored it because he was handling the throttles and propellers for Cooper. Don, lying sideways in his seat, lifted his head to peer at Larson with his good eye. Larson looked mad as hell. For some reason this seemed funny to Don, and he laughed. He decided his right hand worked a bit and slowly lifted his oxygen mask a couple of inches to speak. *What a sorry sight we are,* he gasped. Cooper glanced over at Don in recognition but said nothing to him, they were too busy. Don could see they were in and out of the clouds, somewhere in the approach to Seven Mile airfield, and it was rough. Cooper was flying 686 with his right hand, and Larson was his co-pilot, his left hand. He would need him for the throttles, lowering the gear, the flaps and unlocking the tail wheel once they landed. Even in Cooper's smooth hand, the yoke jerked about with a mind of its own.

Ease the throttles back 300 RPM, watch the tachs and the manifold pressure gauges, both back together. If I ask for throttles back up, I mean right now, but ease them up together, okay? Always together. This thing flies like a pregnant cow for some reason so we might need the power all the way to the runway. When I tell you to, start lowering the gear. Don, listening to Cooper, knew 686 was in good hands, even just one hand. He closed his eye and laid his head back and felt velvet fur slide over his scalp, drawing him back and down.

Moments passed, but he knew it was more like five or ten minutes because 686 was taxiing with its butt down, wiggling it's big ass tail with gusting winds. Cooper spun the airplane around in its parking space, standing on a wheel brake. Larson, still dutifully kneeling between the seats, eased the throttles to idle and moved to the mixture levers. *Pull the mixtures,* called Cooper and 686 coughed and clattered to a buzzing stillness. *Master switch, OFF.* Don turned his head and watched Cooper unbuckle himself from his seat, carefully working around the console with his good arm. *I told you I'd take good care of you, Don,* he said quietly. He patted Don on the shoulder after examining the blood-soaked compresses stuffed under his shirt. *I want the nurses to know you're hurt up here, you've lost a lot of blood. We'll get you taken care of.*

After a few minutes a nurse from the 166th Station Hospital checked him over, ignoring the swollen eye and probed around his chest. Finally she called for the medics and Sergeant Larson, directing them to lift Don out of his seat. They cut away his left sleeve and in the process lifted his left arm. An inch below his elbow, which was about twice its normal size and black and blue, was a huge, thick blister the size of an egg. *What za' hell izsat?* Don babbled, in shock to see something like that on his arm. *Somethin' hot hit ya', Lieutenant, and it cooked away in your arm and the heat raised the blister. That must hurt!*

He was hooked up to an IV once he was on a stretcher in the middle of the aisle in his own airplane. Very carefully they shifted his body so he was lying on his injured lung. When they first lifted him up and lowered him to the stretcher, he could see another nurse gingerly cutting Jack Cooper's shirt sleeve off as he stood leaning against the fuselage. There was a series of deep gashes and punctures from his elbow to his shoulder. Cooper looked completely exhausted now, his eyelids almost closed, as if he were asleep. *Okay*, she said curtly, *you're going to have to spend some time with us, Lieutenant. Both of you look like you got parts of your instrument panel stuck in you.* She caught the attention of one of the medics as they lifted Don up. *Get that one on O2 immediately*. He felt dizzy as they carried him off the airplane, but he smiled as he felt the thick, heavy rain drops slap across his face.

CHAPTER 27

December 10, 1942, 166th Station Hospital, Port Moresby

This was the first day he could think clearly, grasping where he was as soon as he woke up. It was a long series of steps, like smooth stones spaced out across a stream. One could get across but you had to concentrate on each step or you would fall. You had to jump and land on each stone with both feet. The dreams he recognized, that is, he knew they were dreams. He was good at that. Starvation and *Shabu* created his dream world for a time on the Kokoda. He controlled it then so the long hours, days and weeks simply passed. The dreams were simple, almost pleasant and infinitely better than being awake. But the dreams he had now were all slices of butcher shop horror, mutilated faces of men who had died beside him or because of him. They were silent as their bodies, bloated and ripe from days on the side of the trail, drifted by to explode as they fell like rotten fruit, erupting gas and sinew and maggots from every orifice.

His final waking thoughts in Buna were of his coming death. He accepted it, almost welcomed it because he was so alone. In the end the constant bombing reducing their solid coconut coastal bunkers to splinters. There was nowhere to go, so you rolled inside yourself and waited. His last hours were spent among whimpering and crying strangers, fresh infantry with only two weeks on the island. Recruits who still sang and danced, joyful when told victory was near. *Nankai Shitai*, once it returned down the Track, was destroyed as a fighting unit so the individual soldiers no longer had a home. A starving, broken column, the fresh troops avoided them. General Horii was dead, as were most of the regimental officers. The few hundred men who were still standing were dispersed and assigned to the defense of Buna and Gona. Every day the airplanes returned to drop bombs trying to penetrate the thick logs, followed by American and Australian infantry carrying grenades, satchel charges and flame throwers. There was no escape, nothing behind them except the beach. When the bombs came too close there was a flash, numbness then nothing.

When the horror dreams started to fade and he heard voices, his mind was confused but he would search in that direction because it was more pleasant. The voices were foreign; English and female sometimes, confusing him further. The gradual transition to consciousness was hard, he had to focus—on the next smooth rock. The smells gave it away; the alcohol, urine and the sour-sweet odor of blood and bodily fluids. He kept his eyes closed except when he knew it was dark. He did this

322

because as long as he appeared to be unconscious the enemy left him alone. He mentally moved around his body, aware of the numbness or dull pain in several places. His hands and arms were restrained. He was hurting but heavily medicated, with an IV in both arms. Once again the enemy, in their baffling ways, was trying to *fix him*. When he listened very carefully, he could hear someone shift their weight in a chair, someone very close. There was the creak of leather boots and a harness of some kind. Someone was there.

Today he heard a male voice next to his bed. There were several people close by, but this one spoke in English before seeming to direct his speech towards him.

Ohayo! (Good morning!) Ikaga desu ka? (How are you?)

When he didn't open his eyes or respond, the male voice spoke to someone in English. Someone gently pulled his eyelids apart. He rolled his eyes back and stared at nothing, conscious of only two blurry faces close to his. The hand pressed his eyes shut and the voices moved away, murmuring.

Hiroshi Takahashi returned to First Company on Mission Ridge and resumed his role as company commander. He used the radio to report ahead to the BC the Australians were still withdrawing on the unknown south track, and the loss of Warrant Officer Miyamoto and Sergeant Inoue to an ambush. *Kempeitai* losses were not mourned by the regular Army officers and men, so this information raised little attention or tears. The most important consequence for Hiroshi was Miyamoto was the only one who knew how to cook *Shabu*. Corporal Yasuda, Hiroshi's aide, had no idea. It was something Miyamoto did secretly, out of sight. Hiroshi was relieved to find Yasuda did have a large supply of *Nekome-jo* tablets, so he could at least keep his nerves at bay. With the resumed food shortage, *Nekome-jo* was all there was to keep them going.

The few remaining members of Miyamoto's reconnaissance platoon were spread out among First Company's platoons as regular riflemen. With Miyamoto gone they no longer had a mission. Hiroshi's leadership was accepted without question, and not a single soul asked about Miyamoto or Sergeant Inoue once the men heard they were dead.

Third Battalion suffered predictably heavy losses climbing up the face of Mission Ridge. The Second Battalion Commander decided not to pursue the Australians down the south track with just a single battalion. General Horii supported this decision, giving *Nankai Shitai* a short breather before resuming their pursuit. Wounded men needed to be transported back up the Track to the poorly equipped surgical hospital at Kokoda, and there was hope the supply situation could be remedied by stopping the advance. The dwindling native stretcher bearers did what they could to move the wounded, but the ration supply was critical now.

323

The Australians, the decimated 39th, 53rd, 2/14, 2/16 and the 2/27 battalions, kept pulling back and down the Track until they reached Imita Ridge at Ioribaiwa, overlooking Port Moresby only 43 kilometers away. This was the last defendable position before the Australians had to withdraw to Port Moresby itself. 2/14 was so reduced by the time they reached Ioribaiwa the survivors were blended with 2/16 to form a composite battalion.

When *Nankai Shitai* reached Ioribaiwa they were down to 1,500 men. Hiroshi, watching the glowing lights of Port Moresby at night, did so by peeking over the ridge with the remaining survivors of First Company, now comprised of two small platoons totaling 33 men. On September 16 they received the word General Horii was ordered to withdraw *Nankai Shitai* back down the Kokoda Track. Port Moresby, tantalizing close, would never be taken. Reinforcements necessary to take and keep Port Moresby were not coming; one task force directed to assault the tail of New Guinea, Milne Bay, was turned back by the enemy. Another force tasked specifically to reinforce *Nankai Shitai* up the Track was redirected instead to support the battle for Guadalcanal.

There was hushed whispering up the line and Hiroshi glanced around, irritated by the noise because they were so close to the enemy lines. He could not believe his eyes as General Horii crept up beside him. Horii clapped his hand on Hiroshi's shoulder. Hiroshi, honored, bowed and made room for his commander. Horii didn't say anything for several minutes, his thoughts kept to himself as he viewed the shimmering harbor with his field glasses.

"We have come so far, Lieutenant," Horii said reflectively, "our men have sacrificed so much." Horii was quiet for a long time, just watching, before putting his field glasses down. He glanced at Hiroshi and smiled.

"We're going to withdraw slowly, Hiroshi, so the enemy doesn't guess what we're doing. I don't want them pursuing us like we've been pursuing them. We need to buy time to slip most of our men away." Hiroshi suddenly realized what Horii was saying, and a cold hand gripped his heart.

Horii put his hand on Hiroshi's shoulder again. Hiroshi turned towards his commander and nodded in salute.

"We will do our best; do our duty to buy you that time, sir."

"I know you will, Hiroshi. When you slip away and rejoin us, I want you on my personal staff. In fact you are already listed, at the rank of Captain. Congratulations!"

For the next six weeks *Nankai Shitai* withdrew back down the same Track they had rushed up like madmen. A few composite companies formed from the survivors were tasked to slow down the pursuing Australians as much as possible. At first these men staged a series of holding actions, all at great cost, buying the rest of the task force a little cushion to withdraw down the Track. Within a week it was impossible to organize a steady line of resistance because of the crushing, brutal pressure the Australians were now able to bring to bear. The Aussies, using the same technique of a frontal assault combined with a circular flanking attack employed by *Nankai Shitai*, overwhelmed the thin lines of holding units. These rear-guard forces, already out of food, medicine and any hope of survival, continued to fight until they were cornered and killed. Those few who escaped had to abandon dying comrades, believing the Australians would give them no quarter. Their only solace was they made the pursuing Aussies pay a high toll, again, for every meter of the Track they took back.

The Aussies, acknowledging the opportunity to destroy *Nankai Shitai* was finally at hand, sent a fresh new Brigade, the 25th down the Kokoda in pursuit. The battered, nearly decimated 21st Brigade and the 39th Battalion were relieved. The 25th Brigade recognized the real rainy season, *the wet,* was upon them. The rivers and streams crossing the Kokoda Track on the eastern side of the Owen Stanleys' would soon become impassable for either side. Their mission was not to hold or resist *Nankai Shitai* in any way. Their mission was to chase the survivors down like wild animals as quickly as they could and kill them all before they escaped to waiting barges at Buna.

When he was awake now, Hiroshi didn't try to think about those final weeks. His dreams took care of this well enough. The constant hunger, cold and pain of innumerable injuries blended into one endless agony. He lost his men one or two at a time. Some died from gunfire, grenade fragments or when the Aussies got close, bayonets. But some left in the middle of day while leaning against a cold, slick bone white tree root, doing nothing more than shivering from cold, fear, hunger or disease. They shivered and closed their eyes, and then they were gone. At first friends would scrape out a shallow grave and roll their comrades in. No one said words anymore, they just buried them. They were gone, they had escaped. Others slipped out of their friends' grasp attempting to ford roaring little streams they crossed 10 weeks before when it was slow and half a meter deep. Some cried out in fear, many made no sound at all, accepting their fate as a release.

Hiroshi's aide, Corporal Yasuda, died in such a way. He reached across as he stepped on a rock and handed Hiroshi the company satchel, once owned by Captain Hashimoto, containing most of the important records of First Company. Hiroshi accepted the satchel and lifted his hand to help Yasuda, whose face was suddenly full of fear and confusion as he slipped and started to fall. There was nothing anyone could do it happened so quickly. The stream ran flat and fast for five or six meters then dropped straight down a narrow chimney, a racing chute disappearing into the face of a huge boulder. Yasuda didn't even cry out, his head disappeared under the smooth current to be swept over the edge and gone. The man behind Yasuda stopped only to look down the stream before looking up at Hiroshi. Hiroshi, his hand still outstretched, was suddenly grasped by this man and Hiroshi instinctively pulled him across to safety. The loss of Yasuda happened in the blink of an eye, and at first Hiroshi was uncertain himself it actually occurred. His grasp of reality was only tentative sometimes. *Did he dream this?* Later that day when Yasuda didn't appear to prepare Hiroshi's bedroll for the evening, Hiroshi began to accept the finality of the loss. With Hashimoto and Miyamoto gone and now Yasuda, there was no one to turn to, no one to prepare an escape for the evening. Gone with Yasuda was the last of the *Nekome jo*.

The first few weeks without it was very hard for the survivors of First Company. Hiroshi continued to distribute the tablets after Miyamoto's death because of the hunger-dampening qualities. When the *Nekome-jo* was lost all that was left was *Totsugeki-jo*, the green tea mixture existing in limited qualities among *Nankai Shitai*. Hiroshi looked for it too because within a day and a half without it he became very sick. The *Tetsugeki-jo* was a weak, poor substitute for men accustomed to stronger doses, but it dampened the worst symptoms of skull-splitting headaches, insomnia, intense confusion, stomach cramps and severe muscular pain. Troops going through the experience were as useless as soldiers having a bad malaria episode, except this sickness continued for weeks. In most situations it was categorized and treated the same as malaria, that is, the patients were left alone as there was no treatment available.

Being nearly killed by bombs in Buna brought him here, reintroducing him to morphiates. Any relief this may have offered was overshadowed by the severity of his wounds. His chest caused the most discomfort because it hurt so much to breathe. He could tell his ribs were broken, several of them. The most pain was on one side, his left he thought. At some point, if he survived, they would stop giving him morphine as they did when they brought him to Alola. But it would be awhile. Once he was coming out of a dream where he was drowning, suffocating in wet mud. He couldn't breathe at all and he felt hands massaging his chest and some intense, horrifying pain. He had lost consciousness, which was a relief as the drowning dream went away. He awoke sometime later, confused, his chest hurting terribly, but he felt better and could breathe. It was the way it is. He may be dying, but as long as he lay still they kept him sedated. Not enough to shut down his brain, yet enough to keep most of the pain suppressed. It was enough, he accepted it.

The last days on the Track were the worst. First Company was no more. The few survivors by the time they reached Oivi were blended with other companies. After the battles of Oiva and Gorari on the Kokoda, the 144th Regiment was destroyed as a combat unit. True to his word General Horii brought Hiroshi into his inner circle, his personal staff, what was left of it. The loyalty of these men had no bounds, as Hiroshi witnessed them preparing Horii meals from scraps they could have easily consumed themselves. Panic was rustling through the men like a cool breeze as they approached the creeks they had crossed earlier with bicycles. The rain created torrential floods through the same creeks, now 100 meters across with treacherous currents and speed. With the Australians all around them, men attempted crossings with equipment or animals and were drowned. Horii issued orders the men never expected to hear from him. *Bury your weapons to lighten the loads, shoot the horses and mules so the enemy cannot use them.* Many of the men simply could not do it. The animals were turned loose.

The final orders were for all troops to proceed independently any way they could to escape the floods and the Australians. When the survivors made it to the Kumusi River, they were stopped abruptly because there was no crossing the river by wading or swimming. It was too wide and way too fast. Men attempted to build simple rafts and cross the river, but most of these came apart and the men drowned. General Horii, growing impatient, commandeered a canoe found by other soldiers and took off across with a few members of his senior command staff. No one saw it overturn, but Horii and the members of the command staff who accompanied him were never seen again. The rest of the men, Hiroshi included, took the time to build larger, more robust rafts. Although the Australians were in close pursuit, most of the men who crossed the river in the big rafts made it to the other side.

By the time Hiroshi and the survivors of *Nankai Shitai* made it to Gona and Buna, American forces were now engaged, coming up the peninsula from the south, slowly taking over the prime assault role. Barges were being used at night to evacuate the Japanese wounded until this was no longer possible because of air attacks. *Nankai Shitai* blended with the fresh new troops sent weeks before from Rabaul, but the sense of doom was palpable in the air. The Australians, tired and worn, pressed down and hard on the defenders in Gona as US forces pushed up towards Buna. The American Army, fresh but green, moved clumsily, but was becoming better supported by air power as fewer and fewer

Japanese planes seemed to make it over. The barges stopped coming, but men, told they would be evacuated, waited on the beaches day after day until Aussie and US bombers and fighters drove them back to their bunkers. Some, hopeless and desperate, set out swimming and were never seen again.

Hiroshi remembered the beach clearly; loading wounded onto the barges in the dark all night. He was surprised to see men who actually survived the 90 kilometer journey from the Kokoda on a stretcher carried by native bearers. He assumed the natives would toss the wounded men off the stretchers once the going got hard or the overseer wasn't watching. It apparently didn't happen. He sat on the same beach with several of the new troops, fresh in every respect. Clean uniforms, fat faces from good diets, a positive attitude and a complete belief in the inevitable victory. He was in awe of them. They were like aliens from another planet. Hiroshi, in rags and covered with jungle sores, was barely acknowledged except by the collar insignia General Horii had given him weeks before. He was an infantry captain from the non-existent 144th Regiment; this warranted hesitant bows and salutes which he ignored. That same day he walked to the water's edge and kept walking, until the water was up to his chin. The salt water stung his sores and innumerable small injuries, but he stayed out there for nearly an hour, turning a deaf ear to warnings of an air raid that never occurred. His sobbing, when it happened, was never seen by the men sitting by the water's edge 20 meters away, their feet in the cool, lapping surf. Even if they had seen or heard him they would have whispered among themselves and ignored it. He was a strange man to them, like all the ones coming fresh from the Kokoda, men who talked to themselves all of the time.

In his dream Hiroshi saw bobbing heads in the same docile, placid surf. Hundreds of them. He knew every one of them. He saw General Horii, Captain Hashimoto, Lieutenants Tanaka, Nishikawa, Tomita, Shamada, Sergeant Kato, and so many of his men. They were all together, bobbing like surf kelp, keeping time. It was like looking at a company picture of First Company, only there wasn't a Lieutenant Takahashi, and all of their eyes were closed, as if they were sleeping. They seemed at peace and content. It didn't seem right and he needed to be with them. One by one, they sunk below the surface until the last one, Hashimoto, disappeared too. *You left me alone.*

CHAPTER 28

December 11, 1942, 166th Station Hospital

Katie McCutcheon was exhausted. She leaned against the counter in the nurse's station and closed her eyes. The fighting in Gona and Buna seemed to produce many more casualties than predicted, despite the *Armed Services News* and *The Stars and Stripes* stating the Japanese were cornered and beaten. The 153rd Station Hospital staff was officially relieved and replaced by the 166th, but an endless train of casualties continued to be flown to Port Moresby instead of direct to Australia as planned. Close, face-to-face combat with the Japanese resulted in a higher percentage of gunshot wounds than in Europe, they were told, where most of the wounds were caused by artillery, mortar or grenade fragments. Because of it, fewer of the wounded men were immediately air transportable for long distance flights, especially thoracic injuries. A small group of nurses, a few of the malaria-ridden surgeons and most of the administrative staff of the 153rd were already gone. They were preparing the Southport hospital for the large group of casualties who would eventually be flown direct to Australia, either from Dobodura airfield near Buna, or from Port Moresby.

For Katie it was a blessing because she and other 153rd nurses like Sue Culpepper remained theoretically as volunteers. She had no surgical duties, which she detested, and no ridiculous ancillary responsibility like managing the enlisted men in the laundry. This type of nursing she remembered before she joined the Army, basic ward nursing, and she realized with some humor she enjoyed it now. The 166th nurses took over the surgical suites and were trying to handle the crush of patients arriving two or three times a day. All of the 153rd nurses had their orders to depart, but the departure date was open because of the shortage of nurses in the wards, and space on the transports. Only a few of the 153rd nurses chose to remain in their quarters with their bags packed, waiting for the chance to fly out with the transports carrying wounded to Townsville and Brisbane. They volunteered to be one-way, on-duty flight nurses, freeing up medics who were needed at the field surgical hospitals. The nurses traded the short duty for the seven-hour flight back to a clean, safe and sane place. Having spent seven or eight weeks in Port Moresby they wanted nothing more to do with the malaria-infested swamps. Katie understood why they wanted to leave but still held them in contempt.

She knew her orders could be finalized at any moment, but she and Sue kept themselves indispensable by handling this special ward by

329

themselves during the day. At night only a single nurse was on duty, with Katie and Sue on call. Neither of them had succumbed to malaria—yet, but what had been a small overflow ward for high-maintenance patients with a variety of serious injuries turned into a thoracic post-op ward with an international cast. Katie and Sue picked up the ward with six patients, mostly Americans, before gaining an Australian—Sergeant Hickey, then the Japanese prisoner. Three of the original six patients were thoracic cases, gunshot wounds to the chest. Now they had 18 patients, gaining one or two new ones a day, all of them thoracic wounds. Most of these were lung injuries, difficult to treat because if the patient survived long enough to get to Port Moresby, the injured lung was sealed by careful bandaging or needle and thread work by the field surgeon before transport. Unless there was poor debridement at the field surgical hospital, the closed wounds of the lung were left alone to begin healing. Sucking chest wounds, which really was a misnomer, as the big killer was the air leaking out, not sucking in, usually involved large penetrations, shattered rib bones and punctured lungs. It was also rarely survivable. Almost all of the cases here were gunshot wounds with some rib fractures and secondary damage to other organs, but clean, smaller punctures otherwise.

Katie, who was originally trained in psychiatry, was learning fast. Sue Culpepper, who was a thoracic specialist, was a good teacher. The primary function of the nursing staff was to keep the patient's lungs clear of fluids and foreign matter. Besides their other wounds and secondary infections, this was what would kill them. Patients, conscious or unconscious, had to be rolled around to ensure the lungs didn't fill with blood or other fluids. If conscious and able, the patients were leaned up and asked to cough repeatedly several times a day, with all discharges measured and noted on the chart. If unconscious, sometimes the fluid would build in the lungs and the fluid had to be aspirated through a long, large gauge needle. It was a horrible procedure to watch at first, only performed by a surgeon at the bedside, but still difficult to witness if you weren't used to it. After a couple of weeks Katie was starting to get the hang of it. She assisted when it was performed early in the arrival of Sergeant Hickey, then twice on the Japanese prisoner.

In any case it was a quiet ward, as thoracic wounds were painful and debilitating. When it hurt to breathe patients spent their recovery time sedated and quiet, usually about three weeks on the average before being cleared for transport. At least most of the patients. She smiled as she guiltily brushed her hair, using the chrome sides of a towel dispenser to examine her face. She looked tired and worn out around the eyes, not very attractive at the moment. She wished she had used more eyeliner in the morning, but here it was nearly dinner time and she'd been on her feet since five.

Don—Lieutenant Crenshaw, whose face looked like it was worked over by Popeye in the cartoons and also had a neat bullet hole right between the ribs underneath his nipple—was four days out of post-op and already talking. He recognized her and said her eyes were gorgeous and he missed seeing her. Of course he also told Sue Culpepper she had a nice ass. Not exactly those words, but that was a common comment in any ward Sue worked, usually as a whisper, sometimes not. Sue did have a nice bottom, Katie admitted, nothing to be ashamed of, especially since the aviation overalls they wore were hardly form-fitting, with the only sizes being the men's.

She was shocked when they wheeled Don into the ward after his surgery. No one told her in advance it was Crenshaw, she discovered it by accident as she scanned the list of new patients two days earlier. She recognized the name, noted the list of injuries and was surprised at her reaction. They only spoke a few times, spending minutes together here and there. They were planning some form of date before she left for Australia. Not much commitment. There was a strong interest on his part she felt, and she admitted she thought about him every now and then. Now, seeing his name and the associated injuries, he seemed much closer to her than ever before. She couldn't explain it. There was a clutch at her heart and she was on her way down the ward before she read anything about the next new patient on the list.

She had to bite her lip and keep her eyes on Don's eyes, a trick she learned early dealing with young men who were mutilated by their injuries. They keyed on what they saw in your face. Rather, she concentrated on Don's EYE, as his right eye was swathed in a large cotton compress. The medical description on the chart noted small fragments of glass and metal from the instrument panel had slashed the eyeball itself, but no damage was noted to the retina. The wound was soaked with petroleum and the patient warned not to move his eyes around, as it would irritate the wound and create obvious pain. Don glanced up, recognized Katie and looked her way just momentarily with genuine joy, until the inevitable came a split second later. He cried out and moaned, closing his eyes and Katie, inexplicably, wanted to lean down and hold his head to her breast. Sue Culpepper didn't help much as she sauntered over. She took his pulse out of habit and glanced at the chart Katie was holding.

"He's a mess, poor baby. But he is cute as a bug, isn't he? I forgot already. I like this guy too!"

Don Crenshaw, for his part couldn't believe his good luck in drawing the very ward his favorite nurse was working in. With two attractive nurses on duty all day Don couldn't help but recover quickly, he figured. To reduce the injury of the damaged eye, the nurses and doctors attempted to have Don wear a compress patch on both eyes once he was awake and alert. This would reduce movement because he would be less distracted by people and things around him. This lasted less than an hour after his first encounter with Katie. He wanted to see her and learned quickly to move his head instead of his eyes to see things. It was strange to witness, this wooden dummy patient who jerked his head around like an owl, but it seemed to work. Sue Culpepper and Katie McCutcheon laughed when they first saw it, but Don was serious and saw things mostly this way, with a few painful slipups. The chest wound kept him down and sucking oxygen, and his lacerated elbow was tucked in tight. He should have been quieter with all of his injuries but Don loved the attention.

Before Don arrived on the 7th Sue and Katie were spending a lot of time with Vic Hickey. There were only a few patients alert and not heavily sedated, so when they could they would stop by Vic's bed and shoot the breeze with him. They didn't mention the incident involving the Japanese prisoner, which was easy since Vic never brought it up. They hoped he simply forgot about it. The prisoner was still sedated and recovering slowly, so he hadn't been moved yet to a special POW ward set up on the other end of the hospital. If Vic was curious about the MPs who periodically replaced one another farther down the ward, he kept it to himself.

Vic Hickey's unit from the 21st Brigade, the 2/14 Battalion was still in Gona fighting the Japanese. Potty Johnson didn't return to the unit after all, suffering another bout of malaria the day he was scheduled to fly out. He tried to visit Vic every few days when he had the strength. Potty also visited Link and Rocko, whose gunshot wounds kept them at Port Moresby. The MO tagged him for Australia as being too sick to return to duty. Captain Welsh, their company commander, also knocked down with severe malaria, checked in before he was flown out. Jock, Red and Slim, worn out and sick, visited for a few minutes on their way to the flight line. With the exception of Link, Rocko, Potty and himself there was no one left of the original 9 Platoon on New Guinea.

The ward was filling up every day with new patients, almost all of them Yanks. Vic realized the only reason he was still kept in the ward separated from his countrymen was the nature of his wounds, specifically his chest wound. It had something to do with the tendency of medical establishments to congregate like illnesses or wounds in the same place. But he was healing, the constant demands from Lieutenants McCutcheon and Culpepper to get him to sit up, roll around like a beached whale and then cough whatever he could out of his lungs appeared to be working. The rib fractures were painful so coughing was painful as the lungs expanded, but they offered the alternative of a huge hypodermic needle to be punched into his lung to withdraw the secretions if he didn't try hard enough. They showed him where they did it when he was first arrived, and he admitted the spot was very tender. So he coughed as they wiped up the spittle and measured it, noting favorably as the color went from dark brown to red, to pink and now he was dry.

"You're as strong as an ox," Katie McCutcheon said admiringly.

"Aye' bloody used ta' be, Leftenant," he beamed back.

Katie McCutcheon brought it up, his coming transfer to the Australian Army ward here at the 166th Station Hospital, or possibly to the Australian Army Station Hospital a short distance away. It wasn't a sure thing, but she obviously did it because she assumed it would cheer him up and Vic would want to be around his countrymen, which he did. The Australian facility was overwhelmed by the initial casualties from the Kokoda and gladly accepted the US Army's offer of handling overflows at the 166th. Once the Australian casualties recovered enough for transport, they were temporarily transferred over to the Australian Hospital or transported directly from Seven Mile airfield to Australia, then routed to a hospital close to home. In either case, as she smiled in a way that melted Vic Hickey's heart, the message she wanted to convey was clear. *You're going to be okay, and you're going home soon.*

To Vic, her message created a small ache because he was falling for her, he assumed, like every bloody fool Tom, Dick and Harry soldier did with a beautiful Sheila like her, who came into their lives at such a time. He remembered his first sight of her as she tended to him those early days, now seemingly far in the past. Her tangled hair and delicate features were those of an angel, an opinion that had not wavered one bloody bit. When the ward was quiet after the nursing shift change, Katie (she let him call her by her Christian name, as did Sue Culpepper when nobody was around) would sometimes pass on dinner and pull up a chair. They talked about each other's old lives, before the war, and Vic couldn't help but sense the common background of this lovely young woman from a large ranch in Oregon. Sue Culpepper was raised around horses in Texas, so both of them seem to listen to his stories with genuine interest. It was for Vic the first time he could remember where he was beginning to think about a life after the Army, after the war. How bold was that, mate? The war was just bloody starting. It depressed him when he thought about it too hard, so he didn't. He wasn't much of a drinker, but at such times he could stand a pint or two. Especially if he could share one with Katie.

A few days earlier several new patients were brought into the ward, with one drawing a lot of attention from Katie and Sue. After a day or two, considering most of the patients were heavily sedated and quiet, a male voice could be heard joking with the nurses down the ward out of Vic's sight. Katie told him later it was one of the Yank biscuit bomber pilots Vic met a week or so ago. The name and the memory escaped him, it meant nothing to him. Other than he suspected this pilot was someone special to Katie and Sue.

Vic was jealous of the bastard, he would admit to no one but himself, but Katie and Sue divided their time now between Vic and the pilot, and there was more laughter down that way. The flyboy was a Yank, so maybe they had more in common by being Americans. He understood that, and of course the bastard must be an officer, as the Yanks didn't go much for Sergeant pilots like they did in the RAAF.

Captain Welsh, when he visited Vic, mentioned Link and Rocko were slated to be flying home to Oz in a day or two, as was Potty. Vic could expect a visit before they left, they had promised. Today was the day so at least he had something to look forward to. Like Katie and Sue and the Yank flyboy, he could spend some time with his own countrymen, and the last of 9 Platoon.

Sue propped Vic so he was almost sitting up in his bed. Light was filtering in bright and yellow, allowing him to look around as if seeing things for the first time. He was eating well, his catheter was finally gone. His hip and leg hurt much more now, probably, he figured, because he was awake most of the time to be conscious of it. The mosquito nets were tucked up and away for the day, so his view was pretty good considering his unusual bed location. Not that there was anything to see. To his left was a short wall while to his right there was a fabric screen between himself and the next patient. He never heard a peep out of whoever that was, if there was anybody there at all. Only a few of the patients on the other side of the ward had screens on the sides, signifying something special about them. The men inhabiting the beds across the way were inert and didn't sit up or speak. He knew the nurses rolled the patients around their beds like they did for him, presumably to keep their lungs clear, but now that he was more alert and awake, it felt like a morgue.

The day past slowly and Vic began to wonder if he had the day wrong. It was getting to be dinner time soon, as additional lights were beginning to pop on in the ward as the shadows grew longer and darker. He watched casually as a big American MP Sergeant with his sidearm prominently displayed walk quickly down the ward, glancing menacingly to his left and right. When he came to Vic he stared for a moment as their eyes met, probably surprised to find anyone up and awake in this ward. The sergeant, his eyes dismissive, kept going and went down the ward and out of sight. A minute later two officers, one a tall MP, walked down the ward in the same direction with one of the US Army surgeons. The MP officer stared hard at Vic like the MP Sergeant had, a very unfriendly look. Vic knew there was something odd about the entire arrangement, but he couldn't quite put his finger on it. There was a prisoner down there, probably a Yank needing surgery. What else could it be?

After about 10 minutes the MPs left, soon followed by the other officer and the surgeon. This time all of them ignored Vic. A minute or two later Sue Culpepper appeared, beaming, with two pathetic looking characters in tow, Potty and Rocko. Link was nowhere to be seen.

"Well, Sergeant Hickey, I do believe these men are familiar to you! I apologize to all of you for the delay, but the MPs insisted we keep out visitors until they were done with the—uh, special patient we have at the end of the ward. Sorry." She brushed a loose strand of her blond hair out of her face and smiled again. Potty and Rocko, looking for the world like a couple of orphan waifs staring at a descending angel, bobbed their heads in unison.

"No prob' at all, miss," stumbled Potty, "Ewe' 'ave yur' job ta' do. 'Ere soon bound fur' 'ome, so we 'anted ta' see our 'argent." He said this with eyes wide with wonder as did Rocko, even with his neck and one shoulder propped firm in a cast. Sue Culpepper nodded and stepped back.

"Then I'll leave it to you then, gentlemen!" She glanced over her shoulder as she walked away, holding up a slim hand to attract Vic's attention.

"Supper will be served in about 30 minutes, Sergeant. Pork chops and mashed potatoes!"

Vic had to laugh at his old mates, who stared over their shoulders as Sue Culpepper walked away.

"Blimey," said Rocko after a long moment, a man known mostly for his brooding silences. "Ewe' 'ave 'ovely nurses 'or 'ere, Vic!" It was Vic's turn to beam.

"Aye, mate, 'at aye' do!"

Potty and Rocko waited for over an hour for the MPs to come and go. Link, shot through both shoulders, was in no position to walk about and sent along his best wishes from his hospital bed. Potty and Rocko came late because they were informed they were leaving Port Moresby first thing in the morning and didn't want to miss saying goodbye. Rocko looked pretty good considering his neck wound. He was a stubby, gnat of a man in the first place, but hospital food had done him some

335

good. Potty on the other hand looked worst for the wear. His bouts with malaria were short but very intense, he admitted. *Bit like bein' boiled in a pot an' squeezed'ru' a bloody ringer.*

They chatted for a bit before Vic waved his visitors in closer, signaling, without realizing it, for *quiet voices.* Potty, always one for conspiracy, leaned in extra close.

"Ook' mates," Vic whispered, "ewe' kin' satisfy me' curiosity 'ight 'ere an' now." He looked at them before nodded to the right, down the ward. Both Potty and Rocko followed the motion although they couldn't see anything so close to Vic. "Any Yanks 'own there? Any MPs?"

Rocko, close to the end of the bed, backed up and peered down in that direction. He lifted his free hand in a half-hearted wave, grimacing as he came around close to Vic's bed again.

"Aye', des' a Yank MP doon' da' way—noot' a friendly chap, 'fraid!" He shook his head in obvious irritation. "Aye, they all be bastards, 'suppose. Aussie, Brit or Yank!"

"Aye' see," sighed Vic. "Won't be keen on ewe' lookin' in on 'is patient, 'suppose, aye'? Kin' ya' see anythin' at ta', mate?"

"Naw, Vic, patients' goot' a wall on un' side an' two screens un' the three 'oopen 'ides."

Vic let it go, talking to his old friends until Katie, Sue and a couple of medical orderlies started to bring in supper for the few patients who could actually eat. Normally visitors had to leave during meal periods, but Katie saw Potty and she returned his enthusiastic wave. *Stay out of sight,* she said cheerfully, under her breath. Potty watched the nurses and the orderlies pull the trays out of a large central warmer, and had an idea. He winked at Vic and Rocko and casually pulled a tray of food out of the warmer when the nurses and orderlies were not looking. Vic watched Potty disappear down towards the end of the ward where the MP was. Rocko started to follow him but Vic instinctively pulled him back.

Vic heard the surprised verbal warning, obviously from the MP and the scuffling of a chair being pushed back. "Wait a minute! Hold it right there, pal! Don't come any closer! I have a prisoner in this bed!"

"Orry' mate!" This was Potty, apologetic as hell, "Ought' ewe' 'ight want a spot o' 'nner, goot' some spare!"

"Just—just, get back, 'fella! I'm on duty, you can't come any closer, hear? You do, one more step, I'm authorized ta' shoot ya'! Now get da' hell back, goddamn it!"

"What's goin' on!" Vic could hear Katie's voice, obviously distressed. "What are you doing handing out food, Corporal Johnson?"

336

"Goddamn it, Lieutenant, ya' got to get these guys away from my prisoner!"

"I'm sorry, Corporal Smith, I don't think he meant any harm, he probably thought you were hungry!"

"There's not supposed to be any visitors here, Lieutenant, this is a special prisoner, and I have to report this!"

"Do what you have to do, Corporal. I'm sure it was a mistake, but it's my fault, do you understand? I take full responsibility."

"Yes 'mam. But you have to report this immediately to Sergeant Kolinsky who will inform Lieutenant Barrow. Those are my orders, anybody approaches the prisoner other than medical staff has to be reported. I can't leave the prisoner, I have to ask you to call Sergeant Kolinsky. He's my immediate supervisor, Lieutenant."

Katie McCutcheon suddenly appeared in front of Vic's bed with Potty in her firm grasp. She plucked the plate out of his hand. She was not smiling, and her anger was pointed towards Potty and Vic.

"I hope you didn't set him to do this, Sergeant Hickey! Your men have to leave now, and I mean now. Get them out of here before the MPs arrive, or I guarantee these two will not be on any plane tomorrow, they will be in the stockade until this is cleared up. This is my fault. No one is supposed to be in this ward during meal periods in general, but I thought you would have enough sense to keep your head down. I was obviously wrong!"

Vic tried to apologize but if fell on deaf ears. Katie had already stormed away. He looked at Potty sheepishly, hoping to come up with a clever final comment before his men left him. Instead he was met with Potty staring at him as if he had seen a ghost.

"Preciate' what ewe' were tryin' ta' do, Pot, aye' really do!" Potty said nothing, just stared, his face drained of blood. It took a few seconds for Vic to realize something was wrong.

"Whad' ya' see doon' there, Pot?"

337

CHAPTER 29

December 11, 1942, 166th Station Hospital

Once the supper trays were delivered and patients were set up to eat, Katie McCutcheon went to find the MP Sergeant. She didn't want the MP to get in trouble, as she already knew Lieutenant Barrow was an asshole from previous dealings with him. Less than 10 of the patients could actually eat food, with most of them needing assistance, so she needed to get back to help Sue Culpepper and the medical orderlies. Katie stalled as long as she could until she was certain Sergeant Hickey's two visitors were gone. The Australian medic, Corporal Johnson, appeared quite upset and had to be led out by his buddy who was in the neck and shoulder cast.

She called for Sergeant Kolinsky on the phone but got Lieutenant Barrow instead, who was unpleasant and kept interrupting her, finally stating he was wasting his time talking to a nurse and would be coming down to detain and question the Australian soldier visitors. When she coldly told Barrow there was no one to question and the soldiers were gone, she could tell he was speechless. The phone went dead because he was obviously furious. *You let them go?* Lieutenant Barrow was a First Lieutenant and outranked her but his attitude was more than Katie could stomach. *Did you get their names and unit?* She explained with as much ice in her voice as she could, she had no idea who they were. They were visitors of one of her patients, and the entire episode was a misunderstanding, nothing more. The Australian soldier in question thought he was doing the MP a favor. Once he was confronted by the MP, who was doing his job, the Australian soldier returned to the bedside of his friend. They needed to leave so they did.

Barrow then wanted to come down to talk to the Australian soldier in the ward, figuring the soldier would know what units the Australian soldiers were from. Katie swallowed her pride and softened her tone, trying anything to keep Barrow out of the ward. She informed him the patient was severely injured and was probably not even aware of what occurred. What possible point was there in questioning these men, these *allied soldiers* who might take offense to the implications of the probe? She was careful not to mention Vic Hickey's name, hoping Barrow was not aware who he was or where he was in the ward. Sitting up or lying down, Vic was wearing the same blue pajamas as all the rest of the patients and no one would know he was an Aussie until he opened his mouth.

Well, there shouldn't be any visitors at all with a damn important

338

Jap prisoner right there in the ward. Most of those guys layin' in the beds were killin' Japs a week ago and had buddies killed by Japs. The patients are pretty quiet, I grant you that, most of em'. But visitors are a different story, they're all up and walkin' around. They could've killed my MP and the Jap in a heartbeat, dolly, I mean in a goddamn heartbeat!

Katie held her tongue and waited, hoping. There was a long silence on the line, then a heavy sigh. She could hear the metallic rapping of something metal against the receiver as he made up his mind.

Okay, what's done is done. We should've moved this prisoner to the POW room days ago, but one of your docs says he can't get the care he needs over there. Fine. He's not getting the security he needs in your goddamn ward. That's gonna' change right now! I'm responsible for this prisoner and nothing is going to happen to him before we get a chance to talk to em'. I'm gonna' talk to the hospital commander right now and get another MP standing on that ward door, dolly, and I mean in about 20 minutes. No more visitors for anybody without clearance from me. Nobody in and out except medical personal assigned to that ward. Is that clear enough, Lieutenant?

Katie returned to the ward exhausted, frustrated and fit to be tied. She took it, as far as she was concerned, because she had too. They wanted to keep the whole damn thing hush hush and they got it. What did they expect when they plop an enemy soldier right in the middle of a bunch of wounded soldiers? But at the same time she knew it was her fault too, she didn't take the issue seriously enough to consider those very ramifications. *How stupid can a girl get? AND that SON OF A BITCH called me DOLLY two goddamn times! The nerve of the prick!*

First thing Katie went down to the end of the ward to see Corporal Smith, the MP. Sue Culpepper could see Katie was upset, and tried to ease her agitation by giving her the "OK" sign. Dinner was under control. Katie told Smith Lieutenant Barrow was informed of the incident. That was the extent of her report to Smith, who seemed disappointed when he was informed Barrow was not coming down as far as Katie was aware. The incident was closed. Since she was there, she told Smith she needed to check up on the Japanese prisoner. The prisoner was no long visible until you walked around the dividers. The opening used to be at the foot of the bed, so the patient could be seen if you were about six feet away coming down the middle of the ward. The MP apparently slid the side divider to the front, creating an enclosed box around the bed except at the top of the bed near the wall. The MP now had his chair by the small opening.

"Did you move the divider?" Katie asked.

"Yes mam." The MP glanced at her defiantly before following her around the divider. Katie stopped and visually examined the prisoner before checking his vitals and fluid flows. His respiration seemed fast, but what caught her eye was the fluttering of the eyelids. She pulled the penlight from her pocket and lifted an eyelid as she flashed the light. The eyelid blinked once or twice and for a fraction of a second the pupil moved to track her face until she released the eyelid. The eyelid continued to flutter for a few moments before growing still. She opened the other eyelid with one hand without the light, watching the pupil roll back and stay there. She went back to the first eye and opened the eyelid again without the light, watching the pupil roll up and stay there. Once again she released the eyelid, watching it flutter after a few seconds.

The MP, who was apparently under instructions to watch her hands like a hawk, did just that and missed it. She decided right then and there she needed to come back later with Sue Culpepper.

"Okay, Corporal, we need to roll this patient over in a little while, the routine thing, so I have to get the other nurse and an orderly if one's available. We'll be back in about 30 minutes." Katie stepped back and looked at the prisoner's restraints, after lifting the blanket and viewing the body. This man couldn't weigh more than 100 pounds dripping wet, he was so wasted away. She put the blanket down and stared hard at the face, noticing for the first time the rippled scars on both cheeks under the whispy beard. *Whatever he is, this one is awake.*

Katie walked along the beds until she came up to Vic Hickey's. She wanted to be there in case Lieutenant Barrow came along with his additional MP. Nobody was going to mess with her patients, nobody, especially Barrow. Sue Culpepper was coming over with bowls of extra rice pudding and put them in Katie's hands.

"Here, you take over, Katie. Sergeant Hickey is pulling the hollow leg trick again!" Sue could see Katie was still upset, so she leaned in close. "That jerk Barrow yank your chain up and down the hall?"

Katie smiled thinly and nodded, walking over to Vic's bedside, pulling up the chair they used for their chats, placing the rice pudding on his tray table. Hopeful, Vic put his spoon down and cleared his throat until Katie looked up.

"Ook' 'ere, Katie—I mean, Leftenant—I really am 'orry 'bout all this. 'Orry me an' my mates got ewe' n' trouble. Ah' ole' Pot was tryin' ta' do was figur' who da' prisona' was. Well, he 'ound out, an' it bout' kilt em'! It's a matta' of coincidence—impossible coincidence—if ats' true!"

"What do you mean, Sergeant?"

There was a commotion at the main door, so Katie held up her hand and peeked around the wall. She saw Lieutenant Barrow, one of the surgeons, a nursing supervisor and a couple of MPs. Katie told Vic quietly to pretend he was asleep and lay still no matter what. Katie, as she expected, was not consulted as the group was lectured by Barrow. She walked casually across the ward and checked the chart on a sedated patient, watching the nursing supervisor out of the corner of her eye nod her head like a damned Chinese puppet. Barrow was doing all the talking. After a couple of minutes the entire entourage walked down the ward towards the prisoner's bed. Sue Culpepper was captured to join the group and the nursing supervisor gave Katie the 'come along' with her index finger. Katie sighed and tagged along, noticing Barrow giving Vic Hickey the once over and totally ignoring her.

After 10 minutes everyone was gone. The nursing shift supervisor, who was a 166th nurse, knew Katie and Sue were 153rd volunteers so she demonstrated her displeasure by not saying a word to them. The night nurse came on and Sue went to dinner, promising to return in half an hour to help Katie turn the prisoner. Katie didn't mention to Sue she believed the prisoner was awake and pretending to be unconscious. Katie went to the double doors and peeked outside, and sure enough an MP stood there. He nodded respectively and Katie nodded back. She was hungry but her curiosity was aroused so she came back and tapped on Vic's hand. He opened his eyes carefully then smiled warmly when he recognized her.

"The arse 'as gone away?"

"The arse' has gone away, thank God! Now tell me again about this coincidence?"

"Aren't ya' gonna' get sum' suppa'?"

"I'm okay. Come on, tell me."

Vic told her the story *of their* Jap prisoner and the battle by the waterfall. He told her of their blocking force catching the Japs on the road, and the discovery of the wounded Jap in the forest. *We were shootin' the survivors, an' if it were up ta' me, I woulda' shot im' too!* He explained how Lieutenant Edwards wanted a prisoner and this one was an officer. He told her how Potty took it upon himself to treat the Jap just like any other wounded soldier, including swabbing out his eyes so he could see, and shooting him up with morphine for pain.

"Ad' ta' leave em' at Alola, no translators so we couldn't interrogate im' proper, an' in the end no one to 'arry im' out, so we left em' fur' the Japs ta' find. 'Ought that was the end of it until we 'ought da' Japs agin' at Mission Ridge! We were some of da' 'ast ta' 'scape down a secret Track, but Pot, 'arryin' some 'ounded, ran inta' Japs who kilt the men 'round em' with 'ayonets. When a couple of em' tried ta' stab ole' Pot, this Jap—this prisona' he fixed up, recognized ole' Pot, an' tried ta' stop em'. When they didn't stop, he kilt em' both with a pistol!

341

'Ard ta' elieve', but I 'elieve Pot when he says that's what 'appened!"

Katie was ahead of him, her eyes wide. She glanced down the ward and back to Vic, the question on her lips.

"You mean, Corporal Johnson—er, Pot—Potty, as you call him, thinks our prisoner is the same man?"

"Pot says 'ees one an' da' same! He saw em' at bout' two meters, says there's no doubt in is' mind. The man 'aved 'is bloody 'ife, so aye' 'uppose you would 'emember." Vic looked at Katie thoughtfully, and smiled.

"Ewe' seen im', Katie? Kin' ewe' check a thing er' two fur' me? Eee's got some scars on 'is 'ace, like big stars, from some 'urgery, sewin' 'is 'ace oop. Shot thru 'oth 'cheeks. Aye've 'een 'im too, 'lose 'oop." Katie nodded as he spoke, then touched her face with her fingertips.

"That is amazing! So amazing for—Corporal Johnson—I mean, Potty. I'm so glad for him. But I don't need to check, Sergeant. I've seen them, the scars. They're big, one is bigger than the other, and I recognize them as bullet wounds. He had some rough field surgery on both cheeks, lots of scarring."

Vic stared at her for a moment before slowly shaking his head in disbelief.

"Awl' be a bloody ape if awed' 'elieve it myself if awed' didn't know it ta' be true."

Katie thought about this in silence before glancing over at Vic guardedly. He had a distant look in his face, but he seemed to sense what Katie was thinking.

"I don't know if you remember this at all, Sergeant, but about a week ago when they first brought the prisoner in, somebody accidently told you he was a Jap officer and you—you reacted violently. Do you remember?"

"No," said Vic honestly, "Awe' don't 'member a thing. Wha— what did awe' do?"

"Oh, you acted like you would've jumped out of the bed and shot em', I think, if you had a gun, but you had the pulleys and things for your leg and hip, and of course you were in much worse shape then. I thought for sure you hurt yourself, the way you were carryin' on until you passed out. It took Lieutenant Crenshaw and me to keep you in the bed, and you were heavily sedated for a few days because of it. You caught the attention of the MP Lieutenant, that's for sure. I told em' some cock and bull story about how you and Lieutenant Crenshaw were buddies and you got excited somehow when you saw em'."

"Leftenant' Crenshaw, is e' the biscuit bomber pilot, the new

342

'atient doon' the hall?"

"One and the same, Sergeant."

"Awe' see." Vic peered over at Katie with what she saw suddenly as tired, sad eyes. She was struck again at how his brooding, strong features reminded her so much of her Uncle Ted. The dark eyes searched hers for a moment before he smiled.

"Ewe' don't need ta' worry 'bout me doin' anythin' foolish, Katie. Even if awe' could move 'bout, ah' wouldn't 'urt this Jap. If ee's the one who 'aved Potty's 'ife, ee's square with me."

Katie nodded and looked away.

Vic lay back in his pillows and closed his eyes as if he wanted to sleep. It was past 1900 hours, the new ward nurse was making her rounds, turning off unnecessary lights and increasing sedation. Katie wasn't sure how long she sat there in silence. She slowly stood up and leaned close to Vic, touching his hand gently. He opened his eyes slowly when he felt her hand.

"What 'appened to the Yank flyboy?"

"His plane was attacked by a Zero as they climbed out of Buna with a load of patients. Lieutenant Crenshaw was shot in the chest and hit by shrapnel in one eye and an arm. Luckily the plane wasn't disabled or anything and his co-pilot wasn't hurt as bad and flew them back down into the clouds."

"Awed' say ees' a lucky man, al' way 'round." Vic closed his eyes again and didn't open them again until Katie, who stayed close to him for a several minutes, finally walked away.

"A lucky man," he said to himself.

Katie glanced at her watch before rummaging around in the nurse's station for something to nibble on and then quietly walked up the ward towards Don Crenshaw's bed. The lights were already dimmed and the night nurse and orderly were tucking in the mosquito netting around each bed. She could see Don was asleep. They had to operate on his eyelid to smooth out some scaring that was causing him pain, so he was sedated most of the day. She looked up as Sue Culpepper approached. She had a spam sandwich wrapped in wax paper in her hand.

"For you," she said, smiling. "I don't think we're going to be doing this much longer. Barrow made such a stink about your uncooperativeness, the 166th may ask us to get on an airplane and go away."

"Oh?" Katie shrugged and accepted the sandwich. She looked at Sue and grew serious. "I wanted you to come back because we need to check the Japanese prisoner. I think he's awake, pretending to be unconscious." Sue was taken aback.

"Is he dangerous?"

"I don't know, but the MP is right there, he's got a gun. The prisoner is restrained but in order to turn him over we have to remove his restraints. If he's faking, he might try something."

"Damn it, Katie, is he dangerous?"

CHAPTER 30

December 11, 1942, 166th Station Hospital

There was so much activity as it got dark Hiroshi Takahashi was concerned they were coming for him. Normally as the evening progressed it became dim and quiet, the nurses or medics would roll him around, check his O2, vital signs and switch bottles with his IV and catheter. Once they closed the mosquito netting around his bed he wouldn't see anyone again for hours. He could hear the person who was sitting near him shift around in his chair, but this person rarely actually came around the dividers and looked in on him. Hiroshi never saw him because if the chair moved and he sensed footsteps, he feigned unconsciousness. It was probably a guard. Once it got late enough they dimmed the ward lights down almost to twilight. Hiroshi would open his eyes very slowly to peek through his eyelashes until he was certain no one was nearby. Anyone standing outside the mosquito netting would be hard pressed to see his eyes in the dim light, he suspected, but he took no chances. Any sound of footsteps ensured his eyes were closed.

He sensed clarity of thought not experienced by him in months. The unavailability of *Shabu*, of *Nekome-jo* and even *Totsugeki-jo* no longer mattered. What he did know was a veil of some kind was lifted from his consciousness. The first real step came when he was able to distinguish between his dreams and reality. Now even with the morphine he knew was in the IV, his thoughts were no longer clouded with a surrounding fog. He could think about things and not immediately get tired. The dark, bloody dreams didn't automatically intervene to pull him back and down to fearful wakefulness. That was the biggest thing, he could think without fear.

Lying in the bed he felt he was transported from some hellish place where his soul was taken from him. The sense of relief, of rescue was strong, but to where? He was a Japanese Imperial Army officer, a professional, a disciple of Bushido, a soldier in training for nearly a decade to honor his masters and his Emperor. What happened? What happened under the guidance of a true Samurai, Captain Hashimoto? Did he not try to follow in his master's footsteps? Did he not perform the duty as required of him, whether it was Hashimoto, Lieutenant Shamada, Warrant Officer Miyamoto or even General Horii? Did they not teach him what it meant to be a warrior? Did these men not die in honor for the glory of Japan and the Emperor? What was once so clear cut in his mind was no longer so.

Was there honor in death, such as his own death, when you caused the death of your fellow warriors? Hiroshi killed Miyamoto and Sergeant Inoue when they attempted to kill the Australian *kangohei,* the medic who offered kindness to him, and probably saved his life. Hiroshi saved the Australian in turn for saving his life, but took the lives of two of his countrymen to do it. *What madness is that?*

What was crazy was the strange dream he experienced earlier in the day, revealing how his guilt over the incident was still very much with him. At least he knew it was a dream, he could distinguish that now. In the dream he saw the Australian *kangohei,* well and in a different uniform, coming right up to him carrying something flat in his hands, right here in this hospital. In the dream Hiroshi had his eyes open as the Australian came closer, and there was no doubt the man recognized him. He seemed shocked, but was almost immediately confronted by Miyamoto, also in a different uniform. The rolls seemed to be reversed, like Miyamoto was trying to protect Hiroshi. Miyamoto kept his hand on his holster but didn't draw his pistol, speaking loudly to the Australian. He just couldn't understand what they were saying. In the dream the Australian backed away from the divider and disappeared from sight. It seemed so real. Hiroshi woke up later to cautiously open his eyes. The dividers around his bed were all enclosed, there was no way he could have seen the Australian if he wanted to. He knew then it was a dream. He had no idea what it meant, other than Miyamoto was his protector and the guilt he felt was heavy and painful.

Hiroshi could smell the food as they brought it around for some of the patients. There was nothing for patients who were unconscious. They must be feeding him through the IV. It had been so long since he actually ate anything, he could only guess at what the cooked food items were. Some type of meat tonight, perhaps pork. He was beyond the sense of hunger responding to food odors, the dullness in his gut matching his lack of interest. The smells were pleasant but seemed of little consequence. All he knew was his situation was safe for now. He was afraid and wanted to hold out as long as he could. His fear was the enemy considered him more valuable than he really was. He was nothing, with nothing to tell them whatsoever.

In Buna he was no longer part of the command staff and not involved in any of the defensive strategy. A castoff survivor of *Nankai Shitai,* he was deemed useless by the new troops coming from Rabaul. They were respectful because he was an officer, but he wasn't in their chain of command and had no duties. No one knew what to do with him. It made it hard because he couldn't occupy his mind with tasks. He helped dig out the bunker when the bomb explosions collapsed walls, and reset the heavy timbered logs offering the only protection they had.

Their world involved inches of dirt and wood, in some cases stopping or slowing down hot metal whizzing around, getting closer and closer and sometimes men died.

As the attacks came more frequently with infantry assaults following, they couldn't even step out of the bunkers anymore. No one wanted to think about the flamethrowers some of the Australians and Americans carried. If they spotted an enemy carrying the canisters, he was a very special target. Hiroshi was in the same bunker for several days, waiting, like all the rest, for the final bombs to come to end it for them. It was still preferable to the flamethrowers. In either case, they eventually understood they would not survive. There were no barges, no evacuation plan for them. He watched the boys, the young strangers all around him, grow sullen and fearful. Many begin to talk about suicide. In his bunker he was the only officer, so they whispered these thoughts among themselves. He said nothing.

The bombs came and somehow he survived. The Allies pulled his body out with all the rest but he was alive. He could not explain why the Australians or Americans did not simply leave him there or roll him into the common grave with his dead colleagues. He had no idea how many days he was in the bunker with the dead, or how long he had been in this hospital, but he wanted to get his strength back before he faced whatever was coming. He thought he got the act down pretty well, breathing slowly, rolling his eyes towards the back of his head when he sensed they were going to pry his eyelids apart.

When the large group of people converged on his bed he almost panicked. Not a soul touched him, but he sensed their presence and stares. They didn't stay long, but they whispered with agitation and anger, one of them still arguing as they walked away. It took hours before he could breathe normally. As evening fell, the lights were dimmed and the mosquito net was tucked in around his bed. He finally relaxed. Hiroshi was thinking about his company, First Company, an organization and a group of men who no longer existed. He missed them. With his brain and memory functioning so well, he tried hard to remember their names and faces. He knew he was no coward to his men; he stood his ground when the Australians swept their positions time and time again as they fought their holding action down the Kokoda. But he couldn't shake the sense of guilt in his heart he had let them down. Every day there were fewer men lying in the cold wet mud next to him. They believed in him, just as Lieutenant Shamada tried to explain to him long ago when Hiroshi took over the platoon. They believed in him all the way to their graves. *Just as he believed in Captain Hashimoto and General Horii.*

The voices were right outside of the dividers before he was even aware they were there. He clamped his eyes closed just as the nurses and the MP came around to his bedside. It was late. This was not normal, so Hiroshi was very alert. Someone turned on the gooseneck lamp attached to the wall, flooding his bed with light. He pressed his eyelids down hard, trying to focus on not opening his eyes despite the light. He could hear three different voices around the bed, two feminine and one male. He could feel the cool, slim hands of one of the nurses as she pulled the sheet away from his body. The two nurses were whispering, but both seemed agitated as they touched his restraints. He felt one restraint, the one for his right wrist being removed, then the one for his right leg. He felt one of the nurses bumping her way around the bed to the other side, but as she started to release the left wrist restraint the other nurse said something harsh to her. He sensed the hand coming to his face and rolled his eyes up in his head as both eyelids were peeled back accompanied by a bright light.

It hurt and the light was blinding. Instinctively he blinked and jerked his head when a hand reached for his eyes. His right hand was free so he reacted naturally in pushing the hand away. Hiroshi glanced up into the frightened eyes of a nurse who was trying to corral his right hand. He lifted his head and upper body and was surprised when his left wrist restraint came off. Both arms had IVs inserted and now another nurse was pressing in on the left side trying to push him down. Hiroshi, already out of breath, kicked out with his free right leg and connected with someone, who grunted with pain. His oxygen mask slipped off. An American soldier brushed the nurse aside to throw his body weight against Hiroshi, slamming him back down on the bed.

The nurse on the left pinned Hiroshi's arm down but Hiroshi watched the American soldier push himself back far enough to draw his sidearm. It came up on his left side and Hiroshi gasped as the big bore of the American .45 pistol swung towards his chest. Hiroshi, his right hand free again, shoved the barrel away to his left as he faded. There was a brilliant flash of light then blackness.

CHAPTER 31

December 11, 1942, 166th Station Hospital

Vic Hickey was not asleep. Despite the evening sedation he was alert. He lay back in the darkness, thinking about Potty, his father and Katie McCutcheon. The American surgeon was noncommittal earlier in the day to Vic's inquiry about regaining the full use of his right leg. He shattered his femur, which was healing well, but bullets severed the sciatic nerve in his thigh and below his knee. *This would take time to heal*, the doc said slowly, *months before it will be known if you can walk normally.* As soon as he was transported to Australia he would begin intensive neurological therapy, whatever that meant. It was beginning to dawn on Vic he might very well end up a cripple, a man unable to do the simple things like walk down the street without a cane—or worse. Leaving the Army certainly didn't bother him, although he would miss his men. However he always assumed, with the brash optimism of young, healthy men, he would return from the war with a ribbon or two for the Returned Services League clubs, and walk right back into his old job at Ford. *Crimey*, he sighed, *would they take me back?* As a supervisor he had to walk the shop floor, for kilometers on some days. How the bloody hell could he do that if he has a gimp leg?

He lay still as Katie McCutcheon and Sue Culpepper walked purposely down the dimly-lit ward. Neither of them looked his way, no doubt assuming he was asleep like most of the other patients. They were whispering but there was a disagreement between them. He never heard them argue before, so it made him upset. In a few days he would be flown out of Port Moresby for home. The nurses said they understood Australian wounded men were sent to the Australian Army Hospital closest to the soldier's home. His home was in Victoria in the south so he would never see Katie again, since she told him the 153rd was returning to Southport, near Brisbane in Queensland. This depressed him, but he knew it was for the best. Best to cut the ties as cleanly as he could, as soon as he could. *She's aye' bloody officer, ewe' old 'ool*, he thought most uncharitably, *an'there's no gettin' 'round that in 'is 'orld! Fraternization, they 'alled it. 'an't 'appen'!*

From his screened in corner he noted the extra light filtering back down the ward. Katie and Sue had turned on one of the lights over somebody's bed. There was a sudden physical commotion from that direction, so Vic pushed himself up with his elbows. A moment later a deafening blast, a gunshot, echoed through the ward. His ears buzzed. Stunned, he tried to comprehend what just happened. *.45 caliber—he* thought finally, as his brain engaged and fear raced up his spine. *Katie is down there. So is that Jap prisoner!*

There was chaotic screaming down at the end of the ward, soon accompanied by the screams and moans of patients frightened out of their wits from the gunfire. The overhead ward lights flicked full on, bathing the space with yellow glow. The ward night nurse and medical orderly approached cautiously down the ward, slowing as they got closer. The nurse stopped and called out meekly, *is everybody okay?*

A male voice called out: *we're okay, but we have a casualty.* The MP guarding the door rushed in, his face flushed red with his weapon drawn. He slowed when he saw the nurse and orderly stopped. When they saw him, they pointed down the ward and waited for him to go first. A few seconds later they were overwhelmed as other nurses and doctors rushed in, asking the same questions: *What happened? What just happened?* Two more MPs arrived with guns drawn to join the melee. Vic watched an empty gurney wheel by as he pulled his body more erect, frantically deciding if he could possibly get out of the bed. The stabbing pain in his hip and leg as he twisted to see better took his breath away. His lung ached from the deep breathes he was taking and he grew dizzy, but he forced himself to stay up so could see, worried sick about Katie.

A cluster of doctors and nurses wheeled the gurney back up the ward. It was hard to see through the mosquito net. He couldn't identify a face with all the people around the gurney, but he saw a flash of pale skin and a breast, with huge bright red splotches soaking through a white cotton bandage. The thin legs were half in the khaki cotton coveralls the nurses wore. Vic frantically searched the surrounding nurses and doctors, hoping until he spotted the unraveled blond tresses of Sue Culpepper, there was no missing those. His heart sunk like a lead stone and he fell slowly back into the bed. Only two nurses went down the ward, Sue and Katie. They wheeled the gurney right past Vic without anyone so much as giving him a glance.

Vic knew he must have slept or passed out because when he awoke the ward was dark and still again, as if nothing happened. For a moment or two he hopefully considered the possibility it was all a dream, until he heard someone stir next to his bed. He turned and tugged at the mosquito netting until whoever it was sitting there helped him push a part of it aside. It was Sue Culpepper. Even in the dim twilight he could see the sunken eyes of a person who had been crying and suffering. Their eyes met and Vic reached out with his big paw. Sue gripped it with both hands and pressed her head against the raised bed rails.

"Aye's she gone, Sue?" he asked quietly. She pressed hard on his hand as her head bobbed in the affirmative. Vic closed his eyes for a moment, and took a deep, painful breath. He opened his eyes, but they flashed dark and intense.

"Kin' ya' tell me what 'appened doon' there? As' it the Jap that done it? 'Cause if it's true he won't see da' mornin' sun." Sue lifted her head and stared hard at Vic. He couldn't see the blue in her eyes but he saw the unblinking glint in them.

"No, it wasn't the Jap's fault, Sergeant. It was all of us. We approached him all wrong because Katie thought he was faking it. We needed to turn him in his bed and unstrap him, but if he was awake and faking it I thought he might be dangerous, so we asked the MP to be ready. I think we just needed to give him a big dose of morphine to knock him out and not worry about it, and I should have insisted. But Katie wanted to make sure. Anyway, we weren't very coordinated and we had him half unstrapped when we checked his eyes with a bright flashlight. He was faking it, the bright light bothered him, and instinctively he blinked and tried to wave the flashlight out of his eyes. He could do that because we had unstrapped one of his hands." Sue stopped to take a deep breath, shaking her head from the memory.

"I don't know what we were thinkin'. I was on his right side and tried to grab his arm, then somehow the left restraint failed and he started to push himself up and kicked the MP. Katie was around on the left. The MP brushed me out of the way as he dove on the Jap, knocking the wind out of him. Then the MP decided to step back and pull out his gun and point it at the Jap. He said he wasn't intending to shoot the guy, just scare him enough to stop fighting us. When he pointed his pistol at the Jap the Jap must've thought he was gonna' get shot, so he pushed the barrel away to the left with his right hand, which I had let go of when the MP pushed me away. God all mighty, what have we done!"

"So the MP 'ad 'is 'inger on the trigger as the Jap 'ushed it away?" Sue nodded slowly, her head down.

"He must have, I was right there. Katie was leaning over the bed wresting his arm down and she was hit in the sternum. She didn't have a chance. I—I don't think she suffered much."

"Know what 'appened ta' da' Jap?" Vic said after a long pause.

"The MP clubbed him in the head with the pistol and damn near killed em'. He's gone, probably in surgery. But he won't be coming back here! They'll move him somewhere else for security reasons." Sue looked up, Vic could feel her eyes watching him.

"So he's gone, Sergeant. Most of the patients have no idea what happened, and I've been told to keep my mouth shut. I have no idea what the Army plans on telling Katie's parents. As far as the Army is concerned, you don't know anything about it either. You were asleep." Vic could just see the hint of a sad smile on her face.

"But you're a Digger, and none of these guys can really tell you what to do. And I know you cared a lot for Katie." Vic snorted, not really knowing why, other than maybe acknowledging she was speaking the truth. He sighed and laid his head back.

"What 'ya think aye' 'hould do, Sue? Iffen' it was ah' accident, what's ta' do? Katie's gone in any case, aye?"

"Aye. She's gone in any case." They didn't say anything for a few minutes.

"Well, Sergeant, I need to get some sleep. I'm done. I won't be coming back in the morning. The 166th is taking over the ward. I guess this was the kicker. They want all of us gone so they can sweep this under the rug. They've relieved me and are gonna' ship me back to Australia and as far away from this place as they can get me."

He felt the squeeze of her hands as she stood up. She leaned inside the mosquito netting and planted a sweet gentle kiss on his cheek. He could smell her scent, some kind of soap, but no matter. The blond tresses brushed his chin and were gone.

"Alm' gonna' miss you 'ovely sheilas, aye' know!"

"Goodnight Sergeant!"

352

CHAPTER 32

December 14, 1942, Seven Mile airfield, Port Moresby

They woke them up early, fed them before gently placing them on gurneys. The new nurses, all from the 166th, were cool and professional. Nobody called Don Crenshaw 'Don' anymore, it was Lieutenant this or Lieutenant that. Not a whole lot of small talk with these ladies. He was on his way out, just another patient in a bed soon to be replaced with someone else. They wheeled a bunch of them down the corridors until they came to some kind of holding area. Don vaguely remembered it after a few minutes. He walked through it once looking for Katie. He had no recollection of coming through as a patient. It was stripped bare, nothing but double screened doors and clear space, the transition area where the ambulances loaded or unloaded their patients. The thrumming sound on the metal roof declared it was raining, hard.

All of them were deemed 'air transportable', most conscious and aware of their surroundings. It seemed to Don many of the patients were from his ward. Despite the rain and time of day it was hot and humid. As the big double doors were swung back exposing the portico and waiting ambulances, Don felt the damp wave of tropical moisture brush across his face. *The wet.* There was no getting away from it in this place. He wasn't going to miss the humidity and the stink of rot. Just weeks before when he was still flying he remembered the early morning starts. Most of the nasty storms gathered in the afternoon as the thunderstorms developed all around the Owen Stanley ridges. In the mornings it rained sometimes but there was less wind. The clouds, as you punched through them were benign and less turbulent. The Australian flight, which he never got a chance to do, always departed in the morning. It was about a seven hour flight, so if they got off early and didn't have to divert too much around weather, they could make the run to Townsville and sometimes on to Brisbane before sunset.

Other than the business with Katie McCutcheon, Don was feeling pretty good. The IV was out and he only wore a small gauze patch taped to his eye socket. He could move his eyes without much pain now, but they still kept his right eye saturated with ointment because of the friction from the moving orb and the injured tissue. His left elbow, fractured and torn by some hot chunk of cannon shell, was healing nicely and only loosely hung with a sling. He couldn't bend the elbow yet, but his hand worked fine. His lung wound was now just a small slit scar on both the front and back of his chest, and only hurt when he breathed hard.

The fast moving 7.7 copper-jacketed round had punched through the instrument panel and right through Don, skewering his lung and out his back, lodging itself in his seat. Oddly enough, the exit wound was smaller than the entrance wound, and almost sealed itself. He was remarkably lucky, the docs exclaimed. Normally a double penetration through the lung walls meant more air was escaping then could be drawn in, and was therefore often fatal if the air loss couldn't be plugged up. Don didn't know what to say to such a pronouncement. He was feeling poorly anyway you looked at it and hit in three places. *You damned right he was lucky.*

The Jap pilot had only a second or two to depress his nose for his best target, a partial deflection shot hosing the cockpit. His guns were armed, so the SOB was hunting them, following them and tried to guess where they were going to break out. If he'd come up behind them Don wouldn't be lying here thinking about it. But the Jap came up in front of them, nose to nose. With the closing speeds he could only squeeze the trigger for a second and then move the stick over so they wouldn't collide. No suicide plans for that guy. But he could have killed both Jack and him, or missed and shot up one of their engines or fuel tanks. You just don't survive encounters with Jap fighters in clear air flying gooney birds, you just don't. Thank god for Jack diving us back into the clouds, thank god for Jack not losing his cool. Don sighed and shook his head just thinking about it. *You damned right he was lucky.*

He tried not to think about Katie too much, it was still an impossible thing to contemplate. He didn't witness it, didn't have the trauma of viewing her body. Don remembered their last conversation as brief, breezy and casual, just as he was wheeled away for his surgery. She was alive, whole and a woman he wanted. It was the way of the war, people simply disappeared sometimes. His guilt of not being there for her wouldn't go away. He was sedated that night from his little surgical procedure removing some scar tissue and slept through the whole thing. Sue Culpepper, when she came in one evening to visit, said it was total chaos for a little while, with the gunshot and patients dragged out of sleep or sedation screaming in fear. Don was sedated, lightly sedated according to Sue, but never woke up. It made him feel like a heel.

The first he knew something was wrong was in the morning, when he encountered the new nurses. They played dumb and never got out of character. When Don asked about Katie and Sue the new 166th nurses stated the 153rd nurses were gone, probably back to Australia. They wouldn't talk about it and were visibly cool to Sue when she did come around. Sue told him in private she was ordered not to discuss the issue with anyone. She was in violation speaking to him about it, but he

354

had a right to know, she said. The only other patient who knew what happened was the Australian, Sergeant Hickey, because Sue told him. Don vaguely remembered him, but didn't think much about it. *I guess there wasn't a funeral or anything,* Don said lamely. *No*, Sue said shaking her head. *Nothing. They whisked her body away and ordered the hush hush.*

Don was one of the first loaded into the plane, right up near the cockpit. When they left the hospital they were each transferred from a gurney to a stretcher. By the time the ambulances were loaded and they drove out to Seven Mile airfield, the rain had stopped. It was still very grey and the clouds were low and full of moisture, he could tell, but it was good to be unloaded from the ambulance and not drenched by heavy raindrops. He knew from experience, because in half an hour you'd be at altitude and freezing your ass off with your wet clothes. There was no half-way or comfort in New Guinea. God, he hated this place. Don looked up as the pilots sauntered up the aisle, working their way up to the cockpit. *Well, look who's ridin' as a free passenger!* It was the squadron XO, not such a bad guy, but Don certainly didn't feel like talking to him much. He never did call Don about getting on the Australian flight list. Guess he won't be bothering to do it now. They chatted for a couple of minutes as the XO introduced Don to some other admin guy who never flew real missions, but was going to fly right seat to Australia. *Nice meeting you too, asshole.*

The C-47 is a tailwheel aircraft, so the tail sits lower than the main cabin when it's on the ground. Don propped himself up on his elbows to look further down the cabin, his head hitting the stretcher above him, hard making the occupant grunt.

"Sorry, buddy," he apologized.

"Iz' awe' right, mate, we be awe' most hoom'." The second he heard him Don leaned to the right, peering up trying to see the man above him.

"Hey, you an Aussie? Are you Sergeant Hickok?" Don watched the stretcher strain as the man above him shifted his body around until they could see each other. The man groaned, but kept moving. The Aussie stared down at Don for a few seconds then smiled. There was a pain and sadness in the smile.

"Hickey, Vic Hickey. Ewe' be the Yank flyboy. Aye' 'cognize yur' 'oice, suh. 'Ope the eye's awe' right."

"Oh, it's nothing, just got some cuts, I'll be okay to see again soon as they heal up." Don looked at Vic for a long time, realizing the Aussie was sizing him up somehow. The Aussie couldn't move farther so he slowly extended his right hand down to Don. Don looked at the hand, a huge paw, and shook it firmly.

"Alm' glad yur' be awe' right, suh. Be good ta' go 'ome. Ad' 'nough of this war."

"I don't know if I'm done, but I wouldn't complain if they shipped me back to the States."

Vic Hickey pulled his arm back up, shifting his weight to become more comfortable, but his eyes never left Don's.

"Alm' 'orry 'bout Leftenant' McCutcheon, suh'. Alm' gonna' miss 'er too. She 'as a sweet a Shiela as aye' ever knew, she was."

"Katie…"

"Katie."

Neither could finish the conversation, so Don slid back into his narrow stretcher and Vic Hickey did the same. After a few minutes Don pulled up again when he heard a commotion down by the tail near the double cargo doors. He could only see eight patients on this flight and all of them were loaded up forward. They were waiting for something. He couldn't believe his eyes as Sue Culpepper came up the aisle carrying charts and a checklist. She stowed her bag and walked right up to Don, beaming as she looked up at Vic Hickey.

"Hi fellas! Looks like you're still in my care for a little bit longer." Without caring to look who might be observing, Sue touched her fingers to her lips and then touched both Vic and Don's arms. She volunteered for an Australian flight and the 166th was more than glad to get rid of her, apparently, she said, grinning. They were only going with eight passengers on this flight because they were waiting for some special cargo. They chatted until Sue had to get busy, making sure the oxygen canisters for the patients who needed them were on board, and there were sufficient blankets when it started to get cold at altitude.

Don was in a lower stretcher hung just below the level of the windows. He didn't have one right next to his head, he was too far forward, but by lifting and twisting his head he could see out one window on the starboard side, and part of two on the port side. The main fuselage door was on the port side, the pilot's side, and he could see another ambulance backing up to the tail of the airplane. He also saw MPs approaching the airplane. Sue, who was also watching the ambulance approach, saw the MPs and stiffened. *Shit*, he saw the word form silently on her lips.

First Lieutenant Barrow climbed into the airplane and looked around. He saw Sue Culpepper and froze.

"Are you the duty nurse on this aircraft, Lieutenant?" he asked in disbelief.

"I am, Lieutenant Barrow. I volunteered since my orders are back to Australia." Barrow stood still for several seconds, staring.

"There must be some mistake," he seethed, his eyes suddenly darting over his shoulder at the ambulance. He turned back to Sue, his hands now on his hips. "You should not be here, goddamn it."

Another officer stepped aboard the aircraft. Don had to think for a second to remember his name. The intelligence officer, Captain Cox. Lieutenant Barrow motioned Cox to follow him outside, where an argument quickly ensued. The pilot, the XO, could hear the argument too and came out of the cockpit. He winked at Don and walked down the aisle. The XO, a major, wanted to resolve whatever the issue was as quickly as possible. The voice of the XO was now added to the argument, but it was brief. After another minute or so, the XO walked up the aisle again, his face a few shades of red. He stopped by Sue and put his hand on her shoulder in a familiar way, clearly noticed by both Vic Hickey and Don Crenshaw. The XO glanced down the aisle and out the windows before he spoke.

"Don't worry, Sue, you're goin' ta' Australia with us—that jackass MP can go fuck em' self, he has some problem with you being on board with his fuckin' prisoner."

"Prisoner?" Sue asked in a small voice, her eyes widening. She couldn't help herself and looked up at Vic Hickey. Their eyes met. The XO just shrugged, glancing at his watch.

"Yeah, some special Jap prisoner they're taking to Australia to a POW camp. I wouldn't worry about em', the intel guy, Captain Cox, says they have him shackled and he's well sedated. You have that kind of stuff on board, don't you?"

Lieutenant Barrow would not even glance in Sue's direction as the prisoner-patient's stretcher was hooked in place at the far end of the fuselage. The XO signed for the prisoner, and Sue took a deep breath and walked down the aisle to examine him. The prisoner still had a sizeable bandage on his nose where the MP had clubbed him with his .45 pistol. His hands were well secured and handcuffed to the stretcher poles, as were his stick-thin ankles. One IV was inserted. Lieutenant Barrow spoke quietly to the MP assigned to be with the prisoner on the flight, then turned on his heels and left. Captain Cox, the intelligence officer, looked at Sue Culpepper for a moment then smiled.

"I'm sorry about the disturbance. Lieutenant Barrow can be a pain in the ass. He thinks you might be a threat to the prisoner because of what happened to Lieutenant McCutcheon."

"I don't hold anything against this man, it was an accident. It was as much our fault as anybody's."

"That's what you said in the inquest and I believe you." Cox glanced down at the prisoner for one last time then turned to go. Sue touched his arm and he stopped.

"What's going to happen to this prisoner, Captain?" Cox pursed his lips, his eyes moving up the cabin where the pilots were settling into the cockpit. He looked back at Sue, noting the deep shadows under her brilliant blue eyes.

"We asked him some questions through an interpreter, but he's a confused fellow. It's hard to distinguish the truth from fantasy in his head. He was part of the command staff for General Horii on the Kokoda Track. We discovered his name with some buried official documents, so we were pretty excited when we captured him. But he's gone through a lot, this might take some time, and by the time we get some useful information out of him, it won't matter. We tried some drugs to induce— talkativeness, I guess is the way to describe it. Drugs do funny things to people, and this fella was way out there in no time. It was like he lived in a dream world, and when we drugged him he went straight there. Sometimes this incredible stuff came out, and you could tell he just hated himself for whatever he did. He lived his own hell, that's for sure."

Cox knew he needed to help this woman find some peace in the death of her friend, he could tell by the growing look of horror in her face.

"Look, Lieutenant, don't get me wrong, here. We learned a lot— make no mistake about it, and we'll learn more from him once we get him healed up some. These Japs on the Kokoda were special soldiers. They did impossible things getting up to the Kokoda. Once they realized they couldn't make Port Moresby, they retreated, but it was hell on earth for them, hell on earth. They were starving to death, but still fought the Aussies like maniacs. What makes people do that? Understanding these guys help us understand our enemy, so we can beat em'. It just takes time. Once these guys realize we don't intend to kill them, they come around."

Sue was no longer listening, he could tell, but she kept her eyes on him and slowly nodded her head.

"Lieutenant McCutcheon did her job, Lieutenant, just like you and that MP. Nobody wanted it to happen that way."

After Cox left they buttoned up and taxied out to takeoff. Sue Culpepper busied herself with making each of her patients as comfortable as possible as soon as the aircraft established a steady climb. The air was unstable, but Sue wasn't about to pull down one of the folding parachute pans and sit down. She didn't want to sit and start to think.

Don Crenshaw tucked his good arm behind his head and watched Sue Culpepper for a few minutes. This business of having the Jap prisoner here on the same plane with Sue and Sergeant Hickey was too much, so much like the Army to just botch something like this completely. It just didn't seem right to have him on the plane, forcing Sue to take care of the SOB. Even if, according to Sue, he wasn't the one at fault. *Well, who the hell else fault is it?* What the hell were Hickey, Sue, Katie and himself doing on this goddamned piece of shit island in the first place if it wasn't for the Japs?

The C-47 climbed slowly northward from the runway at Seven Mile before beginning a smooth climbing 180 degree turn to the south. Don casually glanced out the windows every few minutes, not able to break the habit of looking outside while flying. They punched out of the cloud deck into bright sunshine at about 3,000 feet, and it was at that point Don realized they had a single P-40 escort. The P-40, an Aussie, had a single central fuel tank hanging between the wings so it could stay with the C-47 for an hour or so. The C-47, Australia-bound, would not fly over any part of New Guinea for the direct flight to Townsville. Few Jap fighters ventured south of Port Moresby, they didn't have the range from Rabaul, but here was the XO's plane bound to Australia with an escort. Don could only shake his head, considering the crews flying direct from Port Moresby to Dobodura and back, day in and day out, with no escort. And of course, every now and then, one of them wouldn't return.

Out the port windows Don could see an odd sight. He had to sit up and stare hard, unbelieving what he was looking at, because it was over 100 miles away, just over the silhouette of the olive-brown Kittyhawk fighter. The Owen Stanley range, with just a stretch of the high peaks visible. They were majestic, beautiful, usually cloud-enshrouded and full of rocks, poking out of the white cloud deck like Everest without snow and ice. The shards of grey gave no hint to the dark secrets below the clouds, the dank, damp and life-sucking Kokoda Track far below the top layers of the green canopy. Don, like most pilots, only flew over it, dropping supplies to desperate men far below them. In the early days when they still landed on the short strips, he remembered the sense of helplessness and fear while they were on the ground, waiting for the Aussies to suddenly dash out of the forest to take the supplies or load the wounded. He guiltily wanted nothing more than to lift out of those strips and leave them behind as quickly as he could. He could not comprehend having to stay there.

Don glanced up to the bottom of the stretcher above him, thinking of Sergeant Hickey and men like him who fought on the Track. He felt a powerful kinship to Hickey, but after a moment remembered the prisoner down near the end of the fuselage. *What about that SOB; he was there too*. In a way, it was too much to get his head around. Hickey fought Japs just like this guy lying in the stretcher 30 feet away. A Jap tried to kill him the other day in a Zero. It was too much to ask of people to be humane, to consider the brutal enemy anything but vermin to be destroyed so you could go home, go back to your life. Katie died because they expected nurses to treat enemy wounded like Allied wounded. Katie got too close.

Don watched the Owen Stanleys' fade away as they flew south. The cloud deck, forever changing, swept away the peaks like a rising tide of rolling white surf. New Guinea disappeared from view. The Pratt and Whitney engines droned on with a comforting, familiar vibration. The XO said they usually flew around six to seven thousand feet crossing the Coral Sea to Townsville, so the airplane wouldn't get too cold or the patients suffer from lack of oxygen. He watched Sue move quietly from patient to patient, tucking blankets around each of them as the cabin grew cooler. About half were on auxiliary O2, and she was adjusting the little valves frequently. The sad pain in her eyes he had seen earlier dissolved as she worked around her patients. Her blond hair, bound tightly in a bun in the back, slowly unraveled, the lovely curls wafting around her head like a halo.

He got it finally, watching Sue, especially when she rotated around to the prisoner. He saw the same steady, professional care given to him she gave to every one of her patients. A SOB, who for whatever reason the Japanese decided to start this war, was ultimately and personally responsible for Katie's death. Her willingness to do this job, as did Sue, was the glue to bring it all around. He didn't understand how they could do it, because they worked on guys who were hurt by these bastards. It was remarkable. Don sighed and wished he could smoke a cigarette. He wished, more than anything in the world, to be able to give Katie a big hug and a kiss. She would be impressed a dumb ass like him got it. She was gone now and would never know he, Don Crenshaw, had figured out how goddamn important women like Katie were for keeping the pieces together. The world wouldn't go on otherwise. Somebody had to normalize things, put them back on the shelf where they belong.

Don watched Sue a few more minutes until some innate sense in women had her glancing up the cabin at him. She stared at him for a moment then beamed her light-the-room smile. Don smiled back but noticed her eyes went up a bit and she grinned again. Don leaned out from his stretcher and peered up at Vic Hickey, who was leering down at him, his big paw pointed towards Sue.

"Aye' say, 'at girl 'as a 'ovely smile, mate!" Don could only nod his head in agreement.

"That she does, that she does!"

About the Author

Into the Wet is Jerry Coker's second book. His first book *First Among Men*, is a historical novel set in 1943 during the invasion of Attu Island in the Aleutians. A former US Marine rifleman, he earned degrees in English Literature from the University of California, Davis and Brown University when he returned from Southeast Asia. He lives in Northern California with his wife. For more information visit http://Pacificwarscribe.com.